Divine

MICHELLE
HOLMAN

Divine

HarperCollinsPublishers

This is a work of fiction. The characters, incidents and dialogues are products of the author's imagination and are not to be construed as real.

National Library of New Zealand Cataloguing-in-Publication Data
Holman, Michelle.
Divine / Michelle Holman.
ISBN 978-1-86950-740-4
I. Title.
NZ823.3—dc 22

First published 2008
HarperCollins*Publishers (New Zealand) Limited*
P.O. Box 1, Auckland 1140

ISBN: 978 1 86950 740 4
Cover illustration and design by Clarisse Odum
Internal text design and typesetting by Springfield West

Printed by Griffin Press, Australia.

50gsm Bulky News used by HarperCollins*Publishers* is a natural, recyclable product made from wood grown in sustainable plantation forests. The manufacturing processes conform to the environmental regulations in the country of origin, New Zealand.

In memory of Pip and Llyween Scrivener

Acknowledgements

I'd like to point out that the town and people of Divine are very much figments of my imagination and bear no resemblance to my hometown of Cambridge. A lot of people helped me with this book — I apologize in advance if I miss anybody out. Thanks to my friends, and to Hamish Wright and everybody at Wrights Bookstore: your support and encouragement have been amazing. Thank you to my neighbour John for his invaluable advice on dairy farming, although I still don't really understand why bulls have to do stud duty in pairs; to Ian McKay, equine vet, for patiently answering my questions — I have wildly embellished on fact for Magic the pony; to Bronwyn Campbell for medical advice *again*; and to Richard Wright for allowing me to steal some of his pranks (you should be writing books!); to Carolyn Parkes, owner/manager of Deli on the Corner, for letting me pick her brain about café life, plus supplying perfect moccachinos and scrumptious food; and to Robyn Brookes from Ooby Ryn for letting me use her beautiful clothes designs for some of Tara's clothes. Thank you to Anna Pickering of the New Zealand Prostitutes Collective, who kindly sent out word when I rang for help on the sex industry. Anna put me in touch with Sue Watkins, who taught me about the complexities of telephone sex, and also Hana Tatere, whose input was invaluable when describing Richard's journey. Ladies, you are awesome! Kate, Lise, Sandra and everybody at HarperCollins, it's not often you get total professionalism with a touch of utter madness — it's been a pleasure. I owe a BIG thank you to Lorain Day, HCNZ's Publishing Manager for her astute advice and limitless patience; *Divine* is a much better book for her input. Finally, *thank you!* to my husband, Les, and my kids, McKenzie and Fleur, for putting up with me when I'm writing. *I love you all the world and a bag of cough candies.*

Prologue

'Tara, I have to tell you something . . .'

Tara Whitehead looked at her husband Richard's pale, strained expression and felt her stomach plummet into her shoes.

'What is it? Has somebody died? Is it Jen? Has something happened to Jen?'

Richard shook his head. 'Nothing's happened to Jennifer. It's something about me.'

Tara's shoulders slumped in relief. Jen was safe. Whatever he had to say, nothing could be as bad as hearing their fifteen-year-old daughter had been hurt.

Or so she thought.

'Tara, I'm leaving you,' Richard said quietly. 'I want to be a woman.'

He'd lied.

Somebody *had* died.

He had.

At first Tara thought Richard was playing some sort of a joke — a bad one. He *had* to be joking. She waited for the punch line, but it didn't come. When it finally registered that Richard was serious, Tara numbly followed him like a faithful dog from room to room, watching as he collected his keys and cellphone in the wide, sunny kitchen overlooking the swimming pool.

She felt dazed. 'Is there somebody else?' While painful, at least that would be understandable.

'No.' Richard's blue eyes swam with tears. 'Darling, this isn't your fault. Leaving you will kill part of me, but if I stay I'll slowly die anyway. I can't pretend any more.'

Tara tried desperately to make sense of his words. 'You mean you're a . . .' She swallowed. *'Homosexual?'*

He shook his head. 'I'm transgender.'

'What . . .'

'It's sometimes called the third sex.'

Tara flinched. She didn't have a clue what he was talking about, but it sounded like a disease. 'So why did you marry me?' she cried.

'Because I love you,' Richard insisted. 'I always will. If I hadn't loved you so much I could never have lived this way for so long.'

This way? What did he mean by *this way?* Tara felt the first stirrings of anger.

Richard continued earnestly, 'Tara, it's as if I've been living in another country. I never really understood the language or the customs, but over time I managed to pretend I was a native. Only, I'm not — no matter how much I pretend, I'm still a foreigner in a foreign country. Everything I hear has to be translated inside my head into a language I understand. *I* have to keep changing to fit in.'

'I don't understand a word you've said,' she whispered.

'I know.' His voice broke. 'I'm so sorry, darling. I'll be in touch.'

And he was gone.

Tara stood at the window watching Richard's car disappear down the driveway, past the landscaped gardens and through the wrought-iron gates.

Her husband of sixteen years had just left her.

He wanted to be a woman.

What had she done wrong? Surely it was some sort of joke?

But Richard's tortured expression told her it was no joke. This was real. It was *really* happening. Richard would never deliberately hurt her. He was a precise man who thought carefully before he committed to something, and that hadn't changed, even as he ripped out Tara's heart and shredded her perfect world into pieces.

Seeing the empty hangers and drawers in the walk-in wardrobe finally punched a hole through her shock, and the outside world suddenly came rushing in.

Richard wanted to be a woman.

He *wanted* to be a *woman.*

HE

WANTED

TO

BE

A

WOMAN.

Tara turned the words around and around in her mind, but still couldn't fathom their meaning. She knew she had been dealt a mortal blow. She was thirty-five years old and her husband didn't want her.

When Jennifer came home from school she found her mother sitting in the study at her father's desk, cuddling his blue cashmere sweater. It needed washing and was one of the few articles of clothing he'd left behind. Tara blurted out the news.

'Oh,' Jen said slowly. 'We've been taught about that at school.'

Tara lifted her face from Richard's sweater. 'What?'

Jen looked as white as her school shirt. 'About sexual orientation and . . . stuff.'

What was Jen talking about? Why was she so calm? What was wrong with her? Tara's anguish boiled over into anger. *'How dare you talk about your father like that?'*

Jennifer began to cry. As Jen's misery penetrated Tara's shock, Tara leapt to her feet to hug her daughter tightly. Tara's heart began to harden against Richard. Jen didn't deserve to be abandoned by her father. How could he *do* this to her?

'I'm so sorry, love!' Tara brushed tendrils of silky blonde hair the same shade as her own from Jen's face. 'I didn't mean to shout at you.'

'It's OK.' Jen swiped her nose with the back of her hand. She hesitated. 'Did you really never think Dad was a bit different?'

Tara was dumbstruck.

As it turned out, Jen wasn't the only person unsurprised by Richard's astonishing announcement.

Tara was in a club all of her own.

Chapter 1

Tara Kemp met Richard Whitehead during her first semester studying for a Bachelor of Arts at the University of Auckland. Richard was completing a Bachelor of Commerce. He was three years older than Tara, and eons ahead in sophistication and maturity. He was blond and blue-eyed, with the face of an angel, and the girls on campus adored him. Richard loved socializing and spent very little time in his student flat, but was clever enough to maintain his studies and grades. Tara thought Richard was as near perfect as a person could be, and she couldn't believe it when he singled her out.

Growing up on Auckland's wild west coast, Tara had spent most of her time on the black-sand beaches of Piha and Muriwai, surfing, drinking beer and partying. She was the epitome of the beach babe: golden-skinned and long-legged, with waist-length silvery blonde hair. She excelled at surfing and just about any sport she turned her hand to, and would have looked right at home in a Beach Boys video doing the twist on a white, sandy beach dressed in a polka-dot bikini. Tara owned a wardrobe full of bikinis, sarongs and cut-off jean-shorts that were swapped in winter for a wetsuit and jeans. Her only fashion indulgence was the high-heeled shoes she spent every spare cent on and only took off when she went to bed or to the beach. Because they seldom saw her barefoot, a lot of people thought Tara was tall when she was in fact only five foot five.

Tara's older sister, Kim, and her boyfriend, Mickey, were the uncrowned king and queen of the surfer crowd. Nobody was cooler than Kim Kemp or badder than Mickey Green. They were notorious party animals, and Tara tripped along gleefully in their wake. Two things distinguished Tara from her big sister, however: she was very bright, and she had difficulty pronouncing the letter 'r', which meant that their parents, Trevor and Sandra, had to fork out for speech lessons. Instead of being teased because she couldn't say *rain* or *rhubarb* or even her own name, now she was teased for sounding stuck-up.

It took a while before Tara developed a thick enough skin to ignore the taunts of the other kids, although being Kim Kemp's little sister helped. Kim socked more than a few kids in the eye for teasing her sister, but she wasn't nearly so supportive out of earshot. 'You'll never get a boyfriend if you sound like you're reading the news.'

But Tara's posh accent ended up being almost as much of a drawcard as her pretty legs and blonde hair, and she never lacked for boyfriends.

Richard Whitehead was an only child. This was a novelty to Tara: there were precious few families in her area with only one kid. Richard's family came from the Waikato, where some time in the latter part of the nineteenth century his great-great-grandmother Sarah Whitehead and her missionary husband, Henry, had settled a large tract of land beside the Waikato River. Sarah had gazed at the lush green bush and broad sweep of the river and announced, 'Henry, this place has been touched by a divine hand.'

Which was how the town of Divine got its name.

Tara was impressed. She didn't know anybody whose family was responsible for naming an entire town. She was also impressed by Richard's blond good looks, wry wit, and gentle, urbane charm. Tara could talk to him for hours without the expectation that she'd finish the night on the back seat of a Holden with her ankles behind her ears after listening to the steady stream of blonde jokes — the nearest thing you got to foreplay from surfer dudes.

'Hey, Tara, why do blondes hate gang bangs? Because they hate having to write all the thank-you notes afterwards.'

No matter how many times Kim heard a joke, or how bad it was, she always laughed, but Tara couldn't be bothered, and this reinforced her stuck-up, snooty image. She became resigned to being the odd one out, always on the fringe of the crowd, accepted only because of her big sister.

Her posh voice wasn't the only mark against her. She completed her homework, passed her exams, and didn't bunk off school when the surf was up. When Tara's application was accepted by Auckland university, she might just as well have announced she was joining an obscure religious sect. Kim took it as a personal insult that her younger sister didn't want to follow in her footsteps.

'Do you have to be so stuck-up?' she complained.

'Do you have to be so predictable?' Tara retorted.

It was the beginning of a rift that developed into a yawning chasm as the years passed. Tara tried to pretend she didn't care.

The first time Richard made the journey to West Auckland to collect Tara and meet her family, he arrived in his customized Volkswagen Beetle.

'What the bloody hell is that?' Trevor, her mechanic father, demanded as Richard pulled into the driveway of their modest three-bedroom home. The front lawn was adorned with two stripped-down cars in different stages of restoration; a third sat beneath the raised deck at the front of the house. Trevor was a petrol-head and would still have been out with the boy-racers every night if Sandra hadn't put her foot down.

Tara was mortified to see that her mother had just hung Kim's and her oldest bras and knickers on the line under the house for Richard to walk past on his way to the front door.

Kim leaned her head and shoulders out of the lounge window to gawp at Tara's new boyfriend and his car. 'Look at the size of the back seat! What could you do in there?'

Tara glared at Kim's bottom. Her jean-shorts had ridden up to reveal a tattoo on her left buttock in the shape of a rose with Mickey's name written in black ink across the middle. Tara had pointed out to Kim the stupidity of putting some guy's name on her bum when she changed her boyfriends as frequently as her knickers, but Kim insisted that Mickey Green was *the one*. 'You'll *know* when you meet him,' she'd informed Tara loftily.

Tara cringed. What would Richard think when he saw Kim sticking out of the window with her breasts threatening to fall out of her halter top? Most guys would enjoy the view, but Richard wasn't most guys, and it was pointless asking Kim to be discreet. Kim thought discretion was something done to the pores around her nose when she got a facial.

'I s'pose it could have been worse,' Trevor observed. 'It could have been a Lada.'

He spread newspaper sheets on the sofa and sat on them in his oil-stained overalls. It was the compromise he'd reached with Sandra to allow him to take a break from working on his cars without having to remove his overalls.

Kim hauled herself back into the room as Richard mounted the steps at the side of the house. 'You definitely won't have to worry about this guy jumping Tara in the back of his car, Dad,' she smirked. 'Bit of a shame really, because he looks quite cute — if you go for the blond Jesus look.' She widened her eyes at Tara. 'Does he wear socks with his sandals in the winter?'

'Kim,' Trevor intoned from behind his newspaper, without really paying any attention to what was being said. He'd realized the futility of trying to stop his daughters fighting a long time ago.

'Shut up, Kim!' Tara hissed. 'Not everybody rates a car by how much room there is in the back seat for a shag.'

'Tara.'

She ignored her father and wiggled her feet into a pair of emerald-green suede stilettos which matched her clinging, green knit dress, and rushed to the front door in the forlorn hope that she might persuade Richard to leave without meeting her family. Her mum and dad weren't so bad, but Kim saw it as her personal mission in life to embarrass the crap out of Tara every chance she got.

'Pardon me for breathing, Lady Muck!' Kim yelled as Tara opened the door. 'I've seen you disappear into the back seat of a few cars!'

'Kim.' Trevor turned the page.

Tara looked up at Richard, her face burning with shame. She wanted to die.

'Er . . . have I come at a difficult moment?'

She shook her head miserably. With her family, there would never be a right moment. Why on earth had she thought she could introduce somebody like Richard Whitehead to them?

Richard's face softened. 'Hey, don't look so sad. Nobody died.'

Tara's trembling mouth curved into a smile, and at that instant she fell in love with him.

Richard coped reasonably well with his introduction to the Kemp clan. Kim flirted outrageously with him, and Richard skyrocketed still higher in Tara's estimation by skilfully rebuffing all her overtures with a polite smile and blank stare. Sandra acted as if Prince Charles had turned up for a visit and rushed out to cut the crusts off the sandwiches, while Trevor was suspicious of a man who refused the offer of a beer because he was driving.

'He's lovely, Tara, just lovely!' Sandra enthused loudly in the kitchen as she made coffee for Richard. 'His family must be stinking rich if they own a whole town! Does he like cheese-and-onion?'

'Not if he's hoping to get a snog tonight,' Kim said nastily, swiping a sandwich from the plate on the kitchen counter. 'He looks like he should be on the front of a knitting pattern with a pipe in his hand.' She frowned. 'Why have you got all the best china out, Mum? And you never cut the crusts off Mickey's sandwiches.'

Tara couldn't get Richard out of there fast enough.

Sandra was the only one charmed by Richard. Trevor and Kim couldn't understand what Tara saw in him, but shrugged their shoulders. Tara had always been different, so what else could you expect? They didn't know how overwhelmed Tara was by university life that first semester. Nobody in her family or immediate circle of friends had ever been, and it was like suddenly finding herself in a strange new country. She was alone and miserable for the first couple of months, and spent money on shoes instead of books, trying to cheer herself up. Only the thought of her proud parents' crushing disappointment if she dropped out kept her catching the bus into Auckland every day. And it gave her somewhere to show off the new shoes.

Richard Whitehead was a godsend. He seemed to see beneath the blonde prettiness of the West Auckland surfer girl to the misery and loneliness she tried to hide, and took her under his wing. He was a lifeline, a breath of fresh air, and very quickly became her best friend. Richard listened to her fears, guiding her through those first awful months at university. He excused her ignorance and was indulgent about her offbeat sense of humour and appalling dress sense. Richard recognized Tara's potential. He saw a rough diamond, a swan just waiting to be born.

Tara was so desperate to fit in that she accepted Richard's suggestions about her clothes and hair, and the books and films he thought she might like. Richard reshaped her and she became his willing acolyte, unaware that he was turning her into the person he wanted to be. Being treated as if she was made from spun glass began to wear thin when by the sixth date he'd done no more than French kiss her and touch her breasts through her clothes. Tara was so desperate to take things to their natural conclusion that she was even willing to brave the cramped back seat of his car.

'Passionate little thing, aren't you?' Richard observed, which Tara interpreted as *What a slut.* She backed off.

He spent hours on foreplay, turning it into an art form, worshipping and stroking every inch of Tara's body, before finally making love to her after they'd been going out for eight long weeks. Tara didn't make Richard wait for her; Richard made Tara wait for him. He spent so much time arousing her that she scarcely noticed that the act of penetration was over very quickly. When Richard proposed to her less than six months after they'd met, Tara giddily accepted. Surprisingly, it was Tara's parents who voiced reservations about the couple marrying so young. Henry and Grace Whitehead were in total support and welcomed Tara with open arms into their charming, gracious house in Remuera, to Sundays spent watching the polo at Clevedon (which Richard loathed) and yachting on Thursday evenings on the Hauraki Gulf. Grace was only too happy to throw herself into the task of making Tara over.

Years later, Tara realized she had been the answer to Grace and Henry's prayers. She'd been too naïve and besotted with Richard and the life he offered her to pay attention to the warning signs. Tara's rose-coloured glasses were super-glued to her face.

The only ripple was caused by a visit to Divine for Richard's Uncle Eric's birthday party. Eric Whitehead looked Tara up and down with a distinctly lascivious expression on his craggy face, before announcing, 'Well, if anybody's going to make a man out of him you will.'

There was an awkward silence while Richard pursed his lips and reddened, and his parents fidgeted.

Tara forgot all about making a good impression on Richard's family and flew to his defence. 'You vile old bugger!' she cried. 'You take that back!'

Henry and Grace were aghast.

Eric studied Tara silently and shook his head. 'What a bloody waste.'

The birthday party was a subdued affair, bearing no resemblance to the parties thrown by Tara's family. Dressed in a short, flirty, cobalt-blue halter-dress that showcased her golden tan and waist-length blonde hair, and a pair of blue-and-white striped high heels, Tara stood out like a brightly coloured alien in the Whiteheads' calm, ordered world.

Most of the women wore pearl necklaces and earrings, and busied themselves offering platters of asparagus rolls and smoked salmon vol-au-vents. There wasn't a bright pink lamington or sausage roll in sight. Tara watched everybody standing around talking politely and sipping wine, and decided it was hardly surprising nobody got up and danced when nothing but James Last, Cliff Richard and The Shadows had been played all night. If she had to listen to 'Apache' one more time she'd scream, but when her suggestion that they change The Shadows for something more upbeat was met with a look of collective shock, Tara realized she'd dropped another clanger.

'They're Eric's favourite group,' Grace explained.

Tara looked at Eric sprawled in a chair by his birthday cake, drunk as a lord, his snores throbbing like a chainsaw, and felt a spurt of annoyance. The man was a bully.

A small, dark-haired woman with eyes the colour of rich, dark chocolate touched Grace's arm. 'Come on, Gracie — Eric's plastered.' She winked discreetly at Tara. 'Let's liven things up a bit.'

Tara smiled gratefully at the woman whom Richard had introduced as his Aunt Connie.

The party livened up considerably after the music had been changed and Henry had put Eric to bed. Tara danced Richard off his feet while his family looked on, unable to believe that this energetic, lovely creature was really Richard's new girlfriend.

When they eventually left the party in the wee hours of the morning, Richard looped an arm about Tara's waist and hugged her to his side. 'God, I love you! I usually loathe family parties, but having you along made it so much easier. None of them could believe you were my girlfriend,' he said with satisfaction, leading her past some garages and through a wide metal gate towards a rough dirt road edged with towering trees.

Tara tripped along beside him in her blue-and-white high heels, ecstatic that this gorgeous man loved her. 'Why wouldn't they believe I'm your girlfriend?'

Richard shrugged and refused to elaborate, instead backing her gently against a broad tree trunk. Tara looped her arms around his neck. 'Do we have to invite your Uncle Eric to the wedding?'

He put his hands under the skirt of her dress and stroked her legs. 'Don't you want to?'

'No! Where does he get off saying things like that?'

Richard shrugged again and slid her knickers down her legs.

Tara was astonished. She'd never known Richard to be so urgent before. But he was erect and inside her almost before she knew it, hooking her legs and frivolous blue-and-white shoes around his naked buttocks and thrusting energetically.

It didn't take long. Richard began to apologize profusely. 'I'm sorry, Tara! I shouldn't have done that, I don't know what came over me. I behaved like an animal. Are you all right? Did I hurt you, darling?'

Tara smiled and stroked his face. She didn't care that she hadn't come. She was delighted that for once he'd let his baser instincts rule him.

Tara married Richard two months after Kim married Mickey Green.

Kim was pregnant.

Tara wasn't.

But within a year of the wedding, Richard and Tara's daughter, Jennifer Jade, was born. She wasn't an accident; Richard had wanted to start a family right away, and Tara had taken it as a sign that he just couldn't keep his hands off her. Despite her reservations, Tara had given in. She would have preferred to wait and finish her degree, but instead, at the age of twenty, she was a stay-at-home wife and mother, and stayed that way for the next fifteen years. Richard's parents saw to it that they never suffered financially, and Richard took a junior position in a bank before working his way up to become a senior economic analyst. There was no need for Tara to go to work, and whenever she talked about it Richard made her feel guilty by saying Jen was too young to be left.

Life was pleasant, if at times a little boring. Tara spent her days doing parent support at Jen's school, raising money for the PTA, entertaining Richard's business colleagues, building up a stunning collection of art, and adding to her wardrobe of shoes. She decorated and refurbished one home after another, until they finally settled in a large house in one of the best parts of Auckland, complete with a swimming pool and tennis court.

Richard worshipped his wife and daughter. His calm, unflappable nature was the perfect foil for Tara's more fiery personality. Their sex life become less active as the years passed, but Richard worked long hours and was often exhausted by the time he got home at night, and Tara's girlfriends gave the impression their husbands were the same. Tara, who had always loved the physical side of their relationship, missed it. She enjoyed making love to Richard and thought he enjoyed it, too. Tara told herself she was a lucky woman, because her husband liked to spend hours stroking and exploring her body rather than just leaping on her and having sex. It wasn't until he'd left that what Tara had seen as signs of Richard's love for her began to seem sinister: his deeply solicitous concern when she got occasional monthly cramps, his detailed questions about her experiences growing up, and the way he'd been so totally absorbed by the changes in her body when she was pregnant with Jennifer.

Tara would have liked more children, but Richard was reluctant to add to their family; he preferred to give the best he could to one child rather than have to divide his time among several, he said. Jennifer was blonde like her parents, and blessed with her father's placid, kind disposition. Right from the moment they brought her home from the hospital, she was the baby who never got colic and who slept through the night, much to her Aunt Kim's annoyance.

'Trust Tara to have the perfect baby,' she complained, struggling to cope with the first of her three boisterous sons.

The only cloud on the horizon was Richard's muted disappointment when Jennifer became something of a tomboy. Richard was unfailingly polite and kind to Kim's noisy, destructive sons, but Tara suspected he felt that the Kemp family genes had surfaced far too strongly in his daughter. Jen was a fearless athlete who excelled in just about any physical activity she tried. Unfortunately, this didn't extend to the ballet classes and recitals her father so looked forward to attending and Jen so grudgingly participated in. Richard had been a competitive swimmer in his teens, had a mean tennis backhand, and was a strong, graceful dancer, so Tara was baffled at his insistence that Jen take ballet classes. 'She's a natural athlete, Richard. Why does she have to attend dancing classes as well?'

He eventually explained that he'd asked to do dancing classes when he was small but Henry had refused to allow it. 'I want my child to have the opportunity to try different things and not have to conform to what society deems normal.'

Tara's confusion showed. But wasn't insisting on ballet lessons for their daughter doing exactly that: conforming to what was considered normal for a girl? Richard clammed up and refused to discuss the subject any further. Later — much later — it made a strange sort of sense. Richard hadn't been allowed to explore his feminine side, and in some sort of an emotional backlash he was worried that Jen wasn't exploring hers.

When she was eight, Jen staged a mutiny and refused to attend another ballet class. 'I hate ballet, Mum! The tutus make me itch!' Instead she asked for a pony and riding lessons.

Tara wasn't wild about the idea but suspected it would all be a five-minute wonder. Richard was utterly opposed. He'd spent hair-raising, miserable school holidays at his Uncle Eric's farm, forced to career around the countryside on unruly, evil ponies with his younger cousins Gil and Alison, paying for the pleasure with broken bones and a serious concussion. There was no way Richard was letting his precious daughter loose on a pony, no matter how well behaved it was. Tara enrolled Jen at the local swim club instead, where she competed successfully for several years, although her heart was never really in it. Right up until she was thirteen, Jen still asked if she could have riding lessons.

When Richard left, Tara realized that she had spent most of her married life apologizing for the differences between her upbringing and Richard's, and felt bitter about how she'd let Jen down in her efforts to please him. She dreaded telling her family that Richard had left her, and why. On the rare occasions Tara and Richard visited her parents in Henderson, Sandra still behaved as if Prince Charles was visiting. Trevor looked at Richard as if he was an alien being, and Kim was always at her obnoxious worst. Tara usually visited alone or with Jen, who adored her Kemp relatives, including her rowdy cousins, Troy, Travis and Trent. Tara loved her family, even if she and Kim did still fight at the drop of a hat.

Surprisingly enough, none of her family was nearly as jubilant or keen to say *I told you so* as she had expected.

Trevor was horrified. 'You mean he's going to get his tackle cut off?'

Tara felt sick. 'Of course not!' she cried.

'Maybe he'll get over it,' Sandra said, as if Richard had a bad case of the flu and just needed lots of bed rest, fluids and some aspirin. 'He's always had such lovely manners,' she added, as if good manners were a sure sign of heterosexuality.

Kim was more forthright. 'The prick! At least Mickey left me for other women. How dare Richard do that to you?'

Tara was touched by their show of solidarity. Until Kim added, 'Bloody insult, wanting his own fanny instead of yours.'

Chapter 2

'The bastard! Why does he want his own vagina? What's wrong with mine?'

Nicole Baxter nervously checked to see if anybody else on the restaurant terrace had overheard Tara Whitehead's comment.

It was a perfect May morning, one of those late autumn days when the sun still shone warmly enough to sit outside. Nicole conceded that Tara had a right to be upset, but she had never been comfortable hearing the *vee* word. Her mother had always referred to it as a *Mary*, which Nicole thought was much nicer.

She watched Tara stab a fork at her Greek salad and thought how dreadful she looked. Nicole had always envied Tara's silver-blonde mane, but at the moment it hung about her pale, wan face in lank strands. There were dark circles under her fine grey eyes, and deep hollows beneath her perfect cheekbones. It wasn't fair that even miserable and unkempt, Tara Whitehead still managed to look like an elegant Afghan hound, all slender limbs and gentle curves. She and Richard had made a striking pair, both lean and blond with an indefinable air of casual chic. People often commented that they could have been mistaken for brother and sister. But Richard came from a distinguished Waikato family and old money, while everybody knew that Tara was from West Auckland. Nicole checked the expressions on the faces of the table's other occupants.

Elizabeth 'Lizzie' Steiner and Ann Levesque were hanging on Tara's every word, watching her like rubberneckers at a fatal car accident, fascinated, horrified and deeply relieved it wasn't them. *Their* husbands, like Nicole's, were at work earning the fat salaries that kept their trophy wives in the manner to which they were accustomed. They might be lusting after their secretary or the photocopying girl, but that was better than lusting after the contents of their wife's wardrobe.

'Do you think Richard might have somebody else?' Ann ventured.

Tara flung her a contemptuous look. 'Well if he has, I doubt it's female.'

Ann bridled.

Nicole pursed her lips disapprovingly. You could take the girl out of the West and all that, but . . .

The only one unshaken by the vitriol pumping from Tara's mouth was Lizzie, who was lapping it up like mother's milk, her mouth hanging slightly open, hazel eyes wide.

Nicole studied Lizzie's eyes suspiciously. She was sure they hadn't been that almond-shaped before Lizzie's eye-lift. (Lizzie denied having had one, but nobody believed her story about banging her face on the side of the baby's cot — *twice.*)

Tara looked at her so-called best friends and felt even more depressed. Ever since Richard had left three months ago, they'd slowly begun to edge her out of their circle, making excuses not to meet for lunch and not always returning her calls. Tara felt as if she'd contracted a terminal illness, and they'd decided not to waste time holding her hand while she carked it but had got straight on to arranging the funeral. If she wasn't careful they'd have her cremated and be planning outfits for the memorial service.

It was yet another thing to hold against Richard. He'd visited Jennifer twice a week after he left, until Tara eventually asked him to pick Jen up and take her somewhere else rather than meet at the house. She couldn't bear seeing the changes in him. He was wearing different clothes, wide-legged palazzo pants in shades of white and grey, and loose, gauzy shirts in pretty pastels. And he was letting his hair grow. Tara wondered how Richard's colleagues at the bank were taking his transformation. She'd imagined things couldn't get any worse, but a week ago Richard had announced that the house would have to be sold to help finance his sex reassignment operation and recuperation.

'You can't just go and get something like that done so quickly!' Tara cried. 'Even *I* know that! You have to have counselling and psychological assessment and things . . .'

'I've been having that for the past six months.' Richard paused. 'And hormone therapy.'

Tara recoiled.

Six months? He had been receiving counselling behind her back for six months? And hormone therapy? Did that mean he was going to grow breasts?

'Tara,' Richard said gently. 'Didn't you sometimes wonder about us these last few years?'

'No.' She shook her head stubbornly. *'No!'*

He sighed. 'I'm afraid we'll have to sell the house, but you should have more than enough money to buy another place and be mortgage-free. I'll provide you with a monthly income for as long as I can, but once I have the operation I'll need time to recuperate and I'll have to give up my job.'

'If they don't sack you first,' Tara snapped.

Richard flinched. 'Yes. Unless they find a way to do that first.'

She hated herself for being so cruel and wished she didn't still care so much. 'I won't be able to afford a house in this area.'

'No, but you could still buy somewhere nice nearby.'

Tara didn't want to live somewhere nearby; she wanted to stay in the same area, close to her friends and Jen's school. Her life had changed enough, and she didn't see why she and Jen had to keep making sacrifices.

'Do you realize Jennifer is being teased at school?'

'I've told her how sorry I am,' Richard said stiffly.

Tara gave him a scathing look. As if that would help.

Surprisingly, Jennifer had never once condemned her father or complained, although Tara could imagine how dire her life must be at school, despite Tara's visits to the school principal and the dean, who'd both looked embarrassed and at a loss to know how to deal with what was happening.

Her wandering attention was dragged back to the present by Lizzie hissing, 'Look! It's Madame Bancroft!'

They all looked across the sunlit terrace at the petite, beautifully groomed woman making her way over the terracotta paving stones on pale lavender suede shoes with four-inch heels. She had long, gleaming sable-brown hair that fell in waves about the shoulders of the pale lavender tight-waisted jacket that matched her knee-length skirt. Her eyes were grey-green, long and slanted upwards (naturally, Nicole thought), and her wide pink mouth curved upwards at one corner in a faintly mocking smile. She didn't so much walk as sway towards the table where Tara and her friends sat, and every man on the terrace turned to watch her glide by.

'Ladies?' Sian Bancroft murmured when she reached their table. 'Enjoying the sunshine, I see.'

Nicole, Lizzie and Ann regarded her suspiciously. Like many of their contemporaries they didn't know what to make of Sian. Marcus Bancroft had divorced her six years ago, presumably because after seven years of marriage Sian had failed to produce the son he needed to shore up his position as the head of the family firm. While other discarded wives tactfully quit the scene, Sian had remained close to her ex-husband and thrived, much to the annoyance of his second wife, Susie, who had conscientiously popped out three little Bancrofts in quick succession, the last being the longed-for boy. Nobody knew exactly what Sian did for a living; she was a successful businesswoman who exuded an air of mystery and mockery whenever she met the women she had once numbered among her friends.

Tara had always been fascinated by Sian and appalled by Marcus's callous treatment. She'd paid a discreet visit to Sian when news first broke of the split, to say how sorry she was for what had happened. Now she looked at the glamorous, beautiful creature standing beside her, feeling ashamed of what a mess she looked, and even more ashamed that her friends wouldn't offer Sian a seat at their table.

Sian cast a languid glance at Nicole, Lizzie and Ann's frozen faces and smiled at Tara. 'Tara, darling, how are you? Have you taken a carving knife to Richard's testicles yet?'

Lizzie and Ann gasped.

Nicole goggled. Her mother had never even *had* a word for those.

Tara choked back laughter. 'Not yet. He's going to pay a doctor in Colorado a lot of money to do it instead.'

'What a shame,' Sian sympathized. 'You could have had your satisfaction and saved money.'

'I hardly think this is the time or the place to discuss something so personal,' said Nicole primly.

Sian regarded her curiously. 'No? What would be a more appropriate venue? A public toilet?'

Nicole's mouth opened and closed like a goldfish.

'Sod off, Sian!' Lizzie fumed. 'Nobody invited you to—'

Her indignation bounced right off Sian, who took a pale lavender business card from her purse and slid it across the table to Tara. 'Make sure you take good care of yourself and that lovely daughter of yours. If you should need anything, don't hesitate to give me a call.' She smirked at the angry faces of the other women and finished the meeting as she'd started, her eyebrows raised in two question marks as if she wasn't entirely sure she was saying the right thing. *'Ladies?'*

With a discreet wink at Tara, Sian Bancroft glided away on her high heels, her hips swaying and her silk stockings whispering sensuously. A tall, dark-haired man with touches of grey at his temples, dressed in a business suit, rose from a table on the far side of the terrace and held out a chair for her.

'The bitch!' Lizzie spat. 'Who the hell does she think she is?'

There was a chorus of agreement from Ann and Nicole.

Tara watched the man bend his head to Sian's and felt a slight easing of the knot of pain and fear that had been her constant companion for the past few months. Under cover of the arrival of their drinks, Tara slipped the lavender card into her handbag.

She didn't really know who or what Sian Bancroft was. But at the moment Tara sensed she might be the closest thing she had to a real friend.

'So?' Sian Bancroft arched a brow. 'I take it the little women don't know you're here.'

She was perched on a pale pink suede sofa wearing white silk lounging pyjamas. The pink polish on her toenails matched the sofa. Sian crossed her legs and spread her arms along the back of the seat. A long flute of golden champagne dangled from her right hand.

Tara sat opposite her on a matching sofa. She still couldn't quite believe she was visiting the infamous Sian Bancroft at her gorgeous, sumptuous home, and fidgeted with the matching flute of champagne that Sian had insisted she accept, even though it was only two o'clock in the afternoon. Tara wished she'd taken more care with her appearance. Her split ends were out of control, and she couldn't recall the last time she'd looked at her eyebrows, let alone taken the tweezers to them.

'The little women?'

Sian took a sip of champagne, rolling it across her tongue before swallowing it and sighing with pleasure. 'Mesdames Baxter, Steiner and Levesque.'

Tara choked on her wine, her eyes watering as it shot up her nose. 'You call Nicole, Ann and Lizzie *the little women?*' she gasped, thumping her breastbone.

Sian smiled languidly. Tara pressed her fingers to her lips and laughed.

'Not just them — *all* of the trophy wives,' Sian explained.

Tara sobered. What a horrible description, but how apt it was. 'And me, too, I guess.'

Sian tipped her head to one side. 'From time to time, but you were always a little different.'

'Why?' Tara asked grimly. 'Because my husband left me to become a woman?'

Sian slid her glass on to the marble table between the sofas. 'Tut tut! Aren't we being just a little melodramatic?'

Tara's eyebrows rose. 'Don't you think I'm entitled to be?'

Sian shrugged. 'He was never the man for you, dear.'

'I beg your pardon!' Tara spluttered. 'I loved Richard! I still love Richard! We were very happy together.'

'Of course you were,' Sian agreed. 'But you both clearly made compromises, and I'm ninety-nine percent sure you weren't *in love* with Richard Whitehead.'

Tara stared. Who on earth did Sian Bancroft think she was to be making such sweeping statements about Tara's personal life? And why on earth had she thought that visiting her was a good idea?

Sian's cool gaze challenged her. 'If you're planning on storming out, please don't slam the front door. The glass is Italian.'

Tara subsided resentfully.

'Well done. See? I knew you weren't really one of the little women.' Sian tucked her pink-tipped toes under her bottom. 'How are you financially? Do you have to sell the house?'

Instead of being offended by the intrusive question, Tara was relieved. She answered every one of the personal and probing questions Sian fired at her.

'It sounds to me as if your best option would be to move away for a while,' Sian said at last.

'Why? Why should *I* move away? I've done nothing wrong. Why should Jen and I be punished for what Richard's doing?' demanded Tara.

'It's not about placing blame. It's about what's best for you and

Jennifer. You said yourself she's having a terrible time at school at the moment and, well, look at you.'

Tara self-consciously ran a hand through her hair. 'I *like* living here. All my friends are here.'

Sian's brows rose eloquently.

'Maybe they're not such great friends at the moment, but they're the only ones I have,' Tara said crossly.

Sian regarded her thoughtfully. 'You won't be able to afford a house around here with your share of the matrimonial property.'

'I'll get a job.'

'It will have to be an extremely well-paying job if you want to buy a house here.'

Tara rubbed her face wearily. 'I know.'

Sian hesitated. 'I could offer you work, but I doubt that you'd accept it.'

Tara looked up hopefully. 'Why not? If it means I can buy Richard out and stay in my house, I'll do anything.'

'Don't speak too soon, Tara.'

Sian topped up their glasses and considered her words. She'd always liked Tara Whitehead. Tara was less pretentious than most of the wives, and Sian had never forgotten Tara's kindness when Marcus had left her. Tara's blonde beauty and perfect diction made an impression on every man she met. It was impossible for them not to wonder if she'd be as cool and self-possessed when she was naked beneath them.

'I'm sure you've wondered exactly what I do for a living,' Sian began. She chuckled when Tara blushed. 'Oh, I know everybody thinks I'm engaged in selling sexual favours.'

'No, not at all—' Tara began hastily.

'They're right.'

Tara's jaw dropped.

Chapter 3

'I don't provide sexual services myself these days, other than for a few old clients who I can't seem to persuade to consider any of my other ladies, but I manage a thriving escort agency for the very top end of the market.'

'You're a — a *madam?'* Tara gaped.

'Yes.' Sian stroked a hand up the back of her neck, lifting her heavy fall of sable hair free of the collar of her pyjamas. There wasn't a trace of grey anywhere in the shining mass. 'And you, my dear Tara, are the kind of woman men wonder about. When they look at all that cool blonde loveliness and hear those proper, perfect vowels, they wonder what you'll be like in bed. They wonder if you'll become unglued, Tara, if you'll scratch and bite and moan.'

Tara's face grew hot.

Sian smiled knowingly. 'Tell me, did Richard ever make you come unglued?'

Tara drew in a breath and looked away.

'Darling!' Sian slid to the edge of her seat. 'I'm so sorry. That was cruel.'

Tara clutched her wine glass. 'I couldn't, Sian, I couldn't — you know . . .'

'I expected you'd say that,' Sian said kindly. 'But what about telephone sex? You'd be perfect for it and, believe me, it can be very lucrative.'

'Telephone sex?'

'Yes. With a voice like yours, you'd make a wonderful dominatrix. You know, for men who basically want to be told they've been very naughty and be threatened with a good spanking.'

'Oh, I couldn't!' Tara gasped.

'You don't have to decide right away. Just think about it.'

'But what if it was somebody I knew?'

'I screen all our clients before accepting them on to my books. It's quite safe. You could do it in the comfort of your own home while you were drinking a glass of wine or sunbathing by the pool. And I'd contribute to expenses.'

'Expenses?' queried Tara faintly.

'Telephone-line rental and things like that.'

'Oh, I see.'

She didn't see at all. How on earth could she sit in her kitchen sipping wine and telling men she was going to spank them? While she appreciated Sian's honesty and support, Tara was absolutely certain she'd never in a million years contemplate taking Sian up on her offer.

'I'll think about it,' she said politely.

Sian frowned. 'Now you're being a little woman and lying to me. All I ask is that you don't repeat anything I've said today.'

Tara looked at her as if she was mad.

'Never in a million years.'

A week later, Tara received a sheaf of papers from a law firm informing her that Eric Whitehead was moving into a retirement home and had decided to leave his house and fifty-eight acres in Divine to Jennifer Jade Whitehead, with Tara managing the inheritance until Jen turned twenty. Tara had only ever met Richard's Uncle Eric that one time, and they'd hardly parted on good terms. When she called the number on the letterhead to tell the lawyers there'd obviously been a mistake, she was told firmly that there hadn't. Her efforts to reach

Eric were unsuccessful. Whenever she called Peacehaven Retreat, the retirement home where he'd decided to live out his remaining years, the matron could never seem to find him.

'We can't locate him at the moment, Mrs Whitehead,' Marion Popplewell told Tara stiffly. 'Perhaps you'd like to call again. Or if you'd care to leave your number I will ensure Mr Whitehead receives your message.'

Tara got the impression that Eric wasn't Matron Popplewell's favourite resident. She had no choice but to arrange to meet with Richard to discuss what was happening.

They met at a favourite café. Tara didn't realize Richard was already waiting for her until a tall woman wearing a dark-blue patterned skirt, ivory cashmere sweater, and navy-and-bronze silk scarf stood up. The scarf was carefully draped to deflect attention from the breadth of her shoulders.

Tara froze in her tracks. *'Richard?'*

He nodded and gestured towards the chair opposite. 'Would you like to sit down?'

She didn't sit so much as fall into the chair.

'I've shocked you,' Richard said in a soft, high voice that sounded nothing like his own. Blonde hair waved against his cheeks and swept across his brow from a side parting. He wore pale blue eye shadow and pale pink blusher and lipstick, and a light beige foundation covered his skin. He looked pretty.

Tara's stomach heaved and she had to look away. 'What have you done?' she whispered in agony.

'I did try to warn you,' Richard said. 'It might have been easier if you'd agreed to see me earlier, but . . .' He shrugged.

'Oh? So this is my fault?'

He shook his head and sighed. 'No, that's not what I said.'

Tara glanced at the people sitting at the other tables, wondering what they must be thinking. No amount of make-up could disguise the fact that Richard was a man dressed up as a woman.

'If you're embarrassed, we could sit in the car,' he said.

Suddenly she knew that wasn't the problem, and she wanted to explain that to him. She saw the odd combination of suffering and peace in his eyes, and wondered how she had ever missed the anguish it had replaced. Tara wished yet again that she could understand and that she didn't still love this person so deeply.

She took a deep breath. 'No. I need to tell you this face to face.' She quickly explained about Eric.

Richard shrugged. 'Who he leaves his estate to is entirely up to him. God knows there was never any love lost between him and me, and especially not now.'

'You mean he knows?'

'Yes. When I made my decision I contacted the family and told them, so everything was out in the open. I wrote letters to everybody and posted them weeks ago.'

He had struggled for days to compose the letter he'd sent to all the Whitehead family circle. What Richard didn't know was that one of the letters was under the passenger seat in his car, where it had fallen on his way to the post office.

Tara wondered if Richard would have been so upfront if his parents were still alive. His mother, Grace, had died of cancer five years ago, and Henry from a heart attack at the beginning of the year. She suspected Henry's death had removed the final barrier to Richard telling the truth about his sexuality, and felt bitter that his parents' feelings seemed to matter more than hers or Jen's. Tara forced herself to focus. 'Do you think he's doing this out of spite?'

Richard pulled a face. 'Who knows? And to be honest, I don't care. I'm happy for you and Jen to have the money. Believe me, Eric will have plenty of reasons for doing this and only one of them will be to get at me.' He changed the subject. 'How are you?'

She shrugged.

'You've lost weight.'

'Your voice has changed,' she replied bitterly.

There was a heavy silence.

'I didn't have a choice about this.'

'Everybody has choices.'

'Not about everything. Some things are predetermined before a person is born.'

The silence grew again.

Richard moved his hand hesitantly towards Tara's and she saw that he was wearing nail polish. 'I have a new name. I call myself Rachel.'

She recoiled, from his touch and from what he was telling her.

It was too much.

It was all too much.

Tara leapt to her feet, sending her chair crashing to the ground behind her, and stumbled away from the café. If she'd looked back, she would have seen Richard sitting at the table with his head bowed.

When she reached home, Jennifer was listening to music. Tara followed the noise of Opshop up the stairs and into Jennifer's bedroom and turned off the CD player.

Jen lay on her bed in her school uniform. She looked up warily at her mother's pale, tense face. 'Mum?' she asked uncertainly.

'How bad is it at school, Jen?' Tara asked. 'Tell me the truth.'

Jennifer hesitated. Her mother's moods had been unpredictable since her father had walked out, and she'd tried hard not to add to Tara's misery by pouring out her own problems. Just because her dad had gone and done what . . . what he had, didn't mean Jen could stop loving him. She didn't want to let him down by turning away from him, but each time she saw him she felt more confused and, although she tried to hide it, more repulsed. She kept trying to be calm and supportive, but she didn't understand. And when her father asked if she wanted to call him Rachel, Jen said she'd think about it when in reality she wanted to scream at him to stop doing what he was doing to her and her mother and, worst of all, to himself. Jen wanted her father back. She didn't want Rachel — and she could tell by the hurt and sadness in his eyes that he knew.

'Tell me the truth. I want to know. I *really* want to know,' insisted Tara.

Jen began to sob. 'It's horrible — really horrible.'

Tara sat on the bed and gathered her into her arms. 'I'm sorry, love, I'm *so* sorry! I've been so caught up in my own problems, I forgot how horrible this must be for you.'

'It's OK . . .' Jen grabbed a tissue and wiped her nose. She was always willing to make excuses for other people. 'It hasn't been easy for you and Dad, either.'

Tara leaned backwards and looked into Jen's face. 'I saw your father.'

'Oh. So you saw . . .'

Tara closed her eyes and shuddered. *'Everything.'* She opened her eyes. 'He told me he wants to be called Rachel — and I bolted like a runaway horse.'

Jennifer bit her lip. A fat tear rolled down her cheek.

Tara clasped her daughter's pretty face gently between her hands. 'Jenny Benny?' she murmured, using her daughter's old baby name. 'We've both tried to tough it out, but I really think it's time to admit defeat.'

'What do you mean?' Jen searched her mother's face.

'How about we run away to the Waikato for a while?'

Chapter 4

Testing — one — two — three—'

'You're a legend, Bevan! Come on, give us a song!' Chook Larby yelled towards the front of the small community hall where Divine's community cop had been struggling to get the microphone and sound system working for the past thirty-five minutes. Bevan Sargeson was a good cop, but he was no electronics expert.

There was a roar of laughter from the men seated on old-fashioned, chipped wooden chairs with brown metal frames in front of the stage. They were gathered for a meeting about a proposed lifestyle-block development on their land.

'If you can do any better, Chook, you're welcome to get on up here.' Bevan tapped the microphone and blew into it for good measure. 'Testing — one — two — three . . .'

Dave Richards pointedly checked his watch and directed his attention to the tall, rotund figure standing beside Bevan with papers in his hand. He was the only person in the room wearing a suit and tie. 'Can you get a move on, Barney? *Survivor* is on in another thirty minutes. I think Steff might get voted off tonight.'

'Hope not,' Chook said. 'I like her.'

Barney Bigelow heaved himself on to the stage, tugging the waistband of his trousers over his paunch. The moment he let go, they slid under his belly again.

Bevan gave up on the sound system and went to sit with the others.

'I think you all know the reason I called this meeting tonight,' Barney began in his booming nasal voice.

They nodded.

'You all know that Eric Whitehead's checked himself into Peacehaven,' Barney continued, a pained expression on his ruddy moon-shaped face. He owned Peacehaven Retreat, Divine's one and only retirement home. He also owned the undertakers next door, much to the discomfort of Peacehaven's residents.

'You know why he's looking like that, don't you?' Chook muttered to Dave. 'Eric moved himself into one of the best apartments, with an *en suite* and private garden, and he hasn't paid Barney a brass razoo since he got there. Barney's fit to be tied, but he doesn't dare turf him out.'

Dave snorted with laughter. 'Yeah, Eric's got him by the short and curlies, all right.'

'Will you two shut up?!' Barney shouted. 'I'm only going to say this once.'

Chook and Dave fell silent.

'What you *don't* know is Eric's left his house and land to his niece.'

There was a stunned silence followed by uproar.

'He can't do that! He's not dead yet! You can only leave things to people *after* you're dead!'

'I didn't know he had a niece! What niece?'

'Is she a local? What's her name?'

Bevan stood up. '*Shut up!!*'

Barney waited until they'd quietened. 'For your information, Norris, you don't have to be dead to pass on your assets. And in answer to your question, Dave, her name is Tara Whitehead. She's married to Henry's boy, Richard.'

The room filled with noise again.

'Is that the blonde sheila with the legs and the big boobs that came to Eric's birthday party that time?'

'Why didn't Eric leave it to his nephew? It doesn't make sense.'

Barney pursed his lips. No need for them to know everything. There were some aces he intended to keep firmly up his sleeve.

At the back of the room, Gil Sorensen noticed Barney's cagey expression and wondered what he was hiding. He'd always had a nagging suspicion that Barney's plans involved a lot more than a few lifestyle blocks, since his block of land was tiny in comparison to the likes of Norris, Dave or Gil's. Something didn't add up. Gil didn't quite know what it was, but he smelled a rat.

'How does this affect the property development then?' Norris Jenkins asked nervously.

Barney rolled his eyes in disgust. *At last.*

'You all know how much we need Eric's land. It's the easiest way for The Country Corners Lifestyle Development to access the main road. Without it, we'll have to spend a fortune cutting in a new road.'

There was a general nodding of heads.

'We haven't spent the past five years pushing this project through to come a cropper now. It's been like pushing shit uphill with a spatula, and we've come too far to let anything stop us now,' Barney stated emphatically.

'So what do we do about the niece? Where is she?' Dave demanded.

'She lives in Auckland.'

This was greeted by groans and head shaking.

A dorklander — just what they needed. Auckland was to New Zealand what London was to England and California was to America: it was where the rest of the country liked to pretend all the extravagant rich fruitcakes lived, as anybody living south of the Bombay Hills took great delight in pointing out to any Jafa (Just Another Fucking Aucklander) who strayed south. For their part, most Aucklanders neither noticed nor cared.

'Well, let's make her an offer,' Chook spoke up. 'With any luck she'll take the money and run.'

There was a chorus of agreement, with the exception of Gil

Sorensen and Dave Richards. Everybody knew Dave had short arms and long pockets, and the thought of spending money was enough to give him heart palpitations. As for Gil, well you never could be sure what he was thinking; he was a man who played his cards close to his chest. Besides which, unlike the rest of them Gil didn't need the Whitehead land for road access, because his two-hundred-acre dairy farm was opposite Eric's place on the other side of the road.

'What are we going to do, Barney?' Chook asked.

In serious financial trouble, Chook was relying on the sale of his land to dig him out of the mess. Ostrich farming wasn't nearly as lucrative as Chook had imagined it would be. When the bank refused to lend him any more money, he'd been forced to swallow his pride and do something he'd always vowed he'd never do: approach Barney Bigelow for a loan. So now, like many of the others in the room, Chook was in the unenviable position of being another one of Barney's yes men. If the Country Corners development didn't start making *real* progress soon, he would lose not just his self-respect but everything he and his wife, Ngaire, had worked for.

'Yeah, what are we going to do?' several voices echoed.

Barney suppressed a smile. He never had to wait long before they turned to him to sort out their problems. This gave him complete control, and that was the way he liked it. The lifestyle-block development was just the tip of the iceberg of his plans for Divine — not that he had any intention of discussing that with them. They were putty in his hands, and never more so than when the shit hit the fan. *Idiots*, he thought contemptuously, *every one of you.* His eyes met Gil Sorensen's steady gaze, and he shifted uneasily. *Perhaps not* every *one*, he conceded. He harboured many grudges against Sorensen, including that Gil wasn't a team player. By his definition, that meant Gil didn't want to be on Barney's team . . . and if they did ever find themselves on the same side, Barney wouldn't be the captain. Gil was also one of the few people in Divine who didn't owe Barney money or a favour. And, despite his name, he was a Whitehead through his mother, Connie.

Being able to claim Whitehead blood mattered a lot in Divine. If you couldn't say you were born one, the next best thing was to marry one. There were some who could truthfully say their family had been in the area before the Whiteheads. Chook quite rightly pointed out that his Maori ancestors had been there way before Sarah and Henry arrived.

Gil Sorensen and Eric Whitehead were the only big players in the community not in Barney's pocket. Ever since Sorensen had got himself some business degree, Barney's suspicions that Sorensen thought he was an idiot had deepened. Barney didn't appreciate being thought of as an idiot.

He'd married Alison Whitehead expressly to establish his power base, and had stayed in their miserable excuse for a marriage ever since rather than lose everything he'd worked for. Not that Alison cared; she treated Barney with utter contempt, when she wasn't ignoring him. On the second of only two occasions Barney ever saw her drunk (the first being the night he got her pregnant), she told him she wished she'd married her cousin Gil.

Barney had never forgiven her, or Gil Sorensen, for reminding him of his lowly origins. His father had been an alcoholic and his mother had run off when Barney was thirteen, leaving six children to fend for themselves. Barney could still remember the pitying, disgusted expressions on the faces of the town tabbies as they dispensed care and advice to Arnold Bigelow's dirty, sullen brood while he spent what money he had at the Long Drop Pub and Sports Bar in town. Barney got a kick out of watching some of the people who had once looked down on him come to him now with their hands out.

He'd climbed out of the poverty and muck by getting Alison Whitehead pregnant when he came across her drunk and alone. Barney wouldn't have used a condom even if he'd had one, and he couldn't believe his luck when he heard that Alison, daughter of one of the town's richest men, was up the spout. Tiffany was their only child. Seen by her father as a way to keep his place at the top of the Divine pecking order, he alternately spoilt and ignored her, which had turned Tiffany into a fourteen-year-old piranha with an eye to the main chance. It didn't help that Alison Whitehead scarcely noticed her daughter's existence.

Barney looked at Gil and mentally crossed his fingers, toes, eyes and anything else he could think of. A lot rested on getting Sorensen to go along with what he was going to say next.

'Apparently, Tara Whitehead is moving down here with her daughter.'

'What?' Dave cried.

'Why would she want to do that?' demanded Norris.

Barney shrugged. 'Who knows? She's from Auckland. Anyway, we need to keep a close eye on her.' He watched Gil Sorensen from the corner of his eye. 'We need somebody to take her under their wing and become indispensable to her.'

'What about her husband?' Chook asked.

'He's not coming.'

Eyebrows were raised as people put two and two together and came up with five.

'She's not going to have a clue how to look after the land and those horses, is she?' Barney continued. 'She's going to need somebody to guide her.' He looked directly at Gil. 'She's going to need somebody to hold her hand and teach her everything she needs to know about horses.' He corrected himself. 'As much as she needs to know without getting too independent.'

Barney stared at Gil.

Gradually, everybody else turned to look at him.

Gil looked warily around the ring of faces. His eyes narrowed as the penny dropped. He shot Barney an accusing look and shook his head. 'Oh, no. I'm not babysitting Richard's missus.'

'Why not?' Norris asked. 'He's your cousin, isn't he?'

'Yeah, that's right,' Chook nodded. 'He's your cousin.'

'He's my cousin about twenty times removed, Chook,' Gil protested, but he knew he was sunk. He looked at Barney and thought, *You devious bastard.*

Barney gloated. 'You're the obvious choice, Sorensen. You're the only single one.'

'No, he's not. What about me?' Norris asked.

Everybody ignored him. Norris was single for a good reason: he was pug ugly and dreamed of a career on the stage as a magician. He was convinced that all that stood between him and stardom was the lack of a beautiful female assistant willing to be sawn in half.

'What do you mean I'm the only single one?' Gil demanded. 'What's that supposed to mean?'

'It means we need you to give your all to make sure Country Corners Lifestyles becomes a reality — the whole nine yards,' Barney said.

Chook sniggered. 'Or the whole nine inches.'

'Nine inches?' Norris echoed disbelievingly.

Chook and Dave laughed.

Gil ignored them. 'Let's get one thing straight, Bigelow. If you think I'm going to become the town gigolo for the sake of a bloody housing development, you're in for a serious disappointment.'

Barney cleared his throat uneasily and looked around his audience. He wasn't used to his authority being challenged. His gaze slid back to Gil: it was obvious that he wasn't going to back down. Gil was several years younger than Barney and as fit as a fiddle from running a dairy farm and riding his horses. Not the sort of man you took on, not that Gil had ever been an aggressive sort of bloke.

Barney cleared his throat again and smiled jovially. 'Nor would we expect you to, Gil. She could be as ugly as that mutt of Norris's.'

The men laughed. The only thing that made Norris's dog Francine's mangy, wall-eyed face bearable was her superior cow sense. Norris loved her dearly, and was still offended every time Francine had a litter and nobody wanted one of the puppies.

Dave Richards checked his watch and climbed to his feet. 'Well, that's all settled then. I'd better get cracking: Trish will be making the tea.'

Chook Larby slapped Gil. 'Never mind, mate, she might not be too much of a dog.'

Gil eyed him sourly. Chook laughed uproariously at his own joke as he left.

When only Barney and Bevan were left, Gil got to his feet and walked across to where Barney was collecting his papers together and Bevan was packing up the sound system.

'Don't you ever pull a stunt like that on me again, Bigelow,' Gil said.

Barney smiled tightly and glanced at Bevan, who watched silently, coiling an extension lead around his elbow and hand.

Barney's lips thinned. The local cop was one of his few failures when it came to collecting yes men. While Bevan attended the meetings because he owned twenty acres of the proposed development, Barney suspected he'd intervene only if fists started flying.

'Don't take it so much to heart, Gil,' Barney said heartily. 'All we need you to do is keep an eye on her. That's not too much to ask, is it?'

'Never again, Bigelow,' Gil repeated quietly. '*Ever.*'

Gil wasn't stupid.

Nor was he about to fall in with Barney Bigelow's plans. The only reason he attended the Country Corners Lifestyles meetings was to keep an eye on progress. Gil had no intention of selling his farm. He loved it too much, and the thought of some of the most productive farmland in the country being turned into lifestyle blocks littered with white-painted post-and-rail fences and architect-designed houses was anathema to him. There was also the issue of how the local infrastructure would cope with the added pressure on sewerage, water, drainage and road systems if Barney got his way and managed to rush things through council. However, Gil was first and foremost a realist, and the Master of Business Administration he'd completed four years ago at Massey University had taught him to think both smarter and outside the square. The result was a steady growth in his personal wealth through investments in stocks and shares both at home and offshore, as well as a tightly run farm. To ensure that Barney and the locals couldn't pry into his finances, Gil didn't keep an account at any of the local banks and so was far more solvent than any of them knew.

Gil's first love would always be the farm. His teenage son, Jake, helped around the place, but his heart wasn't in it, and Gil knew that when he retired Jake would not be stepping into his shoes. It made sense to allow the property to be rezoned, so that when the time came for Gil to be carted out of the house in a wooden box, Jake would get top dollar. It also made sense to keep a close eye on proceedings rather than set himself up in futile opposition.

But it still didn't mean he had to like it.

Chapter 5

Before he moved into Peacehaven Retreat, Eric had asked Gil to keep an eye on his place. Eric made some money grazing horses and occasionally some cattle beasts for fattening.

'All right,' Gil had agreed, pocketing the spare set of keys. 'But you know you'll be back. You won't last five minutes at Peacehaven with Mad Marion.'

Mad Marion, or *Maid* Marion, depending on your personal bias, had been the matron of the retirement home for the past fifteen years. She always reminded Gil of Hattie Jacques from the *Carry On* films his parents sometimes watched. Like Hattie, Marion was tall and well-upholstered, with a round face and several chins above a large bust and wide hips, all wrapped up in a pristine white uniform, white stockings and white shoes. She even had a white starched nurse's cap. Gil doubted she'd ever passed any nursing exams, but she ruled Peacehaven with an iron hand in a latex rubber glove.

Or at least she had until Eric Whitehead moved in.

Gil was puzzled by Eric's sudden loss of mobility and departure to the retirement home. Five weeks ago, Eric had been climbing fences and roaring around on the tractor. Gil hadn't yet figured out exactly what Eric was up to, but the crafty old bugger was definitely up to something. He just hoped for Tara Whitehead's sake that she didn't get caught in the crossfire.

Gil had heard from his mother and father all about how his cousin Richard's girlfriend had stirred up Eric's birthday party years ago. In those days, Gil was building a reputation as an up-and-coming three-day-event rider, and he and his wife Louise had been away for the weekend while Gil competed a promising young horse that had the makings of a successful international eventer. Gil hadn't minded missing the party. In his experience, family parties were little different to family funerals — everybody stood around sipping drinks, talking politely and listening to lousy music.

He was fond of Eric. The old boy's irascibility and delight in shit-stirring the more staid members of his family, including Henry and Grace Whitehead, amused Gil. He and Louise had been married only a few months, though, and given the choice between a weekend away with her to pit himself and a green horse against a challenging cross-country course, or watching Eric cut his birthday cake and get pissed, his decision was a no-brainer: Lou and the horse won hands down.

'She was like a breath of fresh air.' Connie Sorensen's dark eyes gleamed wickedly as she recounted Tara's antics at Eric's party. 'She shocked Henry and Grace rigid by asking if the music could be changed.'.

'Don't tell me. The Shadows?'

She nodded. 'I think it was hearing "Apache" for the tenth time that finally drove the poor girl over the edge. I thought Grace was going to swallow her bridgework when Tara asked to change the record. Fortunately, Eric was plastered by then and Henry put him to bed.'

Connie went on to describe how charming Tara was, and how incredulous everybody had been that she was Richard's girlfriend. 'She looks like she's just stepped off the beach — tanned, blonde, gorgeous figure, and absolutely besotted with Richard, and she wears the most beautiful shoes!'

Gil laughed. His mother's shoe obsession was a family joke.

He shared her surprise that Richard had brought along a girlfriend who seemed to be the real thing and not just window-dressing to keep his parents happy. Gil had always got along well with Richard. In fact, he didn't know of anybody who didn't — apart from Eric, of course. But Gil was far closer to his younger cousin Alison.

Everybody knew there was something different about Richard, but Eric was the only one who said it out loud. Gil often felt sorry for Richard, because Henry allowed Eric to bully him into participating in the family obsession with horses when they visited Divine. Gil was a gifted rider and horseman, and although Alison didn't share his passion she was an extremely competent rider. Richard, however, was terrified of horses. He would be white-faced with fear whenever his father forced him onto one, and it wasn't until Richard had a serious fall resulting in a broken collarbone and concussion that Henry gave in and stopped making him ride.

The family heaved a collective sigh of relief, apart from Eric, who washed his hands of his nephew — until the day he arrived with pretty, blonde Tara in tow.

'She certainly livened things up,' Connie said. 'Eric couldn't believe his eyes. Apparently she took issue with the way Eric spoke to Richard and called him a vile old bugger. It's such a shame she won't stay that way.'

'She called Eric a vile old bugger?' When Gil had stopped laughing, he asked, 'What makes you say she'll change?'

Connie snorted. 'Grace had *makeover* written all over her face. Once she's finished with Tara, you won't recognize the poor girl. She'll turn her into a modern-day Grace Kelly.'

Gil didn't attend Richard's wedding later that year, but his mother showed him photos of Richard and a slender, ethereal blonde who looked as if a puff of wind would blow her over. The main thing Gil recalled was that Richard and his new wife looked enough alike to be brother and sister, which was creepy. A year later, they produced a daughter.

'Can't be his,' Eric insisted. 'It's probably one of them artificial insemination jobs.'

Henry and Grace were cock-a-hoop that Richard had proved his critics wrong. They thrust photographs of their new granddaughter beneath the nose of anybody who stood still for longer than five seconds.

'Jennifer Jade is the image of her father at the same age!' Grace gushed like a broken tap.

By then, Jake was already a year old. Gil and Louise had bought Eric's dairy farm and were too engrossed in their own small family to pay much attention to anybody else's, and Alison Whitehead's shock pregnancy and marriage to Barney Bigelow soon overshadowed Richard's marriage and fatherhood. Gil felt guilty whenever he thought about Alison's disastrous marriage.

Being only children and cousins, Gil and Alison had spent a lot of time together growing up. Gil had no idea that Alison's father Bill Whitehead (who was a cousin to Eric, Henry, and Gil's mother Connie) wanted Alison to marry Gil. He had certainly never encouraged her, and she had never looked twice at him, but she confided to him that she'd overheard her father talking about her to Eric and Henry a few months before Gil started dating Louise Gibbs.

'Alison's a good girl, does as she's told,' Bill said over a whisky in the office he used in the stables on his property, unaware that Alison was listening at the door. 'It would have been better if she'd been a boy, but there you go — nothing I could do about that, although God knows I tried, but Nancy kept losing one baby after another and the damned doctor said we had to stop trying. So long as she marries that boy of Connie's, I'll be happy. At least that way everything stays in the family.'

'What about Richard? He's a Whitehead, too,' Henry protested. 'He's even got the name.'

'Don't be stupid, Henry,' Bill replied impatiently.

Until that day, Alison had adored her father and had foolishly thought that he adored her too, which he did after a fashion; he certainly treated her like his little princess. But she was confronted with the unpalatable truth that Bill's love for her was conditional. Once she got over her shock and anger, she slipped back into her old habit of trying to please her father, and began to look at her cousin

Gil as a potential husband instead of a substitute brother. But by then it was too late. Gil had met Louise Gibbs and was in the throes of first love.

The night of Gil's wedding, Bill got drunk and said some ugly things to Alison about what a failure she had been to let the one decent young man in the family be snatched from under her nose. Alison was spoilt and immature, and her father's unexpected criticism tore a gaping hole in her self-esteem. She needed somebody to shore it up and tell her she was wonderful again, to put her back at the top of the Christmas tree, the pretty, perfect fairy admired and fussed over by all. She started sneaking booze from her father's drink cabinet, but the first time she got drunk she ran off into the night, terrified Bill would find out.

Barney Bigelow just happened to be driving his clapped-out Holden home from his shift at the dairy factory when he spied Alison Whitehead, the town princess, puking her guts up in some trees by the side of the road. It was a gift from God. He was eight years older than Alison, tall and moderately handsome if you didn't pay too much attention to his protuberant blue eyes. He was also sly, cunning and couldn't believe his luck. Barney saw his chance and took it. He listened to Alison's tearful, drunken story, dried her tears, told her she was beautiful, and relieved her of her virginity. Alison mistook Barney's attention for affection and fell like a ripe plum. It didn't occur to her to ask him to use a condom, and Barney wouldn't have anyway; he only had this one chance, and getting Alison Whitehead pregnant would be poetic justice for the way the Whiteheads and the town had treated him and his family.

Six weeks later, when Alison discovered she was pregnant, her father went ballistic — especially when he heard who the father was. He screamed obscenities at Alison and would have hit her if Eric hadn't been there to stop him.

News travels fast in a small town; bad news, fastest of all. Barney had nothing to lose. He asked Alison to marry him, and the rest, as they say, is history.

It didn't take Alison long to realize she'd swapped one tyrant for another, but the final straw was when her new husband asked her to dress up in her jodhpurs and riding boots, tie him to the bed and paddle him with her riding crop. Alison's sexual experience was limited, but even she knew that this wasn't normal. She was so repulsed that she moved out of the room she shared with Barney and back to her old bedroom. When Barney tried to first cajole and then bully Alison back into his bed, she threatened to tell everybody about his sexual preferences. Barney backed down, but only after cruelly telling her she was useless in bed anyway and he'd done her a favour by having sex with her because nobody else would ever want her.

Bill Whitehead died of emphysema within months of Alison and Barney's wedding. Alison nursed her father in the final weeks, putting up with his vicious comments about her jutting belly and useless, arse-licking husband. She wept like an abandoned toddler at the funeral while Barney looked on, trying not to rub his hands together as he thought of the money and power coming his way. It wasn't until Alison almost passed out at the graveside and everybody became worried about her going into premature labour that Barney finally paid attention to his wife. The baby she carried was his insurance policy. When he attempted to put his arm around Alison and lead her from the grave, she lashed out at him and screamed hysterically, 'Take your hands off me, you filthy pervert! I've already told you, you'll never ever touch me again!'

The rest of the mourners hurried forward to usher her away, relishing the sight of the young upstart getting his comeuppance.

Alison pushed them all away, crying brokenly, 'Gil? Gil?'

Gil hesitated and looked at Louise, who held Jake in her arms.

'It's all right. Go on,' she urged.

As he led Alison away from the graveside, Gil felt Barney's gaze and looked up apologetically. He didn't share the Whitehead snobbery and sense of superiority. He disliked Barney because he was an opportunist who didn't care who he hurt or what he had to do to get what he wanted. In Gil's opinion there wasn't much difference between Barney and Bill, Eric or Henry, except that the latter bought their clothes at better stores, drove nicer cars and lived in beautiful homes. Unlike the rest of the mourners, Gil didn't get a kick out of seeing Barney demoralized, but the bitter, furious look in the other man's pale blue eyes warned Gil that he'd made himself an enemy.

This was confirmed when the will revealed that Bill had left everything in trust for Alison, with provision for Gilbert Malcolm Sorensen to manage her inheritance until she was capable of doing it herself. Bill had managed to deliver a huge slap in the face to his son-in-law from the grave. Barney's hatred and resentment towards Gil and the Whiteheads deepened until it was like an oozing sore at the very centre of him. Bill Whitehead might have thought he'd spiked Barney's guns, but all he'd done was firm up Barney's resolve to grab any opportunity that came his way to take down the Whiteheads.

Gil breathed a huge sigh of relief when Alison recovered sufficiently to hand over the management of the estate to a group of advisors recommended by her lawyers. She arranged a monthly allowance for Barney, and eventually gave him permission to tear down her old family home and build a new one, and after that ignored any efforts to involve her in any financial or business matters, instead taking up painting and sculpting. Alison poured all her emotions into her art; and her unhappiness, frustration and loneliness translated into moody, startling abstracts. Alison Whitehead's pieces became sought-after and, as is often the case with people who have no need of money, began to earn her a very good income at home and abroad. She scandalized the town tabbies by spending an entire year producing huge stone phalluses, which were snapped up as fast as she could produce them; years later, stone penises continued to startle the unwary in the gardens of some of New Zealand's more salubrious homes.

Barney loved the status and attention that being the husband of Alison Whitehead the artist gave him, even though he privately had no interest in art and found his wife's work incomprehensible.

'It's all tits and balls as far as I can tell,' he confessed to his cousin Jerry Wallace, the publican of the Long Drop Pub and Sports Bar.

'And cocks,' Jerry replied. 'Don't forget them stone cocks she made.'

Barney scowled. He'd rather forget. 'Who wants to look at that? And if you do, why spend all that money on a bloody painting or a lump of stone or wood when you can get nice, glossy close-ups in a copy of *Playboy*?'

Jerry agreed unreservedly, and for once actually meant it. Barney had done Jerry a big favour by helping him get his publican's license and putting him in charge of the only pub in Divine (Barney had systematically bought out and closed down the competition), and Jerry was safe in the knowledge that, as long as he continued to do things the way Barney liked, he would never have to return to his previous employment as a milk-tanker driver for the local dairy factory. Taking over the pub had been the beginning of the spider's web Barney had spun around Divine. It happened so gradually that the townspeople didn't notice at first, and by the time they did it was too late to break Barney's stranglehold. Rather than watching in frustration as money continued to roll into the Whitehead coffers as regularly as waves hitting a beach, Barney had set about using his position as Alison's husband to build his own personal wealth, using any means at his disposal.

Alison had shown no interest in their daughter, who was born a few months after her father's death. Unfortunately, little Tiffany did not inherit her mother's dark, petite prettiness, instead favouring her father, who was rapidly losing his looks as he settled into the good life. Tiffany suffered from chronic colic and spent most of her first year screaming at the top of her lungs. It was a standing joke that the habit had never left her, and she still screamed a blue streak if she didn't get her own way.

Alison suffered from postnatal depression and it was then that she began attacking huge slabs of stone with sledge hammers, saws and chisels, and turning out tortured, raw sculptures. Barney felt short-changed. He wanted a wife who knew her place and acted like a woman, not one who wore overalls and protective goggles, forgot to wash her hair for days on end or shave her armpits, and wielded a chisel and hammer like a seasoned navvy. He instructed Alison to stop pissing about with rocks and stone.

Alison told him to piss off.

Gil was aware of what was going on between his cousin and her husband, but he was busy trying to meet the mortgage payments on the farm as well as realize his dream of becoming a member of the equestrian team to represent New Zealand at the next Olympics. He had an outstanding thoroughbred gelding called Wordsworth, or Woody, who was winning just about everything. So when Gil was selected as a member of the equestrian training squad, it seemed his goal might be within reach.

On the third night of the training camp, a horrendous storm hit without warning and a whole month's rain fell in twelve hours, turning paddocks into rivers with only the highest ground showing as tiny, sodden, green hill tops. The following morning when Gil and the other riders went to find their horses, Woody had drowned. Gil knew he would never find another horse like him. Horses like Woody came along once in a lifetime, and Gil was sure he'd used up his quota.

He returned to the farm, and quickly forgot about horses and Olympic gold medals when the bottom dropped out of his world.

Louise awoke one morning with a blinding headache. She looked so dreadful that Gil called their local GP, despite her assurances that it must be a migraine and if she stayed in bed and took a couple of tablets it would be gone. Before the GP had even made it to their house, she had lost consciousness and Gil had called an ambulance. By the time Louise reached Waikato Hospital, she was no longer breathing and the paramedics had hooked her up to a portable ventilator. She was admitted to the intensive care unit where a brain scan revealed she'd suffered a brain haemorrhage, and she was taken straight to the operating theatre to stop the bleeding and relieve the pressure on her brain. Louise never woke up again, and was eventually pronounced braindead. Gil gave the go-ahead to switch off the ventilator and numbly agreed to the request that her organs be donated, because he knew it was what she would have wanted.

At the age of twenty-four Gil was a widower with a three-year-old son. The day Louise was cremated, he buried not only his heart but also his youth and his dreams. Connie and Malcolm moved in for the first few years, providing much-needed help with Jake and the farm, and supporting Gil through the dark days when he functioned on autopilot and frequently lost the plot altogether.

When Gil looked at Jake, he figured Louise would think he'd done a reasonable job of raising their son. Jake was fit, healthy, happy, well adjusted, and a source of great pride to his father and grandparents (who spent half of the year at their home in Divine and the other half travelling or at their place on the Sunshine Coast of Queensland). Jake liked having a young father. He could generally ask his dad just about anything without fear of getting a lecture or shocking him.

When Jake began getting more telephone calls than Gil and they were nearly all from girls, Gil decided it was time to give Jake the obligatory sex talk.

'I've learnt it all at school,' Jake announced when he realized what his father wanted to discuss.

'Is that so?' Gil folded his arms. 'Well then, maybe you should tell me everything you know and I'll learn something instead.'

Jake was stumped. He knew that his father was seen as fair game by most of the single women in Divine, and he also figured that the reason his dad dated a few women casually in Hamilton, the nearest big town, was to get laid there rather than have sex with the likes of Glenys Tweedie, the local real estate agent, and be expected to put a ring on her finger. Jake liked to think of himself as mature and able to cope with just about whatever life threw at him, but the thought of Glenys as a stepmother was gross and made him want to gag. However, acknowledging that your father had a sex life was equally gross. It wasn't until he watched *Boston Legal* that Jake realized his father had been a champion of the concept of 'friends with benefits' for years.

'Do we have to do this?' he complained. 'You're going to ask me embarrassing questions, aren't you?'

'Only a couple.'

'OK. Get it over with.'

'Do you have condoms and lube?'

Jake slouched in his chair and mumbled, 'Uh . . . yeah . . . most of the time.'

In fact, he'd had the same pack for an entire year and he was fifteen! A virgin! *At fifteen!* When every other guy his age at school said that he'd already done it, at least twice. Jake really liked Melanie Larby, but had never been able to work up the courage to ask her out.

'Most of the time's not good enough.' Gil accurately surmised the true state of affairs, but didn't want to embarrass Jake any more than he had to. 'If you run out and need more, tell me and I'll pick you up some.'

Like that's going to happen, Jake thought. 'Yeah, OK.' He balanced his chair on two legs and glowered at his feet. He wanted this conversation *over.*

'There are two golden rules,' his father told him.

'Oh yeah?' Jake replied truculently. 'What are they, then?'

Gil lifted a booted foot and tipped the front legs of Jake's chair backwards.

Jake yelped as the chair fell back against the wall, leaving him dangling in midair with his knees beneath his chin.

'Listen up,' Gil said. 'You *always, always* wear a condom, d'you hear me? Apart from the risk of getting the girl pregnant, you've got a chance of catching the clap, HIV, Hepatitis B and C—'

Jake struggled upright. 'OK! OK! What's the other golden rule?'

Gil frowned. 'What?'

'You said there were two golden rules. What's the other one?'

His expression cleared. 'Oh. That. Never buy your condoms in Divine.'

'Why not?'

'Because within twenty-four hours everybody in town will know the brand, colour, how many you bought, and be counting the days until you buy more.'

Jake was appalled.

Gil nodded. 'You get the picture. And lastly, some advice you can either take or leave.'

Jake eyed him warily. 'What?'

'Think really carefully before you get involved with anybody in Divine, because your business is *never* your business in this town.'

'But what about if you really like somebody?' Jake protested, thinking of Melanie Larby's big hazel eyes and soft, round boobs.

Gil shrugged. 'It's your call. I've always made it a rule never to get involved with anybody local.'

Jake was crestfallen. 'Never?'

'*Never.*'

Chapter 6

'Oh my God, we're stuck in a time warp. We've been sucked into the 1970s.'

Tara looked about the kitchen of Eric Whitehead's house in dismay. It was the complete antithesis of her gorgeous home in Auckland, which had once warranted a spread in *New Zealand House and Garden*. Eric's house would never in a million years grace the pages of a magazine, unless it was the *Pig Farmer's Gazette*.

'It's really well maintained,' Jen offered.

'Even worse,' Tara replied dolefully. 'At least if it was peeling and falling apart I'd have an excuse to spend money on redecorating. Come on, let's see the rest of it.'

The house didn't improve. Eric was obviously keen on orange drapes and brown velour chair covers, and in the lounge he'd really let himself go and covered the walls with red flocked wallpaper, to complement the green vinyl sofa with a buttoned back.

'It looks like an English pub,' Tara fretted.

Jen couldn't stop laughing.

The kitchen cupboard doors were covered in high-gloss paint in orange, red and sunshine yellow, and a brown wooden cuckoo clock hung beside the brown aluminium back door set with frosted yellow panes of glass. Eric had given Tara and Richard a similar clock as a wedding present. They'd donated it to a PTA fundraiser. When the cuckoo popped out of hiding to call *Cuckoo! Cuckoo! Cuckoo!* Tara's eyes narrowed.

'I like it!' Jen protested.

The master bedroom had a big, old bed with a cream vinyl headboard and an orange candlewick bedspread. Tara recalled Richard telling her that Eric had never married, preferring instead to cut a swathe through the flower of not only Divine's womanhood but also the surrounding towns. He'd been a randy old goat who saw any woman as fair game, regardless of whether she was married or not. According to Richard, the women had fallen like ripe apples, and Eric had been involved in more than a few punch-ups with irate husbands and had been named in several divorces.

'The mongrel!' Tara had cried.

Richard had nodded. 'Yes. I'm afraid Uncle Eric is the skeleton in the family closet.'

Tara's lips twisted as she looked at Eric's bed. He hadn't been the only skeleton hiding in the Whitehead family closet. She resolved to replace the bed with her own as soon as the moving van arrived. There was no way she was sleeping in Eric's shag pad.

Eric's lawyers had arranged for Tara to collect the house keys from local real estate agent, Glenys Tweedie, who'd led the way in her car to the Whitehead property, which was about five kilometres out of town on the main road. Glenys's navy blue skirt and blazer didn't do any favours for her pear-shaped figure, but her short blonde hair was well cut. Tara would have asked for the name of her hairdresser but for Glenys's patronizing smile and condescending manner.

'The house is very well maintained,' said Glenys. 'Eric was a stickler for keeping the place up to scratch, and he'll no doubt want it to stay that way. Let me show you around outside.'

All very well, but it's still ugly, Tara thought, although she had to admit that the long driveway that dog-legged past the tall shelter belt at the front of the property and beneath a row of silver birch trees to the house was quite picturesque — at least until you set eyes on all that angry red brickwork and the ugly brown aluminium window frames.

The agapanthus plants either side of the driveway nodded and swayed as Tara guided the Lexus past them to park in front of a row of garages with old-fashioned roller doors painted a startling shade of orange. Tara could imagine how pretty everything would look in spring with leaves on the trees and the plants along the drive in bloom.

Jen pointed to the lush green paddocks on either side of the driveway. 'Mum, look at how pretty it is!'

Tara dredged up a smile. 'Yes, it's lovely.'

Glenys smirked and offered to take them for a ride in her SUV to see the rest of the property, but Tara declined. 'We'll do it ourselves tomorrow.'

'The forecast is for rain,' Glenys said.

Tara shrugged. 'That's OK; we'll drive up that road thingie.' She pointed vaguely at a dirt road bisecting the paddocks at the back of the house.

'You mean the race?' Glenys asked disdainfully.

'Is that what it's called?' replied Tara coolly.

Glenys studied Tara's gleaming olive-green Lexus. 'You plan to drive your car down the race?'

'Yes. What's wrong with that?'

'There are some potholes along the way that Eric didn't get around to filling in, and if it rains it'll get slippery. You wouldn't want to get your car stuck,' Glenys said bossily. 'The forecast is for heavy rain tonight. Not that we don't need it; it's been dry as a chip this winter.'

Tara wondered if she could get away with torching the house and collecting the insurance money for Jen.

'Hey, Mum!' shouted Jen ecstatically from behind the house. 'We've got horses!'

Tara picked her way across the uneven ground to stand beside her daughter at a five-strand wire-and-batten fence. Two horses, both brown and huge, watched them from beneath a willow tree on the far side of the paddock. She frowned. 'What are they doing here?'

'Oh, didn't you know?' Glenys replied casually. 'Eric grazes horses. There's about twenty on the property at the moment. No doubt you'll see them when you take your drive tomorrow.'

Tara was dismayed. 'What do I have to do with them? I mean do I have to *do* anything or do they just, you know . . . eat?'

'Just the usual,' Glenys said unhelpfully. 'Well, I'll leave you both to settle in. Don't forget to shut the gates, will you?'

Tara watched Glenys stride away to her mud-splattered SUV and muttered, 'I won't forget to shut the gates if you can remember to shut your cakehole, you old bat.'

'Mum!' Jen reproved.

'Old bag,' Tara insisted, following Jen into the house.

Glenys sat in her car and called Barney Bigelow's cellphone number.

'They're here,' she announced when he answered. 'Tomorrow she plans to drive her big flash car down the *road thingie* and have a look at the rest of the property.'

Glenys listened as Barney spoke.

'Why does Gil Sorensen have to know they're here?' she asked resentfully.

Most people in town had heard that Gil had been assigned the job of looking after Mrs Tara Whitehead and knew that it had something to do with the lifestyle-block development that Barney, Chook, Norris, Dave, Bevan and Gil had been involved in for the past two years. Until he'd decided to move into Peacehaven, Eric Whitehead had been involved, too, and had caused Barney no end of headaches. For the most part, the townspeople of Divine had little interest in the money-making ambitions of Barney and the others, although several were surprised that Gil Sorensen had thrown his hat in with them. Gil and Barney hadn't always seen eye-to-eye in the past, and Gil was very attached to the farm that he and his wife Louise had bought from Eric early in their marriage.

Glenys wasn't very happy with the idea of Gil spending time with willowy, blonde Tara Whitehead. Gil had been a widower for over ten years and Glenys wasn't the only woman in Divine who thought it was high time he remarried, but despite Glenys's strenuous efforts Gil Sorensen remained immune to her charms. Glenys was becoming so desperate that she'd recently accepted a dinner invitation from Norris Jenkins and spent an entire evening watching his repertoire of cutlery tricks and looking at photos of Francine's latest litter of puppies. With so few single, decent-looking and *sane* men in town, Glenys certainly didn't appreciate outside competition.

Barney outlined his plans.

'What do you mean you hope she gets her car stuck?' Glenys demanded. Barney brayed on in her ear. 'Oh.' She stared glumly through the windscreen of the car. 'So Gil has to tow her out.'

Gil knew that Barney was behind Glenys Tweedie telling him that Tara Whitehead and her daughter had arrived the day before — not that Glenys ever needed an excuse to call him. Jake had made Gil swear that he would never date her.

Gil was up early to milk two hundred and fifty cows before returning to the house to wake Jake for school. Jake arrived in the kitchen, yawning, as Gil stood at the sink sipping his first cup of tea for the day.

'Morning.'

'Morning,' Gil replied.

'I'll do the afternoon milking today. It'll give you a chance to meet the new neighbours.'

Gil leant back against the kitchen sink, the mug of tea cradled against his chest and a hand in the pocket of his overalls. 'Put a sock in it, you little smart-arse.'

Jake snorted and helped himself to the first of the five bowls of cereal he ate every morning, followed by half a loaf of toasted bread. It was costing Gil a fortune to feed him.

'You never know.' Jake added milk to his bowl. 'She might turn out to be hot.'

'I know what she looks like. Your grandmother showed me the wedding photos when she married Richard.'

'What was she like?'

'Blonde and skinny. She and Richard looked so much alike they could have been brother and sister. It was creepy.' Gil looked at Jake. 'There's a teenage daughter. I don't know her name, but I expect you'll come across her at school sooner or later. Keep an eye on her, will you?'

'OK,' Jake mumbled around a mouthful of cereal. 'Are you going over there, then?'

'Nope.'

'What about the horses? I thought Eric asked you to keep an eye on them.'

'I can do that without Mrs Whitehead being any the wiser. I'll be buggered if I'm going to rush over and introduce myself after the stunt Barney B pulled.'

Gil would have stuck to his guns if he hadn't recalled the potholes in Eric's race that needed filling.

And if Tara Whitehead hadn't got her big, flash car stuck in one of them.

It had rained heavily overnight, just as Glenys Tweedie had predicted, but unlike Auckland, which was one big clay pit, Divine was located in sandy loam soil and the resulting puddles drained away in no time. Tara thought this was a sign that it would be fine to take the Lexus for a drive along the race.

She was wrong. Less than ten minutes into the journey, one of the front tyres got stuck in a rain-filled pothole. Tara tried unsuccessfully to reverse out of the hole, and when that didn't work she put Jen behind the steering wheel and got out to push. All she got for her trouble was a face full of mud, and dirty water and dollops of mud sprayed down the front of her white jumper and cream jeans.

'Oh shit!' She held her arms out from her sides and stared at the stinking brown sludge decorating her clothes. 'I'll never get the stains out!' Her teeth began to chatter as the icy wetness seeped through her bra and her nipples exploded like popcorn kernels against the front of her sodden jumper.

Jen climbed out of the car and came to look. 'Why didn't you wear some old jeans and a pair of the gumboots from the garage like I did?'

Tara glowered at the old pair of jeans and gumboots Jen was wearing, but was unable to answer with the truth, which was that lately the reckless streak in her nature that she had worked so hard to subdue for the past sixteen years had resurfaced with a vengeance. Richard had affectionately called it her 'wild Westie streak', but Tara hadn't been fooled; she knew he became uncomfortable when she was impulsive and reckless. Driving an expensive car along a potholed mud track and wearing cream jeans and high-heeled Scarpa boots on a farm outing was retaliation against Richard and what he had done. Anyway, one look at the ugly selection of worn old gumboots had made Tara suck in her breath in dismay. How could a woman who worshipped shoes be expected to put her feet into something so ugly?

'Because I don't *have* an old pair of jeans, and I *refuse* to wear a pair of those disgusting, ugly old boots! Why should I have to lower my standards just because I've come to live in the bloody country?' she snapped.

'Do you need a hand?' enquired a low, deep voice.

'Aaahh!'

Tara and Jennifer clutched each other and leapt into the air.

Jennifer landed squarely on the soles of her rubber gumboots.

Tara wasn't so lucky. The stacked heels of her Italian boots skidded in the mud and she fell flat on her bum in the oozing, brown slime. She whimpered as the mud seeped through her designer jeans and into her Elle MacPherson thong, while a strange man watched her from the other side of the fence that ran alongside the race.

'Where did you come from? Who are you?' Tara demanded, fear sharpening her voice.

They were two women alone in the middle of nowhere with a

strange man they'd never set eyes on before watching them. Jen edged closer to Tara and reached down a hand to help her up, as Mr Country Calendar swung himself over the fence and dropped onto the race in his big, brown, scuffed work boots.

Tara thrust Jen behind her.

'I'm your neighbour, Gil Sorensen,' he said evenly. 'Eric asked me to keep an eye on the place.' He jerked a thumb over his shoulder. 'I live on the farm across the road.'

Tara eyed him suspiciously, wondering if she detected a glimmer of amusement in his dark eyes and that mild voice. Her brow furrowed. Gil Sorensen? She had a feeling Richard had a cousin by that name.

Gil waited patiently while she studied him.

Tara had never seen anybody made up of so many shades of brown: brown eyes, brown skin, and tufts of dark brown hair sticking out from beneath a dun-coloured woollen beanie pulled low over his brow with *Divine Diggers — Give 'em Hell* picked out in orange letters on the turned-up cuff. Even his waterproof jacket and leggings were brown. The deep grooves bracketing his mouth and the lines fanning out from the corners of his eyes attested to long hours spent outdoors. Tara eyed his broad shoulders, large hands and long legs uneasily. She didn't realize that Gil Sorensen had been studying her just as thoroughly, as he looked fixedly at her face to keep from staring at the two hard little nubs pebbling the front of her filthy jumper.

'Do you ladies want a hand to get your car out?' he asked.

Jennifer smiled. 'Yes, please!'

Tara hesitated.

'I'll go and get the tractor. You're cold,' Gil said. The instant the words were out of his mouth he wanted to call them back again.

Tara glanced down and hastily hugged her arms across her breasts. A dull flush crept up her neck and into her face as she glared at their unwanted saviour.

Gil thought about apologizing, but the look on her face told him he'd be wasting his time. He climbed back over the fence and headed across the paddock, brushing curious horses aside as he went.

'How's that for luck?' Jen exclaimed. 'He seems really nice.'

Tara glowered at Gil Sorensen's departing figure and kicked the wheel of the car. 'He seems very brown.'

Jennifer looked at her oddly.

About fifteen minutes later, Gil came down the race driving a faded blue tractor which effortlessly pulled the stranded Lexus out of the pothole. He smiled when Jen punched the air and yahooed.

Tara wrinkled her nose at the smell of the diesel and said, 'Thank you very much.'

'You're welcome.'

Tara looked at him sharply, certain she could detect amusement in his voice. She was unaware of the picture she made, with her hair and face caked with mud, and her pale peach lipstick-covered lips pursed irritably in the middle of the mess. She turned her back and removed her muddy jumper, turning it inside-out so she could sit on it for the return journey instead of ruining her car's leather upholstery. Beneath the white jumper she wore a thin, long-sleeved cotton T-shirt, which Gil noted was, of course, *white.* Tara beckoned to Jennifer, her shoulders hunched in an attempt to hide her rigid nipples. 'Come on, Jen.'

Jennifer lingered beside the tractor, eyeing the controls curiously.

On impulse, Gil asked, 'Do you want a ride back to the house?'

'OK!' Before Tara could stop her, Jen had clambered up beside him.

He looked over his shoulder at Tara and called, 'Just keep your speed steady and stay away from the right-hand side. The ground is softer there.'

Tara watched her daughter and new neighbour disappear off down the race towards Eric Whitehead's ugly house on the smelly, chugging tractor, and mimicked resentfully, '*Stay away from the right-hand side!* Bloody mud! *Bloody men!*'

By the time she'd parked the Lexus in front of the garage, she'd calmed down sufficiently to remember her manners. Jen was standing beside the blue tractor talking up a storm with Gil Sorensen. Hugging her arms across her chest, Tara went to join them. 'Would you like to come in for a cup of coffee?' she asked politely.

He just as politely declined. 'No, thanks. Maybe some other time.' Then he smiled at Jen and put the tractor in gear. 'Bye, Jennifer. Give me a call and we'll sort out a time.'

'What was all that about?' Tara asked as the tractor roared off along the driveway leaving the agapanthus plants reeling in its wake.

Jennifer beamed. 'We've got a tractor and Mr Sorensen is going to teach me how to drive it.'

The woman's about as useful as a one-legged man in an arse-kicking contest, and bloody rude, too, Gil thought as he headed through the underpass beneath the main road that linked his property to Eric's. Back when Gil's dairy farm had belonged to Eric, the underpass had been used to move the herd safely across the road from one part of the property to the other. Gil still used it to bring the cows over to graze Eric's paddocks during spring and summer to help keep the weeds and grass down. Gil doubted that Mrs Whitehead would be asking for the arrangement to be continued.

He drove the tractor towards the house that he and Louise had begun building fifteen years ago after spending the first two years of their marriage living in the half-round barn, which stood on the driveway opposite the house. Gil had finally finished the place three years after Louise had died, and it still saddened him that she had never seen it completed. After she'd died, he'd toyed with the idea of selling the farm and letting somebody else complete it, but Gil's parents and Eric had insisted that Gil owed it to Louise's memory to finish her house. Gil could honestly say that blood, sweat and tears had gone into the final result, a long, low building of dark-brown wood, with doors opening from every room on to wide brick patios bordered by sweeping green lawns. A wooden pergola that would soon be festooned in lilac-coloured wisteria shaded the tall wooden front door, and fantails flitted from beam to beam, making their characteristic squeaking. Two pukeko stalked across the front lawn, flicking their tails to reveal a flash of white as they poked at the grass with their stubby red beaks. They were the bane of farmers' lives, getting into feed and generally making nuisances of themselves, but Gil had reached a compromise by feeding the pair so that they restricted their activity to the garden.

He was still thinking about Tara Whitehead as he parked the tractor by the barn and got down. What idiot went out on a farm on a wet, muddy day wearing white clothes and high-heeled boots? He didn't rate her chances when it came to cleaning the mud and cowshit off her clothes and those boots. If ever there was a high-maintenance woman, Tara Whitehead was it. Gil's mother had been right: apart from the pale, silken blonde hair, Richard's wife had changed from the girl he'd seen in the wedding photos. For one thing, she wasn't skinny any more, judging by those boobs and the curve of her bum. He suspected that if she smiled she'd be pretty, but the pinched, irritated expression on her face looked permanent, as did the droop of her mouth and the misery in her light-coloured eyes. Separation and divorce were a bitch, but Tara Whitehead looked more like she'd suffered bereavement. Gil had seen that same look of desolation on his own face after Louise had died. It irritated him that he felt so damned sorry for Tara. Leaving Richard wasn't the same as him dying. She could still see him, smile and talk to him again one day. For all he knew, it might be some kind of trial separation and they'd be back together again in a few months.

Gil kept picturing her nipples beneath the sodden white wool and scowled. 'Probably implants,' he muttered.

He liked the daughter. She looked a lot like her mother, except that she had Richard's blue eyes and none of her mother's sourness. Gil didn't know why he'd offered to teach her to drive Eric's tractor. Perhaps it was because he felt that all that unbridled enthusiasm and sweetness deserved a reward. It couldn't be much fun living with Tara, although Gil supposed she must be a good mother if she'd managed to raise such a nice daughter.

'Somebody in that house needs to know what they're doing,' he said aloud as he headed inside. 'And it doesn't look like it's going to be the mother.'

Barney Bigelow telephoned later that night.

'You met Mrs Whitehead then.'

It wasn't a question. Gil wondered how he did it. Did he have spies hidden up every tree in Divine? 'I pulled her car out of a pothole,' he said flatly.

'That's good.'

'Why?'

'What do you mean *why?*' Barney sounded annoyed. 'You're her nearest neighbour. She needs to know she can call on you for help.'

'What if I don't want her to call on me for help?' Gil replied. Barney had a way of getting right up his nose, and his demand that Gil supply more than neighbourly help still angered him.

'Don't be like that, Gil. You know how it is in the country.'

Yeah, he knew. You helped your neighbours out in times of need and watched each other's backs, but that didn't include providing sex on demand. When he recalled the way Richard's missus had looked down her nose at him, Gil nearly laughed out loud. Tara Whitehead had been infuriated at the prospect of Gil pulling her out of the mud, so the odds of him actually *pulling her* were extremely long. Besides, he didn't like stuck-up women, even if they did have nice knockers and a heart-shaped bum.

'Barney, I thought I made myself clear the other night. If you persist in shoving Mrs Whitehead at me, I won't be responsible for my actions — so back the hell off, do you hear me?'

There was a long, tense silence while Barney waited for Gil to apologize. When he didn't, Barney hung up, fuming. He'd always suspected that Gil Sorensen could be a loose cannon.

Barney didn't want any cannons loose in his town, not unless he was directing their fire.

Chapter 7

Jen met Jake Sorensen two days later, as she waited at the end of the driveway for the school bus. Her mother had telephoned to check that Jen was eligible for the free service and to find out exactly where she had to wait.

'That's handy,' Tara said brightly. 'Door-to-door service, and it'll give you a chance to meet kids who live nearby.'

Jen murmured assent. Her mother was more worried than she was about her changing schools. In Jen's opinion, getting the school bus was the only difference between going to All Saints and her school in Auckland. She still had to wear an ugly uniform and she would still never be one of the in-crowd. Despite that, she was relieved to be away from Auckland and all the knowing stares and whispering behind hands about her father.

As she stood waiting, a tall, dark-haired boy wearing grey trousers, white shirt and a navy tie came strolling down the driveway opposite. His navy blue jumper had the same white All Saints emblem that Jen had on her navy blue school blazer. A bulging backpack was slung over one shoulder, and his other hand was deep in the pocket of his trousers. He stopped opposite Jen, dropped the pack between his chunky black shoes and raked his hair back with his hand.

They studied one another across the road.

He lifted his chin in greeting. 'Hiya. You just moved into Uncle Eric's?'

Jen nodded warily. He was definitely older than her, at least a Year Twelve or Thirteen — and the way his shoulders and chest filled out his school jumper made him look more like a man than a boy. She looked at the driveway behind him and guessed he must be Gil Sorensen's son; he certainly looked a lot like him. Her mother said Gil was her dad's cousin, which would explain why this guy called Eric 'uncle'. Jen's gaze slid back. He was really cute, with dark hair gelled into spikes on his forehead and a nice smile. Cute — but not nearly as handsome as his dad. Jen had developed a big crush on Gil.

'I'm Jake Sorensen.' Jake jerked a thumb over his shoulder. 'I live on the dairy farm opposite. I think you met my dad the other day.'

Jen blushed. 'He pulled our car out of a pothole.'

She waited for a smart remark about townies in the country.

Jake watched her expectantly. 'Have you got a name?' he asked.

'Oh!' Jen's cheeks burned. 'Yeah — it's Jen — Jen Whitehead.'

He nodded affably. 'We're cousins.'

'I guess,' Jen agreed doubtfully.

Jake grinned. 'No, we *are* — about fifty times removed or something. Uncle Eric and my grandmother are right into the family tree and all that kind of stuff and they'd know for sure.'

Jen smiled back. It might be cool to have a cousin at the same school. In Auckland, her cousins Trent, Travis and Troy lived out west, which meant they went to different schools. Aunt Kim didn't have the money to pay for private education like her parents. 'The boys', as they were known in the family, were almost always in trouble and spent more time in detention than they did in class, not that it improved their behaviour. Jen's father disapproved of them and didn't like her spending too much time with them or her Aunt Kim. It was one of the few things that her mother and father fought about. Jen privately liked her rowdy, naughty cousins and irrepressible, loud-mouthed aunt, and she loved staying at her grandparents' house and hanging out with her mother's family. Her Kemp relatives were drama queens. They turned the simplest thing into a major event, and Jen spent most of her time in fits of laughter. As the only girl in the family, she was spoilt rotten and the boys approved of her because she was pretty *and* really good at sports *and* she didn't squeal when they misbehaved.

The bus came into sight and slowed with a squeal of brakes and a belch of diesel fumes on Jake's side of the road. He hefted his pack over his shoulder and looked across at Jen. 'You coming?'

'Mmm? Oh! Yeah!'

She grabbed her backpack, hurried across the road and climbed aboard ahead of him.

The bus was already half-full, and everybody stared at her. Jen sank into the nearest seat and was grateful when Jake sat down beside her.

'So.' He sprawled in the seat, his long arms and legs taking up his half and a portion of Jen's as well. 'What's your mum got planned today? D'you reckon she'll need pulling out of any potholes?'

Jen smiled and shook her head. 'She's had enough of potholes. She said she's going to spend the day buying a pair of gumboots.'

'It doesn't take a whole day to buy a pair of gumboots.'

Jen rolled her eyes. 'You don't know my mother.'

Tara was in her element. For years she'd made a career out of buying outrageously beautiful footwear, and she assured herself that somewhere there had to be a pair of gumboots (shudder — what had she come to?) which would make her feel as wonderful when she put them on as her beloved Sergio Rossi boots, Alexander McQueen wedges or Hugo Boss pumps.

She discovered a small shop in the main street of Divine that sold absolutely beautiful shoes and matching handbags. It was almost a religious experience. The moment she crossed the threshold, her feelings of alienation and confusion disappeared. She was no longer lost in the middle of the Waikato countryside, but standing on familiar territory. She instantly recognized a kindred spirit in the beautifully dressed and shod shop assistant.

Tara cast covetous looks at the other woman's iridescent peacock-coloured dress with its unusual belt fastened beneath her breasts. 'Where did you get your dress?'

'Ooby Ryn.' She smiled and explained, 'A Waikato-based designer. I bought it right here in Divine. Her clothes are just gorgeous.'

Tara felt a stirring of hope. 'You'll have to tell me where the shop is.'

Divine looked much the same as any other small rural town in New Zealand. There were no traffic lights, but a roundabout covered in flowers lay at each end of the main street. Outside the town hall stood a clock tower and war memorial, and beside that was a village green with the police station at one end and the office of the local paper, the *Divine Flyer*, at the other. Peacehaven Retreat was on the other side of the green beside the Presbyterian Church and the undertakers.

There was one pub, the Long Drop Pub and Sports Bar, one supermarket, and a racecourse five kilometres outside of town. The Lean and Mean Gym, the undertakers and the pub were all owned by Barney Bigelow, who believed in offering a cradle-to-grave service. A selection of shops, cafés, restaurants and banks were housed in the old buildings adorned with dark green historical plaques situated on either side of the main street. Wrought-iron lampposts painted the same dark green as the plaques were hung with flower baskets, and matching green wrought-iron benches were evenly spaced along the pavement edge.

Stepping into the little shoe shop was like stepping through a black hole into another universe. There wasn't a single pair of gumboots in sight. The glass shelves were artfully arranged with a tumble of shoeboxes frothing with brightly coloured tissue paper and gorgeous sandals, pumps, boots and evening shoes. Tara tried on eight different pairs before settling on beautiful saffron-coloured suede sandals with saucy gold-chain ankle straps. She knew she couldn't really afford them and that some time soon she would have to stop indulging herself. It was even more depressing to think she didn't have anywhere to wear them.

'I don't suppose you stock gumboots?' she asked as the shop assistant wrapped the sandals.

'No. Why don't you try The Warehouse?'

Tara sighed. 'I live on a farm.'

'Don't we all?' the woman replied cheerfully as she handed back Tara's credit card.

Tara examined the selection of navy, green and black rubber boots at the big red shed. The only ones she could see herself in were in children's sizes, so she drove into Hamilton and ruthlessly combed the two malls in the city centre before eventually finding just what she wanted in a shop that sold everything from quiche dishes to lovely little shovel-and-spade sets in their own wooden cases complete with floral gardening gloves. It was the floral gardening gloves that first caught Tara's eye; they exactly matched the red gumboots decorated in yellow and green flowers standing on the floor beside them. The sight of the flowery boots soothed Tara's soul.

'I'll take them and the gloves, please.' She handed over the credit card for the second time that day, wondering when Richard would cancel it.

The sun was shining when she reached Eric's place, but it was still colder than Auckland and Tara shivered. She put on her new gumboots, red Hero jacket, Ralph Lauren jeans and a pair of large, black sunglasses, and pulled her hair into a ponytail high at the back of her head. When she looked in the mirror, she tried to remember the last time she had worn a ponytail. Tara knew that she should be ashamed for spending so much on the saffron sandals, but buying them had cheered her up. She set off on foot to explore as much of Eric's property as she could before Jen got home from school. It would be nice to pretend for a while that everything was fine and her biggest problem was where to wear the new sandals.

Tara strode past the garages, knowing she looked ridiculously overdressed but not caring. It was all part of her rebellion, and better than feeling sad and depressed. She marched along the race, stopping beside a large, round, corrugated-iron shed that looked like a drum that had been cut in half. The door wasn't locked. A quick peek inside revealed that this was where the owners stored bridles, saddles, horse covers and tall bins of what looked like the horsey equivalent of muesli. The back of the barn was stacked high with hay bales, and Tara inhaled the sweet scent of the hay.

Outside, she dodged potholes and cut across the culvert full of rainwater running alongside the race. She criss-crossed back and forth from one paddock to the next, some filled with horses and some empty. Most had large, impressive-looking willow trees sprouting new leaves, and Tara imagined how they would look in the summer with their full heads of hair trailing to the lush, green grass below. Fantails flitted around her floral gumboots in the hope she would unearth some insects. She smiled. 'Clever birds. You obviously appreciate a gorgeous pair of boots.'

Peep! Peep! cried the fantails.

She smiled and marched on.

Her father had often taken her and Kim walking in the Waitakere Ranges when they were younger, and they'd got to know most of the names for the native trees and birds. When his grandsons and granddaughter were big enough, he'd done the same with them. Tara admired a glossy puriri tree and wondered why she'd never thought to go along on any of their walks. Eventually she reached the river and what appeared to be the boundary of Eric's property.

The spot was hauntingly beautiful. Tall, glossy tree ferns with fronds curled tight as a newborn's fist sat alongside khaki green and red-streaked flax and stands of toetoe grass. Tara sat on a tree stump and watched the feathery white plumes of the toetoe waving to and fro in the breeze and tiny green silvereyes investigating the flax. Small black-and-yellow-striped finches with scarlet faces sat in rows on the branches of a nearby tree, rising in a cloud when one was disturbed.

Tara sat for a long time, watching the river slide gently by and letting the place work its magic on her agitated soul. The lush, fecund beauty of the Waikato seeped into her pores, stroking a gentle finger along her tortured, knotted nerves. She didn't know that she was in the exact spot where Sarah Whitehead had sat boiling a billy of water over a campfire almost a hundred and fifty years earlier, before making her pronouncement about the land being touched by a divine hand. For a little while things almost made sense. Auckland seemed a long, long way off. Through the soles of her gumboots, Tara felt the silent heartbeat of these three stunningly beautiful islands tucked away at the bottom of the earth, cradled by the Pacific Ocean. The heartbeat of the land kept rhythm with the pump of her solitary, lonely heart. People would come and go, but the land would always endure.

Peep! Peep!

Peep! Peep!

The fantails interrupted her thoughts. Reluctantly, Tara left the riverside and made her way back down the race.

She'd counted fifteen horses and ponies in the paddocks and wondered how much income they generated. *I need a job*, she thought as she wandered slowly along, oblivious to the darkening clouds overhead that promised more rain. As the wind picked up, the tall trees along the side of the race began to creak and sway.

Tara looked at them and suddenly remembered.

This was where Richard had taken her after Eric's party. She walked slowly across the race and laid her hand against one of the tree trunks, wondering if it was the one that had scraped the skin of her bare shoulders and back when Richard had lifted her up and made such mad, precipitous love to her. He'd wanted her so much that night, so much that he'd pulled off her underwear and pushed himself inside her without trying to arouse her or worrying about using a condom.

Tara ran her palm across the rough bark and whispered, 'You used to love me. You used to want me.' Tears blurred her eyes and her voice cracked. 'What did I do wrong, Richard?'

A sudden noise made her turn.

Gil Sorensen stood in the middle of the muddy race, dressed in his uniform of brown overalls and jacket. He didn't move, just watched as Tara stared at him with grief-stricken eyes awash with tears that spilled over onto her cheeks. He'd been about to call out to let her know he was there, but she'd touched the tree and spoken before he could get the words out.

Tara snatched her hand from the tree and swiped at her face with her palms. 'You shouldn't walk up on people like that! What are you? Some kind of stalker?'

Gil ignored her hostility. He knew what that kind of pain felt like, but he was taken aback to find that haughty, icy Tara Whitehead knew, too. 'Sorry,' he said gruffly. 'I just came over to look at the potholes to see how much aggregate I'll need to fill them.'

She'd shrunk. Gil looked at the ridiculous red, green and yellow flower-strewn gumboots. Without her high heels, Tara looked small and surprisingly vulnerable.

'I don't recall asking you to fill my potholes!' She sounded ridiculous, but there wasn't even a glimmer of amusement in Gil Sorensen's dark, all-seeing eyes, only deep sympathy. Tara's stomach churned. She could have coped with his derision far better than his pity.

'No. Eric did.'

'Oh. I see.'

Tara didn't want this man with his keen, observant gaze seeing into the corners of her soul. She stiffened as a thought struck her. Did Gil feel sorry for her because he'd received one of Richard's letters? Tara dropped her gaze to the toes of her floral boots, her face burning with humiliation. She didn't want to look into his face and see her biggest fear confirmed. Her nose prickled with more tears. *Oh God, not again.*

'Tara?' Gil said quietly.

Suddenly she broke into a run, sprinting past him down the muddy race, fleet as a deer despite her silly flowery gumboots.

Gil spun around as she sped past. 'Tara!'

She ran faster, as if the hounds of hell were after her, stumbling and righting herself before she fell. He watched helplessly as she wrenched open the metal gate and ran across the grass and on to the concrete in front of the garages, then disappeared from sight into the back garden behind the house.

Gil waited on the race for another five minutes to give her plenty of time to make it inside, before slowly making his way back to the gate. He paused and looked towards the tree where Tara had been standing.

You used to love me. You used to want me. What did I do wrong, Richard?

The grief and pain in her voice made his chest feel tight. Tara Whitehead had opened up old scars, reminding Gil what it was like to feel so utterly hopeless and empty that getting through the next minute was a struggle, let alone a day, a month or a year. Jake had been Gil's saving grace, and he suspected that Jennifer was Tara's. She was the reason Tara got out of bed each morning when all she wanted to do was bury her head under the pillow and hide.

The forlorn note in her voice and the agonized expression on her face had floored Gil. What the hell had happened between Richard and his wife? Like most people, Gil had assumed that Tara had done the leaving. Now, he wasn't so sure. He swiped a hand across his face. He didn't want to know. More importantly, it was obvious that Tara didn't want him to know.

Gil headed towards the underpass. 'I don't need to know,' he told himself. 'I promised I'd keep an eye on the place, but that's all I'm doing. Richard and Tara Whitehead can sort things out for themselves. I refuse to get roped into their mess, whatever it is.'

But try as he might, he just couldn't wipe from his mind the picture of Tara Whitehead's luminous, silvery grey eyes spilling tears down her soft, porcelain cheeks.

Chapter 8

'I *really* think you should pay Mr Whitehead a visit,' repeated Marion Popplewell for the third time.

Tara gritted her teeth.

She'd been meaning to visit Richard's uncle, but kept putting it off. Whenever she recalled the one time she'd met the old bugger, Tara found an excuse not to drive into Divine. But it appeared her reprieve was up; Marion Popplewell obviously wasn't going to take no for an answer, but Tara wasn't about to give in easily. If Matron Popplewell thought she could jump on the blower and summon Tara whenever Eric Whitehead played up, she was in for a shock. Tara didn't see why she had to be responsible for Richard's vile, old uncle, just because she was living in his house.

'Has there been some kind of problem, Mrs Popplewell?' she asked coolly.

'It's *Miss* Popplewell, although I prefer to be called "Matron" if you don't mind,' Marion replied primly.

'Fine,' said Tara flatly. 'But am I right in assuming there is a problem?'

There was a pause.

'Matron?'

'Well . . .' Marion drew a deep breath. 'There is the small issue of the cost of Mr Whitehead's accommodation . . .'

No way was she going to be responsible for Eric Whitehead's bills. Her money from the sale of the house was sitting in a high-interest account while Tara tried to think of a way to double it before the year was out, so that she could return to Auckland and buy a house in her old neighbourhood.

'Well, that's something you'll need to take up directly with Mr Whitehead,' she said firmly.

There was another pause while Marion tried to force Tara to squirm and make promises she'd regret. She soon discovered that Mrs Whitehead was made of sterner stuff.

'I see,' Marion said resentfully.

She didn't know what Barney would say when she told him what the Whitehead woman's response had been to her gentle probing about Eric's unpaid bills. Marion wasn't used to being gainsaid, and she was upset that she couldn't take better news to Barney Bigelow, a man she had been devoted to for years, despite his often callous treatment of her. Marion believed Barney when he told her that, had it not been for his fourteen-year-old daughter, Tiffany, he would leave his wife, Alison, to be with Marion. In another four years, Tiffany would be eighteen and hopefully off to university — if she didn't end up in a youth detention centre — and Barney would be free to leave his heartless, uncaring wife to be with her, the love of his life.

She chose to ignore the fact that Barney had another long-time mistress, Elaine Selwyn, who worked at the council offices. The relationship was an open secret in Divine, but in Marion's opinion Elaine was just an aberration who would disappear when Marion could take her rightful place alongside Barney. Marion knew that a man as good-looking and successful as Barney Bigelow would always attract *that sort of woman*, and she understood that she couldn't always be there to give him the love and attention he needed. Elaine Selwyn might be younger than Marion, with a mane of brown Farrah Fawcett hair and a fondness for faux-leather jumpsuits and plunging necklines, but on the increasingly infrequent occasions when Barney shared the silk sheets of her frilly white bed, Marion reassured herself that the relationship they had was on a far higher plane than the tawdry sex a creature like Elaine Selwyn could offer.

'Matron? Is there anything else you wanted?'

Marion started. She'd completely forgotten about Tara Whitehead on the other end of the telephone. How dare she behave as if her time was more important!

'Yes, there is. There's the issue of the mobility-scooter group.'

'Mobility-scooter group?' Tara echoed. 'Does Eric have a mobility scooter?'

'No. But he's been upsetting all the residents who do by telling them they should form an action group and assert their rights.'

'What rights?'

'I have no idea. All I know is that whenever Eric Whitehead is involved *bad things happen.* He's been asking to see you.'

Tara's heart sank. 'He has? Why?'

'I do not pry into the private business of the residents,' Marion lied. 'Perhaps it would be best if you took the time to visit your uncle and ask him yourself.'

Tara knew she was trapped, but she wasn't about to give in without a fight. 'He's not my uncle.'

Two hours later, Tara reluctantly walked into the reception area of Peacehaven Retreat accompanied by a curious Jennifer. She'd heard about her father's notorious Uncle Eric, and none of it had been good. Judging by the orange, brown, red and cream floral carpet on the reception area floor, Eric should feel right at home.

Tara approached the receptionist behind the desk. 'Hello, we're here to see Eric Whitehead.'

The receptionist's gaze sharpened behind her rimless glasses. 'Are you his niece?'

'By marriage,' Tara conceded in a pained voice.

The woman took her time looking at Tara's Country Road trousers and Karen Walker trench coat, and decided that Richard Whitehead's wife looked like a snooty cow. She turned to Jennifer and smiled. 'You've got your father's eyes.'

Tara frowned.

Jennifer smiled uncertainly. 'Thank you.'

'How is—'

Tara interrupted the receptionist. 'Can you tell us the way to Mr Whitehead's apartment, please?'

As they walked away, Jennifer whispered, 'That was rude, Mum. People are bound to ask about Dad.'

Tara didn't answer.

They found the door to Eric's apartment at the end of a corridor on the ground floor. Tara knocked and a male voice barked, 'If that's you, Mad Marion, or *you*, Barney Bigelow, you can bugger off!'

Jen's eyes widened.

Tara grimaced. Eric obviously hadn't improved with age. She shoved the door open and glared at the tall, raw-boned man sitting in a brown leather La-Z-Boy chair beside the window. His fair hair had receded and held more grey than the last time Tara had seen him, but apart from that Eric Whitehead looked hale and hearty at seventy-two years of age. He was wearing a red-and-white checked shirt beneath a brown cardigan, with brown trousers, and brown corduroy slippers on his large feet.

Eric frowned at Tara and Jennifer for several moments before recognition dawned. 'Oh. It's you. Richard's missus. Or should I say Rachel's missus?'

So, Richard really had written those letters. Tara wondered just how many people in Divine knew the whole sorry story. She could call Richard and find out exactly who he'd written to and what he'd said, but Tara wasn't sure if she would be any better off knowing.

Jen flung her arm about Tara's shoulders and cried, 'Shut up, you wicked old bugger! Don't you dare talk to my mother like that!'

Tara was astonished: Jennifer rarely lost her temper, and it was the first time Tara had ever heard her swear.

Eric chuckled. 'You look like your father, but I'm pleased to see you've got your mother's guts. You know, she said almost exactly the same thing the first time she met me.'

'Why?' Jen demanded. 'Who were you tormenting then?'

'Jen!' Tara gasped.

She shared a long look with Eric, silently begging him not to tell Richard's daughter what he'd said about Richard the day that he and Tara had met.

Eric shrugged. 'Could have been anybody. It keeps me entertained. You might as well come in and close the door.'

Trying in his own way to be hospitable, he said, 'I've got some toffees in me top drawer over there.'

Once riled, Jen was not easily mollified. 'I'm fifteen, Uncle Eric, not five.'

'How am I supposed to know what girls your age are interested in?' he complained. 'Now if you were a boy, it'd be a different matter. I'd buy you a box of condoms.'

'Eric!' Tara snapped. 'One more word and I swear we'll be out that door and you'll never see us again. Jen is *fifteen years old* for God's sake! Show her some respect!'

Eric looked sheepishly at Jen. 'Sorry, love.'

She nodded and tried not to giggle.

Eric considered himself forgiven. 'Have you met your cousin Jake? He lives across the road from you with his dad.'

Jen nodded. She sat with Jake on the trip to and from school every day, which had made her unpopular with a lot of the girls at school, in particular with Tiffany Bigelow. As well as being cute, Jake was captain of the First Fifteen and there were a lot of girls who wanted to go out with him and didn't appreciate a stranger poaching on their territory — cousin or not. They'd come to the conclusion that Jen and Jake were going out together, but this couldn't have been further from the truth. Jen thought Jake was really good-looking, but so were her cousins in Auckland and she didn't fancy them either. She and Jake had quite a lot in common, particularly being an only child and wanting to have a brother or sister. At the moment, Jen needed friends, not boyfriends. Jake didn't have a girlfriend right now, and a guy would have to be blind not to notice how pretty his new cousin was, but she wasn't Melanie Larby. It amused them both to see the confusion on the faces of the other kids.

'He gets the school bus with me,' she told Eric.

Tara's ears pricked: Jen had never mentioned Jake Sorensen.

'Good-looking boy,' Eric observed slyly.

Jen shrugged. 'The girls at school think so.'

'Looks just like his father did at the same age.'

The mention of Jake's father brought a blush to Jen's cheeks that talk of his son hadn't.

Tara missed the blush. She was too busy thinking that if Gil Sorensen's son was as handsome as Eric said, she doubted he took after his father. Gil had been over to the house twice more since he'd seen her talking to the tree on the race, both times to teach Jen to drive Eric's tractor, and each time Tara had hidden inside. She didn't like the race, because every time she set foot on it Gil Sorensen appeared and she made a complete tit of herself. She supposed he might have a decent body beneath his ugly overalls and waterproof clothing, but apart from those deep-set, dark eyes the face beneath the ever-present beanie was hardly memorable. Besides, Tara's feelings about men were horribly confused at the moment.

She changed the subject. 'How closely related is Jen to Jake?'

'They're both the great-great-great-grandchildren of Henry and Sarah Whitehead. Gil's great-grandmother was Henry and Sarah's youngest daughter, Mary, and Richard's great-grandfather was their eldest son, Joseph.'

Tara swallowed. Gil was one of Richard's cousins and had probably received a letter. She'd never been all that interested in the Whitehead family tree before, but she gave Eric her full attention now.

'Mind you, that little tart Tiffany Bigelow is a cousin, too,' Eric sniffed. 'Her great-great-grandfather was Henry and Sarah's son Henry.'

Tara felt sick. Another cousin, and another potential recipient of one of Richard's bloody letters. 'Who're her mother and father?'

Eric pulled a face. 'Alison Whitehead and Barney Bigelow.'

'Of course! Richard's cousin is Alison Whitehead, the artist.'

'If you call somebody who turns lumps of stone into gigantic pri—'

'Yes, thank you, Eric!' she interjected hastily.

Alison Whitehead's brief series of stone phalluses were highly sought-after as garden ornaments, but Tara far preferred Alison's oil paintings and later sculptures. When she'd discovered that Alison was one of Richard's cousins, Tara had asked if they could visit her, but Richard made excuses not to go. 'I haven't seen Alison in years, Tara, and from what I've heard she's a virtual recluse. She had a disastrous marriage, and now she spends all her time on her art. If you met her husband, you'd understand why her work is so tortured-looking.'

'So Tiffany goes to All Saints, too?' Tara asked before Eric could launch into a tirade about stone pricks.

Tiffany was in the year below Jen, but from what Jen had seen so far Tiffany acted as if she owned the place. She ruled the roost and her gang of lame friends because she was Barney Bigelow's daughter, although Jen didn't know why that was such a big deal. For some reason Tiffany seemed to have it in for her, and Jen didn't think it was just because of her friendship with Jake. She was puzzled at first by the other girl's hostility, but had a feeling it was because she was a Whitehead while Tiffany was a Bigelow. Jen couldn't believe how important being a Whitehead was in Divine, and had said as much to Jake on the bus trip home after she'd been at All Saints a few days.

'Didn't your father explain how things work down here?' he asked her, his knee banging against Jen's as the bus bounced across the road.

She shook her head. 'We never came down here. I always got the feeling Dad didn't like the place very much.'

Jake put one of the earpieces from his iPod into his ear and offered Jen the other. 'Don't blame him. My dad says most of the family are a bunch of old women. You'll probably like my Nan and Grandad, though. They're away at the moment, but they'll be back for the summer. They're cool.'

Jen plugged the earpiece in and wondered if Jake's father or his grandparents had received one of her dad's letters. The fear of being confronted by somebody who knew the truth kept Jen and Tara from mixing with the local community. Jen really hated it; she wanted to make new friends and a new life. Jake didn't act as if he knew about her dad, but Jen cringed when she imagined what his reaction might be if he ever found out, and the thought of what Tiffany Bigelow might do with the information made her want to throw up.

She looked at her great-uncle. He obviously didn't like Tiffany, which was pretty cool; usually old people went on about how you couldn't like everybody, but how everybody had something nice about them. Jen doubted anybody could find anything nice about Tiffany.

Jennifer smiled at Eric and he winked back. 'Can I have one of those toffees please, Uncle Eric?'

'Help yourself. They're in that top drawer next to me erection pills.'

'Eric!' Tara snapped.

'What do you expect? I'm seventy-two.'

Jen helped herself to the toffees and went out into the small garden beyond the patio doors that opened from the living area. She closed the door behind her, popped a toffee in her cheek and laughed.

Tara glared at Eric. 'I'm warning you, Eric, Jen's every bit as lovely on the inside as she is outside. Don't you dare corrupt her with your foul mouth and dirty mind.'

He watched Jen through the window. 'She's a beautiful girl, all right, the sort that needs a father to keep the boys in line when they come sniffing around. Richard always was about as useful as a spare prick at a wedding.'

Tara got to her feet.

'Sit down, sit down!' Eric cried testily, waving a hand at her. 'I'll try and keep me thoughts to meself, but it's hard when I see you and that girl alone and at the mercy of every mongrel in Divine, and believe me this town has more than its fair share.' He paused to consider her. 'You've grown even better looking, Tara. I knew you would.'

Tara eyed him dubiously, but he seemed sincere enough. She slowly sat back down. 'Why did you suddenly decide to leave your place to Jen?'

'It was time,' Eric said evasively.

'Time?'

'Time for me to move on, I'm getting too old to run that place all alone, my heart wasn't in it. I had . . . other things I wanted to do.' His gaze became hooded.

Tara waited, but he didn't elaborate.

'So, Gil pulled you out of a pothole.'

She scowled. 'How do you know that?'

'Everybody knows about it. Divine's a small town. If somebody farts at seven o'clock in the morning, you can guarantee the rest of the town will have heard about it by seven o'clock that night. It's not like Auckland down here.'

Tara rolled her eyes and thought, *Tell me about it!*

'And Gil's been teaching Jen how to drive the tractor.'

Tara sighed.

'You want to keep on the right side of Gil: he'll be bloody useful to you, and he's as honest as the day is long.'

And brown all over and boring, Tara thought. *And far too perceptive.*

'He knows everything there is to know about horses and taking care of the land.'

Better and better, Tara mused sourly, but she did take note of Eric's comment about the horses. So far she'd done nothing but look at them and watch the people who owned them come and go. Each horse earned Tara and Jen twenty dollars a week in grazing fees; not a huge amount of money, but it still helped pay the bills. Tara wanted to increase the number of horses and her weekly income, but she wasn't sure how many horses she could accommodate.

One of the owners, a woman named Pat Warner, had come to Tara only the day before to complain about the paddocks not being mucked out. She was a very tall, awkward woman, who didn't look her best in jodhpurs and rubber riding boots. Her beaky nose was covered in broken red capillaries, and Tara was certain she cut her own hair — and then ran one of her horse's brushes through it.

'Felix and his paddock mates are probably full of worms. Eric always saw to it that the manure was picked up and disposed of. If you're not careful, the paddocks will soon be horse-sick, and if that happens I'll move Felix somewhere else.'

Tara thought the woman was having her on just because she was an Aucklander. She'd heard of stables being mucked out, but she refused to believe that paddocks had to be cleaned.

'Would you like me to polish and dust, too?' she enquired with saccharine sweetness before shutting the door in the woman's astonished face.

'Eric, how many horses could be grazed on your land?' she asked. 'There's none in those two front paddocks at all.'

'That's because they're full of weeds.'

'No, they're full of grass.'

'They're covered in buttercup,' Eric corrected. 'Weeds. Ask Gil.'

Tara stared at him in dismay. She didn't want to ask Gil Sorensen for anything, but was reluctantly coming to the conclusion that she might have to. He'd filled in the potholes in the race despite her bizarre behaviour the other day, and Tara wanted to thank him and ask how much she owed him.

They left soon after, with Eric accompanying them as far as the front door on his walking frame. Tara felt guilty. She hadn't realized how frail he was. She and Jen walked along slowly either side of him as they passed through the communal lounge on the way to the reception area, trying not to disturb the group of women in their yoga session. A skinny, balding man wearing grey carpet slippers and an orange paisley shirt and blue cardigan was fast asleep in a chair, oblivious to the noise and activity going on around him, his head tipped back and his mouth wide open, snoring.

Tara spied a set of pink-and-white dentures on the table beside him. She nudged Eric. 'Is he deaf?'

Eric tore his gaze away from the yoga group. 'Stan? No, he's probably just got his hearing aid turned off.'

'And we are row-row-rowing the boat! Come along, ladies, row those boats!' the middle-aged female instructor called out. She wore a pink leotard over black leggings and was seated on the floor, holding the big toe of one foot, sawing back and forth as if it was the oar of a boat.

Tara and Jen looked doubtfully at the elderly women on the floor struggling to reach their big toes, let alone row with them. They all seemed to be taking it very seriously, though, except for one woman who had given up and was shaking with helpless laughter.

'Miss Gillickson! You *must* focus!' the instructor cried.

'Silly bitch,' said Eric loudly.

The instructor stopped in mid-row and glared at him.

Jen and Tara smothered giggles.

'*Mr* Whitehead,' the instructor said icily. 'This room has been booked for a yoga session and is closed to the rest of the residents until five-thirty.'

Eric ignored her. His gaze was firmly fixed on Miss Gillickson, who still wasn't focused. 'Hello, Miss Gillickson,' he said in a voice that had probably made more than a few hearts beat faster over the past fifty-odd years.

Tara and Jen raised their brows at one another behind his back. Eric didn't seem to be having any problems focusing. They took a closer look at Miss Gillickson. She was petite, with silver-grey hair and beautiful skin. She nodded primly at Eric and tugged her skirt over her knees. 'Mr Whitehead.'

Tara suddenly had a good idea of what one of the other things that Eric 'wanted to do' might be.

He reluctantly followed them from the lounge to the front door.

'Before you go, I've got something I need you to do.'

'Oh?' Tara asked warily, remembering Marion Popplewell's comment about his unpaid account. 'What's that?'

'I want you to buy me a mobility scooter.'

After Tara and Jen left, Eric went through the motions of making his way slowly back to his room, leaning heavily on his walking frame. Mad Marion intercepted him as he approached his apartment.

'I hear you've had a visitor,' she announced, forcing a smile.

Eric looked at her white false teeth and at the bright red lipstick on the mouth framing them and shuddered. How Barney could give Marion one was beyond him.

'Have you now, Marion?'

'Hopefully it will improve your disposition, Eric.' Marion smiled determinedly, mindful of Barney's instructions not to upset Eric Whitehead, or at least not until they'd secured his land for the Country Corners Lifestyle Development.

'It might for a little while, Marion, but the sight of you would put anybody in a shitty mood so I wouldn't hold your breath,' Eric advised.

'You tight-fisted, evil old man!' Marion hissed. She hastily checked to see if anybody had overheard her. She went to great lengths to cultivate her saintly, caring image, which was why some people called her Maid Marion.

Eric grinned. 'Tut tut, Marion, your halo just slipped.'

'You are the most loathsome creature I have ever had the misfortune to meet, Eric Whitehead!'

'That must be excluding Barney.'

'Barney is worth a thousand of you any day, you old arsehole!' Marion snarled.

'Yeah, yeah,' Eric continued on his way to his apartment. 'Why don't you just climb back on your broom and piss off, Marion? There's a good matron.'

Marion closed her eyes and sunk her top dentures into her bottom lip to keep from swearing at his departing back.

Eric smirked at her just before he closed the door, then, pressing his ear to the wooden panel, he laughed as he heard a strangled cry of fury.

Chapter 9

Throwing the walking frame aside, Eric strolled across the living area and into his bedroom, where he collected his cigarette makings before opening the door on to the small patio area. One of the reasons Eric had insisted on this particular apartment was because the garden wasn't overlooked. It was also one of the most expensive, and it would drive Barney insane having Eric living in it for free.

He strolled across the patio, stroking his tongue along the seam of a roll-up, then pressed it closed with his thumb and perched on the edge of the retaining wall. Eric patted the pocket of his red-and-white shirt and pulled out a box of matches. He lit the cigarette and inhaled deeply, picturing how Lillian Gillickson had looked sitting on the floor at her yoga class, her pretty face flushed with embarrassment as she tugged demurely at the hem of her skirt.

Eric could spend all day looking at Lillian if she'd only let him — which she wouldn't. She was the very first woman to spurn his attentions and actually mean it. But he had made some progress since moving to Peacehaven; Lillian was sympathetic to his apparent loss of mobility.

Lillian had moved into Peacehaven earlier that year to be closer to her sister, who had been a resident until she'd died unexpectedly four months ago. Eric had got to know Lillian when she'd joined the

Bridge Club, and was smitten; not a particularly pleasant experience for a man who'd spent his life chasing other men's wives. But at the age of seventy-two Eric Whitehead was in love for the first time, with a retired spinster schoolteacher who was unimpressed by his family or his notoriety. Lillian Gillickson was a strong-minded woman with firm moral convictions, the kind of woman Eric had always avoided. Women like Lillian expected marriage and fidelity — two things that had always made Eric recoil in horror. However, the thought of spending the rest of his life married to Lillian didn't seem so terrible.

When Lillian began to make noises about leaving Peacehaven and moving to Wellington to be closer to her relatives, Eric knew he had to act promptly. Richard had already sent Eric the letter outlining his plans to leave his wife and daughter to become a woman named Rachel. Like most of his generation, Eric had a limited understanding of human sexuality. As far as he was concerned, you were either a poofter or you weren't, and if you were you should do everybody a favour and stay in your closet. He'd always had his doubts about his nephew, and was perplexed when Richard had managed to catch himself such a lovely, feisty wife. Even though Eric had met her only once, she'd had the temerity to chew him out for the way he spoke to Richard, and Eric liked Tara a whole lot more than he liked her husband. It hadn't been a difficult decision to contact his lawyers and change his will to leave his property to Richard's daughter, Jennifer. Eric liked the neatness of his plan because it killed two birds with one stone: it got him closer to his beloved Lillian, and it threw Barney Bigelow's plans into disarray.

If Eric did say so himself, sometimes he was a genius.

He intended to keep an eye on Tara and her daughter from afar. Eric knew he could rely on Gil to step in if they got into any kind of trouble, because Gil was the kind of man who wouldn't let a bully like Barney Bigelow browbeat somebody smaller and weaker. Eric just hoped Gracie and Henry hadn't got their hooks too deeply into Tara and neutered her the same way they had Richard.

Eric smoked his cigarette and wondered what Gil made of Richard's wife. She deserved a proper man. And it was about time Gil let go of Louise and found himself a woman to warm his bed. In the meantime, Eric had plans of his own. Lillian suffered from arthritis and was waiting for a knee replacement operation. Eric wished he could tell her outright that he'd pay for it whether she wanted him to or not, but he knew she'd refuse. She was a proud, independent woman, and although she'd softened towards him since he started using the walking frame, she continued to refuse his invitations to dinner. Eric hadn't quite decided how he was going to stage his miraculous return to full mobility when the time came, but he'd figure something out. Lillian's arthritis meant she got about on a walking frame or mobility scooter, and she was a member of the Divine Area Mobility Scooter Group — a bunch of old farts in Eric's opinion. However, if the only way to woo Lillian was to join the mobility-scooter group, Eric was up for it. He'd picked out the model he wanted and the colour.

All he needed was for Tara to arrange for it to be delivered.

Barney Bigelow gave Tara Whitehead a few weeks' grace before presenting himself at her door. It was important that his visit seem like that of a kind, helpful neighbour, which he was, since Eric Whitehead's property fronted the parcel of land Barney owned that was part of the Country Corners Lifestyle Development. The thought that all that stood between Barney's land and the vital road frontage was Eric's paltry fifty-eight acres always made Barney reach for his antacids. He'd tried to buy Eric's land at the same time he'd purchased the hundred-acre block behind, but Eric wouldn't play ball, although he had taken great delight in stringing Barney along for almost a year before announcing that he had no intention of selling.

Eric Whitehead was a mongrel and no mistake.

Barney lived on the other side of town, on land left to Alison by her father. The house he had built ten years earlier was known locally as Bigelow Towers. He was extremely proud of the red brick and glass monstrosity, which he'd designed himself after two architects had quit in protest at his questionable taste and the realization that it would be professional suicide to have their names associated with the end result. The house had eight bedrooms (each with an *en suite* bathroom), a games room, an indoor lap pool, gym and conservatory, plus stables and an indoor dressage arena for his daughter, Tiffany, who was horse-mad.

The front of the house sported a brick turret at each corner. Tiffany's bedroom was in one of these turrets. Her friends thought it was cool, but Tiffany hated it — it was impossible to arrange bedroom furniture in a room with no corners. Her white four-poster bed with *broderie anglaise* canopy and curtains stood in the middle of the floor, with her CD player, desk and computer, and book shelves in a circle around it. It drove her nuts, but her father refused to let her move into another room.

The *pièce de résistance* of Bigelow Towers was undoubtedly the matching indoor and outdoor fountains: one in the middle of the circular driveway by the towering double doors at the portico entrance, and the other in the marble-floored hallway in the reception area behind them. Barney was the only person in town who ignored the water restrictions imposed in years of drought; his fountains kept on bubbling right through until the rains finally came at the end of autumn. The consensus among the Divine population was that Barney had built such a large house so he and Alison didn't have to meet.

Alison hadn't paid any attention to Barney's house; she'd been too busy designing her art studio. When she eventually realized what the finished house was going to look like, her artistic soul shrivelled. She'd become so adept at tuning Barney out that he'd fallen off her personal radar years before, but the house regained her attention as surely as if she'd been run over by a train. There was no way on earth Alison could live within the walls of Bigelow Towers, and this gave her the perfect excuse to remove herself physically from Barney as ruthlessly as she had removed herself emotionally. She immediately changed the plans of her studio to include a bedroom, bathroom and kitchen.

When Barney got wind of this, he tried to put a stop to her escape by blocking council consent for the studio plans. Alison surprised him by stirring herself enough to drive down to the council offices to corner the mayor, Simon Unwin, and insist that Divine Town Council approve the plans for her studio. Barney never forgave Simon for caving in to Alison's demands when she'd reminded him that he was her cousin and could do with showing some family solidarity. Simon liked to remind people that he *was* related to the Whitehead family, through his great-great-grandfather Theodore Unwin, Sarah Whitehead's profligate brother.

'Don't you go forgetting which side your bread's buttered on, Unwin,' Barney warned menacingly after the fiasco with Alison.

Simon wished he had the guts to stand up to Barney, but he wasn't known as 'Oily' Unwin for nothing. He lived deep inside Barney's back pocket, where he spent most of his time kissing Barney's flabby white arse. However, Simon didn't intend to remain in a backwater like Divine forever. He had dreams of becoming mayor of Auckland or Wellington one day — if for no other reason than that he was far more photogenic than the current incumbents.

Alison moved into her studio, leaving Barney and Tiffany to keep one another company in the big, ugly house, furious that Barney still thought he could control her. To mark the occasion, she made a sculpture especially for her husband and had it set at the foot of the outdoor fountain while he was out for the day.

That evening, when Barney swept through the electronic gates and along the curving driveway towards the marble fountain that sent water arcing high into the air in front of his castle, he was met by a sight that made him stamp hard on the brakes of his car. At the foot of his glorious fountain stood one of his wife's famous stone phalluses, but this piece was unlike her previous soaring, primal creations.

It was small. It was misshapen. And it drooped to one side.

Barney took to it with a sledgehammer, destroying a piece of art that would have fetched thousands.

Alison didn't care. She'd made her point. It was the talk of Divine for months, and Chook Larby famously said that if he wanted a dick on his front lawn all he had to do was invite Oily Unwin over.

For Barney, it was yet another score he needed to settle with the Whiteheads.

He had planned to leave his visit to Tara Whitehead until the end of the month, but a conversation with his daughter about Jennifer Whitehead made him revise his plans.

'Have you made friends with Jennifer Whitehead yet?' Barney asked at the breakfast table, his head bent over the loaded plate of bacon, eggs, fried bread and sausages he ate every morning.

Tiffany was slouched in a chair opposite, stirring cereal idly around her breakfast bowl, her head propped on one hand. She was so terrified of getting fat like her father that she'd taken to eating less and less, and if she did ever empty her plate she went straight to the toilet, shoved her fingers down the back of her throat and threw everything up.

Neither of Tiffany's parents noticed that she was losing weight, because neither of them ever really looked at her, leaving her plenty of opportunity to do pretty much what she liked. Tiffany rather liked her new role as a poor little rich girl. She'd convinced herself that people either liked or disliked her because of her parentage. Her Whitehead blood meant people were nice to her, and her Bigelow blood meant they weren't, although most people kept that to themselves for fear of Barney finding out.

Until recently, Tiffany had relished her father's power and made full use of it. She'd grown up watching him operate, which had given her a distorted view of human relationships. But lately she'd begun to hate being Barney and Alison's daughter. Adolescence had dented Tiffany's formerly bullet-proof confidence. For the first time she was looking at her friends and wondering if they *really* liked her. She conveniently forgot her often cruel treatment of the other kids at school, kids who had gone to kindergarten, primary and intermediate school with her and had long memories.

Tiffany eyed her father warily, wondering why he was so interested in Jennifer Whitehead. Barney didn't ask idle questions. The only time he showed any interest in Tiffany's friends was if he thought they weren't good enough to rub shoulders with his daughter. Tiffany felt a surge of warmth. Perhaps her dad thought Jennifer Whitehead wasn't good enough, which would suit Tiffany just fine. She'd hated Jennifer the moment she set eyes on her; by having the Whitehead name, Jen outranked Tiffany. Jen Whitehead was also tall, slim and extremely pretty, *and* she had a 'nice personality'. Tiffany, on the other hand, looked like her father. Worst of all, Jake Sorensen had wasted no time in making friends with Jennifer when he hardly gave Tiffany the time of day.

'She says they're just friends,' one of Tiffany's inner circle reported when Tiffany sent her to find out what the story was with Jen and Jake Sorensen.

Tiffany's lip curled. 'Yeah, right.'

Her friends laughed. In their minds, any girl with half a brain knew that the only way you hung on to a guy who looked like Jake Sorensen was by having sex with him — unless of course you were Melanie Larby and planned to stay a virgin for the rest of your life. Perhaps Jennifer Whitehead was just as lame as Melanie.

Tiffany had always gone out of her way to be nice to Jake; initially, because her father had impressed on her that Jake was her cousin and he wanted Tiffany to be friends with him. Later, as Jake Sorensen grew to be one of the cutest boys in school, Tiffany had her own reasons. She'd lost her virginity a week after her fourteenth birthday to Dale, one of her Bigelow cousins; she'd chosen him because he was cute, dumb and scared of Tiffany's father, so there was no way in hell he'd ever spill the beans. Tiffany had done it to get back at Barney when he refused to buy her the new horse she wanted. She didn't really like sex all that much, but she enjoyed the kissing and hugging part, and was impressed how popular being sexually active made her with guys. Tiffany made it clear to Jake that he only had to ask and she'd have sex with him, but Jake hadn't even been tempted.

Tiffany tried to tell herself that he only disliked her because his father did.

If Tiffany did have a passion, it was horse riding. Her mother had put Tiffany on her first pony when she was two, and Tiffany had taken to it like a duck to water, going on to win everything at pony club in her age group, and then to beat kids much older than her. She still recalled coming home from her first-ever ribbon day, clutching a blue ribbon and excitedly telling her father she had come second in Best Trained Pony.

Barney, who was on his way out to a meeting, brushed her aside saying, 'Second? Tell me when you've come first.'

Tiffany turned into the pony club kid from hell, alienating the other members and her own mother in her determination to come first. The day she presented Barney with a clutch of red ribbons and a photo of herself in the *Divine Flyer*, he promptly took over her equestrian career, spending large amounts of money on lessons and horses as Tiffany rose in the ranks. Alison relinquished her only remaining involvement in her daughter's life.

Last year, Barney had managed to get Gil Sorensen to give Tiffany riding lessons, but it had been an unmitigated disaster. As Barney's daughter, Tiffany was used to being told how good she was, but Gil criticized her hands, her seat and her lack of patience.

'You'll never get anywhere if you're not prepared to put in the work,' he'd told her when her new thoroughbred mare fluffed a dressage movement for the third time. 'And it's no good blaming the horse, it's not her fault. Your aids aren't clear.'

Frustrated and humiliated, Tiffany yelled, 'Well if you're so bloody good, let me see *you* do it!'

When Gil's face froze into a mask of disapproval and disgust, Tiffany sucked in a breath and caught her bottom lip between her teeth. 'S-sorry, Mr—'

'Get off that horse,' he said, stalking towards her.

Tiffany got off.

Gil adjusted the stirrups, climbed aboard the fractious, worried mare, and within a few minutes had her performing one flawless dressage movement after another, several of which Tiffany didn't even know the mare could do.

Gil Sorensen never gave her another lesson.

Tiffany recalled her humiliation at the hands of Jake's father, and added it to the growing list of personal grievances she had against Jen Whitehead, who had Jake Sorensen eating out of her hand with nothing more than a smile and her 'nice personality'.

Barney was waiting impatiently for an answer to his question.

'No,' she said truculently, mashing cereal against the side of her bowl. 'Jennifer Whitehead's not my type.'

Barney's knife and fork stalled above his plate. 'What d'you mean, she's not your type?' His pop-eyed stare skewered her.

Tiffany shifted nervously on her chair and faltered, 'What I mean is, we don't have a lot in common, that's all.'

There was a long silence.

Barney's icy disapproval whistled through the cavernous dining room like a polar wind.

'Well, you'd better find something that you *do* have in common with her. I want you to become best friends with Jennifer Whitehead, d'you hear me? Get her over here for a sleepover or something, and make it soon.'

She dug the tip of her spoon into the middle of her sodden cereal.

'Tiffany!' Barney snapped. 'Did you hear me? I want you to get Jennifer Whitehead over here for a visit.'

Tiffany nodded sullenly. 'Yes, Daddy.'

Chapter 10

When Tara opened Eric's front door to Barney Bigelow she had no idea she was meeting the self-styled king of Divine. All she saw was a tall, ruddy-faced man with receding sandy hair, stooped shoulders and a paunch beneath which was belted a pair of expensive grey trousers that he somehow managed to make look cheap. His red-cheeked face reminded Tara of a clown, and she only just stopped herself checking his feet to see if he was wearing an outsized pair of red shoes. When he opened his mouth to speak, his big, yellow teeth and booming, nasal voice confirmed the impression.

'Mrs Whitehead?' Barney smiled and held out a large, hairy paw. 'I just wanted to introduce myself and welcome you to town. I'm Barney Bigelow.'

He paused to see if his name would elicit any response from the delectable Mrs Whitehead, while thinking that Richard Whitehead deserved to have his bollocks off for kicking this stunning creature into touch. Barney had read the letter that Richard had sent to Alison about his marriage break-up and his plans to become a woman. He hadn't been entirely surprised: everybody knew that Richard Whitehead was as camp as a row of tents. Alison didn't see the letter, because Barney regularly sifted through her mail, taking anything that looked important or interesting. He was enjoying being one of the few people in Divine who knew the truth about Richard and

Tara Whitehead's failed marriage, although he suspected old Eric was in the picture, and possibly Gil Sorensen, because Richard had said he was sending letters to all of his closest relatives. Barney was sure Simon wasn't in the know, because he would have mentioned it; besides, none of the Whiteheads considered Simon a member of the family — apart from the odd occasion when it suited their purposes. Barney was still scratching his head trying to decide if Gil Sorensen knew, but, since Gil wouldn't piss on Barney if he was on fire, finding out was virtually impossible.

Barney looked at Richard's wife, his hooded, watery blue eyes taking in the high, sculpted cheekbones, luminous grey eyes and wide, full mouth, before moving on to her round, generous breasts and the place where her long legs met. Barney wondered if she was a bottle blonde or the real deal, and felt his groin twitch. Chances were, Tara Whitehead hadn't got laid in a *long* time. She touched his hand briefly before snatching hers away again. He followed the length of her legs in their black trousers to the floor, and stared transfixed at her black pointy-toed shoes with big bows on the front and wickedly high heels.

Barney felt his tongue thicken in his mouth and his heart began to flop about inside his chest like a freshly landed snapper. He had a fetish for icy, dominating women in stilettos. In fact, until recently he had paid substantial amounts of money to visit a dominatrix named Madame Olga, who sneered and belittled him before she walked all over him in black, needle-heeled boots, carrying a long, black riding crop which she flicked at his naked, pasty body while he squirmed with excitement. Madame Olga hailed from Eketahuna and had never been any closer to Eastern Europe than a trip to Norfolk Island, but that was neither here nor there. Her recent retirement from the profession had left a huge hole in Barney's life, and so far the escort service hadn't been able to offer him another dominatrix who even came close to her in nastiness and vitriol. He'd got Marion to dress up in her nurse's uniform and hat and wield a riding crop in a desperate attempt to fill Olga's place, but that had been an abject failure. Olga had been a taut, fit, almost cadaverous-looking woman who weighed fifty-two kilos, whereas Marion was twice her size. Although Marion wore white rubber-soled nurse's shoes instead of thigh-length, high-heeled PVC black boots, the pain of having her clambering up and down his naked back had been excruciating. Barney wanted to be demeaned and subjugated — not squashed like a bug.

He gazed at Tara Whitehead and wanted to howl with frustration. *Here* was the woman of his dreams; *here* was the woman who could finally fulfil every one of his fantasies. And he had handed her over to that prick Gil Sorensen. Once again Sorensen was going to get the attention of a woman Barney thought should be his. All Barney's old feelings of inadequacy and fury resurfaced, sending his gastric reflux into overdrive. He rubbed the heel of his hand against his chest and swallowed the sour taste in his mouth.

Tara wanted to slam the door on him. The way this man's eyes slid over her made her think of a scaly lizard flicking its tongue over its prey. She shuddered and wondered how she could get rid of him. There was a meeting of the PTA at Jen's new school that night and Tara planned to go along. Although she was reluctant to spend much time in town getting to know the natives, checking out Jen's school was a different thing entirely.

Tara was heartily sick of the steady stream of visitors who had made their way to her door over the past few weeks. It was as if somebody had fired a gun and there was a race on to see who could visit her first. She didn't know that Barney had given the go-ahead to Chook Larby, Dave Richards, Norris Jenkins and their ilk to roll out the welcome mat for her.

'Why now?' Dave complained at one of their meetings in the community hall.

'Because she's had time to settle in and start worrying about how she's going to manage Eric's place, *that's why,* you idiot. Don't worry, Richards,' Barney said sourly. 'You don't have to put your hand in your pocket and take her a housewarming present or anything.'

'I'll go and see her first thing in the morning,' Chook Larby grinned. 'I saw her last week in town getting some groceries and she's no dog.'

Mention of Mrs Whitehead's lack of resemblance to canines pulled Norris from his contemplation of Francine's suspected pregnancy. He looked about the room and asked, 'Where's Gil?'

Barney scowled. 'Sulking.'

'You can give me the job of babysitting Mrs Whitehead if you want,' Chook offered.

'Who're you kidding?' Dave asked. 'Ngaire'd have your balls in a vice.'

Chook sighed deeply, his deep brown eyes filled with laughter. 'Why does Gil get all the good jobs?'

Barney looked at Tara Whitehead with rapt attention. Her cold, pale stare and her refusal to touch him after their initial handshake excited Barney almost as much as his visits to Madame Olga had.

Tara repressed another shudder at the glazed expression in Barney's protuberant eyes. He seemed to be panting slightly, but she told herself she must be imagining it. Behind her back she covertly wiped the hand he'd shaken on the seat of her pants while she said firmly, 'Thank you for taking the time to stop by and say hello, but I'm afraid I'm on my way out. I'm due at my daughter's PTA meeting.'

Barney seemed to come out of his trance. Knowing she was wiping her hand on herself behind her back escalated his arousal even further. 'Fancy that.' His delight oozed towards Tara like the contents of a broken sewerage pipe. 'My daughter, Tiffany, attends the same school and I'm going to the meeting, too. Can I give you a ride?'

Tara wanted to tell him to get stuffed, but was worried about upsetting the parent of one of the girls at Jen's new school. She had a horrible feeling, though, that the ride Barney Bigelow was offering didn't just mean a lift in his car.

Gil Sorensen sat back in his chair, his arms folded across his chest, and watched as Tara Whitehead walked into the boardroom of All

Saints College accompanied by a gloating, excited Barney Bigelow. To Gil's knowledge it was the first time Barney had deigned to attend a PTA meeting, and he had a pretty good idea why Barney had suddenly decided it would be tonight.

Gil hadn't spoken to Tara since he'd found her crying on the race, and had only seen her once from a distance, when he went over to teach Jen how to drive the tractor. A quick scan of her pale, set face now indicated she wasn't all that happy with her escort. Gil tried to watch Tara discreetly in case Barney jumped to the wrong conclusion, and wondered why Barney hadn't put his own hand up for the job of sleeping with Tara; he was all but panting as he trotted along behind her, the fingers of one pudgy, white hand pressed against the small of her back as if she couldn't navigate her way around the boardroom table without his assistance.

Gil saw Tara arch her back and lengthen her stride in an effort to evade Barney. As usual, she was immaculately and expensively dressed; this time in black trousers and a burgundy wool jacket that hugged her narrow waist. Her silvery blonde hair lay across her shoulders, gleaming in the light. A pair of small, silver hoop-earrings and an expensive-looking jewelled watch strapped to her left wrist were her only jewellery; for the first time Gil noticed that she didn't wear a wedding ring. A swift glance at the floor revealed she was wearing a pair of black high heels with lethal-looking stiletto spikes.

Gil remembered how small she'd been in her floral gumboots. In her high heels, he estimated she'd only be about four inches shy of his own six feet. How on earth did the woman stay upright in the damned things? The soft floppy bows on the front didn't disguise the fact that they were a pair of kick-arse shoes — or, to borrow a phrase Gil had heard from the teenage daughter of one of his women friends, come-fuck-me shoes. He was alarmed when he had a sudden vision of Tara naked but for her high heels. Gil stared at the pale rose lipstick on her lips. She had the kind of soft, full mouth a man imagined sliding his tongue and other parts of his anatomy into. He was appalled. Here he was, at a PTA meeting, fantasizing about Tara Whitehead. What the hell had got into him? Gil covertly checked to see if anybody else in the room was watching him, but they were all staring at Tara as if she were a celebrity dropped into their midst.

Barney herded her around the table towards Gil.

Gil's face hardened. Tara saw Gil Sorensen's stony expression and slowed. She almost didn't recognize him in tidy clothes and minus his beanie. Tara was shocked to see that without his overalls he was quite presentable.

She glanced over her shoulder at Barney Bigelow and back at the two empty chairs beside Gil and tried to decide what would be worse: sitting beside a man who couldn't seem to keep his hands to himself, or being next to one who looked as if he would rather have his nostril hairs pulled out one by one than sit next to her.

Gil forced a smile. It wasn't Tara's fault that he was horny and irritable and that she was a fruitcake. 'Evening, Tara.'

'Hello, Gil.' She slid reluctantly into the chair beside him, leaving Barney to take the one alongside her.

Gil turned away to speak to Annabelle Archer, the president of the PTA.

Annabelle was a widowed dairy farmer with two boys at All Saints, and, judging by the disapproving, suspicious look she was giving Tara Whitehead, she wasn't too impressed by the newcomer. Annabelle's idea of dressing up for the meeting was plum-coloured polyester slacks with an elasticized waist, and a blue-and-white patterned polyester blouse with a large pussy bow collar that bunched beneath her prematurely wrinkled brown chin. Annabelle was a staunch supporter of polyester: any manmade fibre was a winner in her book. She simply couldn't understand other women's fixation with natural fibres. Annabelle was a busy woman with cows to milk twice a day and no time to iron, so what would she do with all those wrinkly linen and cotton clothes? She did, however, find time in the evenings to knit, and the fluffy mohair cardigan she wore in a rainbow of colours with a black and white panda on the back was her handiwork. Annabelle had already decided that Tara Whitehead was a natural-fibres type of woman — and as for her shoes, Annabelle didn't know *what* the woman was thinking, or if she was thinking at all. Her nose twitched. Tara was trouble with a capital T. Annabelle could smell it a mile off.

'D'you wanna read the minutes, Elaine?' she barked at Elaine Selwyn, the PTA secretary and Barney Bigelow's long-standing mistress, who worked at the council offices as Oily Unwin's secretary. 'Elaine!'

Elaine started. She tried to concentrate on the minutes from the last meeting, but she was entranced by Tara Whitehead's beautiful clothes and gorgeous shoes. So far, Elaine had only seen Tara from a distance and had once waved shyly, but Tara either hadn't seen her or had ignored her. Elaine longed to update her look to something more elegant, but Barney loved her long, brown Farrah Fawcett hairdo and had a fondness for zip-up jumpsuits cinched with thick belts. However, at the age of thirty-seven, Elaine really felt her *Charlie's Angels* days were over.

She was growing increasingly disenchanted with her relationship with Barney, and was beginning to wonder if he really would leave his wife when Tiffany finally left home. Elaine had been twenty-five when she met Barney, who, trapped in his miserable excuse for a marriage, eagerly poured out his story into her sympathetic ear. Elaine had fallen hook, line and sinker. She truly loved Barney, but as the years went by she was finding it increasingly difficult to turn a blind eye to the roughshod way he rode over people to get what he wanted. She was a kind, loyal woman who had given Barney her youth, but was no longer so certain that she wanted to hand over her middle years to him as well, particularly when he seemed to value her less and less as the years passed.

Elaine was tired of being treated as a bit of a joke by the people of Divine. Barney insisted on pretending that they weren't having an affair, saying that it didn't fit with his image as a moral, upstanding pillar of the Divine community. When Elaine once pointed out that it was common knowledge that they were lovers, Barney had lost his temper and refused to speak to her for a month. Elaine learnt her lesson and never mentioned it again. But that didn't mean her feelings of resentment and ill use had gone away.

'The minutes, Elaine! The minutes!' Annabelle snapped.

Elaine dutifully began to read out the minutes, which were seconded by Gil, who smiled at her and winked to soften Annabelle Archer's rudeness. Elaine smiled back. Gil Sorensen was one of the nicest men in Divine, and certainly one of the best-looking. She sighed. Gil would definitely never treat a woman the way Barney treated her. She gave Chook Larby and Dave Richards's apologies for being unable to attend the meeting.

'Rubbish!' Annabelle cried. 'I saw their cars outside the Long Drop. It'd serve them right if somebody went over there and hauled them out by the ear.' She looked hopefully around the ring of faces at the table, but nobody seemed to agree, and Gil Sorenson even had the cheek to laugh at her. Annabelle made a sound of disgust. 'Come on, then, let's get on with it.'

Simon Unwin suddenly stood up and beamed across the table at Tara Whitehead. Elaine couldn't recall Simon ever giving her that smarmy smile, but it was the one he wore just before he made a speech. Like Barney and Annabelle, Simon regarded Elaine as a doormat just waiting to be walked on. Not that Elaine would ever *want* Simon to look at her the way he was looking at Mrs Whitehead at the moment. Working as closely as she did with Simon meant she knew all his secrets.

For instance, she knew that Simon could never love anybody as much as he loved himself, which was the most likely reason why at the age of forty-six he'd never married or even lived with a woman. She also knew that he had to have his back waxed regularly, and that the reason his dark hair always looked so gorgeous was that he had subtle chestnut foils put through it every six weeks and wore a hairnet to bed. Elaine was responsible for booking Simon's waxing and hair appointments in Hamilton, and buying his hairnets at the supermarket. After all, Simon couldn't risk being seen purchasing his 'slumber-nets' (as he preferred to call them) himself. Elaine had long ago become resigned to people thinking she wore a hairnet to bed.

'I'd just like to welcome Mrs Whitehead to the meeting and Divine,' Simon began with an unctuous smile, tilting his head so that the fluorescent light brought out his chestnut highlights. 'May I say . . .'

Tara nodded politely, but Elaine got the feeling she wasn't listening to their illustrious mayor. She wondered why Barney's chair was so close to Tara's. As usual he hadn't acknowledged Elaine when he'd entered the room, even though she kept telling him that his habit of ignoring her only raised people's suspicions rather than quelled them. As Elaine watched, Tara inched her chair closer to Gil's.

Gil studied the town mayor critically. He had never been able to find out why Simon Unwin was on the PTA. He was unmarried, had no children and contributed only what Barney told him to. Trust Oily to grab the opportunity to ingratiate himself with Tara Whitehead. With that greasy smile on his weak-jawed face it was a wonder he didn't slide right off his damned chair when he sat back down. It turned Gil's stomach to think that he and Simon were distantly related. Simon Unwin was all hair oil and no socks.

'Thank you.' Tara shifted her chair a couple of inches closer to Gil's. That got his attention, considering she had so far treated him as if he carried bubonic plague.

Simon stopped to take a breath.

'Finished with the socializing, Simon?' Annabelle cut in. 'Good. Then let's get on with it. We've all got homes to go to.'

Simon sat down sulkily.

For the next hour they ran through the planned fundraisers and the upgrade to the audiovisual suite.

Barney Bigelow slowly but steadily edged his chair closer to Tara's, and Tara slowly but steadily edged hers closer to Gil Sorensen's in an attempt to avoid Barney. She stopped listening to Annabelle somewhere between the fundraiser for the netball trip to Fiji and the cost of resurfacing the tennis courts. Short of sliding under the table and out the other side next to Simon Unwin (and didn't *he* look a dodgy piece of work!), Tara didn't know how to escape Barney. She could stand up and denounce him, but the thought of the embarrassment it would cause to Jen if word got around that her mother had made a fuss at the PTA meeting made Tara grit her teeth and tell herself that the meeting had to end soon. She felt helpless and impotent, two emotions that had become her almost constant companions ever since Richard's startling announcement.

Tara sat like a statue, her hands clenched in her lap, stirring only when she had to once again move her chair, and hoping that Gil Sorensen was too engrossed in the meeting to notice. He hadn't spared Tara a glance since his initial greeting. He sat with his chair pushed back from the table, slouched low in his seat, his long legs stretched beneath the table and his arms folded across his chest.

After the embarrassing incident on the race, Tara had planned to be polite but distant when she next saw him. Instead she was almost climbing on top of him. 'Sorry!' she whispered each time she bumped Gil's shoulder or knee, her pale face flushing. Eventually, after a particularly violent jostle from Barney, the inevitable happened and Tara tipped sideways into Gil's lap to land with her nose buried in his crotch.

Simon leapt to his feet and peered across the table to see where she had gone.

Annabelle and Elaine followed suit, while, under cover of everyone's shocked surprise, Barney scuttled sideways until he was a respectable distance from Tara.

Gil lifted his folded arms and looked down bemusedly at Tara Whitehead's blonde hair spilling across his lap. He could feel her warm breath fanning the front of his zipper and her breasts pressed against his right thigh. If it hadn't been for the weight of those breasts and the heat of her breath, Gil would have been certain he was at home asleep, dreaming about Tara Whitehead. His erection unfurled against her cheek. Gil knew Tara felt it because her nails dug into the side of his leg, but shock rendered him temporarily immobile.

'Mrs Whitehead!!' Annabelle shouted. 'What on earth do you think you're doing? This is a public meeting!'

Tara flailed about and tried to sit up.

Gil grabbed her by the shoulders and lifted her from his lap, catching sight of Barney's excited, glistening gaze over her head. Gil recoiled, his hands still on Tara's shoulders.

Tara braced her hands on his thighs and tried to catch her breath.

'Mrs Whitehead!' Annabelle's voice rose another decibel. *'Get off Gil!!'*

'Shut up, Annabelle!' Gil snapped.

Annabelle's mouth dropped open in shock.

Gil stood, lifted Tara and sat her down in her seat.

'Are you all right?' Elaine rushed around the table. 'Do you want me to get you a drink of water or something?'

'No, thank you.' Tara swiped her hair from her eyes.

She wanted to die. What if Gil Sorensen thought the same as the stupid woman with the panda cardigan? Tara pressed her shaking palms together between her thighs and glared at Barney Bigelow. The pervert needed locking up.

Barney nervously shuffled some papers on the table and tried to ignore Elaine's shocked, accusing stare and Tara and Gil's furious glares. He didn't know what had come over him and he blamed Tara Whitehead. Ever since she'd opened the front door of Eric's house, Barney hadn't been acting like himself, at least not his *public* self.

Gil had a fair idea why Tara had landed in his lap, and he was tempted to kick Barney's fat arse out the door, but that would only make things worse for Tara. By tomorrow it would be all over Divine that Tara Whitehead had put her face in Gil Sorensen's lap at the PTA meeting.

'I'd like a cup of tea now, Elaine!' Annabelle was angry at Tara's behaviour and at Gil for shouting at her. Her friend Glenys Tweedie had warned Annabelle that Tara Whitehead was a troublemaker. Just wait until Annabelle told Glenys what had happened tonight.

Elaine dutifully headed towards the small sink area concealed behind double doors at the far end of the boardroom to make tea and coffee, while Gil wondered what the hell had got into Barney. Gil had been so intent on ignoring Tara that he'd failed to notice what was happening. If he hadn't seen the lascivious, sickening expression on Barney's face, he would have suspected it was a ploy to quite literally throw him and Tara together.

Gil noticed the bleak expression on Elaine's sweet face as she handed around the teacups, and realized that he wasn't the only one who knew what Barney had done.

Simon went to visit the toilet and Annabelle got up to help herself to the best biscuits from the plate that Elaine was preparing.

'I'm sorry, Barney, but we've run out of filter coffee,' Elaine called from the other end of the room. 'I'm afraid there's only instant.'

Barney frowned at her. 'Eh?'

Gil used the diversion to touch Tara briefly on the arm.

She jumped. 'What?'

'Do you want to make sure Barney doesn't give a repeat performance?' he asked quietly.

Elaine tried to placate Barney. 'It's that special coffee. You know, the one with the girl in the ad that you like?'

'What do you think?' Tara said flatly.

'Do you want to change seats?'

Her eyes flashed. 'No! I wouldn't give him the satisfaction.'

'It's still bloody instant, Elaine!' Barney complained.

Gil smiled. Maybe Mrs Whitehead would kick Barney's arse out the door instead. 'Great weapons, high heels. A stiletto heel down a shinbone makes a helluva mess.'

Tara stared at him.

Gil raised a brow.

Tara felt the hard edge of a man's shoe creep its way up her right calf. She gritted her teeth. Gil was on her left. Barney was on her right. Tara could tell by the way Gil suddenly tensed that he'd guessed what Barney was up to. She clutched his arm to stop him grabbing

Barney. Her head whipped around so fast that the ends of her hair flew across Gil's face.

'You pervert!' she snarled softly at Barney, and raked her heel the length of his skinny shin, tearing a hole in the leather over his instep with the tip.

Barney howled and fell forward across the boardroom table, clutching his leg.

Elaine rushed across the room. 'Barney! Barney! What's wrong, love? Is it your heartburn again?'

Barney looked up at Tara, his cheek pressed against the wooden surface of the table, his eyes glazed with lust.

Tara shrank closer to Gil.

Gil decided he'd had enough. He stood, grabbed Tara by her elbows and lifted her into his chair. 'Sit here!'

'Now what's wrong?' Annabelle cried through a mouthful of Mallowpuff as Simon re-entered the room. 'Sit up, Barney, and stop making a fool of yourself! Elaine! Do something!'

'What's happened? What's happened?' Simon cried excitedly.

Everybody ignored him, even Elaine.

Barney behaved himself for the rest of the meeting, knowing that if he didn't Gil Sorensen would kick him out.

Chapter 11

Tara was grateful for the stalwart barrier Gil provided between her and Barney Bigelow for the remainder of the meeting. She was also relieved that Gil knew it wasn't her fault that she'd ended up face-down in his lap.

Tara was surprised that he'd helped her, and kept getting distracted by how he looked when he wasn't wearing waterproof clothing, that hideous beanie and cow dung. His clothes were presentable and matched: beige moleskins, caramel-coloured shirt, and a huge black sweater that hugged his chest and shoulders. He was younger than Tara had first thought, with long, luxuriant black lashes fringing his eyes, and his short, dark hair only lightly touched with grey at his temples.

Each time Tara recalled the moment she had found her nose pressed against Gil's zipper she wanted to die. But she also thought about the telltale stirring she'd felt against her cheek and was appalled by the frisson of sexual excitement she felt low in the pit of her belly. Tara tried to concentrate on the meeting and not on Gil, who ignored her — until Tara was just about to put her foot in it again.

They were closing with a discussion about the date and time for the next PTA meeting.

'Nope!' Annabelle asserted. 'Can't make that! I'll still be calving.'

Tara's brows rose in surprise. She wouldn't have thought Annabelle was the artistic type, but then again there was that ugly panda sweater. 'What are you carv—'

Gil interrupted swiftly. 'Yeah, my cows will still be calving then, too, so I'm out.'

Comprehension dawned. Tara flushed and subsided miserably into her chair. Could things get any worse?

They could. When she was outside in the car park watching Elaine help a limping Barney to his car, Tara realized she had no way of getting home. The perfect end to an appalling night. It was freezing and the wind had picked up, and she wasn't dressed for the long walk home. She'd lingered in the toilet to make sure everybody had gone before she finally ventured outside into the deserted car park again. The only people Tara thought might have given her a lift were Simon Unwin, who was almost as creepy as Barney, or Elaine Selwyn, but she was too busy playing nursemaid to Barney. Gil Sorensen had disappeared, and Tara thought she'd more than used up her quota of favours in that department, anyway.

She flipped up the collar of her burgundy jacket, shouldered her black leather handbag and set off towards the road, trying to ignore the quiver in her stomach. Country roads were not nearly as well-lit as city ones.

Gil finished locking up and stepped into the car park.

Tara strode past him.

'Where are you going?' he called.

She screamed and dropped her bag. 'Stop doing that!'

Gil picked up her bag and gave it back. Christ, the woman was a basket case. A quick scan of the car park revealed that his was the only vehicle left. 'Where's your car?'

'I came with Barney,' Tara said. 'Not by choice, I might add.'

Gil smiled wryly.

Tara stared. He had a very nice smile. Getting into a car with Gil might be just as dangerous as getting into one with Barney, but for entirely different reasons. 'Good night.' She hurried away.

Gil watched her go. It was cold as a witch's tit and she was walking home. He shook his head. The woman didn't have enough brains to give herself a headache. Sighing, he set off after her.

'You're going to walk all the way home?'

'Yes.'

A sudden gust of wind swept in from the road, sending Tara back a few steps and halting Gil momentarily in his tracks. He saw her shiver before she put her head down and ploughed stubbornly onwards. Gil followed.

'I live right opposite your house.'

'I've noticed.'

Her snooty reply made him stop and grin.

Tara strode onwards like a supermodel on a catwalk.

Gil admired the sway of her hips and pert bottom, and the swing of her legs. Damn! How did she walk in those heels? He jogged after her. 'I'll give you a lift.'

'That won't be necessary—'

An even stronger gust of wind drove her right back into his chest. Gil caught her by the elbows as fat, icy raindrops dropped on to their faces.

Tara gasped. 'Where're you parked?'

Gil grabbed one of her hands. It was freezing. 'This way.'

Together they ran back towards the car park and Gil's black ute as the skies opened and rain pounded them, blown in all directions by the swirling wind. Tara held her handbag over her head and matched Gil stride for stride. It wasn't until they were inside the ute that he remembered her high heels. He brushed raindrops impatiently from his hair. 'How the hell did you run in those and not break your neck?'

'Easy.' Tara looked about the interior of the ute and was taken back to her teenage years on Piha beach — not that she thought Gil Sorensen would be trying to entice her into the back of his ute for sex. In Tara's place, Kim would have been trying her hardest to jump him. She liked dark, rugged, outdoor types.

Outside the car, the wind howled and the rain splattered the windscreen as if somebody was throwing buckets of stones at it. The darkened interior gave an impression of intimacy. Tara watched Gil from the corner of her eye. He'd been an absolute gentleman at the meeting. She didn't know what she would have done without him. 'Thanks for helping me out tonight.'

Gil shook his head. 'I don't know what got into Barney.'

'Pervert!' Tara fumed.

'I'm the last person you'd ever hear defending Barney Bigelow, but I've never seen him act like that before. Barney likes to think of himself as a pillar of Divine's community. I'm sure he takes off his halo and polishes it each night before he goes to bed.'

Tara smiled sourly. 'Well he wasn't acting like a pillar of the community tonight.'

Gil started the engine, turned on the windscreen wipers and headlights, and drove out of the car park. 'He was out of order. How's the heel of your shoe?'

Tara wiggled her foot. 'I nearly broke it on his shin.'

He laughed deeply.

Tara felt it all the way down to the tips of her stiletto heels. 'And thanks for stopping me from asking Annabelle what's-her-name what she was carving. It never occurred to me she meant *that* kind of calving.'

'I know.'

They drove in silence for a few moments.

'Tell me,' Tara asked, 'why aren't there any teachers on the PTA?'

'Annabelle scares off the quiet ones and fights with the others. So Elaine acts as the go-between for the PTA and school management. It's better that way; things get done and we get to keep our teachers.'

Tara laughed, and covertly studied Gil, wondering if he'd received one of Richard's letters.

The bottom half of his face was illuminated by the lights from the dashboard. Tara thought about the hardness of his thighs when she'd gripped them, and shifted uneasily in her seat. He was so different from Richard — darker, a couple of inches shorter, and more solidly built. But then Richard was different to just about everybody, she reminded herself bleakly.

They completed the rest of the journey in silence. Tara hated the inky blackness of the countryside at night. It still unnerved her to drive without city streetlights to guide her, and for once she was glad to sit back and be a passenger.

When they reached Eric's, she thanked Gil for the ride and again for his help at the meeting. 'Don't worry, it won't become a habit,' she said, mindful that the last time he'd seen her was when she'd been crying like a baby on the race. She didn't want to be seen as an emotional weakling who needed a man to rely on. Tara was adamant she would never rely on any man again.

Gil looked puzzled. 'What won't?'

'Me needing to be rescued. I'm quite capable of taking care of myself.'

'I don't think anybody at the meeting tonight would question your ability to take care of yourself, Tara,' he replied curtly.

'Yes . . . well.' Tara coloured and stared at the handbag in her lap. 'Thanks again and goodnight.'

She stepped from the car, slammed the door, and holding her bag over her head sprinted to the house where Jen waited with the front door held open.

Gil watched Tara skip through the puddles and mud and up the steps, his breathing suspended as he waited for her to slip and break her neck. He released his breath slowly when she disappeared inside, and returned Jen's friendly wave before putting the ute in gear and turning down the driveway beneath the storm-tossed beech trees.

I'm quite capable of taking care of myself.

Gil felt offended. She'd made it perfectly clear that she didn't want his help. Mouth set in a straight line, he headed up the driveway to his house vowing that 'Mrs Whitehead' would have no reason to repeat the warning.

It was some time later that Tara realized she might have spoken too soon about not needing rescuing. Right now she needed rescuing from herself, before she murdered Pat Warner, owner of Felix the Wonder Horse and self-appointed head of the group of horse owners Tara was beginning to call the Horse Triad.

'There's too much grass! When are you going to start strip-grazing?' Pat demanded, her size-ten feet firmly planted on Tara's back doorstep and her weather-beaten face pinched with anger. Had the woman never heard of moisturizer or sunblock?

Tara decided Pat must be an idiot. She was paying for grazing, wasn't she? So why was she complaining about there being *too much* grass? How could there be too much?

'*Everybody* knows you strip-graze in the spring,' Pat continued. 'Eric *always* strip-grazed as soon as the spring grass arrived.'

'But it isn't spring for another couple of weeks,' Tara replied.

'It's got *nothing* to do with the calendar,' Pat cried impatiently. 'Look at the grass! It's an *early* spring.'

Tara didn't have a clue what she was on about. The grass looked fine to her, and the calendar on the kitchen wall showed there were still a couple of weeks of August left. She was pissed off and worried, because Jen had returned from one of her weekend visits to Richard to report that he had undergone yet another round of plastic surgery, which didn't come cheap. Tara took it out on Pat Warner.

'You want me to *strip?*' she demanded, arching an eyebrow in disdain while her conscience shouted, *Bitch!*

A crimson flush climbed Pat's mottled neck and lit up the broken capillaries on her cheeks like a string of Christmas lights. She squirmed, hating her huge feet and hands, and hating Tara Whitehead and her effortless, blonde prettiness most of all. 'That's not what I said! I said that Eric always strip-grazed the horses in the spring!'

'Did he now?' Tara wondered if having too much grass meant she could graze more horses.

'Yes! You've got too much rye grass. Everybody knows what the mycotoxins in rye grass do to horses at this time of year.'

Everybody except Tara.

The mention of mycotoxins bothered her, and she didn't really enjoy baiting Pat Warner. She might not know the names of all of the animals in the paddocks, but Tara didn't like to think of them suffering because of her ignorance.

'So what are you going to do about it?' Pat persisted.

Tara considered. She didn't want the owners taking advantage of her ignorance. 'To strip or not to strip, that is the question.'

Pat blinked and Tara noticed that her lashes were so fair that they almost didn't exist. Tara wondered what Pat would look like if she bothered to have them dyed, and groaned inwardly. No, no, *no!* She mustn't think about making over Pat Warner.

'I beg your pardon?' Pat asked.

'Tell you what, Pat, I'll think about it.'

Tara closed the door and went in search of a glass of wine.

Jennifer, who'd overheard the exchange, followed Tara into the kitchen.

'That wasn't very nice, Mum. She's right — we should be strip-grazing.'

Tara scowled at the back of the fridge as the cuckoo clock suddenly burst into life. She tried to ignore it and search for the bottle of chenin blanc she'd begun chilling earlier. 'Pat Warner isn't very nice.'

'You can't keep closing the door in her face, Mum. We need the money. Dad is planning on having facial feminization surgery done next and—'

Cuckoo! Cuckoo! Cuckoo!

'No!' Tara backed out of the fridge clutching her precious bottle of wine, shaking her head wildly from side to side. '*No.*' She licked her lips, knowing she was failing Jen by refusing to talk to her about what was happening to her father. She knew they should both have counselling, but the thought of baring her soul to a stranger made Tara break out in a sweat, and Jen refused to go if Tara wouldn't.

Tara changed the subject. 'When did *you* become an expert on strip-grazing?'

Cuckoo! Cuckoo! Cuckoo!

She would kill it! Dumping the wine bottle on the table, Tara snatched a chair, dragged it across the ugly brown linoleum and climbed on it.

'What are you doing?' Jen asked.

Tara pressed the heel of her hand against the clock's little wooden door. 'Shut up, you little shite!'

'Mum! That's cruel!'

'It's made of wood, Jennifer.' The door beat repeatedly against her palm. With any luck the damned bird would decapitate itself. When it finally stopped, Tara climbed down from the chair, ignoring Jen's look of disapproval. 'You were saying?'

Jen pursed her lips. 'I've been talking to Jake and Mr Sorensen about the horses.'

Tara scowled. Mr Sorensen and his son were a source of irritation and concern. Ever since the night of the PTA meeting, Tara had only set eyes on Gil Sorensen as she pulled out of her driveway, when he was in one of his paddocks either riding a tall grey horse or speeding around on a motorbike. Gil nodded politely, and she nodded back before putting her foot down on the gas pedal.

Jake Sorensen often came over to hang out with Jennifer, and you didn't have to be psychic to realize his appeal for a fifteen-year-old girl. Jake was as tall as his father and already had the body of a man. The beginnings of a beard sprouted on his jaw and upper lip, right alongside a sprinkling of pimples that did nothing to detract from his dark good looks. Tara suddenly remembered what it felt like to be fifteen, and what she would have thought of a boy like Jake Sorensen. Even worse, she recalled the things she had got up to on Piha beach with sixteen-year-old boys and her maternal alarm bells went off. When Jen insisted they were only friends, Tara told her to pull the other one.

Jen lost her temper. 'I am sick and tired of people thinking that just because I hang out with Jake Sorensen I must be having sex with him!'

Tara was outraged. 'Who said you've been having sex with Jake Sorensen?'

'Tiffany Bigelow and her pathetic little group of friends.' Jen dropped her head and mumbled, 'And Mr Sorensen.'

'Mr Sorensen? How dare he!'

'He doesn't think it *now!*' Jen cried hastily. 'He knows now that I'm just Jake's friend, but he was worried like you because we spend so much time together. He doesn't like it if I spend too much time down in Jake's bedroom.'

'Neither do I!'

'We're only listening to music!'

'You'd better be,' Tara muttered darkly, feeling reluctant gratitude that Gil Sorensen obviously remembered what it was like to be sixteen.

Despite her concerns, Tara liked Jake. He was funny, easygoing and charming, and attended to odd jobs around the property that Tara and Jen didn't even know needed doing. He also emptied the fridge of leftovers.

When Tara realized that, unlike Auckland, a rubbish-collection truck would not pull up to her front gate once a week, Jake patiently explained what to do. For some inexplicable reason she felt annoyed that Gil hadn't taken the trouble to tell her, which was ridiculous when she'd gone to so much trouble to make it clear she wanted to have as little to do with him as possible. It just irked her that he seemed to feel the same way.

'See that white post on the other side of the trees there?' Jake pointed to the far corner of a paddock. 'That's the pick-up point for the rubbish truck. If you dump your bags each Friday morning, they get picked up around lunchtime.'

'You mean we have to *carry* our rubbish bags across a paddock and climb over a fence? What am I paying rates for?' Tara protested.

Jake shrugged. 'Some people have to drive a couple of miles to get to their drop-off point. You could always drive around in the car.'

She wasn't putting smelly rubbish bags inside her immaculate Lexus, and she could tell by the look in Jake's dark eyes that it would be considered a cop-out.

Jake also explained the etiquette of the 'country wave' when Tara drove him and Jen into the library in Divine one afternoon to do some homework.

'Ah . . . Tara?'

He spent so much time around the house that Tara had finally convinced him it was OK to call her by her first name.

'Mmm?'

'You probably didn't realize it, but Dave Richards waved at you when he went past in his car just then.'

Tara frowned at Jake in the rear-view mirror. He sat beside Jen, filling most of the back seat with his long legs and arms and man-sized torso. She couldn't believe he was only sixteen. 'Dave who?'

'Dave Richards. He owns a dairy farm on the opposite side of the river to your place.'

Tara had a vague recollection of a sour-faced man dressed in the ubiquitous brown waterproofs among the parade of well-wishers who had beaten a path to her door in the weeks after her arrival. If her memory served Tara correctly, he'd wanted to know how much her Lexus had cost, and if it had been purchased new did she get a tax write-off? She also recalled being struck by how much better Jake's father filled out his brown waterproofs than Dave Richards.

Tara pushed the thought away. 'He didn't wave at me.'

'Yeah, he did.'

'No, he didn't. He looked at me, but I'm sure he kept both hands on the wheel.'

'But he flicked his finger at you,' Jake said.

'He gave me *the finger?*'

'No!' Jake glared at Jen when she began to giggle. 'He lifted his finger — like this—' He leaned across the back of the passenger seat and demonstrated by briefly extending his right index finger, an earnest expression on his handsome young face.

Tara took pity on him. 'OK, I believe you. Thousands wouldn't.'

'Have a look at the next person who comes past.' He settled back into his seat, red-faced. 'All the locals do it.'

Tara and Jen's gazes met in the rear-view mirror, their eyes brimming with laughter. 'OK,' they said together.

Jake muttered something about 'girls' and subsided.

Tara was on full alert for the next local to drive past her, and sure enough, just before they passed, the driver saluted them by briefly raising his forefinger.

Tara waved enthusiastically back.

The driver recoiled in shock and stared hard at her as he drove by.

'What did I do wrong?' she demanded indignantly.

Jake and Jennifer were in stitches in the back seat.

'I think you were a bit too enthusiastic,' Jake explained diplomatically.

Jen giggled. 'You did an Auckland wave, Mum — way too effusive!'

Tara rolled her eyes and ignored the kids and any finger-flicking for the rest of the journey. Whoever heard of a code of waving anyway?

Jake was easier to be around than his father, and she certainly didn't care nearly so much when she made a fool of herself in front of him. Tara was sure one of the reasons why Gil had helped her at the PTA meeting was because he disliked Barney Bigelow. Somehow she'd got caught up in their pissing contest. Jen, however, thought Gil was absolutely wonderful. So far as she was concerned he was the oracle of everything, which pissed Tara off no end. She could recall a time when Jen had felt the same way about her, but unfortunately that had only lasted until Jen was eight. But when it came to the subject of strip-grazing, Tara had to admit that Gil Sorensen did have the upper hand.

'Mr Sorensen is strip-grazing his horses to stop them getting too fat, and he gives them something to mop up all the toxins they get from the grass,' Jen announced.

'Does he now?' Tara thumped the bottle of wine and a glass onto Eric's ugly old Formica-topped table. She'd put most of his furniture into storage and replaced it with hers, except for the red monstrosity in the kitchen, because her own streamlined glass-topped twelve-person table didn't fit. 'I thought he was a dairy farmer.' Tara set to work opening the wine.

'He is.' Jen took a seat at the opposite end of the table, her eyes warm with admiration. 'But he occasionally trains horses and gives a few lessons in his spare time. Jake told me that his father was going to represent New Zealand at the Olympics but his horse died.'

Tara stared. 'Really?'

Jen nodded eagerly. 'He was really good, apparently; a lot of people thought he was just as good as Mark Todd.'

'Well why didn't he go later? On another horse?'

'Because then Jake's mother died. Jake was only three.'

'Oh.'

Tara had wondered why nobody ever mentioned Gil Sorensen's wife, and now she knew. She poured herself a glass of wine. There was no need for her to concern herself with the grieving widower when Glenys Tweedie had such a firm handle on the job.

Tara had to admit that Jen did have a point. It was becoming increasingly obvious that there was more to this grazing lark than chucking out a few carrots every so often and making sure the water troughs were full. Pat Warner was still yapping about the paddocks becoming 'horse-sick', whatever that was. The woman had an absolute obsession with worms and talked about them incessantly.

'I went to the library yesterday and got out a couple of books that seemed like they might be useful,' Jen said.

'What about? Fifty ways to kill off your neighbours and horse-faced women without getting caught?'

'*No.* One of them explains all about stock rotation and weeds — did you know that buttercup is a weed? And the life cycle of worms and how—'

Tara raised a hand. 'Thank you. I've heard enough.'

'You should read it, Mum,' Jen insisted. 'We live in the country now.'

'Only until I can raise the money to buy a house in Auckland.'

Jen didn't answer.

Tara peered at her. 'You do want to go back to Auckland, don't you?'

Jen shrugged. 'I don't know.'

Tara was aghast. 'You mean you *like* it here?'

'It's not so bad. I like my school here a lot better than the one in Auckland.'

Not only was the wind taken out of Tara's sails, the bottom of her boat struck rocks and started to take on water. 'Surely you're not going to tell me that learning to drive a tractor and having a lot of horses nodding at you over the fence has made you fall in love with country life?'

'What's wrong with it?' Jen was wearing the dogged, mulish expression that usually spelt trouble. 'It's fun.'

'But . . . but what about all the things you've left behind in Auckland?'

'What things? The only thing I miss is Dad.'

'Your . . . your friends!'

'Hah! Fat lot of good they were when I needed them.'

Tara thought about all the unanswered messages she'd left on Lizzie, Anne and Nicole's answering machines. It was as if she had dropped off the face of the earth. The only people who called were her mother and sister, although Kim spent most of her time complaining about her out-of-control sons and what a useless father Mickey was, and asking sly questions about dairy farmers. Tara hadn't mentioned Gil, or Kim would have been down in a flash.

Clutching at straws, she cried, 'The beaches!'

Jen remained unimpressed. 'It's just over an hour to Mount

Maunganui. By the way, can I learn to surf in the next school holidays? Jake goes surfing all the time, and he said there's a really good surf school in the summer.'

Tara didn't understand. They'd barely had time to unpack, and Jen was already making plans for the summer.

'There's something else I wanted to ask, too, something I've wanted to do for a long time that Dad would never let me.'

'What?' Tara asked wearily, flopping down into one of the red vinyl chairs.

Jennifer's unwavering blue eyes reminded her so much of Richard that Tara wanted to cry. Sometimes, when Jen held her head at a particular angle or pulled a certain expression, it was like a physical pain. Richard and Jennifer spoke regularly, but all contact between him and Tara had stopped.

Just the night before she'd dreamt again that Richard was alone in a hospital bed after the sex reassignment operation he planned to have. The walls of the room were made entirely of glass, and Tara could see that the operation had gone wrong and that Richard was part-man and part-woman. He was pleading for help, but nobody was coming. When Tara tried to get to him, Marion Popplewell closed and locked the glass door to his room, and dropped the key in the pocket of her big, white uniform, saying, 'You can't go in there. You wouldn't listen to him when he wanted to talk to you, and you can't change your mind now.'

Tara had woken up sobbing and couldn't get back to sleep. Richard was all alone. At least she had Jen.

Despite the hour, Tara had dialled Richard's cellphone number and got his voicemail. It was a big mistake. Richard's voice had become even higher and softer than when she'd seen him at the café. And his voicemail message had been painfully different.

'Hello. This is Rachel Whitehead. I'm sorry I've missed your call but it is important to me, so please leave me a message and I will contact you as soon as I'm able to—'

Tara had thrown her phone across the room. Anything to distance herself from that soft, feminine voice and the message. She didn't tell Jennifer she'd tried to contact her father.

'I've been talking to Gil—' Jen began tentatively.

Tara started. 'What?'

'I've been talking to Gil,' Jen repeated.

Tara glowered. 'Since when did you begin calling him *Gil*?'

'He told me to,' Jen said. 'Anyway, *Gil* said he'd be willing to give me some riding lessons in exchange for me doing some relief-milking in the afternoon.'

'Oh, did he?' Tara was still smarting about Jen's preference for country life and about her husband renaming himself Rachel.

Jen jumped up. 'I knew you'd be like this! Just because you and Dad hate horses doesn't mean I have to! I've always wanted to learn to ride!'

'I don't hate horses! In fact, I rode bareback in a bikini the entire summer I was thirteen.'

Jen's mouth fell open. 'You did?'

'Yes. My friend Kerry Milbeck had two ponies and we spent the entire six weeks of the summer holidays galloping up and down Muriwai beach. I rode Pepper and she rode Salt.' Tara didn't add that Kerry had also taught her how to smoke.

'Mum! I never knew you could ride!' Jen exclaimed.

'I didn't say I could. The reason we spent so much time on the beach was because it provided a nice soft landing every time I fell off.'

'So can I have some riding lessons with Gil?' Jen persisted.

Tara knew when she was beaten. 'Oh, I suppose so. But I want to see the horse first.' Not that she'd know what she was looking at.

She drained her glass and refilled it.

Tonight seemed like a good night to get drunk.

Chapter 12

Apart from visits to pick up groceries and get money from the ATM, Tara avoided Divine. Visits from Barney Bigelow, Chook Larby and the others had made it clear that Tara and Jen's arrival in town had caused a lot of interest. Tara didn't want to be the centre of attention after what had happened in Auckland, but she took Jen into Divine on a flying visit to get her a riding helmet, and boots and a pair of jodhpurs for her riding lessons. Aware that money was tight, Jen offered to forego the jodhpurs.

'Honestly, Mum, Gil said the only things he insists on me getting are a helmet and boots. I don't mind wearing my jeans.'

'If you're going to do this, you might as well be comfortable,' Tara insisted.

On the way home, Jen asked when Tara wanted to see the horse Jen would be riding. A face-to-face with Gil Sorensen held little appeal for Tara. When she recalled the humiliating moment when her face was pressed against his crotch, her mind played tricks, and Tara began to wonder if Gil really believed that Barney Bigelow had pushed her. The story had obviously made the rounds, because Jen had come home not long after the PTA meeting and asked what had happened there.

'Why?' Tara asked warily.

'Because there's a weird story going around about you putting your face in Gil's . . . ' Jen hesitated, '. . . *lap*.'

'It was an accident!' Tara protested. 'I was pushed and *fell* into his lap.'

Jen looked disapproving.

Tara sighed. 'Come on: out with it, Jennifer. You might as well tell me what people are saying.'

She reddened. 'They're saying that you were giving Gil a — a — that you had your *face* in his — *you know*.'

'I was not giving Gil Sorensen a blowjob!' Tara cried. She briefly explained the whole sorry episode: '. . . and then Barney Bigelow pushed me sideways and I ended up with my face in Gil's . . . er . . . lap. I bet that old trout Annabelle Archer spread the rumour about a blowjob!'

'Barney Bigelow?' Jen frowned. 'Is he Tiffany Bigelow's father?'

'I think so, and he's a pervert.'

'Tiffany Bigelow is an evil bitch. She's the one who's been spreading the story at school.'

'Jennifer! Watch your language.'

Jen pulled a face and changed the subject. 'I'll understand if you don't want to come over to Gil's. And I'll make sure everybody at school gets to hear what Tiffany's father did to you. That'll shut her up. I can't believe anybody would believe something like that about Gil; he's not that sort of person.'

'Neither am I!' It hurt Tara that Jen seemed to have a higher opinion of their next-door neighbour than of her own mother.

'Of course you're not.' Jen patted her arm and disappeared to her bedroom.

Tara wondered indignantly what Jen would have to say if Tara mentioned the hard-on that *Saint Gil* had got while she was draped across his thighs. In different circumstances, Tara suspected that he wouldn't be opposed to doing *that* at all. She imagined what Gil and Annabelle Archer would have done if she'd gone ahead and unzipped his fly.

Her stomach flipped.

Tara looked guiltily about the kitchen.

Your husband has left you to become a woman, she lectured herself, *which hardly makes you a* femme fatale. *How on earth can you even contemplate oral sex with a dairy farmer who has an unlimited wardrobe of brown clothing?*

Tara was definitely *not* going anywhere near the Sorensen place.

Unfortunately, Gil Sorensen came to her.

Tara was struggling to untangle a length of electric tape from a large blackberry bush. She hated electric fences because she kept forgetting to switch the unit off in the garage and then zapping herself in the paddocks. This time the unit was off, but her hands were full of thorns. Tara was sick and tired of Eric telling her to go ask Gil every time she questioned him about something around the farm.

'Bugger, bugger, bugger!' She sucked blood from her thumb. 'I hate you, Eric Whitehead! You're no bloody help at all! *Go ask Gil! Go ask Gil!*' she mimicked. 'He's not the bloody oracle!!'

Tara wrested the last of the tape from the bush and turned to dump it on the grass.

Gil stood behind her, watching.

She almost jumped into the blackberry bush. 'I am sick of this! Why don't you make some noise? Don't you have feet like ordinary people? Or are you on wheels?'

Gil nodded at the blackberry. 'That needs spraying.'

'I *know* that!' Tara lied.

'I came to see if you wanted me to bring the cows through.'

'Bring the cows through?' she echoed.

'Yes, to get on top of the grass in those paddocks at the far end of the race. Eric usually gets me to bring them through every now and then to keep the grass down.'

Tara felt ashamed. 'Thank you, that's very nice of you.'

'Helps me out, too: free grazing.' He paused. 'By the way . . .'

'Yes?' she asked warily.

Gil pointed at his brown boots. 'No wheels — just feet.'

Tara wanted to crawl into the blackberry bush and never come out again.

If Jennifer hadn't insisted, Tara wouldn't have accepted Gil's offer of free riding lessons. When Jen left for her first lesson, Tara sat at the red table in the kitchen, counting off the minutes until the hour was up and her precious daughter would return intact. It was a shame she'd got off on the wrong foot with Gil, because she really did need some advice about the property and the horses.

An hour and a half later, when Jen still wasn't home and Tara was ready to bite the bullet and cross the road, Jen danced through the door red-cheeked and glowing.

'It was *brilliant!*' she gushed. 'Gil is *so* patient and Magnum is just the best! He's supposed to be twenty-three but he doesn't act it and I walked and trotted and Gil said I have really good balance and I got the hang of rising to the trot *really* quickly and . . .'

Seeing Jennifer's shining eyes and huge smile, Tara could forgive Gil Sorensen just about anything.

'I'm going to get up both mornings this weekend to do the milking with Jake so I can start learning the ropes,' Jen said.

Tara smiled indulgently.

She was still smiling an hour later when Bevan Sargeson phoned to say that Eric Whitehead was causing a public disturbance outside the Long Drop Pub and Sports Bar and would she kindly come into town to collect him.

'*What* have you been doing, you old bugger?' Tara snapped when she set eyes on Richard's uncle on the pavement outside Divine's only pub.

'What d'ya mean?' Eric drew himself up on his mobility scooter. 'I haven't done anything. None of us have. All we wanted was a few drinks and that ratbag manager Jerry Wallace said we couldn't come in because we was wearing patches!'

Tara decided she'd misheard. Which was possible, considering all the noise going on around her. No fewer than seven other mobility scooters were parked on the pavement with their red-faced, angry owners sitting on them. A long bench beside the path was filled with elderly men and women with walking sticks or frames, all of them residents of Peacehaven Retreat.

Marion Popplewell was the noisiest of the lot. Her face was puce with fury above the starched white uniform over which she'd hastily flung a brown checked coat that closely resembled a horse blanket. She flitted from one group to the next, trying to soothe frayed tempers and pour oil on troubled waters. Unfortunately, none of the residents were having a bar of it.

'Mr Skinner, I'm sure you're only getting so upset because you've missed your afternoon medication,' she cooed to a wizened little man sitting on the bench. He wore a cloth cap and gripped a walking stick tightly in one gnarled hand.

'I don't want me bloody medication! I want a bloody drink!' he fumed.

The decibel level rose as several others agreed.

Marion looked as if she was going to have a fit. In the blink of an eye she went from cajoling to bullying. 'Miss Gillickson! Lillian!' she shouted. 'I'm ashamed of you! Escaping to indulge yourself in alcohol!'

Lillian opened her mouth to defend herself, but Eric beat her to it.

'Shut up, Marion! You leave her alone! You're not running bloody Colditz and we aren't children! Lillian is a *lady!*'

Lillian gave him a startled look.

Tara discovered that her dislike of Marion at that particular moment outstripped her dislike of Eric. In her opinion they were both bullies and deserved one another, but the same couldn't be said for the rest of the Peacehaven residents.

'Are you trying to say that because they live at Peacehaven they can't come and go as they please?' Tara demanded.

Marion looked as if she wanted to skewer Tara with the scissors she wore clipped to a chain draped across her fat stomach. 'It's for safety reasons, Mrs Whitehead,' she said icily, her little button eyes boring into Tara. 'It is essential that I know exactly how many residents are in the building at any given time.'

'Why can't you have a book for the residents to sign in and out?'

'Exactly!' Mr Skinner nodded. 'I've been saying the same thing for years.'

'And I have *explained*, Mr Skinner, that it would not do.'

'What you mean is you think we're all too senile to remember to sign in and out — *that's* what you mean,' a lady sitting beside Lillian Gillickson remarked.

Marion clenched her fists. 'Bevan!' she screeched at the community constable. 'I really think we need to get everybody home!'

Back in Eric's apartment, Tara heard the whole story.

Eric had joined the mobility-scooter group, which met in the lounge at Peacehaven every Wednesday afternoon.

'*You've* joined the mobility-scooter group?' Tara asked.

'Yeah. Why shouldn't there be?' He scowled. 'You bloody youngsters think we're all just a joke, but before you know it you'll be an old fart, too.' He pointed at a leather pouch hanging on the back of a chair in the small kitchen beside the lounge area. 'Do us a favour and get me smokes, will you?'

Tara retrieved the pouch and watched as he began to roll a cigarette. 'You're not supposed to smoke in here.'

His lip curled. 'Get a life.'

She was so surprised, she laughed. 'Marion can probably sniff out a fag at a hundred metres,' she warned.

'You're not wrong,' Eric agreed. 'Open that door up.'

Tara rose and opened the door leading to the patio, then returned to her seat. 'So, tell me more about the mobility-scooter group.'

Eric dipped his head to light his cigarette, inhaled, and blew smoke towards the patio. Dropping his matches into the pocket of his checked woollen shirt he settled back into his armchair.

'They're a bunch of old farts who sit around complaining about how long they've been waiting for their hip or knee replacements and how much they've got put by for their funerals.' Eric shook his head in disbelief. 'Bugger me! Who cares about your funeral? It's not as if you're going to be able to enjoy the booze you've paid for at the party, now, is it?' He puffed on his cigarette and thought of Lillian. 'Some of them are all right, but there's a few that could do with having a lid nailed down on them.'

Tara raised her eyes to the ceiling. Good old Eric, overflowing with the milk of human kindness.

'Anyway, I started going along to the meetings and suggested that perhaps they could put their time to something more useful, like raising the profile of mobility-scooter users: you know, things like making sure there's enough room to get your scooter past if there's tables and chairs out on the pavements. Corrine always makes sure there's plenty of room each side, but some of the other buggers aren't so good.'

'Who's Corrine?' Tara waved smoke from her face.

'Corrine Cathcart, the owner of the Mud in Your Eye Café in town.' Eric peered at her through the smoke. 'Don't you know anything?'

'I *do* know I have no intention of getting lung cancer from your second-hand smoke, you old sod,' Tara snapped, and dragged her chair closer to the open door.

Eric shrugged. 'Anyway, I said the group needed a new name and one of them mission statements, and then some of the ladies decided to embroider patches—'

'Patches? You really *do* have patches?'

'Yes.' He leaned over and grabbed his navy blue jacket from a nearby chair. 'Divine Area Mobility Scooter Action Group — DAMSAG for short.'

Tara took the jacket from him. A round embroidered emblem, complete with a little scooter and a spray of lilies with DAMSAG in pale blue letters at the top, was attached to the top of one sleeve.

Eric's rascally blue eyes gleamed. 'Lillian did mine.'

He definitely had his eye on Lillian Gillickson. The *poor* woman.

Tara returned the jacket. 'Did the manager of the Long Drop really refuse to let you in because you were wearing embroidered patches?' It was hard to believe. After all, they were a group of elderly people driving mobility scooters — not a biker gang.

Eric snorted. 'Jerry Wallace is so wet you could shoot ducks off him. He's Barney's cousin.'

Tara threw up her hands in disgust. 'This town is so incestuous it stinks! You're all related to one another.'

Eric was deeply offended. 'I *am not* related to Barney bloody Bigelow! The only reason that mongrel got a toehold in the Whitehead family was by knocking up young Alison. If Alison hadn't been so sour grapes over Gil marrying Louise, she wouldn't have looked twice at Barney. We all knew Bill wanted Alison to marry Connie's boy, although if you ask me Gil never saw Alison as anything other than his cousin.'

Tara sighed. '*Give me strength . . .*'

'What?' Eric demanded testily.

She shook her head. 'Tell me how the police ended up getting called to the pub.'

'Marion called them.'

'*Marion Popplewell? The matron?*'

He nodded.

'Why would she do that?'

'To knock us into line — make us behave,' Eric explained.

Tara's stared at him. 'What?'

'You heard me. She runs this place like Colditz.' He stabbed the two fingers holding his cigarette towards her. 'You know Fred Skinner? The little bloke with the walking stick?'

'Yes.'

'Him and Felicity Ringwald want to move into an apartment together, but they don't want to get married because they're better off on two single pensions than on one, besides which they don't see why they should have to tie the knot at their age. Anyway, Marion and Barney won't let them have a two-person apartment, *even though* there are at least two empty at the moment, unless they agree to get married. Fred's eighty and Felicity's eighty-one — well over the age of consent, and it's hardly as if Felicity's likely to end up with a bun in the oven, is it?'

Tara looked pained.

'You bloody young 'uns,' Eric grumbled. 'D'you think you're the only ones who have sex? And that's another thing. Mad Marion is refusing to get me erection pills — so you'll have to get them instead.'

'*What?*'

'You heard me, I need you to go get me prescription filled.' Eric ground out his cigarette and pulled his wallet from the pocket of his jacket. 'It's in here.'

'But who—' Tara stopped when she realized she'd been about to ask about Eric's sex life.

'Nobody at the moment.' Eric held out a folded piece of white paper. 'But I'm stocking up.'

She slowly reached for the prescription.

Lillian Gillickson had no idea that Casanova was alive and kicking — well, perhaps not quite kicking — just along the corridor.

The front page of the *Divine Flyer* carried a photo of the Peacehaven Retreat residents outside the Long Drop Pub with Bevan Sargeson, Marion Popplewell and Tara among them.

Bevan looked peeved. Marion looked apoplectic, her white frilly cap askew on her helmet of brown curls. Tara had her mouth open, yelling at Eric, who sat on his mobility scooter smiling for the camera like an evil genie. She hadn't even noticed the photographer. The headline read: *DAMSAG Members Banned From Local Public Bar*

Over Patches. It was agreed that owner/editor Dick Cathcart had outdone himself with the accompanying article.

> Last Wednesday evening, twelve members of the Divine Area Mobility Scooter Action Group, or DAMSAG for short, were refused admission to the Long Drop Pub and Sports Bar by manager Jerry Wallace because several of the group were wearing 'patches' embroidered by some of the lady members. All of the group are residents at Peacehaven Retreat, the retirement village situated in Divine.
>
> Eighty-one-year-old Mrs Felicity Ringwald, a widow who has resided at Peacehaven since the death of her husband, Roy, three years ago, explained that the DAMSAG members had decided to visit the pub for an afternoon drink at the end of their regular weekly meeting.
>
> 'Upon completion of a very productive and pleasant meeting held over tea, coffee, pikelets and Mrs Judd's lamingtons, our newest member, Mr Eric Whitehead, suggested we all adjourn to the local public house for the gentlemen to enjoy a beer and the ladies a shandy. You can imagine our shock and dismay when we were banned from entry because we were wearing our DAMSAG emblems. I was particularly upset, because Miss Lillian Gillickson and I had spent many hours embroidering the emblems. The design was selected following a competition won by Mr Fred Skinner — a very clever, artistic man. However, Mr Wallace told us that he was under explicit instructions from the owner, Mr Barney Bigelow, not to allow anybody wearing gang patches onto the premises. I was deeply hurt to have my embroidery likened to gang patches,' a tearful Mrs Ringwald said.

Dick devoted his entire editorial to DAMSAG, including its mission statement — Tara was dumbfounded to discover there really was one. He also alluded to the totalitarian regime being run by the management at Peacehaven Retreat, under which elderly people were being treated as children rather than being accorded the respect and dignity they deserved.

He ended his editorial by saying:

> I ask the people of Divine: Is this how we want the retired, elderly members of our community to be treated? Do age and infirmity mean that a person must be stripped of the rights and respect any adult takes for granted? Letters and comments to the Editor, *Divine Flyer*, PO Box 41, Divine 3499.

Marion was livid, particularly when her suspicion that it had been Eric Whitehead's idea to visit the pub in the first place was shown to be correct. She was up for two nights while her stomach ulcer bubbled and spat like a Rotorua mud pool. Her constitution wasn't helped by Barney, who was having just as much trouble with his heartburn after reading the article. As usual, he took his fury out on Marion.

'How the fuck did they get out in the first place, Marion, you stupid cow?' he snarled.

'I don't know, Barney! They must have just sneaked out.'

'How can a group of old farts on mobility scooters and walking frames bloody well *sneak* out? What are you? A moron?'

Marion burst into tears. 'It's that awful Eric Whitehead! He's nothing but trouble! He won't listen to me!'

'I'm warning you, Marion, you'd better get this sorted.'

'But how?' she wailed.

'Change the combination on the bloody locks or something! Just make sure they don't get out again, d'you hear?'

Clearly Marion was losing control of Peacehaven's inmates, and Eric Whitehead was a shit-stirrer. Barney was so incensed by the thought of the peasants in his kingdom revolting that he decided that it was time to put Eric in his place. With this in mind, he paid Eric a visit in his apartment that very same day.

'There's the small matter of your unpaid bill, Eric,' Barney began with a genial smile.

'Small?' Eric was rolling cigarettes and dropping them into an empty tobacco tin. 'I would've thought it'd be bloody massive by now.'

Barney's smile slipped a fraction at Eric's couldn't-care-less tone. 'We charge a hundred and fifty dollars a day to stay in an apartment — that's including food, ground rent and utilities.'

'Over a thousand bucks a week?' Eric snorted. 'You call that shit they serve up at the dining room food? I wouldn't feed it to Norris's dog, Francine.'

Barney's lips thinned. 'You've been here for months now, Eric,' he snapped. 'You owe me a fortune in unpaid rent.'

'Do I now?' Eric ran his tongue along a cigarette paper and flattened it with his thumb. 'You're right, Barn; things can't go on like this.'

Barney forced a smile. Even after all these years, dealing with a Whitehead always made him feel like the dirty, snot-nosed kid of the town drunk, and he hated it. 'I'm sure we can work something out.'

Eric nodded. 'Of course we can. Tell you what, how about I pay you off a bit each week?'

Barney beamed. 'That'll be fine. The first payment . . .' he prompted gently.

'I'll be in touch with my accountant first thing in the morning to get it all sorted.' Eric nodded at the door. 'Now if you don't mind showing yourself out, I've a few things I need to get on with.'

Barney swallowed his anger at being so peremptorily dismissed. He'd managed to bend Eric, the head of the Whitehead clan, to his will. It wasn't until he checked the Peacehaven bank statement the following week that Barney discovered he'd been royally screwed.

There *was* an entry for E.R. Whitehead.

It was for five dollars.

Chapter 13

Apart from the banks, Barney had an interest in nearly all of the businesses in Divine, the only exceptions being the *Divine Flyer* and the Mud in Your Eye Café, which were owned by a husband-and-wife team. Dick and Corrine Cathcart had moved to the town ten years earlier, with enough money from the sale of their Auckland business and property to thumb their nose at Barney and generally become a thorn in his side.

Dick Cathcart was an irreverent, eccentric Englishman who believed that no good journalist operated without a bottle of good Scotch in the bottom drawer of his desk. He had been in the business for forty years and the *Divine Flyer* was his swansong. He was past worrying about the press council or the Barney Bigelows of this world. Dick intended to have fun, and pissing off the pompous, overbearing little officials of Divine kept him entertained. He wrote pithy, stirring editorials criticizing Barney, Simon and the councillors, and so far Barney had failed in his covert bids to close the *Divine Flyer* down.

Corrine Cathcart ran the Mud in Your Eye Café like a home away from home. The food was superb, the wit sharp and the welcome warm; and if a lot of the acerbic one liners delivered by the staff flew over the heads of the majority, the select few who understood more than made up for them.

Corrine was a woman who made a person think of good things; she was full-breasted and round-hipped, with a permanent twinkle in her brown eyes that hinted at fun and naughtiness. When she had applied to the town council for permission to open her new café, Barney had suggested she might like to call it the Little Country Café. He wanted Divine to project an aura of country wholesomeness, and had named several of the businesses in town accordingly.

Corrine Cathcart was no fool. She saw through Barney Bigelow's urbane, chummy exterior to the bully beneath, and promptly named her new business the Mud in Your Eye Café — fortunately the interior didn't need changing, so she didn't need planning permission or a building permit.

Barney was furious when the café was an outstanding success. He still smarted every time he saw the purple-and-white sign perched on the black-tiled roof above the hanging baskets (Corrine defiantly planted purple petunias instead of the pink and white impatiens preferred by council). The sign had a grinning, fat purple pig scooping mud from its eye as it wallowed in muck, with *Mud in Your Eye Café* emblazoned in black lettering above. Rumour had it that Corrine had provided the artist with a photo of Barney as a model for the pig, and judging by the protuberant eyes, receding hairline and sagging paunch of the creature he'd been wildly successful.

Tara was convinced that living in Divine would turn her into an alcoholic. The article in the *Divine Flyer* was responsible for her polishing off her last good bottle of wine. If she hadn't been suffering from a hangover *and* if her very expensive German coffee-making machine hadn't gone on the blink, she would never have ventured onto the main street of Divine, let alone inside a café. The rumours about her and Gil Sorensen at the PTA meeting had only just died down when the article in the *Divine Flyer* once again was shooting her to notoriety. Tara was so desperate for a shot of strong, black espresso to dull the ache behind her eyes and wash away the sour taste in her mouth, that she didn't notice how every eye fastened upon her when she walked into the café, a little after nine in the morning.

Corrine, who was manning the counter, took one look at Tara's pale face and the pinched look around her mouth and said, 'Oh dear, I hope it was a really good bottle of wine.'

Tara lowered her sunglasses to peer at Corrine uncertainly, and, seeing only amusement twinkling in the merry brown eyes watching her, gave a ghost of a smile in return. 'I think it was. I really don't remember. I just need something hot, strong and dark.'

'I'm sorry to say I don't have Cliff Curtis or Denzel Washington on the menu, but how would a double espresso do?' Corrine asked kindly.

'Sounds perfect.'

Tara took the silver contraption holding her order number to a discreet corner beside the wide, deep window overlooking the tables on the pavement. The plastic number clipped to the silver holder bore the legend *Singing in Tune Will Be Firmly Discouraged.* On closer inspection, Tara saw that the café had a collection of pigs — stuffed toys on the windowsills and others on the sofa and chairs grouped in a corner — and the signs on the walls were also decorated with pigs in all shapes and sizes. Tara's favourite was a pink pig in black silk stockings and suspender belt, with fake eyelashes, pouting red lips and a long tortoiseshell cigarette holder in one trotter, reclining on the window ledge beside her. A pink plastic name badge clipped to her pink pig cleavage read *Tina Trotter.*

Corrine was singing Gloria Gaynor's 'I Will Survive' behind the big silver coffee machine, her head wreathed in puffs of steam. When she got to the *hey heys* she belted them out with gusto, making Tara jump, although a quick check of the other customers indicated that Corrine's recital was nothing unusual.

A short time later, Corrine carried a steaming, fragrant cup of coffee to Tara, who fell upon it with a cry of relief.

'You must be Tara Whitehead,' Corrine said, the ever-present smile curving her lips.

Tara swallowed a mouthful of coffee and nodded warily.

'I'm Corrine Cathcart, another import.' She gestured to the chair opposite. 'Do you mind?'

Tara shook her head.

'So, how are you finding our little piece of paradise?' Corrine asked, folding her arms on the table.

'Er . . . very nice.'

'Really?' Corrine's large, brown eyes widened.

Tara didn't know what to make of her. She looked about the café. Only a few of the tables were occupied so early in the morning, but there was a roaring trade in takeout coffees. Hungover or not, Tara wasn't stupid enough to risk having her opinion all over town by the end of the day. She liked the look of Corrine, but was still smarting from the DAMSAG article.

'My husband Dick is the editor of the *Flyer*.'

'Oh,' Tara said sourly. 'Is he?'

For obvious reasons, the editor of the *Divine Flyer* was high on her personal shit-list at that moment.

'Yes.' Corrine seemed unperturbed by Tara's hostile response. 'You're his heroine.'

Tara glowered. 'I wish I could say I was flattered.'

'You should be,' Corrine assured her. 'This town needs more people who're willing to stand up to Barney Bigelow and his cronies. Dick and I moved here ten years ago and have watched that monster undermine anybody who has different ideas and opinions.' She shook her head. 'I'm continually surprised at what a hotbed of gossip and intrigue small towns can be.'

'I'm afraid I don't buy the idea that Barney Bigelow is solely responsible for the cesspit mentality in this town.'

'Oh, you mean about you trying to give Gil Sorensen a blowjob at the PTA meeting?' Corrine enquired.

Tara choked on her coffee.

Corrine leapt to her feet and pounded Tara's back. 'There, there!' She handed Tara a paper napkin. 'Do you want a glass of water?'

'*No!*' Tara rasped.

Corrine sat down.

Tara looked at the earth mother figure opposite and decided there had to be something in the Divine town water supply that gave the local inhabitants the idea they could say whatever they liked. In Tara's experience, normal people did not talk about oral sex on first acquaintance, but Corrine hadn't finished.

'Most people don't believe you were trying to have oral sex with Gil — well, at least *not* at the PTA meeting.' She paused thoughtfully. 'Although I wouldn't put it past Glenys Tweedie to try.'

Tara stared at her.

Corrine patted her arm. 'Besides, you're a lot better looking than Glenys. People are beginning to realize they can't keep turning a blind eye to the things Barney B does. A lot of them have relatives living at Peacehaven, and the DAMSAG article made them face the fact that Barney and Marion Popplewell are running a very unfriendly regime for the old folks. You made them sit up and take notice.'

'Me?' Tara protested weakly. 'I didn't do anything. It was Eric.'

'Yes, you did. Your face in that photo got everybody's attention, because they're all obsessed with the Whiteheads.' Corrine shook her head. 'I've never quite understood it myself.'

You and me both, Tara thought.

'I don't think you realize that you could easily become a force to be reckoned with in this town if you choose to.'

Tara searched Corrine's face. *She's serious. Absolutely, totally serious.*

She looked down at her nearly empty coffee cup. Perhaps there was something in the coffee. Perhaps in a few moments she would wake up back in her bed in Eric's bedroom with its horrible orange, cream and brown swirly-patterned curtains. She changed the subject. 'Mud in Your Eye is an unusual name for a café.'

Corrine beamed. 'Isn't it? If it hadn't been for Barney Bigelow, I doubt I would have been so inspired. I owe him such a debt that I even put him on the sign outside.'

Tara sighed. Everything always led back to Barney bloody Bigelow. She didn't have a clue what Corrine was on about and didn't want to know either.

'Oh yes?' She finished her coffee in one big gulp, eager to make her escape.

Corrine looked amused.

'Yes. King Barney wanted me to call it the Little Country Café, which I wasn't having a bar of. He wanted it to exude an aura of twee charm and wholesomeness, and that was hardly likely to happen with somebody like me at the helm now, was it?' Corrine widened her eyes. 'So I put my thinking cap on and came up with Mud in Your Eye Café, which has had Barney Bigelow's boxers in a twist ever since the sign went up.'

Tara pulled a face at the thought of Barney's underwear and Corrine laughed. Tara was beginning to suspect there was nothing wrong with Corrine Cathcart's mental faculties and that she'd be more than a match for Barney. 'But isn't the pub called the Long Drop Pub and Sports Bar?' she asked.

'Yes. But it already had the name before Barney bought it, and in his opinion a pub and a café should be clearly delineated in the public's mind, a bit like a virgin and a hooker.'

Tara had another coughing fit.

'Dear me, I'm beginning to think that coffee's got bones in it.' Corrine stood up. 'Must get back. Make sure you come in again, whether it's post-hangover or not. I'll do my best to get Cliff or Denzel on the menu for you. By the way, *love* the boots.'

Tara looked down at her powder-blue suede boots. 'Thanks.'

She watched as Corrine's black peasant skirt and apron-clad figure slipped between the tables, and noticed the ruby-red sequinned slippers on her little feet. It made sense that Corrine would be wearing a pair of shoes reminiscent of Dorothy's in *The Wizard of Oz*. Maybe it explained why so many of the townspeople seemed out of their tiny minds.

Tara stopped to look at the purple-and-white sign mounted on the roof above the café as she left, and burst out laughing as she recognized the face of the grinning purple pig.

Her next stop was the supermarket.

As far as Tara was aware, her mother was the only person who enjoyed supermarket shopping. Tara shot around the aisles like a madwoman, high on espresso, anxious to avoid the curious stares of other people. She worried that if she stood still for even a second, somebody would approach her to discuss Gil Sorensen's purported blowjob or DAMSAG's storming of the Long Drop Pub.

She stopped at the bottle store (owned by Barney Bigelow, of course) across the road from the supermarket to take advantage of a special on one of her favourite wines.

'Excuse me, how many bottles of the Kim Crawford Sauvignon Blanc will you sell to one person?' Tara asked the boy behind the counter.

It was the first time Neville Tweedie had seen Tara Whitehead up close. His mother said Tara Whitehead was the same age as her, but Neville didn't believe it; his mother didn't look as good as this glamorous creature. He sold Tara a whole case of wine, although he'd been instructed to restrict sales to three bottles per person. Neville offered to carry the wine to Tara's car, and was disappointed when she said she could manage, then smiled and left the store.

Gil was heading into the bottle-store car park as Tara emerged. He hadn't seen her since he'd offered to bring the cows over to Eric's and overheard her calling him the oracle. Gil didn't know why he kept offering to help her. He was frantically busy at this time of year and scarcely set foot off the farm. If Tara had been trying to lie low, she'd failed miserably by getting her photograph on the front page of the local paper.

When Gil first saw the article about DAMSAG and the picture of Tara surrounded by the Peacehaven residents, he'd almost inhaled his morning cup of tea. Seeing snooty Mrs Whitehead caught in the act of screaming at Eric like a fishwife was priceless, and for the rest of the day every time Gil thought about it he laughed. But when he considered what Barney's reaction would be, he stopped smiling and started worrying.

Although Tara had made it clear she didn't want his help or

interference, she had no idea what Barney was like. He was a bully, more cunning than clever, who gave good manners and decency a token nod as he bulldozed his way towards his goal. Barney would try doing things the nice way once — briefly — and when that didn't work he would get out a big club and beat the living daylights out of his opposition until they saw things his way. Whenever Gil thought of Tara and Jen Whitehead, alone in the house across the road and clueless about the pitfalls of caring for the animals or the property, he felt uneasy. Pat Warner and several of her cronies were threatening to take their horses away, but Tara didn't seem to care. Jen had mentioned it to Gil when she came over for one of her riding lessons and, although she'd been careful not to criticize her mother, it was clear she was worried.

'Mum is a city person,' Jen explained.

Gil wisely kept his mouth shut. You only had to look at Tara's high heels and clothes to know she was most at home among the skyscrapers, carbon monoxide and baking tarmac of Auckland. Gil wouldn't have been surprised to hear that she wore high heels to bed, and was annoyed when the thought of Tara naked on white sheets but for a pair of stilettos aroused him.

'Ah, hell, Sorensen!' he grumbled. 'You need a trip to Auckland yourself.'

A couple of years after Louise had died, Gil had made a conscious decision to fulfil his sexual appetites well away from home. His father was fond of saying that it paid not to mess in your own nest, and Gil wholeheartedly agreed. When he finally came out of the fog that Louise's death had left him in, he cultivated friendships with several single women in Hamilton and Auckland who were attractive and discreet and understood that Gil Sorensen really meant it when he said he wasn't looking for anything more meaningful than a fine meal and wine, some good conversation and some even better sex to finish the night off. A few had fallen by the wayside when they'd tried to shift the relationship from a casual footing to something more permanent, but on the whole Gil's sex life was satisfying, if infrequent.

The old adage that still waters run deep summed up Gil Sorensen perfectly.

He had a feeling that his policy of non-involvement with regard to Tara Whitehead was about to come to an end. While all about him had taken sides and begun building trenches, Gil had foolishly believed he could be Switzerland; but Tara wasn't the kind of woman who inspired neutrality. Barney was gunning for Eric, and, because Eric had him backed into a corner, he would turn his sights on Tara and her daughter as the weak link in Eric's defences. Gil wasn't sure exactly what shape Barney's revenge might take, but he wasn't about to let nice little Jen Whitehead be blindsided by a prick like Barney Bigelow.

Although he wasn't so sure that her snooty mother might not deserve all she got.

Then when Pat Warner and two of the other women grazing horses at Eric's place visited Gil to complain about the way Tara was running things, he realized he was fooling himself if he thought he could remain uninvolved.

'She refuses to take me seriously when I complain!' Pat fumed.

Gil didn't tell her that he had the same problem. 'What do you expect me to do about it, Pat?'

Pat's high, bony forehead puckered. 'I thought Eric had left you in charge?'

'No.' Gil shook his head. 'He asked me to help out — nothing more.'

'Oh.' She looked crestfallen. 'I don't know what to do, Gil. Felix has lost weight. It doesn't matter how often I worm him, I'm sure he's riddled. Tara Whitehead makes no effort to pick up the manure or harrow or *anything!*'

'We're thinking about taking our horses away,' Kathy Smith chimed in. 'If it wasn't for the lack of grazing around here, we'd all be gone by now. The moment I hear of somewhere, I'm taking Godiva and never coming back.'

Joanne Reed, the third member of the delegation, nodded agreement. 'And we're not the only ones. Most of the owners are looking for new grazing. In fact, Barney Bigelow offered to let me graze Bart on his land on the other side of the river.'

Kathy and Pat looked shocked.

'He didn't!' Kathy cried.

Joanne smiled smugly. 'He did.'

Gil's lips tightened. Barney was like an evil puppeteer pulling on everybody's strings. By slowly undermining Tara until she lost what income Eric's land generated, Barney clearly thought that he could sidle in and offer her a ridiculously low amount of money and send her packing back to Auckland.

Jen Whitehead didn't deserve to be diddled out of her inheritance.

She was an absolute delight. Gil didn't always enjoy giving riding lessons, but he liked teaching Jen. She loved being around horses, was enthusiastic, and had natural talent, which made his job a lot easier.

He'd been a bit concerned by the amount of time she and Jake had been spending together, but Jake assured him that they were only friends, and Gil knew Jake still carried a torch for Melanie Larby. That didn't stop Gil insisting that Jake's bedroom door remain open whenever he took Jen down there to listen to music. Gil felt duty-bound to hang around in the house when Jen was in Jake's room, and wasted precious time he really needed to spend outside. He made regular trips to and fro, offering cups of coffee, tea, soft drinks, milk — anything he could think of — most of which Jen politely refused.

Gil overheard her ask Jake, 'Does your dad like cooking?'

'No, he's just really worried because you're in my bedroom.'

Jen refused to come over for the rest of that week, much to Jake's annoyance.

'Are you happy now?' he asked Gil. 'Jen is really hurt. Why can't you believe me when I tell you we're just good mates?'

'Don't you pin this on me,' Gil retorted. 'Sometimes you've got the IQ of a green banana. It was you and your smart-arse comments that upset her.'

He really couldn't believe that two such good-looking kids weren't sexually attracted to each other. 'You can't tell me you haven't noticed how pretty Jen is. If I'd had a girl like her for a friend when I was your age I would have wanted more than just friendship.'

'Yeah? Well, that's you,' Jake said. 'Maybe I'm different.'

Gil regarded him incredulously.

Jake scowled and blushed. 'I know it'll sound weird, but even though I know Jen is hot I don't think about . . . you know . . .' He mumbled and looked away. 'She says she feels the same way about me. It's the first time I've had a friend who's a girl and it's kinda cool. Normally I just want to . . . you know.'

Yes, Gil knew. He enjoyed indulging in as much 'you know' as he could find the time for, which with his responsibilities around the farm and the source of his closest 'you know' half an hour's drive away in Hamilton was precious little. He stared at Jake long and hard, but the boy seemed sincere enough. Gil guessed he should just be glad he had a teenage son instead of a teenage daughter, because if Jen Whitehead was his daughter he'd lock her into a chastity belt and greet every pimply-faced, testosterone-overloaded teenage boy that darkened the front door with a Neanderthal growl and promises of castration if they even considered 'you know'. A girl as pretty as Jen should have a father watching out for her, but there had been no sign of Richard since she and Tara had moved to Divine, which perplexed Gil.

'Her mum's pretty hot, too — for a middle-aged woman,' Jake remarked.

'You reckon?' Gil replied coolly, not fooled for an instant by Jake's guileless expression. 'What's that supposed to mean?'

'Nothing. I just said that Tara's hot, that's all.'

Gil levelled a finger at him. 'Don't even go there, Jake.'

As soon as the rumours began to circulate about Tara Whitehead giving him a blowjob at the PTA meeting, Gil had told Jake exactly what had happened.

Jake nearly wet himself laughing.

Chapter 14

The thought of Jennifer prompted Gil to speak to Tara about the management of Eric's property, even though he doubted she'd listen. But the memory of Tara's heartbroken expression when he'd found her crying had a nasty habit of intruding on Gil's memory every time he told himself what a pain she was. So when he saw her coming out of the bottle store, it was as if fate was telling him some things just couldn't be avoided. With a sigh, Gil parked his ute and walked towards the shop.

The moment Tara saw him, she stopped and looked nervously about the car park, which was empty except for her car and Gil's ute. She looked as if she was considering making a run for it.

Gil was annoyed when he considered the help he'd given her at the PTA meeting and the trouble he'd gone to afterwards to squelch the rumours.

Tara reluctantly began walking towards him. She was wearing high-heeled blue boots and a skirt of the same colour, which hugged her hips and thighs. The mounds of her breasts pushed out the front of her pale blue fluffy sweater, and Gil thought how much he'd enjoy warming his hands on them. The weather had grown warmer over the past couple of weeks and Gil was wearing a T-shirt. The weather in subtropical Auckland was warmer than the Waikato, however, so newcomer Tara hadn't given up her winter woollies yet.

She nodded cautiously when she reached him. 'Gil.'

'Tara.' Gil couldn't help himself. 'I think I prefer "the oracle".'

Tara reddened. 'I was having a bad day.'

He wondered if she ever had a good one. At least they were now on a first-name basis, but then it was hard to be formal with a man whose lap you ended face-down in at a PTA meeting. He tried to lighten the atmosphere. 'Still wearing the high heels, I see.'

'Still wearing brown clothes, I see,' Tara drawled. She almost sounded friendly.

Gil looked down at his brown T-shirt and trousers. 'What's that supposed to mean?'

Tara shifted the heavy box of wine on to her hip and turned towards the Lexus, saying over her shoulder, 'Just that it seems you have nothing but brown trousers, brown sweatshirts and brown quilted jackets — oh, and let's not forget the ubiquitous brown beanie.'

'What's wrong with brown? It's practical. It doesn't show the cowshi— mud.'

Tara smiled in amusement. This man had twice dug her out of a hole — literally *and* figuratively — and was providing free riding lessons for Jen.

'Cowshit is *not* brown; it's green. I should know: I've got a ruined pair of white jeans to prove it.'

Gil was fascinated by the sound of her posh, refined voice saying 'cowshit'. It was the first time he'd seen her smile properly. 'I had a black jumper on at the PTA meeting,' he said.

Tara's face fell. Why did he have to bring that up?

'What was wrong with my black jumper?' Gil asked.

She aimed her keyring at the car and popped the boot. She was being too nice. If she was rude, he'd probably go away. 'Nothing,' Tara said shortly. 'It's just a shame you had to wear it with brown trousers and a brown shirt.' Although he *had* looked rather tasty. She balanced the case of wine on the edge of the boot and began to clear a space among the grocery bags.

'Let me take that,' Gil offered.

'There's no need.'

Gil watched her bottom beneath the clinging blue skirt. He had work waiting for him at home and didn't really give a damn about clothes, but he'd keep right on discussing them if it meant he could watch Tara Whitehead's luscious arse. It dipped and swayed, mesmerizing him.

'What's wrong with brown?' he asked.

'Nothing — if you're a mole.'

'We don't have moles in New Zealand.'

Tara continued to rearrange loaves of bread and tin cans, cradling her precious box of wine against her side. 'Rabbits, then.'

'They're grey.'

It dawned on her that Gil might be winding her up. Tara raised her head to look at him and whacked her skull against the edge of the boot. She yelped, lost her hold on the box of wine, and stumbled backwards clutching the top of her head. Gil dived forward, scooped up the box and caught Tara as she tottered backwards into him, managing to stab him in the foot with one of her heels for good measure.

'Oww! Shit!' He snatched his foot away. As the pain subsided, Gil noticed that something warm, round, soft and fluffy filled his right palm. He tentatively flexed his fingers. It sure as hell wasn't a rabbit.

Tara sucked in a breath and the soft warm flesh swelled. Gil realized he was holding her breast. Her breath hitched again and he felt a hard little nub blossom against the centre of his palm. He needed to let go. They were in a public place and, following hot on the heels of the PTA fiasco, it was not the kind of publicity either of them needed. But he was a guy and she felt so good that it was several seconds before his brain managed to forward a message to his hand, as if his personal internet was down.

Finally, Gil's fingers sprang apart as if he'd been jabbed by an electric cattle prod. He jumped backwards, still clutching the case of wine, and cast a belated look around to check whether they'd been seen. It would be just his luck if Annabelle Archer was driving by.

Gil could hear her on the phone to her cronies: *I couldn't believe my eyes! First oral sex at the PTA meeting, and now heavy petting in the bottle-store car park!*

'Sorry! I didn't mean to—'

Tara spun around, her arms crossed over her breasts and her eyes huge. 'It's OK. I—'

'I was trying to catch the wine and you and—'

'Yes!' She nodded vigorously. 'I said it's all right!'

'I grabbed you to stop you from falling and didn't mean to grab you by the . . .' Gil gestured helplessly.

Tara wished he'd shut up.

'It was an accident, like my fall the other night!' she exclaimed. 'Will you just let it go?'

'I thought I did,' Gil blurted.

He grimaced and waited for a tirade of abuse, and was amazed when Tara doubled over, laughing until she was gasping for breath.

'Glad you find it so funny,' Gil said.

She looked up at him through a veil of blonde hair. The sight of his disgruntled expression sent her into a fresh bout of hilarity.

'Sorry!' Tara pressed a hand over her mouth. 'It's just your *face* . . .'

And she was off again.

Gil began to smile. It was impossible not to. Suddenly he saw the girl at Eric's party who his mother had described to him all those years ago: the carefree, golden surfer girl, eyes glowing and lips curving, the misery and despair wiped from her face, leaving a glowing, lively, beguiling woman. Gil was bemused by the change.

Tara straightened and wiped tears from her eyes. She couldn't recall the last time she'd laughed so hard. She felt light as a feather, filled with happiness. 'Can I have my wine back?' Tara asked.

'Your wine?' Gil repeated stupidly.

'Yes, my wine.'

He looked at the box under his arm. 'Yeah! Sure. I'll . . . put it in the boot.'

Once the box was safely stowed, Gil repeated, 'It really *was* an accident.'

'Oh for God's sake: shut up, Gil! Anyone would think it was the first time you've had a boob in your hand.'

Mention of it made Gil's fingers curl in memory. In a desperate attempt to redirect the conversation into safer territory, he asked, 'How long do you think those boots will stay blue on the farm?'

Tara looked down at them. 'What's wrong with them? Ah — don't tell me — they're not brown.'

'Brown clothes are practical on a farm, unlike three-inch high heels,' Gil replied. Something about Tara Whitehead and her high heels affected parts of him they shouldn't.

'I can handle a pair of high heels, thank you very much. I've been wearing them since I was thirteen,' she said haughtily.

'*Thirteen?*'

'Yes.

'You *never* take them off?'

'*Never.*'

Gil thought it better not to mention her floral gumboots. He watched Tara bristle and her eyes begin to flash, and felt better. He wondered why he'd ever thought she was a cool blonde.

'Never, ever?' he needled.

Tara glared at him. She didn't understand why Gil had the ability to send her emotions swinging from one extreme to the other. Just when he'd made her so angry she wanted to grab a bottle of wine from the boot and brain him with it, his dark eyes would gleam and he'd smile his one-cornered smile and suddenly she was imagining herself in a very compromising situation with him.

'Oh . . . *shut up!*' Tara spluttered. 'Who on earth are you to criticize my shoes when your own wardrobe is so appalling? I've a good mind to — to —'

Gil smirked. Push the right buttons and she went off like a rocket. 'What? Complain to my parents? Sorry, they're both away at the moment.'

Tara refused to succumb to his charm, but faced with that smile and those melting dark eyes, her heart skipped and her stomach fluttered in response.

'Perhaps I should take you clothes shopping with me next time I go,' Gil said.

'I've got better things to do with my time than go shopping with you,' Tara replied tartly.

'I go shopping for clothes every three years. You're sure I can't pencil you in for next year?'

She was incredulous. 'You're having me on.'

'No, it's the truth.' Gil studied her boots. 'Perhaps you should take me with you the next time you go shopping for shoes.'

Tara burst out laughing. '*You? And me? Shoe shopping?* I *don't* think so!'

Gil's imagination went into overdrive all over again, and he had to look away.

'I'll be long gone before you need to buy clothes again.'

He stared at the bumper of the Lexus and thought, *Good.*

An awkward silence fell.

'I wanted to thank you for giving Jennifer the riding lessons,' Tara said, finally.

Gil shrugged. 'That's OK. Thanks for letting Jake hang around your place so much.'

'Not at all. He's a nice kid.'

He inclined his head. 'And Jen's a lovely girl. I was a bit concerned about the amount of time they were spending together.'

'Yes, Jen told me. She said you make regular checks on them when they're in Jake's bedroom.'

'It's not that I don't trust them or think that Jen's the sort of girl who would . . . what I *mean* . . .' Gil raked a hand through his hair and grimaced. 'Oh hell, perhaps I'd better stop while I'm ahead.'

One of the things Tara most missed since she'd split from Richard was having somebody to talk to about Jen. Like her, Gil was a single parent.

'They really *do* seem to just be friends. Do you think it's for real? I mean — they're nice-looking kids and at the age when all they have on their minds is the opposite sex — well, at least it's all *I* remember having on my mind at that age,' she stumbled on, blushing.

Gil took pity on her. 'I'll let you in on a family secret.'

Tara raised her brows enquiringly.

'Jake's had a crush on a local girl ever since he found out in kindergarten that she could stick more crayons up her nose than he could. I think she managed five to Jake's four.'

She smiled. 'I'm impressed. The best Jennifer ever did was three.'

Gil eyes wandered across her warm, glowing face. 'Be sure to send Jake home at mealtimes or he'll eat you out of house and home.'

'And have a fridge clogged with three-day-old leftovers?' Tara shook her head. 'I don't think so.'

'As long as you're sure?'

She nodded. 'Jen loves having riding lessons. She wanted to learn years ago, but . . .' She shrugged. 'Richard was never keen.'

Gil watched the glow fade from her face.

'Richard was terrified of horses. Henry deserved to be shot for allowing Eric to force Richard onto them whenever he came to stay.'

Of course Gil would know all about Richard's dislike of the animals; they had shared childhood holidays together. Tara wondered nervously what else he knew about Richard. 'I don't want her getting hurt, she's precious to me.'

'Of course she is, but you can't wrap her up in cotton wool,' Gil said.

Tara decided she could listen to his deep, mellow voice all day, it was so soothing.

'She's doing really well. You should come and watch the next time she has a lesson.'

She nodded. 'I will.'

'Jen said you used to ride when you were younger.'

Tara snorted. 'Like hell! I rode for one summer and fell off all the time.'

Gil grinned. He loved the sound of her plummy voice crying *Like hell!* Ribbing Tara Whitehead and watching her lose her temper could easily become one of his favourite pastimes, but there were more important matters he needed to broach. 'I had a visit the other day from Pat Warner and a couple of the other women with horses at your place.'

'Oh yes?' she said sourly. 'Owner of Felix the Wonder Horse?'

'That's her.' Gil chose his words with care. 'I know she can be a pain, but that horse is all Pat has. She's never married and she looked after her elderly mother until she died last year. She has no close family, so Felix fills the gap. She's owned him since he was a foal. You and I have got Jen and Jake; Pat has Felix.'

'Oh.' Tara digested this in silence. 'I just wish she wouldn't insist on talking to me about the life cycle of worms every time I'm planning to eat.'

When Gil tipped back his head and laughed, Tara wondered how he'd look in Armani or Hugo Boss and decided she needed her head read. She really didn't understand why she was attracted to him. He wasn't even her type.

'If you ever want a hand around Eric's place or have any questions, feel free to ask.'

'It's very kind of you to offer,' she replied politely.

Gil felt as if a door had been slammed in his face and was annoyed that it mattered so much to him. What did he care about stuck-up Mrs Whitehead anyway? She was, to use one of Chook's favourite sayings, about as useful as a fly-screen on a submarine.

'Thank you again,' Tara said coolly.

'Don't mention it,' Gil replied flatly.

A sleek green sedan driven by Barney Bigelow pulled into the car park. His bulging blue eyes widened with pleasure when he saw Tara, and he smiled, waved and aimed the car at her and Gil.

'Oh shit!' Tara cried.

'Calm down, Tara,' Gil said coolly. 'You've got your high heels on, remember?'

'High heels!' She ran to the door of her car. 'A howitzer was more what I had in mind!'

Leaping into the Lexus, she gunned the engine, swerved around Barney's Ford and shot out of the car park like a Formula One driver.

Barney climbed out of his car and frowned after the departing Lexus. 'You're s'posed to be getting on the right side of her, Gil, not upsetting her!'

'Maybe I'm just not the man for the job, Barney,' Gil replied. 'But I think you're right — something *did* upset her.'

Barney looked at him sharply.

Gil turned away. 'Better get on into the store before you put the price back up on my favourite beer. See you at the next meeting.'

'Smart-arse prick,' Barney muttered as Gil walked away.

Gil's laughter drifted back to him.

Barney retreated to Bigelow Towers to brood over the problem of Eric and Tara Whitehead.

Things weren't going to plan. Eric continued to pay him five dollars a week, and showed no sign of taking seriously Barney's increasingly unsubtle hints about changing his will and selling his fifty-eight acres, and Gil Sorensen was being just as stubborn by refusing to get up close and personal with Tara Whitehead and point her in the direction of Auckland.

Barney couldn't figure Gil out. Richard's missus was a knockout, and having read the startling contents of Richard's letter to Alison, Barney was certain that Tara was just gagging for some male attention. He deeply regretted he couldn't be the one to provide it.

His behaviour at the PTA meeting had scared him. Barney prided himself on his self-control and his ability to pull the wool over people's eyes, but Tara Whitehead spoke to something in his soul. Despite his long-standing affairs with Elaine and Marion, Barney was a firm believer in fidelity in marriage, certainly for the woman, and he laid the blame for his own wandering eye at Alison's doorstep. In Barney's opinion, if Alison had been a more attentive wife he wouldn't have needed Elaine and Marion. They didn't count; they were like his car or the clothes he wore, convenient and easily changed.

Tara Whitehead would be quite a different kettle of fish. Her haughty stare and icy tone made Barney's mouth go dry and his hands shake. Gil Sorensen needed his head read. He pursed his fleshy lips. He was beginning to think he'd have to seduce Mrs Whitehead himself. The memory of her repulsed expression and the way she'd snatched her hand away when he'd knocked on her front door flashed into his mind, but Barney thrust it aside. He'd never let anything as trivial as a woman's feelings deflect him from achieving his goal. A person only had to look at Alison to see that. Tara Whitehead had better come to heel soon.

If she knew what was best for her.

Chapter 15

On a scale of one to ten, Tara thought that this time she'd come out ahead of Gil following their encounter at the bottle store; this time *he'd* made a bigger fool of himself than she had. Whenever Tara recalled the feel of his big, warm hand cupping her breast, however, her pelvic floor muscles clenched in response. She looked in the mirror above the Rose and Heather kauri dresser in her bedroom. Who was she trying to kid? If *only* he hadn't squeezed her so gently. If *only* she hadn't wanted him to keep on doing it.

'Hussy!' she told her reflection. 'That part of your life is over!'

Tara concentrated instead on the thing Gil had brought to her attention — other than the resurrection of her libido: the worrying news that Pat Warner and company were planning on taking their horses elsewhere. She couldn't afford to let that happen.

'Where are those books you wanted me to read about horses and stuff?' she asked Jennifer.

Jen rushed off to get the books from her room, and thrust them eagerly at Tara. 'I've finished them, so you can keep them as long as you want. I'll phone the library and renew them for you.'

Tara studied the books with tepid enthusiasm. 'Thanks.'

Jen pointed. 'That one is *really* good!'

'I can hardly wait. Has it got a happy ending?'

'Mum!'

'Oh, all right,' Tara grumbled. 'But I hope you realize I'll have to miss *Boston Legal* and *Outrageous Fortune* to read them.'

'Auntie Kim always records *Outrageous Fortune* — you can get her to send you a DVD.'

One of the few things that Tara and Kim shared was a love of the local drama set in West Auckland. Kim had a particularly soft spot for Pascalle West, because she reminded her so much of herself at that age. Tara had to admit that promiscuous, selfish, blonde, not-too-bright Pascalle bore an uncanny resemblance to Kim.

Jen's books became Tara's bedside reading, usurping *Fashion Quarterly*, *House and Garden*, and her favourite Deborah Challinor. With a heavy heart, Tara closed the page on the mind-bogglingly beautiful pair of Pierre Hardy wedges that she had been hopelessly lusting for, and marked the spot in *Kitty* where the feisty heroine had finally been about to drop her frilled Victorian drawers for the scrumptious Rian. She was soon engrossed in looking at pictures of weeds and reading detailed explanations of the life cycle of a tick and how to castrate a lamb. It was enough to turn anybody to drink, but she was trying her best to cut back.

Tara was amazed to discover that paddocks really could become horse-sick. The author advised harrowing in large paddocks, but in small paddocks the only option was to pick the manure up *by hand* every day or two. Due to the excess of grass, Felix and the others were being strip-grazed, which meant the 'by hand' deal was the only option.

'You have *got* to be kidding!' Tara spoke to the page as if her indignation could be directly transmitted to the author. Was this what her life had come to? She was going to become a toilet attendant to a bunch of old nags who farted and crapped like there was no tomorrow.

'I'll help, Mum,' Jen said.

Her lessons at Gil's had made her even more passionate about riding, and her progress had been so good that Gill had moved her on to another horse.

Tara had been poring over the employment adverts and kicking herself all over again for not completing her degree, although that hadn't made her any less determined to get a job to supplement their income. After reading the books, however, Tara became painfully aware that if she was going to keep any money coming in she was going to have to do a lot more work around the property, which meant she wouldn't have the time for another job.

To top it off, Richard called out of the blue. Jen came into the living room with the cordless phone in her hand one night after school, looking nervous. 'Mum? It's Dad. He wants to talk to you.'

Tara stared at the black receiver as if it was a weapon of mass destruction. Each time she heard Richard's voice — his *new* voice — she felt like another part of her died. 'What does he want?'

'I don't know, but he says it's important and he really needs to speak to you.' Jen looked at her pleadingly. *'Please,* Mum.'

Tara silently took the phone and waited for Jen to leave the room. Her stomach was in knots as she put the phone to her ear. 'Hello?'

'Hello, Tara.'

She shook her head soundlessly at the sound of the high, soft, feminine voice.

'Tara? Are you there?'

'Yes.'

There was a prolonged silence while the line seemed to vibrate with suppressed emotion and pain.

'Are you all right, Tara?' Richard said softly.

Tara clamped her forehead between the fingers and thumb of one hand and closed her eyes. How could this be him? How could this be true?

'Tara, *please* say something.'

Richard sounded a lot like Jen had a moment ago when she'd pleaded with Tara to speak to him. The thought of Jen made Tara pull herself together.

'Yes, Richard, I'm fine.' She cleared her throat. 'How are you?'

'I'm . . . fine.'

Tara was instantly suspicious. His hesitation told her that he wasn't fine at all. 'What's wrong?' she asked sharply. 'Are you sick?'

Please spare me any embarrassing details, she prayed.

'No . . . no, I'm not sick,' Richard said firmly. 'In fact, I'm extremely well.'

Tara translated that as 'I've never felt better' and her concern turned to anger. Why did he need to rub it in?

'You called me the other night but didn't leave a message.'

'Did I?' she replied carelessly. 'I must have dialled the wrong number. What can I do for you, Richard?'

Don't you dare ask me to call you Rachel.

When he spoke again, Tara could tell he was annoyed.

'I wanted to tell you I've left my job and won't be able to send you as much money as I have been.'

She closed her eyes and clenched her jaw.

It had only been a matter of time. Tara was surprised that Richard had lasted at the bank so long. She could imagine the dilemma that Richard's coming out had caused for the ultra-conservative directors.

'When?' she asked abruptly.

'I beg your pardon?'

'*When* will the monthly payments stop?'

'I didn't say that they'd stop, just—'

'Let's not beat about the bush, Richard,' Tara interrupted. 'We both know that they'll eventually have to stop because your operation and recovery will mean you'll have to start digging into your money from selling the house.'

As angry as she was with him, Tara didn't want Richard to become destitute.

'I'm afraid my operation simply isn't negotiable. I'm sorry but—'

'Rubbish,' Tara snapped. 'You're not sorry at all. How much longer have I got before you stop paying?'

'I won't stop supporting Jennifer!'

'All right: *me*.'

'We could tap into some of our investments.'

'No.' Tara was adamant. 'I'd rather not touch those, and, besides, I don't want you supporting me.'

Richard sighed impatiently. 'Why do you always have to be so stubborn?'

'Don't blame me, Richard. Jen and I are in this position because of you!'

There was a taut silence.

'I can probably manage until Christmas,' he said stiffly. 'I really wish you wouldn't fall back into your old habits and be so confrontational.'

'What exactly does that mean? That I'm reverting to my wild Westie roots?'

'That's *not* what I said.'

'You don't need to. I know how you think.' Her breath hitched. 'Or at least, I used to.'

'I really don't want to fight with you,' Richard said quietly. 'I miss you.'

Tears stung her eyes. 'Don't do that.'

'What? Don't pretend that I still love you? *I do*.'

Tara gripped the phone so hard it was a wonder that it didn't break in half. She was torn between her old love and her new hatred for him. In the end, the hatred won out. 'Go to hell, Richard!' she cried. 'Go to hell!'

Jabbing a finger on the END CALL button, she flung the receiver across the room and let the tears fall. At some point, Jen brought in a box of tissues and a cup of coffee and sat and held Tara's hand until she stopped crying.

'I'm sorry, Mum,' she said miserably. 'I shouldn't have made you speak to him.'

'No. It's not your fault. What's between your father and me has nothing to do with you, Jennifer. I've been a lazy old tart.' Tara sniffed and rubbed the end of her nose with a sodden tissue. 'It's time I got my act together. We live here—' she sent Jen a warning look '—for now, and we need to get on with making ourselves a new life. I'm going to get things sorted out around here, and then after Christmas I'm going to find some sort of a job in Hamilton.'

'I'll get a job after school,' Jen offered.

'No. You concentrate on your homework and passing your NCEAs. It's my job to bring in the money.'

'Mum?'

'Yes, love?'

'I told you Dad's been having operations.'

Tara wanted to stick her fingers in her ears. 'What kind of operations?'

'He's had some plastic surgery done. On his brow, and he had his Adam's apple shaved.'

'I see.' She didn't really. Tara pictured her poor, sweet daughter visiting Richard only to discover that he'd been butchered by some money-hungry plastic surgeon. 'You told me about it, didn't you?'

'I tried, but you get so upset whenever I mention him.' Jen shrugged. 'He's getting breast implants done next month.'

'Oh, Jen . . .' Tara hugged her. 'I'm so sorry!'

'It's OK. When I visited the first time after he'd had something done it was a bit freaky, but I'm getting used to it now. It makes him happy.'

Tara wished she could get her hands on Richard. She'd rearrange his face for free. 'You don't have to visit him if it upsets you.'

'No.' Jennifer sat back. 'I *want* to see him. He's still my parent.'

Tara felt humbled by Jen's loyalty to her father and the guts it took to visit him in Auckland every other weekend. She was being so brave and mature while Tara sulked and hid.

Tara tucked a strand of Jennifer's long, blonde hair behind her ear. 'OK, love. But don't feel you've got to keep all this to yourself. I know I've got to come to terms with what's happened.'

'He's still a good person, Mum.'

Yes, but you call him your parent now, not your father, Tara thought sadly.

'Tara, darling, how are you finding country life?'

Tara's brow wrinkled as she listened to the languid tone on the other end of the phone. 'Sian? Is that you?'

'Of course it is,' purred Sian Bancroft. 'I've been meaning to call you for ages, but I've been flat on my back and time just got away from me.'

'Flat on your back?' Tara repeated innocently. 'What's wrong? Have you been sick?'

Sian chuckled.

'Oh! I see.'

'Tell me, have you heard from any of the little women?'

'No, but I know how busy they are.'

'Of course. Fitting in visits to the gym, hairdresser and beauty therapist can run a person ragged.'

Tara clenched her teeth.

'I'm on my way south on Wednesday, and thought I might stop in to see you and stay the night if I was welcome. Am I welcome, Tara?' Sian asked.

Was she welcome? A visitor from *the real world?*

'Yes! Yes! Absolutely!' Tara shrieked. 'Are you sure you only want to stay the night?'

Sian gave her throaty chuckle. 'We'll see. Now, what can I bring you as a treat from Auckland?'

'All the gossip — especially about the little women.'

Chapter 16

Sian arrived, driving a brand-new gold Mercedes Benz convertible and wearing a black Donna Karan suit she'd bought on a recent visit to New York. She smelled so intoxicating that Tara asked for the name of her perfume.

'It's called "Sian". Marcus has it made for me in Paris.'

Tara didn't get it. How did Sian manage to remain on such good terms with her ex that he had a perfume made for her in Paris? In Tara's opinion, Marcus Bancroft was a prize shit, and she didn't understand why Sian didn't agree with her. How any woman could love a man who'd dumped her because she couldn't provide him with a child — a man who'd coolly married a younger woman and impregnated her three times in as many years until she produced the longed-for son and heir — *and* then welcome him back with open arms for sex and whatever else he wanted mystified Tara.

'So show me around,' Sian insisted after she'd surprised Tara by changing into a pair of well-worn jeans and a black T-shirt.

'Well, you've seen the house.' Tara gestured unenthusiastically at the kitchen. 'It's just more of the same.'

Sian looked at the red Formica table. 'Yes. The décor might be a tad dated, but somebody has taken very good care of the place.'

If there had been a breeze, Tara's jaw would have flapped in it. 'It's bloody awful!'

Sian shrugged. 'Nothing that can't be fixed, and anyway, it's not the house that matters — it's the land.' She looked at Tara expectantly.

'You want to look at *paddocks and horses?*'

'Of course, but you'll have to lend me a pair of gumboots.'

Sian shook her mane of long hair back over her shoulders, and Tara noticed there were new lines on her smooth, exotic-looking face that hadn't been there the last time she'd seen her. She wondered what had put them there.

Once outside, Sian wasn't content to stand at the gate and gaze at the horses. She went right on in and marched boldly among the animals, confidently rubbing inquisitive noses and firmly pushing aside the more persistent of them. 'That's enough now!' She flicked her fingers and hissed, and they instantly moved out of her way.

'Are you used to horses?' Tara asked.

'Not especially,' Sian replied serenely. 'I'm used to cows, but the principles are the same.'

'Cows?'

'Yes. I was raised on a dairy farm in Taranaki. I'm on my way down to see my parents.'

Who would have thought that sultry, languid Sian Bancroft had been brought up on a dairy farm?

Sian smiled wryly. 'You look just the way Mater and Pater Bancroft did when Marcus first brought me home.'

Tara hastily rearranged her features. 'I'm just . . . surprised.'

Sian's laughter was hard-edged. 'So were the Bancrofts. They were utterly appalled that their darling eldest son was hooking himself up with a girl from Taranaki whom they were absolutely certain still had cow manure clinging to her boots and would walk it all over their Aubusson carpets and Persian rugs.' Sian gave an unladylike snort and set off across the paddock. 'Let's see the rest of the place.'

They ended up going all the way down to Sarah Whitehead's spot by the river, and, as it became more and more obvious that Sian knew a lot about land and animal management, Tara began to explain her concerns and pump her for advice.

'It's good land,' Sian said approvingly, her eyes following the riverbank as the water slid by. 'You've done well, Tara.'

Had she? Had she really? Tara looked about her and felt a stirring of pride.

On the way back down the race, Sian started talking about the Bancrofts again.

'I made them eat crow by the time I'd finished. I was the most sought-after hostess and on the board of so many charitable trusts that they had to smile and pretend they just *loved* me, when all the time they were fuming because I'd beaten them at their own game.' She smiled. 'Of course I couldn't have done it without Marcus. He never wavered. He stood between me and their vileness like my very own Berlin Wall.' She slanted a sideways look at Tara. 'D'you know, his brother tried to have an affair with me? It was Mama Bancroft's master plan when all else failed. They were going to arrange for Marcus to discover me and Kenneth in bed together.'

'No!' Tara was so shocked that she stopped walking.

Sian flung a mocking smile over her shoulder and Tara hurried to catch up.

'Yes. But I spoilt things by telling Kenneth to piss off and threatening to tell Marcus if they didn't back off. And they did — for a while.' Sian pursed her lips and watched her feet hit the soft brown mud of the damp race.

'Eventually, Mother Nature came to their aid when I couldn't get pregnant. I didn't even have so much as a miscarriage to show for such an outstanding sex life. And believe me, it *was* outstanding. Marcus Bancroft is the best fuck I ever had.'

Tara blushed.

Sian laughed. 'You are *such* an innocent, Tara! No wonder men go gaga for you.'

Tara couldn't understand why Sian kept saying that. 'What happened?'

They had reached the gate at the end of the race that led to the wide sweep of lawn in front of the garages. Sian rested her hands on top of the gate and gazed pensively at a kingfisher sitting on the washing line, his iridescent jade-and-cream body and long, sharp beak lit by sunshine.

'Marcus hated Kenneth and his wife, Emily. He was determined to have a son so that Kenneth wouldn't get his hands on the bulk of the family business, because Kenneth was not only a shit but also a lousy businessman and would have ruined everything that five generations of Bancrofts had built up. There was no alternative. I divorced him and he found himself a fertile young wife whom his mother utterly adores and who has given him two gorgeous daughters and the longed-for son.'

'Oh, Sian,' Tara said softly. 'I didn't know the half of it. I'm so sorry.'

Sian looked at her and smiled. 'Don't be. Susie Bancroft might be the mother of Marcus Bancroft's children, but I'm his wife.' She touched her heart. 'Here.'

Tara still thought that Marcus Bancroft was a shit.

'Well, well . . .' Sian purred in her cat-that-got-the-cream voice. 'Who's this?'

Tara looked up: Gil Sorensen was trotting towards them through the underpass on his grey horse. Tara was no expert, but even she could tell he was a very good rider, rising and falling effortlessly in the saddle, the muscles in his thighs bunching beneath the fabric of his rough brown trousers, which were tucked into black half-chaps and riding boots. The horse glided along, its long, tapered ears pricked and its muscled neck arched as its hooves covered the ground. When he reached them, Gil stopped.

'Hi, Tara.'

'Hello, Gil.'

He nodded politely at Sian, who stared boldly back. Tara was annoyed to see Gil's mouth begin its little upward curl, and Sian's sultry smile indicated that she knew she was the reason for it.

'Did you want something?' Tara asked brusquely.

Gil looked away from Sian and raised a brow in mild rebuke. 'I'm supposed to be giving Jen a lesson tonight,' he explained. 'But I've got to go into Hamilton to get a part for the tractor. I was over this way, so I thought I'd see if you were around to let you know so you could tell her when she gets home.'

'OK. I'll tell her,' Tara said flatly.

'Thanks,' replied Gil, just as flatly.

Sian watched them curiously. She stepped forward to run a hand along the grey's neck. 'I'm Sian Bancroft.' She smiled up at Gil, her palm doing a slow slide down the horse's neck and shoulder to stop by Gil's knee. 'What a beautiful animal.'

Tara wanted to kick her. It was obvious Sian wasn't just talking about the horse. The woman was incorrigible. Or had she been in the sex business so long that she couldn't stop herself reacting when she set eyes on an attractive man?

Tara glowered up at Gil, wondering when exactly she had started thinking of him as an attractive man. He was her neighbour, a man who went shopping every three years and bought ugly brown clothes. He was the man who had groped her breast and then apologized awkwardly. But there was nothing awkward or unattractive about the smile he was giving Sian. Gil Sorensen had sex appeal. It was in his smile, the gleam in his dark eyes, the stubble on his jaw, and the way he filled out his rough work clothes. Mother Nature even lent a helping hand by sending a breeze to lift his dark hair off his forehead.

Gil was too busy smiling at Sian to notice Tara's moody stare. When the horse began to fidget, he smoothed a hand slowly down its neck and it instantly quietened. 'Thank you,' he said in a low, intimate voice.

It took Tara a moment to realize Gil was thanking Sian for complimenting his horse.

'You're most welcome.' Sian's gaze followed the path of his hand.

If she started stroking Gil, Tara was going to slap her.

'I'm a friend of Tara's from Auckland and you are . . .' Sian lifted a brow enquiringly and continued to pet the horse, her hand inches away from Gil's.

Gil extended a hand. 'Gil Sorensen. Tara's neighbour.'

Sian shook his hand lingeringly.

Tara made a fist to keep herself from slapping their hands apart.

For the next few minutes Gil and Sian talked acreage, dairy herds and milk yields. Tara might just as well have disappeared. She had no choice but to wait while they continued their little *tête-à-tête*. The horse looked as bored as she felt, so she stroked it on the nose. It looked back at Tara with large, soft brown eyes and blew gently into her palm.

'He likes you,' Gil said.

Sian smiled and thought the horse wasn't the only one who liked Tara, judging by the sparks flying between her and her neighbour.

He gathered up the reins. 'I'd better get going if I want to get that part before the shop closes.'

'Absolutely,' Sian murmured. 'Nice meeting you, Gil, and you too, Lazarus.'

Tara guessed Lazarus must be the horse. She'd been so miffed at the way Gil and Sian were gobbling one another up with their eyes that she'd missed most of what they'd been saying. As Gil and Lazarus disappeared beneath the underpass, she felt obliged to explain, 'He's teaching Jennifer to ride. He's supposed to be a brilliant rider.'

'Oh, I'm *sure* he rides brilliantly,' Sian drawled. 'In fact, I wouldn't mind a few lessons myself.'

Sian behaved impeccably in front of Jennifer; in fact, Jen fell in love with her.

'I never heard you talk about a friend called Sian before,' she said when Sian absented herself to take a call in her room.

Tara found it hard to believe that Sian was a prostitute, and even harder to believe that they had become friends, but the more time she spent with Sian the more Tara enjoyed her company. Unlike Tara's so-called friends, Sian had kept in touch.

'Sian, promise me you won't let on to Jen what you do for a living,' Tara said before the school bus arrived.

Sian looked offended. 'Of course I won't! What on earth do you take me for?'

'I'm sorry!' Tara hastened to explain. 'You're so open about it that I wasn't sure if—'

'I do have standards, Tara,' Sian said coolly.

'OK. I said I'm sorry.'

Sian was all too happy to pass on advice and suggestions on how to improve things around the property. It was Sian who identified a set of harrows lying in a corner of one of the garages.

'Harrows? Are you sure?' Tara peered at the pile of chains and metal and did a little jig of delight around the garage.

'If I'd known you were so easy to please I would have pointed them out sooner,' Sian remarked dryly.

Tara danced her around the tractor. 'Do you realize what this means? I don't have to pick up horse manure by hand!'

Sian obligingly did another round of the tractor. 'You might find it quite cathartic, darling: unlike most of the shit in life, it can be picked up and thrown away.'

Tara stopped dancing. 'Good point.'

That evening, while Jen was in her room listening to Fall Out Boy and doing homework, Tara and Sian sat at the kitchen table drinking coffee. Sian once again broached the subject of money.

'I know Richard was kicked out of the bank, and I know you must be starting to hurt financially. If you're really serious about moving back to Auckland, you'll have to do it sooner rather than later, or the housing market will be out of your reach.'

'I know,' Tara agreed glumly.

'My offer still stands.'

'What? You mean . . .' She lowered her voice. 'Telephone sex?'

Sian sipped her coffee. 'You can do it from the comfort of your own home, there are no overheads, and it pays extremely well. What have you got to lose?'

Tara tried to think of all the reasons why she'd turned down Sian's offer in Auckland, but they seemed far less important now than they had then.

'Of course, you could always get a job on the checkout at the local supermarket. They'd even supply you with a uniform,' Sian suggested.

Tara visualized herself dressed in an overall, sitting at the checkout desk while she passed tins of baked beans across the electronic beeper, her eyes glazed with boredom. Why oh why had she never finished her degree? She glared at Sian. The cow, she knew exactly what she'd just done.

'What exactly would it entail? I wouldn't have to meet any of them, would I?'

Sian gave a satisfied smile. Her carefully baited hook had been swallowed whole.

'I wouldn't have to touch them?'

'Not unless you know a way of doing it through the phone.'

'What if I bumped into one of them and he recognized my voice?'

'It's highly unlikely. With the adrenaline pumping, men don't pay attention to things like voices.'

'How much does it pay?'

Tara just about had a heart attack when Sian told her. It would solve her money worries and set her well on the way towards a good deposit on a house in her old stomping grounds in Auckland. And she would have done it herself, without relying on a man. Let the little women stick that in their pipes and smoke it.

'And I can do anything at all while I'm taking the calls?'

'Sweetheart, you can wear your slippers and dressing gown and do the dusting for all I care.'

Tara still hesitated. 'I can't do any . . . you know . . . dirty stuff, Sian.'

'The men who will call you don't want to hear "dirty stuff", Tara. They want to be told what bad boys they are and how angry you are with them. Just think of public school boys and you'll be away. Believe me, it's a great way of dealing with premenstrual tension.'

'All right,' Tara said slowly. 'I'll do it.'

Sian seemed surprised. 'Really? I thought I would have to make at least another two visits before you agreed.'

'What made you so sure I would?'

Sian raised her fists above her head and gave a luxuriant, feline stretch. 'I only back winners, darling.'

It was a long time since Tara had felt like a winner.

Sian swept briskly onwards, brushing aside the last of Tara's niggling concerns with the sheer force of her energy and her absolute certainty that Tara was going to be wildly successful.

'You can decide how many hours you want to work and when you're available, although I would advise that you stick to regular hours — that way, you'll be able to build up a regular clientele.'

'A regular clientele? Why on earth would I want one?'

'Because they'll pay extra for the privilege.'

'They will?' Tara looked doubtful.

'Of course. The only way they can ensure that you'll be available is to book ahead and reserve your time, which costs extra.'

'You make it sound like going to the dentist.'

'Far more pleasurable, darling.'

Just before she left the following morning, Sian said, 'I'll get my office manager to send you a contract. I'll give you a call to arrange two days to complete your training and orientation on my way back to Auckland. Do give my best to your DDF, Tara.'

Tara stared at her dazedly. Sian had an office manager? She was going to get orientation and training? And what on earth was a DDF?

'My . . . DDF?'

'Your Divine Dairy Farmer, darling — Gil Sorensen.'

'He's not *my* dairy farmer!'

'Tara, Tara.' Sian clucked her tongue and shook her head. *'Don't* be a silly girl and let a man like that slip through your fingers when he's right across the road.' She sighed. 'I almost wish I had the time to stay longer and do something about him myself.'

'Are you suggesting I have sex with Gil Sorensen?' Tara cried indignantly.

Sian looked baffled. 'Well, of course. What else would I be suggesting you do with him?'

Tara flung her hands in the air. It wasn't even worth trying to explain. Sian regarded sex the way most people regarded food or drink: necessary and to be enjoyed. When a gourmet meal was on the menu, you indulged yourself to the max; and apparently in Sian's book Gil Sorensen was *cordon bleu.*

'So, Tara, promise me that when you eventually get over your silly scruples you'll give your DDF your *very* best. Because, believe me,' Sian slid her sunglasses down her nose, 'if you don't, *I* will. That man has the look of somebody who knows how to give a woman a good time between the sheets. He looks like he could rise to the trot for *hours.*'

With a smile and a wave, Sian sped off along the drive in her gold Mercedes.

Chapter 17

Sian's visit made Tara face up to some hard, cold facts. She had to stop burying her head in the sand and treating their stay in Divine like a bad dream from which she would eventually awaken to find herself back in her old life. Her old life was gone for good, and if she continued to let things slide she was going to have to start digging into her house fund.

Tara knew she had only herself to blame when Kathy Smith and Joanne Reed moved their horses. No amount of soft-soaping was going to change their minds; in fact, Tara sensed that they enjoyed telling her that they were taking their business elsewhere. Surprisingly, when Pat Warner overheard the nasty way they spoke to Tara she apologized on their behalf.

Tara looked in surprise at Pat's weather-beaten face with its beaky nose and out-of-control eyebrows. She knew she wasn't Pat's favourite person in the world, and guessed it must be Pat's glowing approval of Jen that made her turn a blind eye to Tara's shortcomings. Ever since Jen had started having riding lessons, she spent a good portion of her spare time yakking to Pat and sometimes riding Felix under Pat's watchful eye. At first Tara had been worried — Felix was built like a medieval war horse to accommodate Pat's six-foot frame — but the horse lived up to his reputation as a gentle giant, so much so that Tara had become rather fond of him.

'It's OK, Pat. I know it's my own fault. I *have* let things go a bit around the place,' she admitted.

Pat's brows rose slightly at Tara's 'a bit' summation. 'It wouldn't take much to sort things out around here. I could help.' She wore a navy blue jacket decorated with a stylized horse's head above her left breast, and banana-coloured breeches tucked into green gumboots.

Tara was surprised to see that Pat actually had a decent set of boobs hidden away beneath all her layers of horsey clothes. She was touched by Pat's offer and smiled. 'Thanks, Pat.'

Pat beamed back, displaying large tombstone teeth that were very straight and even. It was the first time Tara had smiled at her, and the smile went a long way towards alleviating the feeling of inferiority Pat always experienced around beautiful, confident women, the kind of women Pat was well aware were nothing like her.

'Why don't you learn to ride like Jen?' she suggested eagerly. 'It's so much fun and you'd get to know a lot more about horses and how to look after them. Why don't you ask Gil? I'll — I'll even lend you Felix if you like.'

Why was this woman being so kind to her when she really didn't deserve it? Tara knew what Pat thought of Felix and what her offer meant. She also knew she would never in a million years ask Gil Sorensen for riding lessons. 'That's really sweet of you, Pat. Perhaps some time in the future.'

Pat nodded enthusiastically, her smile so wide that the corners of her mouth almost touched her ears.

Sian returned the following Wednesday morning wearing her idea of country chic: a pair of Ralph Lauren trousers, a Caroline Sills sweater, and tooled Spanish leather boots.

As soon as Jen had left for school, Sian took a seat beside Tara at Eric's ugly kitchen table, and laid what appeared to be a manual with a lavender cover the same shade as her business card on the red Formica surface.

'What's that?' Tara asked.

'Your training manual,' Sian replied crisply.

Tara's startled gaze flew to Sian's face, her lips curving in a smile which rapidly faded when she saw that Sian was really serious. 'My *training manual?*'

'Of course. Did you think I would allow you to start working for me without teaching you what will be expected of you? I'm running a business, Tara, and you'll be representing me. My standards are very high, and I expect the people I employ to live up to them. Now.' Sian opened the manual. 'Shall we begin?'

Tara nodded meekly.

The next few hours made her head ache and her cheeks burn. Sian hadn't been joking when she said she expected high standards. She was a perfectionist.

'We want the clients to keep coming back.'

'You can say that again,' Tara chortled.

Sian wasn't amused. 'Don't be smutty.'

Tara reddened. 'Sorry.'

Sian explained the different types of services offered and the variations. 'Fantasy, erotica, straight, gay, bisexual, chat rooms—'

'Chat rooms?' Tara interrupted. 'You mean people have *group* telephone sex?'

'Of course, with one of my staff supervising to ensure that people with similar requirements are in the same group. People phone in from as far away as South Africa and India. Last month we began a new "All Comers" service which has proven very popular with our overseas clients.'

Tara goggled at her.

'My most experienced workers supervise the chat rooms and also screen the calls to ensure that clients are connected to the staff member most suitable for their needs. It also provides an opportunity to stop any abusive or unsavoury types from becoming members.'

'Members? They have a membership?'

'Yes.'

'What else do they get? Air points?' Tara asked sarcastically.

'What an excellent idea!' Sian got out her BlackBerry and made a note.

'I was joking!' Tara protested.

'I know.' Sian put away the BlackBerry. 'I keep telling you, this is a business just like any other. Every one of my staff has key performance indicators, an annual performance review and a pension plan, and after three years they automatically get free medical insurance.'

Tara's jaw flapped. 'A performance review? Key performance indicators?' she gasped. 'What are their key performance indicators?'

Sian sent her a withering look. 'Use your imagination, Tara.'

She glanced up at Eric's cuckoo clock to check the time, and saw a strip of duct tape over the cuckoo's door. 'What have you done to that clock?'

Tara had her head buried in her training manual and barely spared the clock a glance. 'It failed its performance review so I taped the door shut. That cuckoo drove me demented, popping out at all hours of the day and night, and Jen keeps pulling the chains and winding it up because she thinks it's funny that it winds *me* up. So I taped it shut.' She looked up and frowned. 'I hope you're not going to accuse me of animal cruelty. It's made of wood.'

Sian shook her head. 'You definitely need some mental stimulation, Tara.' She returned her attention to the training manual. 'Speaking of wood—'

'Now who's being smutty?'

Sian ignored her. 'You get paid by the minute, so the object of the exercise is to keep the client on the phone for as long as possible.'

'What's the longest anybody has ever managed?'

'I've known experienced workers to keep a client entertained for seven hours.'

'Seven hours!' Tara squawked. 'How do they do that? I mean the guy can't be — you know — the whole time. It's not physically possible!'

'Of course not. They'll probably come three times during a session of that length.'

'But — but what do they do in between . . . ?'

Sian shrugged. 'Talk about the weather, the rugby, whatever he wants. An experienced operator knows when the time is right to begin arousing them again. I have one particular worker who regularly wins Operator of the Month.'

Tara didn't dare smile. She wondered if the winner got a trophy and a badge.

'No, we don't have a photograph in the office, nor are they awarded a badge,' Sian said tartly. 'They have the choice of a massage, a facial, or tickets to see the Warriors, and if they've had a *really* big month, I splash out and send them for a weekend at a health spa in Queenstown.' She smiled coyly. 'I know the owner.'

Tara could guess how Sian knew the owner and was sure Sian didn't have to pay the full rate.

Sian began to talk about what she saw as Tara's speciality: dominatrix telephone sex.

'How will I know that's what they want? I mean, what if they want straight — *you know* — and not — *you know?*' Tara asked nervously.

Sian sat back in her chair and folded her arms. 'For God's sake, it's called *sex* not *you know!* If you're too squeamish to even say it, then you really shouldn't even be contemplating doing this.'

Tara thought of her rapidly diminishing weekly income and straightened her spine.

'Good girl.' Sian nodded approvingly. 'Now, in answer to your question: they tend to open the conversation by calling you Mistress or Madam. Let's do a run-through with me as the caller . . .'

After two minutes, Tara was a sweating, gibbering wreck.

'You don't *suggest* he's been a naughty boy, Tara!' Sian said scathingly. 'You *tell* him he has!'

Tara flung herself face-down across the table and moaned, 'I can't do this!'

'Of course you can! Now, let's try again.'

She grilled Tara for the next three-quarters of an hour, critiquing her performance in minute detail, until Tara was so pissed off that she was red-faced and shouting 'YOU WILL NOT TOUCH YOURSELF!'

Sian smiled gently. '*Much* better.' She checked her watch and cooed, 'I'd love a coffee if it isn't too much trouble, darling.'

She left just before Jen got home from school, after doing her best to soothe Tara's nerves. 'Tell me, darling, do you suffer from premenstrual tension?'

'Occasionally. Why?'

'What do you usually do for it?'

'What every woman does: I eat chocolate.'

'I think we'd be wise to cash in on that. From now on, instead of eating chocolate mid-cycle perhaps you could make yourself available for a few extra shifts instead. You're just too nice, sweetie. Now remember what I told you,' Sian continued. 'You're providing telephone services to customers, just like hundreds of other people around the country. That should help you keep everything in perspective.'

Tara doubted it, but was glad she hadn't mentioned she also drank wine *with* the chocolate. Sian would have been faced with a rebellion if she'd tried to get Tara to give that up.

'I'll call you soon to arrange a start date for next week. Bye bye, darling!'

Sian drove away, leaving Tara with the problem of where to hide the training manual from Jen.

Jennifer was disappointed to find that Sian had left. 'Where's Sian? She hasn't gone back to Auckland already, has she?'

'About an hour ago.'

'I like Sian.' Jennifer helped herself to an apple from the fruit bowl. 'She's really interesting.'

Tara thought it was just as well Jen didn't know *just* how interesting Sian Bancroft really was. Or that her mother was becoming a sex worker and even had a signed contract to prove it. She made sure Jen's bedroom light was out later that night before she replaced one of the farming manuals with the lavender-coloured training manual, hoping like hell that Jen didn't suddenly knock on her door.

A steady litany ran through her mind as she turned the pages: *I'm going to be crap at this. I'm going to be crap at this. I'm going to be crap at this!*

Closely followed by: *What am I doing? What am I doing? WHAT AM I DOING?!*

Tara turned into a regular little swot.

She pored over her training manual until she knew it by heart, reread the books that Jen had given her, took out a subscription to a farming magazine, and dutifully read the weekly rural newspaper when it arrived in the mailbox. She'd always been a good student. All she needed to do was apply herself and find the answers to her multitude of questions. Plus drum up some more business to replace the two horses that had gone, and reassure the remaining owners before the trickle of those leaving turned into a torrent.

Tara was curious to know where the other women had found grazing, but nobody seemed to know — or at least, nobody was saying. The land surrounding Divine was mainly used for dairy farming, and dairy farmers were not big fans of horses: they were hard on the land, soured the grass, and produced nothing but horse manure. Gil Sorensen was an exception.

Tara was concerned enough to put aside her instinctive dislike of Barney Bigelow when he turned up unexpectedly with a horse needing grazing. Sian had chosen the following afternoon for Tara's debut as a telephone sex worker, and Tara was sick with nerves, welcoming any diversion.

'The pony's called Magic.' Barney flashed his big yellow teeth and Tara repressed a shudder. 'His owner is a dear friend of the family and dotes on him. When she told me she'd just lost her grazing, straight away I thought of you.'

'Thank you,' Tara replied in her best hostess voice. 'It just so happens we do have a space.'

Barney lowered his lids to hide the combination of lust that the sound of her snooty, clipped tone evoked in him, and sour amusement at her choice of words. He knew damn well Tara Whitehead had 'space', as she put it, because Joanne Reed and Kathy Smith's nags were grazing on his land across the river at this very moment. He'd whispered something to the two stupid cows about keeping it a secret between just the three of them, saying 'I don't do this for just anybody.'

'Of course, Mr Bigelow!' Joanne had cried. 'We *know* that.'

She and Kathy were thrilled to get so much attention from the most powerful man in town, and it would serve that stuck-up Tara Whitehead right if everybody moved their horses, which they would encourage the other owners to do. Barney knew Kathy and Joanne were close friends of Glenys Tweedie and that Glenys's knickers had been in a knot ever since she'd heard that Barney wanted Gil Sorensen to keep an eye on Tara. Barney thought that by now Glenys would've figured out that Gil wasn't remotely interested in her and never would be, but it suited his purposes for Glenys and her mates to be spreading nasty little rumours about Tara Whitehead, so he'd made himself listen to Kathy and Joanne's complaints and offered them free grazing on the neglected piece of land he owned across the river. Barney wasn't surprised when they accepted — after all, being in his good books could pay dividends, while turning him down paid dividends of an entirely different nature.

Tara was unaware of all this as she stood looking at the small, fat white pony munching grass in her driveway. The end of his lead rope was held by Barney's sulky-looking daughter, Tiffany, and parked behind her was a big red Pathfinder and double float. Magic was so small that at first Tara had thought the float was empty.

Jen stroked the pony's nose. 'Oh, Mum, he's gorgeous!'

Tiffany smirked and looked away when her father glared at her.

Tara didn't notice. She *had* noticed that, despite attending the same school, Jen and Tiffany hadn't exchanged a word of greeting, and that Tiffany had unfortunately inherited her father's bulging eyes and long jaw, which all the make-up plastered on her face failed to disguise. She was blonde, short and petite, with a surprisingly large bosom for such a tiny girl. Tara was sure the diamond stud in her nose was real; it matched the ring on the middle finger of her right hand. The expensive, sophisticated jewellery was at odds with the tight pink dress worn over black jeans and chunky-heeled black boots.

So this was the notorious Tiffany Bigelow, yet *another* of the Whitehead cousins.

Tara returned her attention to Magic, who was daintily accepting the grass Jen was offering him, and smiled. He *was* cute, with his little black hooves and long white fringe dangling over his eyes. And even more importantly, his arrival meant more money.

'Of course he can graze here.' Tara took care to keep a good ten feet between her and Barney. 'It's twenty-five dollars per week, with a month paid in advance. Will that suit your friend?'

Barney's smile slipped a fraction. Tara had deliberately added an extra five dollars to the weekly fee to let him know he couldn't just arrive on her doorstep uninvited and expect her to do him a favour. Tara had Barney Bigelow's measure. He was a bully *and* a pervert.

Tara raised a questioning brow at Barney.

He clenched his teeth and smiled. 'I'll write you a cheque before we go.'

It wasn't until Barney and Tiffany were leaving that the subject of Jen's lessons came up.

'Are you going to start riding?' Tiffany asked in a half-hearted attempt at conversation prompted by the dagger looks her father was sending her.

Jen shrugged and said nothing.

Tara looked at Tiffany's smug, round face and wanted to smack it. 'Jen's been having lessons with Gil Sorensen,' she said.

Jen closed her eyes and winced.

Tiffany looked shocked. 'Gil's giving you lessons?'

Jen glared at Tara and nodded.

Tara saw the look of fury on Barney's face just before he smoothed his expression into the usual benign expression. *Uh oh! Big mistake!*

Barney looked at Magic and smirked. 'Let us know how Magic gets along.'

Tara watched them drive away before turning to Jennifer. 'Did I say something wrong?'

'Tiffany used to have lessons with Gil, until he refused to teach her because she's rough on her horses and blames them for all her mistakes,' Jen explained. 'Jake said his father was sick of watching her ruin beautiful animals because she was too lazy and selfish to put in the work to improve her riding. Apparently, he had a big row with Tiffany's father. Mr Bigelow thinks Tiffany is destined for a gold medal at the Olympics. Jake said Tiffany still tries to grease up his dad whenever she sees him so he'll start teaching her again.' She wrinkled her nose in disgust. 'But Gil won't take the bait, and besides, he doesn't teach much any more, so I'm really lucky. Mr Bigelow and Gil don't get on.'

Tell me about it, Tara thought.

The smirk on Barney's face before he left concerned her. She looked at the little white pony as Jen led him away towards a paddock and told herself not to be so stupid. How much trouble could one small animal be?

A lot, as it turned out. *An awful lot.*

Chapter 18

The next morning, Magic managed to escape from the paddock by neatly inserting himself under the electric wire on the fence. Tara almost had a heart attack when she went to hang a load of washing on the clothesline and a small white muzzle suddenly poked itself at her between two sheets. She was so sick with nerves at the thought of her first session with Superior Services in the afternoon that she hadn't been able to eat breakfast, so it didn't take much to send her into sensory overload. She screamed and leapt into the air, dropping the basket full of wet laundry in the mud.

Magic promptly trotted over it, then wound his way through the towels and sheets that Tara had already hung out, smearing them with the mud he had accumulated on his journey beneath the fence, before spreading his legs, raising his tail and releasing a steady stream of bright yellow urine, which splashed up from the ground onto Tara's brand-new jeans.

'You little bastard!' she shrieked, lunging at him.

Magic turned his hindquarters, kicked up his heels and galloped away, farting.

Spring had announced its arrival with torrential rain and swirling winds. Blossoms burst out on trees like pink popcorn alongside manuka bushes smothered in tiny cerise stars. The cabbage trees in

Eric's back garden wore spiky bonnets of white flowers that wafted a sweet, heady perfume into the warm air.

The day had dawned clear and bright, the sun turning on a show of summer-like heat. Tara was soon drenched in sweat from chasing Magic, who treated her pursuit as if it was entertainment that Tara had laid on especially for him. He would mince up and stretch out his neck for the carrots and apples she held, and just before she managed to slip a halter on to his nose he would snatch the goods and bound away again on his nasty little black hooves.

By lunchtime Tara was forced to admit defeat. She opened a bottle of wine and sat on the concrete steps at the back of the house, swearing and drinking. She was pissed off, furious, and stank of sweat.

Magic waited at the narrow gate leading into the back garden, his eyes glued to the bottle of wine in Tara's hand.

'Bugger off, you little swine!' she yelled. 'As soon as I can catch you — and I *will* catch you — you're going straight back to Barney bloody Bigelow! I don't *care* about the money! There isn't enough money in the world to make it worth my while to—'

Brrp! Brrp!

Brrp! Brrp!

Tara belatedly remembered Sian's instructions to be ready to take calls from twelve-thirty. When Tara had suggested that lunchtime on a weekday might not be an ideal time for a spot of telephone sex, Sian had replied, 'Of course it is: time for a spot of R&R before settling down to an afternoon of long, tedious meetings or hours spent staring at a computer.'

Tara's stomach began churning like a washing machine on its spin cycle. The phone rang and rang. She walked into the kitchen, dragging her feet.

Outside, Magic stealthily made his way along the path past Eric's prized renga renga lilies and hostas towards the bottle of wine sitting abandoned on the bottom step.

Tara picked up the phone.

'Hello? Is that Tara?' asked a cheery, friendly woman's voice.

Perhaps I've made a mistake about the time or the day, Tara thought hopefully.

'Yes.'

'This is Rona, office manager at Superior Services. I'm just calling to let you know that we'll begin putting calls through in five minutes. Is that all right?'

'Yes,' Tara mumbled.

She disconnected, laid the phone on the kitchen table and waited, her heart thumping in time with her churning stomach.

Brrp! Brrp!

Tara wiped her sweating palm on her filthy jeans and picked up the phone. 'Hello?'

A tearful male voice quavered, 'I've been so dreadfully, dreadfully bad, Mistress! I'm so ashamed!'

'Er . . .' Tara turned to look out the open kitchen door. Magic had his front hooves propped on the bottom step and his muzzle jammed against the neck of her bottle of wine, slurping greedily. She gasped in outrage. '*You little prick!*'

There was a pause.

'Mistress? How did you know that?' the caller whispered.

Tara listened with half an ear, her attention focused on Magic who was lovingly licking the now empty bottle and keeping Tara firmly in his sights so he could scarper if she made a move towards him.

'You *disgusting* animal!' she snarled. 'How *dare* you do that?'

'But Mistress, I haven't even told you what I've *done* yet.'

Ooops.

Tara thought rapidly, trying to recall what the man had said — *if* he'd said anything important so far.

'Do you think—' She cleared her throat nervously and continued icily, 'Do you think I need *you* to tell me that you've behaved atrociously? That you've spent all day imagining doing things you know you shouldn't be doing? Do you?'

Magic the man gulped and breathed heavily across the phone.

'You're right, of course, Mistress! You're *always* right! But I still want to tell you. Can I tell you? Please?'

Tara crept towards Magic the pony.

He lifted his head and backed up.

Bugger! He was going to make a run for it. She was stuck between a rock and a hard place. Magic was income and he'd just downed the best part of a bottle of wine, but the caller on the end of the line was income, too, and Tara didn't want to get sacked on her first day. She suddenly recalled Sian saying men who wanted dominatrix services needed to be demeaned and subjugated. Did she dare?

Magic trotted out of the garden.

'I can't — I mean, I don't want to talk to you at the moment!' she announced coldly. 'I'll be back when I've finished . . . er . . . what I've got to do. In the meantime, *you will wait for me!*' Another piece of Sian's training popped into her brain. 'And *do not* touch yourself! Do you hear me?'

'Yes, Mistress! I promise, Mistress!'

Dumping the phone on the table, Tara set off in hot pursuit of Magic. She had his measure now: she took a bottle of wine along with her and managed to lure him close enough to catch him. He laid back his ears when he realized he wasn't going to get a second helping.

Tara tried to check his pupils, but didn't know what was normal for a pony. And then there was the question of how she was going to explain to the vet how a pony in her care had consumed the best part of a bottle of wine, plus how much the vet would cost, and the flak it would cause if word got out to the other owners. She figured Berocca tablets and coffee were out of the question. By now it was fifteen minutes since she'd spoken to Magic the man.

'Oh God! You're going to get me sacked on my very first day!'

Magic yawned widely, displaying yellow, grass-stained teeth before lowering himself into the grass beside the clothesline to sleep it off.

Tara watched anxiously in case he vomited and choked, all the time acutely aware of the man waiting on the phone. She didn't want to abuse Sian's kindness by letting her down. When Magic appeared to have dozed off into a drunken stupor, she trudged back to the kitchen and picked up the phone to disconnect the call.

The sound of heavy breathing came clearly down the line.

'Er . . . hello?'

'Hello, Mistress,' Magic the man whined. 'Can I *please* talk to you now?'

Including the fifteen minutes spent catching Magic, Tara managed to keep her first caller on the line for twenty-six minutes. She almost felt sorry for him when she realized he had been waiting for her the whole time, and was relieved that he was quite happy when she adopted a bossy, motherly attitude for the remainder of the call and told him basically to pull his socks up and not be so naughty again.

Sian was utterly delighted with her debut, and passed on the news that the client wanted to know when Mistress Fury would next be available for a chat.

'Mistress Fury?' Tara echoed.

'Yes. I think that's your new moniker. Don't blame me for it: he chose it.'

Sian was very understanding when Tara asked if she could forego any more calls because she had a drunken pony on her hands. 'How on earth did it get drunk?'

'It's a long, long story which you really don't want to know, Sian.'

'Probably not,' Sian agreed.

Tara raced outside to check Magic, who was on his side snoring, with his legs outstretched. She fetched a lead rope from the garage and clipped it to his halter. 'Come on! You've got to walk it off!'

Magic wasn't keen on cutting short his afternoon snooze, but Tara hauled him up. Barefoot, she marched him up and down the race several times, feeling increasingly worried by how slowly he was walking. He'd definitely flunk a breathalyser test.

She looked at the underpass that led to Gil's property and checked her watch. Jen wouldn't be home for at least another two and a half hours, and she dared not tie Magic up and go inside to call a vet for advice, because, even smashed, the little devil would probably not be past untying himself. There didn't seem to be a knot that he couldn't undo.

Tara straightened her blue T-shirt, finger-combed her hair, rinsed her feet beneath the outdoor tap, and donned her floral gumboots. She didn't intend to face Gil Sorensen again looking as if she'd been dragged through a paddock by her hair. She had her pride and, besides, it was becoming tedious. She headed for the underpass, towing a reluctant Magic behind her, hissing over her shoulder, 'If you live, I hope you have the mother of all hangovers, you little lush!'

Gil had just finished moving some calves to another paddock and was heading up the race towards his house when he saw Tara appear from beneath the underpass, leading a white pony. She was wearing a blue top with tiny sleeves, jeans, her floral gumboots and her snootiest expression. When she spotted Gil, she began towing the reluctant pony up the race towards him.

Gil watched curiously, wondering what on earth could have brought her across the road to seek him out and how on earth she managed to make gumboots look sexy. But when she finally reached him, Gil saw that Tara wasn't nearly as calm and collected as she had at first appeared. He sniffed discreetly. Sweat overlaid with floral deodorant and perfume. Although he knew he shouldn't, Gil couldn't resist asking, 'Problems with another pothole?'

Tara pursed her lips. 'No.' She pointed at the pony. '*Him.*'

He whistled soundlessly. How had she ended up with Magic?

Her breasts rose and fell agitatedly beneath the thin blue top. Even sweaty, she trumpeted hot, luscious femininity. Gil wanted to trumpet right back. Instead, he forced his gaze away from the creamy scoops of flesh swelling over the neckline of the blue T-shirt and tried to concentrate on Magic.

'I have a slight problem,' Tara said.

Me, too, Gil thought. 'Uh huh.'

'It's probably nothing, but I thought I should check.'

He waited. Whatever it was, it was bound to be interesting.

She took a deep breath. 'I think I've poisoned this pony.'

Gil looked closely at Magic, who was munching contentedly on grass. Apart from Magic being overweight, Gil couldn't see too much wrong with the pony. Magic was notorious for his total lack of respect for humans, horses and anything in between. A lot of people in Divine would think Tara had done them a favour if she *had* poisoned the little bugger. 'What makes you think that?'

'He got out. I've been chasing him all morning, and I got so angry that I sat down outside and had a glass of wine, and before I knew it . . .' Tara trailed off.

Gil nodded encouragingly. 'Before you knew it?'

'He got to the wine bottle and drank quite a lot.' She gave up trying to look unconcerned. 'I know I should have been paying attention, but I was so furious and tired and — and —'

'About to commit murder?' Gil suggested.

'Yes!'

He nodded. 'Magic has that effect on people. He's nothing but trouble. You know that kid's party game Pass the Parcel?'

Tara frowned. 'Yes.'

'Well, Magic's like the parcel, only nobody wants to be left holding him.' Gil studied the pony. 'You must be acquiring some polish in your old age, Magic. In the past it was always Waikato Draught.'

'It isn't funny! He finished off my last bottle of Mills Reef Reserve!'

'Well at least you can't accuse him of being cheap.'

Tara swept on. 'Every time he lies down I'm terrified he'll vomit and choke.'

'Horses can't vomit.'

'Oh. I didn't know that.'

'So, tell me, how did you get him?'

'Barney Bigelow,' she hissed. 'The swine!'

Gil wasn't sure if she meant Barney or Magic. He reached out and took the lead rope from her. 'Hello, Magic.'

Magic stopped eating and looked warily at Gil. Tara could almost see the horsey equivalent of *uh oh!* going through his nasty little head. He dug in his little black hooves, humped his back, and tried to snatch the lead out of Gil's hand as he had done so successfully to Tara several times already. Gil gave one short, sharp jerk on the rope and said '*No!*' sharply, before relaxing his grip again. Magic tried the same trick twice more, and each time received the same treatment. Tara was piqued when he gave up and walked quietly alongside Gil up the race towards the house she could see on the rise above.

Tara followed behind. 'I don't want to take up too much of your time.'

'No worries, just page the oracle.'

'You love rubbing in everything I do wrong, don't you?'

'Some things are just too hard to resist.'

Like you, Gil thought.

Tara was distracted by the sight of Gil's house. It was long, low and built from wood with lots of bi-fold doors that opened out on to gardens bursting with spring colour. A pergola smothered in lilac wisteria extended from one end of the house above a bricked courtyard. Two pukeko were scratching around a large birdbath that stood in the middle of a wide expanse of lawn at the front of the house. The lawn swept on downwards to end at the driveway leading to the race and underpass nearby. A large half-round barn stood on the other side of the driveway opposite the courtyard. Tara could see a long row of sheds, housing the tractor and other farm implements and Gil's black ute. Everything was tidy and well maintained. The house was every bit as beautiful as her house in Auckland.

Tara longed to see inside. Her lips curved and her eyes glowed in her filthy face as she gazed at it wonderingly. *This* was Gil Sorensen's house? Gil, of the ugly, brown clothes and god-awful beanie?

'The halter's on inside out.'

'Hmm?'

Gil pointed a thumb at Magic. 'His halter — it's on inside out. The buckle is digging into his nose.'

‘Oh.’ Tara reddened. ‘Sorry, Magic.’

Gil led the pony past the house and into the barn and tied him up. ‘I’ll get another halter to put on him while we sort this one out, just in case he decides to do a runner.’

He disappeared into a tack room next door.

Tara wondered if he was collapsed in a corner, rolling around in silent laughter. She didn’t need a mirror to know she looked an absolute mess, and she could imagine that that tickled Gil Sorensen no end, although he’d been a complete gentleman and refrained from mentioning it, much to her surprise. She went to check Magic’s halter, wincing when she saw the buckle pressing against his nose. ‘Sorry, Magic,’ she said again softly. ‘Do you think the wine will hurt him?’ she called out to Gil.

He reappeared, carrying a large blue halter.

‘It’s Lazarus’s,’ he explained when Tara looked puzzled. ‘It’ll do to keep him tethered for a few moments.’ He flipped the longest strap around the pony’s neck and adjusted it and the nose strap to fit before clipping the lead rope to it and removing Magic’s red halter, which he held out to Tara. ‘Here you go.’

She refused to take it. ‘No, you do it. I might hurt him again.’

‘No you won’t. I’ll talk you through it.’

‘Pat’s shown me dozens of times already.’

‘You mean you’ve stood and watched while Pat did it.’

Tara nodded reluctantly.

Gil took her arm and guided her closer to Magic. ‘You’ll never learn by watching somebody else. You need to do it yourself. Come on. If it makes you feel any better, he’s drunk.’

Tara looked down at the warm, callused fingers encircling her arm and smelt the scent of man and sweat and soap.

Gil dropped his hand. ‘Find the long strap and practise doing it up so that the buckle is on the outside.’

It took several attempts before Tara got it right, not because she didn’t know what to do, but because having Gil standing so close turned her into an imbecile. She felt like crawling beneath the hay bales stacked in a corner of the barn, but Gil was explaining how to set up an area for Magic with an electric fence to stop him escaping again.

'Do you know how he got the name Magic?' he asked when Magic was once again wearing his red halter.

Tara studied the strong column of his throat, only half-listening. 'No.'

'Because he can take a perfect day and turn it to shit.'

She laughed.

Gil watched her. There she was again — the surfer girl, grubby, smiling, *sexy*. 'Do you need a hand to set up the electric fence?' he asked gruffly.

'No, I'm beginning to get the hang of it.' Tara looked through the doorway. 'Who designed your house?'

'A local guy, G.M. Sorensen.'

Her eyes widened in amazement. '*You* designed your house?'

Gil nodded.

She stared at the house. 'It's wonderful, Gil, absolutely wonderful.'

He looked embarrassed and pleased at the same time. 'Thanks.'

'No, *thank you.*' She led Magic out of the barn.

Gil followed her into the sunshine. 'You know where I am if you need me.'

Tara nodded. But as she led Magic home she told herself that, despite all the help and knowledge he had to offer her, spending time with Gil Sorensen would be a very bad idea. Tara was beginning to realize that beneath the dusty brown clothes and unprepossessing manner there was a very attractive, intriguing man.

Gil could become addictive.

Magic was confined to barracks in a paddock by the house where Tara and Jen could keep an eye on him. He still managed to get out, but only did it so he could spend the day following Tara around the property. For some inexplicable reason he'd developed a fixation on her. When she sat outside in the sun taking calls for Superior Services, Magic grazed in the back garden or curled up beside her chair, snoring.

'I suppose I should make you cover your ears,' Tara said the first time Magic listened in. 'But you're such a little ratbag it isn't worth the worry.'

Magic heaved himself onto his back, his fat little belly wobbling as he rolled ecstatically around with his legs in the air, flattening a nearby agapanthus. His owner hadn't once called or visited, but the money for his next month's grazing had arrived in Tara's account and she was secretly growing quite fond of him. Magic was devoted to her. He never bothered to abscond when Tara went out in the car, as if he knew she was beyond his reach, but he sulked and ignored her when she left him alone for the day. Tara allowed him one can of Waikato Draught a week for good behaviour.

Jen was miffed because Magic wasn't as attached to her as he was to her mother.

'Maybe he likes blondes,' Jake said.

'*I'm* blonde!'

'Maybe he likes older women.'

Jen hoped Gil didn't, or at least that he didn't have anything against younger women.

On Friday after school, Tara dropped Jen at the bus stop to catch the bus to Auckland to spend the weekend with Richard. Jennifer's weekends with her father were a continuing source of worry and resentment for Tara; worry that Jen was too young to deal with such a complex situation, and resentment because Richard had put them in the situation in the first place.

Chapter 19

Tara got up the next morning after a sleepless night, a dull headache pounding at her temples. She planned to hook up the harrows to the tractor and give Jen a surprise when she got back on Sunday night to find the paddocks were done. So far, Tara hadn't driven the tractor. When she went out and tried to start it, it wouldn't go, but she refused to run across the road and ask for Gil's help. Magic's imminent death was a different kettle of fish to a tractor that wouldn't start.

So Tara had no choice but to put on her floral gumboots and matching gardening gloves, take the wheelbarrow out into the paddocks, and do the job by hand. Some of the owners stopped to stare when they saw stuck-up Mrs Whitehead picking up horse manure, but nobody offered to help. It was back-breaking work, trundling the laden wheelbarrow across the paddocks to the manure heap, and the gloves weren't waterproof so her hands kept slipping on the handles. Tara struggled on, with sweat dripping into her eyes and the muscles of her shoulders and back screaming with the effort. To make things even worse, it began to rain.

'You are not going to beat me!' she panted, glaring at the towering pile of horse manure quivering atop the wheelbarrow and picturing Richard instead. Gritting her teeth and digging the heels of her boots into the soft, dark earth, she strained towards the manure pile. Suddenly her boots slipped and, losing her grip on the handles of the barrow, she fell to her knees. The wheelbarrow teetered and fell sideways, dumping its contents on to the sodden grass.

Tara climbed to her feet and stared at the pile of horse dung. With a howl of fury, she began to kick the manure across the paddock. She was so enraged that she didn't hear Gil's motorbike come through the underpass and up the race. She noticed him only when his brown boots were suddenly in the way of her next kick.

Tara glared up at him through a curtain of wet, dripping hair, panting from her exertions. 'Whaddayouwant?' she snarled. 'Getouttamyway!'

Gil surveyed the horse manure scattered about. 'What are you doing?'

'What does it look like I'm doing?' Her eyes zoomed in on a substantial pile next to his left boot that she'd somehow missed. 'I'm harrowing, now get out of my way!' She started forwards, her floral gumboots slipping on wet grass and flattened manure, only to be brought up short when Gil didn't move. Putting her hands on his chest, Tara gave him a shove. 'Move!'

'No.'

She stared up at him incredulously. 'What do you mean: *no!*'

Gil looked down at her. 'You need to calm down, Tara.'

How dare he? *How dare he?* Who the hell did he think he was? If she wanted to throw a tantrum like a two-year-old, that was her business.

'I don't want to calm down!' Tara yelled, banging her nose on Gil's chest when her foot slipped.

He caught her elbows, steadying her. 'You like kicking horseshit around the paddock?'

She wrenched her arms away and narrowed her eyes. 'Only when I don't have anything else to kick, but you're beginning to look like a better option. Now get out of my way!'

Gil sighed and shook his head.

Tara swore and kicked the side of the wheelbarrow so hard that it righted itself, stubbing her big toe in the process. She sucked in a pained breath and jammed her heel into the mud.

'Feeling better?' Gil asked.

'SHUT UP!!' howled Tara.

'No?' He sighed again. 'Ah well . . . '

Gil bent forward, hooked an arm around Tara's hips and tipped her over his shoulder.

She let out a scream that sent the horses in the nearest paddock bolting madly to the opposite side and must have been heard in Hamilton. Finding herself dangling upside-down with her face to Gil's back, Tara grabbed hold of his buttocks and tried to lever herself upright. 'Put me down!'

Gil tightened his grip and tipped her knees higher.

She shrieked and clutched his thighs, certain she was about to be catapulted to the ground.

He started across the paddock towards the gate.

Upside-down, half-smothered and with the breath being knocked from her with each step Gil took, Tara could only splutter furiously against his shirt. She watched his buttocks rise and fall one at a time as he strolled along. Tara reached down and dug her fingers in, squeezing as hard as she could.

Gil slapped her on the bottom.

Tara reared up, snarling, just as Gil bent forwards, and then she was flying through the air, arms flailing. 'Ahhhhh!!'

He cushioned her fall into the slimy wheelbarrow, where she landed in a jumble of arms, legs and floral gumboots. Gil loomed over her, his hands braced on either side of the barrow. Tara furiously shook her hair out of her eyes and opened her mouth.

Gil leaned forward until they were almost nose to nose. 'Don't. Say. A. Word.'

She swung a foot at his knee and missed.

He growled in the back of his throat, lifted the barrow and began pushing it towards the gate.

Tara clutched the metal sides to stop herself sliding out on to the grass. She considered protesting again, but Gil's warning look made her rethink that idea. Wet, cold horse manure seeped into the seat of her jeans and Trelise Cooper thong. When Tara whimpered and squirmed, Gil deliberately steered the wheelbarrow into a pothole and out again, making her bounce and skid in the cold, wet slime.

They didn't stop until they'd reached the garages. Tara glared up at him through a hank of green-tinged blonde hair. The arrogant swine wasn't even breathing hard. Gil dropped the handles with a thud and surveyed her with his hands on his hips. His lips curved, then he tipped back his head and began to laugh.

Tara tried to struggle out of the wheelbarrow, but her pants were stuck to it as if she was sitting in glue — which wasn't too far from the truth. When she swatted away Gil's helping hand, he grabbed her by the wrists and hauled her out anyway. There was an ominous sucking noise as her bottom parted company with the wheelbarrow.

Tara moaned.

Gil laughed harder.

'You are a total bastard!' she snarled, plucking the seat of her filthy, wet jeans away from her bum.

Gil wiped tears from his eyes. 'Harrowing, eh?'

'Shut up!' She made her way gingerly towards the house like a bandy-legged cowboy. The last time she'd walked like that was just after she'd given birth.

'I came over to fix the tractor,' Gil called after her.

Tara stopped. 'How do you know the tractor isn't working?'

'Jen told me yesterday that it had broken down and I promised I'd have a look when I had a couple of spare minutes.'

Anger rolled off Tara in waves. It would have been nice if her daughter had thought to mention it to *her*.

'Why don't you take the tractor and drive it right up your arse?' she yelled.

Gil laughed.

He was still laughing when Tara slammed the back door of the house.

Tara headed straight to Eric's hideous salmon-pink bathroom and ran a hot bubble-bath. She was lying in the water, trying to soak away the smell of horseshit and thinking up ways to torture Gil Sorensen, when he called her name from right outside the bathroom window.

Tara squawked and jack-knifed upright, pulling her knees to her breasts and clutching her shoulders. 'What are you doing?' she cried, sending water splashing on to the tiled floor. 'Where are you?'

'Calm down. I'm outside. I can't see you.'

'I'm *in* the bath!'

'I know. I heard you. Why do you think I'm talking to you through the window?'

Tara stared at the frosted glass pane. He couldn't possibly see her because he was standing on the path beneath the window. 'What do you want *now?*'

When Gil had finally stopped laughing, he'd started feeling guilty about the way he had manhandled Tara out in the paddock. He didn't make a habit of grabbing women, throwing them over his shoulder, slapping them on the butt and dumping them in wheelbarrows. Tara was his cousin Richard's *wife*, his *cousin* by marriage — although Gil didn't really know what that had to do with anything. He felt ashamed. His behaviour towards her hadn't been any better than Barney Bigelow's at the PTA meeting, and that was a bitter pill to swallow.

He looked up at the window. 'I wanted to apologize. I shouldn't have thrown you in the wheelbarrow.'

There was a silence.

'Or over your shoulder,' Tara said.

'No.'

More silence.

'*Or* slapped me on the bum.'

'You pinched me on the arse.'

'That didn't hurt! Your bum is like a rock.' Tara hoped he didn't take it as a compliment.

'Yes, it did.' Gil tried to sound aggrieved. 'You've got long nails. I'll have bruises and cuts for the rest of the week.'

Tara imagined what that hard butt would look like naked, and shifted restlessly in the water.

'I only pinched you because you slapped me,' she muttered.

'Pardon?'

She raised her voice. 'I said you deserved it.'

A corner of Gil's mouth curled upwards. 'I've fixed the tractor and put the harrows over the last few paddocks. Have you managed to scrub the horse manure off your—'

'None of your business!'

When he didn't say anything more, Tara assumed he'd gone. She lay back in the cooling bathwater feeling oddly disappointed.

'Tara?'

She started and sat up again. 'I thought you'd gone!'

'Why were you having a meltdown out in the paddock?'

'I wasn't having a meltdown. I was just a bit upset.'

'You were shouting at a pile of horseshit.'

'Thank you so much for reminding me.'

'Don't go getting on your high horse, I'm trying to help.' Gil paused. 'I know a couple of the owners have moved their horses.'

'Gee, good news travels fast.'

'You know, you don't have to do everything on your own. Asking for help isn't an admission of failure.'

Gil stared at the window and waited. When there was no answer, he shook his head and tried to work up the courage to broach the other subject he wanted to talk to her about, but he kept getting distracted by imagining how she looked lying naked in the bath. He'd bet his bottom dollar she used bubble-bath. Gil pictured her stretched out in the tub, her long, blonde hair piled haphazardly on top of her head, naked and pink and glistening. His penis unfurled and stretched as if it was waking from an afternoon snooze.

'They all know I haven't got a clue what I'm doing — the owners — *everybody.* I can't even *wave* properly.'

Gil's expression softened at the pain and confusion in her voice.

'Gil?' Tara called softly. 'Are you still there?'

'Yeah, still here,' he answered. 'You don't seriously believe everybody wants you to fail?'

'That's how it feels.' She was speaking so quietly that he had to strain to hear her. 'If it was just me I wouldn't care, but Jen loves it here. One day it will belong to her.'

Gil thought grimly that Eric had a lot to answer for. 'Have you told Eric how you feel?'

'Yes.'

'And what did he say?'

There was a pause.

'He told me to talk to you.'

'So why didn't you?'

More silence. Gil pictured her shrugging one elegant, naked shoulder, and another wave of lust punched him in the gut and shot straight to his groin. It was just as well she couldn't see him.

'We haven't exactly . . . hit it off.'

'We don't really know one another.' He was amazed at how calm and reasonable he sounded while he was thinking about opening the back door, stripping off his clothes and climbing into the bath with her. He drew in a ragged breath and dragged his palms down his face.

'Every time I see you, I make a fool of myself and usually end up filthy.'

The thought of Tara filthy fried Gil's brain.

Tara misinterpreted his silence. 'Don't you dare laugh at me!'

Thank God she can't see me.

Gil collected his scattered thoughts. 'You can't blame me for that. You were already muddy when I saw you with Magic the other day, and by the way — nice gumboots.'

'Shut *up*, Gil.'

Tara rested her chin on the edge of the bath. It was titillating talking to him while she was stark naked. She pressed her breasts against the smooth, cool surface of the bath and swirled a leg gently about in the water.

Gil listened to the sound of her splashing, his heated imagination conjuring up all sorts of fantasies. The tension in his groin ratcheted up another few notches. He had to leave before he said or did something he'd regret.

'How about I teach you to ride?'

Like that.

'What?' Tara sounded as shocked by the suggestion as he was.

'If you know what you're talking about, it'll be a lot harder for the owners to try and pull the wool over your eyes, and to be honest, Tara, if you showed a little more interest you'd find most of them are OK.'

'I don't know if that's such a good idea,' she said doubtfully. 'I mean, I think it's a good idea for me to learn more about the horses, but I don't know if you teaching me to ride would be very wise. We don't always see eye to eye.'

'There won't be any problem: I'll tell you what to do and you'll do it.'

'Oh, I see. Silly me. Why didn't I think of that?'

Gil smiled. 'I'm a very patient teacher — just ask Jen.'

His amusement faded as he recalled that Jen was one of the reasons he was here, but he was worried about offending Tara or sounding as if he had an inflated ego if he said what was on his mind.

'Jen thinks the sun rises and sets with you, so she'd hardly be impartial.'

There it was: the perfect opening.

'OK, then,' Tara said, and the moment was gone.

Coward! Gil berated himself silently.

'OK what?' he repeated gruffly.

'OK, you can teach me to ride. But I want a nice, quiet horse.'

'And a helmet and a pair of boots,' he said with resignation.

'A new pair of shoes! Every cloud *does* have a silver lining!'

'Where the hell are you, Richard?' Gil muttered irritably as he rode home on the motorbike. 'Why aren't you keeping an eye on your wife and daughter?'

It was as if Richard had disappeared off the face of the earth. Tara never mentioned him; and Jennifer only if she absolutely had to, like saying she was going to stay with him for the weekend.

Gil hadn't seen Richard in years, but knew that he occasionally contacted Alison, or Gil's parents Connie and Malcolm, who were due back this week from their latest overseas jaunt. Gil didn't see a lot of Alison, but they could not see one another for months at a time and then pick up again as if they'd spoken only yesterday.

Gil blamed his current predicament on Richard's absence from his daughter's life. If Jennifer had her father around, Gil was certain she wouldn't be looking for a replacement and choosing him for the job. At least, he *hoped* that was what Jen was looking for, because the only other explanation for the way she looked at him, smiled at him and kept popping up everywhere he went was that she had a crush on him.

He wasn't a vain man, but neither was Gil stupid, and in his experience teenage girls generally wore lip gloss and uplift bras to get a male's attention. For weeks he'd been hoping it was for Jake's benefit, but Jen made the biggest effort on the days Gil gave her riding lessons. He rubbed his hands over his face, muttering '*Christ*.'

When Gil got home, he called Alison at her studio. The phone rang repeatedly before she finally picked up. Alison refused to have an answering machine, and if she was busy working she ignored the phone until the caller gave up. Gil knew that if he waited long enough she'd eventually answer.

'Hello, Alison Whitehead speaking.'

'Hello, Gil Sorensen speaking.'

Alison sounded muffled and Gil could hear a muted roar down the line. 'Are you all right? You sound strange.'

'Gil! How are you?'

'Good. What's that noise?'

'Noise?' Alison repeated vaguely. 'Oh! I've got a blowtorch in my hand and a welding mask on. Hold on a moment . . .'

Gil imagined Alison wafting about her studio with a lit blowtorch in one hand and a cordless phone in the other. The roaring noise stopped and Alison came back on the line sounding a lot clearer.

'Gil? Is that better?'

'Perfect. What are you building now?'

'I'm not *building* anything; I'm *creating*,' she replied in a deliberately affected tone.

'OK, what are you *creating* now?'

Alison became vague as she always did when she attempted to describe her work. 'A metal piece . . . a town, I think . . . or maybe I should say a city . . .' Her voice faded, and Gil could imagine her looking at her creation. 'It keeps getting bigger and bigger, so I guess . . . it's more of a city than a town . . .'

'Sounds fascinating – be careful not to burn the studio down while you're at it.'

'I'm not a complete imbecile.'

Gil spoke quickly to reclaim her attention before she was lost again in the realm where only she and her art existed. 'Ally, have you heard from Richard lately?'

'Richard? Richard who?'

'Richard Whitehead,' Gil said patiently. 'Our cousin.'

'Oh, him. No. Why?'

Gil told her about Richard's marital split, and that Tara and Jennifer were living at Eric's. He wasn't surprised that Alison had no idea they were living in Divine. She was so immersed in her art that the world went on around her largely unnoticed. A lot of people made the mistake of thinking Alison was stupid, but Gil knew better; she wasn't stupid, just not interested in the things that made most people's lives meaningful. For the most part, Ally just didn't care.

'Uncle Eric's living at *Peacehaven?*'

'Has been for the past few months.'

'Nobody told me! Why didn't you tell me? I was there just last week to visit Miss Gillickson.'

Lillian had taught several generations of Divine children, including Alison and Gil, when they started at Divine Primary School. The townspeople held her in high regard, and many of her former students still visited her, Gil among them. He could still remember the look on Jake's face when he came home after his first day at school and said in an awestruck voice, 'My teacher said she taught you when you started school!'

'That's right.'

'Wow! She must be at least a hundred years old!'

Alison's voice brought him back to the present.

'I haven't heard a word from Richard in almost two years, and I only met his wife once, at that birthday party at Uncle Eric's. She was a golden wild child.'

Gil thought of his glimpses of the surfer girl Tara tried to keep hidden. She no longer looked as if she'd just stepped off a beach, but the beautiful wild child was still there if you dug deep enough. He liked the surfer girl far more than the woman who looked as if she'd just stepped out of the pages of some glossy magazine.

'It's as if Richard's disappeared off the face of the earth,' he said.

'He was always strange. Beautiful — but strange,' Alison replied dreamily. 'I bet their daughter is just gorgeous.'

'She's nice inside and out.'

'Really? How extraordinary.'

It probably is if you have Tiffany for a daughter, Gil thought.

In one of her lightning changes of topic, Alison announced, 'I'm thinking about doing some sculptures of vulvas.'

Gil frowned. 'Pardon?'

'*Vulvas*: you do know what a vulva is, don't you, Gil?'

'Of course I do. I'm a bloody dairy farmer, remember?'

'No need to get defensive.'

'What on earth are you up to now, Alison? Are you trying to wind me up?'

Alison grinned. 'Do you remember my penis sculptures?'

'How can I forget?' Gil replied dryly.

'Well, I've been thinking: why not do a series of female genitalia?'

Gil's brows rose. 'Stone fannies?'

'Yes. I'm sure they'd sell.'

He was sure they would, too — to men who kept life-sized blow-up rubber dolls in their closets. It wasn't the first time he'd listened to Alison spout off about one of her ideas, although most of them didn't come to fruition. She'd had the audacity to ask Gil to pose for her penis sculptures years ago and sulked when he'd flatly refused.

'Have you heard the saying "thinking outside the square", Gil?'

'Yes. Have you heard the one about "things turning pear-shaped"?'

'Honestly, Gil, when did you turn into such a *petit bourgeois?*' Alison chided.

'Honestly, Alison, when did you turn into such an anarchist?'

'You're not supposed to know what a *petit bourgeois* is. I blame that bloody MBA. You learnt too many big words and suddenly got smarter than me,' she complained.

'Dead right. I use "wheelbarrow" and "marmalade" all the time now.'

Hearing her laugh made Gil smile. Alison didn't laugh enough.

Just before he hung up, she asked, 'Auntie Connie and Uncle Malcolm get back home soon, don't they?'

'Yes, this week.'

His mother, Connie, was a big supporter of Alison's art. Gil's father was a retired journalist who'd owned the *Divine Flyer* until he'd sold it to Dick Cathcart. Alison was close to Connie, who filled the place left by her dead mother, Nancy, and felt sorry for Alison. Gil privately thought it was well past time Alison got over what had happened, stood on her own two feet and started taking some responsibility for her daughter, but Alison seemed to have a blind spot where Tiffany was concerned.

'Goody!' Alison cried gleefully. 'I've missed them.'

Chapter 20

Gil always cheered Alison up. She'd been feeling a little down recently, which happened whenever she allowed herself to think about Barney and her daughter.

Barney utterly repulsed her, and had done ever since Alison finally understood what he wanted from her in the bedroom. She had been such an innocent, so cosseted and immature that she hadn't realized that people like Barney existed, people who got their sexual kicks out of being beaten and hurt. Alison was shocked enough by what had happened to her the night she lost her virginity, but it was nothing compared with the things Barney wanted her to do to him after they were married. She coped by tuning him out of her world; she made the bogeyman go away, and had become so good at it that for large tracts of time she simply forgot she had a husband.

That wasn't the case with Tiffany. Every time Alison looked at her daughter she felt torn in two by her conflicting emotions. She was deeply aware that she'd failed her only child by allowing Barney to raise Tiffany without lifting a finger to stop him passing on his twisted morals and total lack of scruples. And Alison was just as aware that she disliked her daughter.

Tiffany treated Alison with contempt, poking fun at her and sniggering with her friends whenever they came to visit. She knew her mother couldn't stand the sight of her, and Tiffany hated Alison for looking such a frump and acting so weird. Alison was only thirty-four, but with her flyaway, wispy dark hair threaded with grey, and ugly work clothes streaked with clay and paint, she looked closer to fifty. She would wander into town with mismatched shoes, sometimes forgetting her purse and frequently not even noticing when the locals said hello. The more charitable people in Divine called Alison eccentric, but there were others who thought that Barney Bigelow's wife was a few sandwiches short of a picnic. If it hadn't been for Tiffany, Alison would have left Barney years ago; she certainly wasn't dependent on him financially, which infuriated him, because it meant he had no control over her.

The moment Tiffany left home, Alison planned to make her escape. Until then, she stayed out of sight and largely out of mind in her studio in the grounds of Bigelow Towers, watching in case there was any sign of Barney's brutish temper being unleashed on their daughter. Alison knew first-hand how lethal he could be if he was thwarted, and it was fear for her personal safety that had made her create a sanctuary away from the main house. At the moment, Tiffany was still Barney's little princess, a female version of him and a reflection of his success and wealth. But Tiffany was growing up and beginning to show signs of rebellion. More worryingly, she was losing weight. Alison doubted Barney had noticed that, but he *would* notice if Tiffany tried to buck his authority. Barney didn't tolerate rebels — and most certainly not a rebellious daughter. So Alison waited, watched and worried, but for the most part managed to tune the big house and its inhabitants out of her world.

She was still smiling about Gil's response to her vulva sculptures when she went into Divine to pick up some art supplies and collect a parcel from the post office.

'You really don't need to come all the way into town, Miss Whitehead,' the postal worker told Alison yet again when she was at the counter. 'We can arrange for any large packages to be delivered direct to BT.'

'Why on earth would I want my parcels delivered to British

Telecom?' Alison replied frostily. 'I'm quite happy to come in and pick them up.'

The woman behind the window stopped smiling.

BT? And people call me *mad!*

Alison hated the way a lot of people in Divine bent over backwards to ingratiate themselves with her because she was Barney's wife. This particular postal worker had once made the mistake of calling her 'Mrs Bigelow'. The look Alison had given her snap-froze the marrow in her bones. 'My name is *Whitehead,*' Alison said coldly. '*Miss* Whitehead.'

It's a queer set-up at Bigelow Towers, the postal worker thought, not for the first time. She was unaware that Alison knew that Barney went through her mail if she didn't get to it first. Alison had repeatedly asked for her post to be delivered direct to her studio, but it was a waste of time; Barney bribed the postie to bring everything straight to him.

Alison collected her parcel and headed out of the post office, checking the sender address on her package and squinting at the heavily taped cardboard box. She turned it from side to side, her steps slowing as she pictured the partially completed metal city spread in bits and pieces across the work table in her studio. She wasn't entirely happy with it, because she couldn't visualize the completed project.

Inspiration struck.

She needed boxes, lots and lots of boxes, in all different shapes and sizes, to build a city, to create a skyline of buildings! Why hadn't she thought of it before?

Muttering to herself, Alison spied Barney's liquor store across the road and headed towards it, oblivious of the car driving towards her. The driver braked abruptly, shook his head and rolled his eyes before continuing on his way.

Neville Tweedie almost did the same when he saw his boss's weirdo wife come into the shop, but he knew that if he wanted to keep his job he'd be wise to keep his thoughts to himself. Neville had been born and raised in Divine and was too accustomed to Alison's eccentricities to be surprised when she launched into speech without bothering to even say hello.

'Boxes! I need boxes — lots of them — big ones, medium ones, small ones. Have you got any?'

Nutty as a fruitcake, Neville thought. 'Only what's round the back in the dumpster. How many did you need, Miss Whitehead?'

After he'd helped Alison load the boxes into the back of her car, she surprised him by asking, 'Has Tara Whitehead been in?'

'Yes. She comes in to buy wine and . . .' Neville looked puzzled, '. . . sometimes Waikato Draught.' Tara Whitehead wasn't the kind of woman he'd expect to drink Wakas. Everybody in Divine was fascinated by the glamorous, reclusive Mrs Whitehead, especially his mother.

'Waikato Draught?' Alison's forehead creased. 'You'd better give me a bottle of red and a bottle of white and . . . half a dozen cans of beer.'

'Do you mind me asking if this is a gift for Mrs Whitehead?'

'Why?' Alison demanded rudely.

Neville flushed. 'Because she only drinks white wine. I know her favourites.'

'Two bottles of white, then, and the beer. Do you gift-wrap?'

Neville selected two bottles of wine and began to wrap them, but Alison waved him away and took over when she didn't approve of his efforts.

'Do you want the beer wrapped, too?' he asked.

'Don't be stupid,' Alison said.

Neville clenched his jaw and placed the bottles of wine and the beer inside a plastic bag, then tapped on the cash register. 'That'll be—'

Alison scooped up the bag and left the shop without a thank you or a backward glance. She had no intention of paying Barney for the wine. He owed her far more than that.

Once again she narrowly missed being run over as she crossed the road, only this time the driver lowered the window and shouted a string of abuse. Alison gazed at him in surprise — obviously not a local. She turned the car in the direction of Eric's house to pay a call on Richard's wife.

Although she was a huge fan of Alison Whitehead's work, Tara had only met her once, at Eric's birthday party all those years ago. Her recollection was of a small, dark girl who stood in a corner nursing a soft drink. Richard always spoke fondly of her but he didn't keep in touch, and when Alison became famous he didn't like her art, saying it was too raw and assertive for his tastes.

'But that's what makes it so beautiful!' Tara protested.

He turned away. 'Beauty has nothing to do with it. Just pain and suffering.'

When Tara asked him to explain, Richard wouldn't answer, but he did buy her one of Alison's paintings. Called 'The Matador's Cloak', it was a vermilion splash of colour on a stark white background. The folds of the 'cloak' were boldly and simply depicted in black and shades of grey, but the longer the viewer looked at the cloak the more they saw; within it was the silhouette of a charging, wounded bull and the arrogant, ruthless face of the matador. Tara loved it. She had hung it in Eric's bedroom because she couldn't stand seeing it competing with the red flocked wallpaper in the lounge.

When Alison knocked on the front door, Tara was sitting in the kitchen sipping a cup of coffee and studying her bank statement, which was looking a whole lot healthier since she'd started working for Sian. The sound of somebody knocking on the front door made her frown. She hoped it wasn't another irate owner come to tell her that they were moving their horse. Instead, a small, plump woman who could have been anywhere between thirty and fifty stood on the concrete deck, watching her with bruised pansy-blue eyes. She was untidily and badly dressed in paint-splattered jeans, a faded red shirt several sizes too big for her that flapped about her knees, and a pair of old white sports shoes decorated in a rainbow of colours from splotches of paint. In one hand she carried a plastic bag. Tara eyed her warily, bracing herself for a confrontation with yet another of Divine's deranged inhabitants.

'Are you Tara? Richard's wife?' the woman asked abruptly.

Tara stiffened and clutched the door, convinced her worst nightmare had come true and somebody had found out about Richard. 'What do you want?'

'I'm Alison.' She brushed impatiently at a wisp of limp, grey-streaked hair hanging over her left eye. It promptly fell back again. 'Richard's cousin.'

Tara stared.

'Alison?' she repeated, wondering if she'd perhaps misunderstood. 'Alison Whitehead?'

'Yes.' Alison nodded and waved a hand at the disobedient strand of hair as if it were a fly. 'Can I come in?'

Tara was so surprised that she simply stood back and watched bemusedly as one of the most famous contemporary artists in the country swept past her, leaving a trail of muddy footprints on the red, orange and brown paisley carpet. Apparently Alison didn't leave her shoes at the door like most people. She obviously knew her way around the house and disappeared in the direction of the kitchen. Tara closed the door and hurried after her.

Alison was standing by the kitchen table, looking about with a faintly baffled expression, when Tara joined her. 'Where are Uncle Eric's things?'

Tara felt a spurt of irritation. Famous artist or not, it was none of Alison's bloody business. 'They're in storage. I replaced them with my own furniture.'

Her annoyance seemed to penetrate Alison's shell. 'Of course you would.' Her eyes continued to rove around the kitchen. 'Eric's taste is so bad it would be impossible to be surrounded by his things all the time, although I *did* like visiting him just to see it occasionally — it was like visiting a museum.'

Tara relaxed slightly and stopped measuring the distance between her and the wooden block of knives on the kitchen counter. It appeared that Alison wasn't completely off her nana after all, but Tara was still worried about the reason for her sudden visit. Had she received one of Richard's letters? 'Can I get you anything?' she asked cautiously. 'A cup of coffee?'

'Mmm?' Alison shook her head and seemed to recall what she had come for. Dragging a chair from beneath the table, she urged Tara towards it. 'No, no! Sit down.'

Tara's lips tightened. Cheeky bitch! Who the hell was she to be inviting Tara to sit down and talk at her own table? She slid another look at the silver handles of the knives in the wooden block and reluctantly approached the table.

Alison was staring at the cuckoo clock on the wall. 'What have you done to Uncle Eric's clock?'

Tara sat down opposite her. 'Given him a holiday.'

'That clock is Eric's pride and joy. It's the real thing — he got it sent all the way from Switzerland,' Alison said.

'Really? Perhaps as part of the holiday I should send it back to see all its relatives.' Tara stared at her. 'Unless of course you'd like to give it a home for a few months?'

Alison's laughter sounded rusty, like a door hinge that hadn't been oiled in a long time. She studied Tara curiously. 'So, why did you leave Richard?'

Tara tensed. She didn't know what to make of this woman and was annoyed that she thought she could ask personal questions after only a few minutes' acquaintance, but Tara was relieved that Alison didn't seem to know about Richard's decision to leave to live as a woman.

'That's none of your business,' she said coolly. 'It's between Richard and me.'

Alison's eyes widened in admiration. She thought Richard's wife was magnificent: she'd gone ahead and done what Alison had only dreamed about doing: taken her daughter and upped and left her husband to move to a strange town and a new way of life. It was the reason Alison wanted to visit her. The lure of meeting a woman who was strong enough to make the break fascinated her. She wished she was more like Tara, but she was Alison Whitehead, Bill Whitehead's little princess. People did things *for* her. She didn't do anything for herself.

Alison placed the plastic bag on the table top. 'I brought you some wine.'

'That's nice,' Tara said flatly.

'You're angry with me.'

Tara gasped mockingly. 'No! You think?'

'I've gone about this all wrong — I always do. I would have come and seen you sooner if I'd known you were here, but I didn't find out until Gil told me.'

Alison watched Tara blush. Although she was too self-centred and wrapped up in her art to engage in a meaningful relationship with anybody, when her attention was caught and focused — usually when she was painting or sculpting — she was deeply attuned to her subject. As an artist, Alison saw nothing interesting in Tara's perfect features; the unusual or, even better, downright ugly attracted her far more. Barney, for instance, would have made a *wonderful* model.

Alison watched as the pale skin over Tara's cheekbones turned pink and was intrigued. Richard's wife fancied Gil. She wondered if it was reciprocated.

'Do you see much of Gil?'

The flush crept down Tara's face and into her neck. She shrugged. 'Off and on. Eric asked him to help.'

Alison changed the subject. 'It was a huge surprise when I found out that Uncle Eric had moved to Peacehaven.'

'Tell me about it,' Tara replied sourly.

'Don't you like Divine?' Alison asked.

Tara stared at her. 'It's not the place, it's the locals.'

Alison burst out laughing again, the years and strain melting away to leave a pretty, pansy-eyed woman in her thirties who was old before her time. Tara suddenly noticed a resemblance to Richard and, now she thought of it, to Gil Sorensen. Alison had the Whitehead smile, mesmerizing, beguiling and utterly charming.

'I've got one of your paintings,' Tara said.

Alison rolled back a paint-stained cuff. 'Which one?'

'The Matador. Richard bought it for me for my thirtieth birthday.'

Alison looked at Tara thoughtfully and began to tell her about her metal city. Usually she hated to talk about a work in progress, preferring to hug it to herself like a wonderful secret that only she knew. Tara was entranced and even asked sensible questions. She unbent still more when she saw the actual bottles of wine that Alison had brought, and the beer.

Alison watched her curiously. 'The boy at the bottle store said you like beer, too.' She tried and failed to remember what Gil drank.

Tara guessed that Alison thought she had a secret lover and, although she was tempted to tell her that the beer was for Magic, she decided against it. Let her sweat.

'I buy it for a friend,' Tara said smoothly.

She glanced at her watch.

Alison took the hint. When it came to socializing, her attention span was limited. She was anxious to get back to her studio and begin planning her metal city.

After Alison had gone, Tara wondered if anybody could explain to her why so many nutcases lived in Divine.

Chapter 21

As Sian had predicted, Tara was building up a regular clientele, and her callers almost always rang back asking for her.

Tara's first caller of the day was Percy Feather. Percy had a fetish for cleaning and feathers. He was stone deaf and shouted when he spoke. When he got really excited he had a tendency to wheeze, and on several occasions Tara became concerned that Percy was going to cark it in the middle of their call and she would be tracked down and charged with murder.

'I have a little problem with feathers, Mistress!' Percy yelled, the first time they spoke.

'Do you?' Tara yelled back. 'Are you allergic to them?'

'No!' he bellowed. *'They excite me, Mistress!'*

Oh dear God.

Percy could talk about dusting and vacuuming for hours. The thought of cleaning Tara's house really got his motor running. 'I want to dust for you, Mistress! I want to clean your house from top to bottom so that it's a fitting setting for your perfection!'

Tara noticed a long string of cobwebs hanging in a corner of the living room and wished she could take Percy up on his offer. Most of her callers liked to discuss what they were wearing. 'Oh yes? And what did you plan on wearing if I allowed you the privilege of cleaning my house?' she shouted.

Percy wheezed with excitement. 'Nothing, Mistress, I'd be naked. All except for a feather in my—'

'I get the picture, Percy!'

'—teeth!' he yelled.

Percy called every Tuesday without fail to give a progress report on the list of cleaning tasks that Tara had allotted him the previous week. She was really rather fond of Percy, and wished he'd spend his money on buying a new hearing aid instead of discussing cleaning products with her. He was lonely. *Barmy*, but lonely. Percy wouldn't go into detail about where he lived, but Tara gathered he was in some sort of a nursing home.

'What do you want me to do this week, Mistress? *Everything* is dirty!'

Tara looked at her list. The trick was to give him enough to keep him busy without overtaxing him. This week she ordered Percy to wash the fabric covers on the arms of the chairs, and told him off when he pleaded to be allowed to take down the net curtains and wash them instead. The thought of him falling out the window petrified her.

Percy clearly felt cheated. 'I *could* wash the curtains, Mistress!'

'Are you *arguing* with me, Percival?' Tara snapped.

'No, Mistress! Never, Mistress!'

'And you can scrub down the windowsills . . .' Tara paused for effect. 'With an old toothbrush.' She estimated that should keep him busy for the best part of the week.

Percy wasn't her only client with a cleaning fetish. Walter, a retired chicken farmer, was similarly obsessed, but unlike Percy he wasn't interested in feathers. This seemed a shame, considering he presumably had access to a steady supply. Tara was tempted to introduce them to one another.

Walter liked watching other people cleaning rather than doing it himself, so once a week he paid Tara for the privilege of listening in while she cleaned Eric's house. Tara was quite happy to get paid while she did her own vacuuming and dusting, and Walter was as harmless as Percy. He didn't want a dominatrix service — more a Mrs Mop.

The first thing Walter always asked when Tara answered the phone was what she was wearing.

'A long white apron with a frill around the bodice, and yellow rubber gloves.'

The gloves had to be yellow; he'd almost hung up when Tara made the mistake of replacing her old ones with a pink pair.

'What are you cleaning?' he asked dreamily.

'The kitchen. I'm free-ranging my way along the bench with a damp sponge . . .'

She liked to drop in an occasional reference to his former career when she could, and Walter seemed to appreciate the gesture.

'What colour is the sponge?' Walter asked nervously, the incident with the pink gloves still fresh in his mind.

'Yellow.'

He sighed with pleasure.

Tara had actually done the housework on the weekend and was crouched on a kitchen chair painting her toenails. She stabbed the vacuum cleaner button with a toe to switch it on, almost knocking her bottle of Raspberry Ripple nail varnish over.

'Bugger!' She jabbed the button to switch off the machine.

'What happened?' Walter cried.

Tara swiped the little nail brush upwards along the bottle, scooping spilt varnish inside and thinking quickly. 'A sudden backdraft from the vacuum cleaner wafted right up my apron.'

Walter swallowed audibly.

'I have to tell you, Walter, it gave me quite a surprise,' she confided.

'Oh . . . yes . . .'

That was about as suggestive as Tara got. Any caller wanting smut, perversion or a discussion about animals other than their pets did not call twice. Tara had standards. Her callers paid to be put in their place.

When Tara told Jen about Alison's visit, she asked, 'Is she as horrible as her daughter?'

'Jennifer!'

Jen shuddered. 'She sucks. Suddenly she wants to be friends and keeps inviting me over to her house to ride her horse. She's creepy, Mum. Just because you like her mother doesn't mean I have to like her.'

'Of course it doesn't, and, between you and me, her mother is a bit weird, too,' Tara confided. 'I'm beginning to think most of the Whiteheads in this town are.'

'Jake isn't and Gil isn't,' Jen insisted. 'Gil's been wonderful to us.'

Tara chewed her lip thoughtfully. The last thing she wanted was for Jen to start seeing Gil Sorensen as some sort of father figure. Jen was spending far too much time over at the Sorensen house, what with riding lessons, relief milking and feeding the calves.

Jennifer saw her mother's face and decided to change the subject. 'I saw Uncle Eric today. He's really miserable.'

And that was another place she was spending too much time — visiting Eric at Peacehaven.

'I know he is. He's been that way his entire life.'

'No, I mean he's really *unhappy*. I think something's wrong.' Jennifer gazed at Tara with wide, innocent eyes. 'Maybe you should go and see him.'

'Oh no you don't! I get his bloody *erection* pills for him. Don't expect me to visit him as well. I've a good mind to stop you visiting the old—'

'—bugger,' Jennifer finished.

Tara's conscience got the better of her. She reluctantly went to visit Eric, thinking as she went that he was like a spider sitting in the middle of his web reeling them all in whenever it suited him. When she reached Peacehaven, the receptionist directed her to the communal lounge.

Tara looked about the room twice before she realized that Eric was sitting in a wheelchair in a patch of sunlight by the French doors with a crocheted rug over his knees. Behind him, the man called Stanley, who had been asleep in the lounge with his teeth on the table the last time Tara had visited, was moving from one chair to the next, removing the covers from the arms. She looked at Eric in dismay, studying his unshaven face and slumped shoulders. He was notoriously vain about his appearance, but at the moment he looked utterly pathetic. Jen hadn't mentioned that he'd deteriorated to the point of needing a wheelchair.

Tara walked towards him, exchanging a smile and a nod with a group of four women sitting on the other side of the room playing cards. The group included Lillian Gillickson and Felicity Ringwald. Lillian's eyes slid to Eric, a small vee of concern etched between her brows before she determinedly returned her attention to her cards.

Pulling a tufted pink chair closer, Tara sat down beside him. 'What's wrong with you? Why are you in that wheelchair?'

He glared up at her from pouchy eyes like a debauched old basset hound. 'Because I need it. Now piss off.'

'That's a relief,' Tara observed. 'You're only depressed, not suicidal.'

'I don't know what Richard ever saw in you,' Eric said viciously. 'No wonder he turned into a fruit.'

She sucked in a breath and was surprised to discover that, although the pain was still there, she no longer felt as if she was bleeding from a mortal wound. Tara stared at the carpet and bit her lip, thinking that yet another part of what she'd had with Richard had gone.

'I'm sorry. I shouldn't have said that,' Eric said gruffly.

Tara was so surprised she thought she must have misheard him. He looked uncomfortable and defiant and . . . apologetic.

Stanley paused beside Eric's wheelchair.

Eric scowled. 'Piss off, Stan! It's a wheelchair; it hasn't got any covers on the arms.'

Stanley scrutinized the chair closely before shuffling away, clutching his covers.

Tara watched him go. 'What on earth is he doing?'

'Cleaning,' Eric replied disinterestedly. 'He's a fruitcake.'

His apathy concerned her. 'What's wrong, Eric?'

He shrugged. 'Nothing.' His gaze drifted towards the women playing cards.

'Have you fallen out with Lillian?'

Eric looked away. 'None of your bloody business!'

Stanley had finished collecting the covers and was dusting along the windowsill towards them. He stopped when he reached Eric's chair, which was in the way.

'What d'you want now?' Eric snapped.

Stanley silently pointed the feather duster at a cobweb hanging above Eric's head.

'Can't you see I'm talking to me niece? Bugger off and come back later.'

Stanley departed, looking disgruntled.

Tara watched him go. 'Why is he cleaning?'

'He's always at it, especially dusting.'

She shrugged. 'What did you do to Lillian, Eric?'

He scowled. 'Nothing.'

Tara crossed her legs and began to swing one of her pink sandals to and fro. For once it had been warm enough for her to break out the summer sandals and slip on a dusty-pink summer dress and tiny raspberry-pink cardigan. She had plenty of time. If she waited long enough, she knew Eric would crack. Smothering a yawn behind her fingers, she said idly, 'I can't say I'll miss making the trip to the chemist to get your prescription filled.'

Eric snapped to attention. 'Who said you won't be getting me pills? Did you hear me tell you to stop? Did you?'

'Why do you need it anyway if the woman you want to . . .' Tara gestured discreetly in Lillian's direction, '. . . get to *know* better won't speak to you?'

'How do you know Lillian isn't speaking to me?'

Tara pounced. 'Aha! So you *have* upset her.'

He muttered something under his breath and looked away.

'What did you do, Eric?'

There was a pause.

'It's about the fiasco outside the pub. Ever since then, Lillian won't have anything to do with me. She thinks I manipulated everybody and . . .'

Mutter, mutter, mutter.

'What?' Tara leant forward. 'I didn't quite hear you.'

'She thinks I enjoyed all the uproar and getting my picture on the front page of the *Flyer* — as if it's the first time that's happened! The Whiteheads have sold so many copies of that rag that Dick Cathcart should be paying *me* to read it and not the other way around! Lillian says I don't take anything seriously, and that I'm a selfish, unprincipled, arrogant man,' Eric finished petulantly.

'You are.'

'I might have known it!' he cried bitterly. 'Bloody women! You're all the same!'

'Thank God all men aren't like you, you old sod,' Tara shot back. 'Yes, I totally agree with Lillian, and *yes*, I'm willing to help you sort things out with her. Unless of course,' she raised a brow enquiringly, 'you'd prefer to shove your foot further down your throat.'

'If I shove me foot any further down me throat I'll have to stick me toothbrush up me bum to clean me teeth,' Eric replied, mournfully.

Tara fought back laughter. 'Tell me what you've done to make amends.'

He'd said sorry, but Lillian hadn't believed that he was sincere or that he understood the hurt he had caused to her and her friends. Which, if he was honest, he didn't.

He'd bought her flowers, the first time he'd *ever* bought flowers for *any* woman in his life, the nearest equivalent being when he'd picked a bouquet from the now-closed Botanical Gardens in Divine for Mother's Day when he was ten. Lillian thanked him politely, threw away the card with Eric's personal message of contrition, and placed the flowers in the communal lounge for everybody to enjoy.

He attended housie even though he hated it, in the hope that he'd snag a seat next to Lillian and have a chance to show her how much he'd changed. Lillian was polite and distant and always managed to move to a seat on the other side of the table, invariably leaving Eric sitting beside Felicity Ringwald, her best friend.

Desperation had driven him into a wheelchair, convinced that Lillian's kind heart would melt in the face of his sudden deterioration. Unfortunately, Lillian was made of sterner stuff, and Eric had an awful feeling she was suspicious about his lack of mobility. He was pretty sure it had been Lillian's idea for Felicity to crochet him the lap rug that was draped across his knees. Eric knew he had nobody to blame but himself. He was stuck in a bloody wheelchair with a fucking lap rug like an old tabby and he didn't have a single bloody idea how to go about getting out of it. Of course he didn't confide this last problem to Tara, although he did tell her who'd made the lap rug when she asked.

'Now bloody Fred Skinner thinks I'm making a play for Felicity and keeps threatening to thump me!' Eric smiled maliciously. 'Mad Marion's really got her knickers in a knot over it — and they're not exactly small knickers.'

Tara didn't know what tickled her more, Marion's reaction or the thought of Fred and Eric fighting it out over Zimmer frames and wheelchairs. It sounded to her as if Lillian was playing hard to get. Her suspicions were confirmed when she saw how often Lillian's eyes strayed from her cards to Eric when she thought he wasn't looking. Felicity and the other two ladies at the table giggled and whispered to one another while Lillian maintained a dignified silence.

'She hates me,' Eric said dolefully.

'No, she doesn't.'

He cocked his head. 'Why'd you say that?'

'Because she keeps looking at you.'

He looked eagerly across the room. 'She does?'

'Don't look at her!'

'Why? I like looking at her!'

'You're *too easy.*'

'I'm a bloke, I'm meant to be easy,' Eric protested. 'It's women that aren't s'posed to be easy.'

Tara rolled her eyes. 'Listen to me. She's interested, but you're making all the running. Back off, maintain a dignified silence for once in your life. Get her *thinking.* Do you think you can manage that, Eric?'

He looked doubtful. 'D'you really think she's interested?'

'Yes! God knows why, but yes.'

Tara got to her feet.

'Where are you going?' Eric demanded.

'To visit Lillian Gillickson.'

She headed in the direction of the women.

He sat up straighter in his wheelchair and smiled his evil-genie smile. That was what he liked about Tara — she was a woman of action.

Chapter 22

Tara returned half an hour later, looking pensive.

'Well?' Eric asked eagerly.

Tara didn't rate his chances with Lillian very highly. Lillian was nobody's fool and most definitely not up for Eric's shenanigans. But Tara sensed that Lillian was not immune to him, and when she considered the competition offered by the four other male residents Tara had to admit Eric did have a distinct edge — he had all his own hair, a still-strong physique, and remembered to put his teeth in each morning. He also had his own set of wheels.

Eric was insulted by Tara's observations. 'What do you mean my shenanigans?'

'I mean if you think you're going to buy Lillian Gillickson a couple of shandies and get her into bed, you're in for a big disappointment,' Tara said tartly.

He was outraged. 'How dare you speak about Lillian like that! Bloody kids! You don't have any bloody manners!'

'If you're serious about this, you'll have to stop swearing all the time. Lillian doesn't like it. She also doesn't like people who smoke. She thinks they're idiots and the money could be spent on much better things.'

Eric scowled. 'Like what?'

'Like community projects or sponsoring a child in a Third World country. Lillian sponsors three,' Tara lied. Actually, it was one little girl in Bangladesh.

'But I like a smoke!'

She shrugged.

Eric looked desperate. 'Well, what *does* she like?'

'Embroidery, walking — once her knee's been fixed, of course — and Engelbert Humperdinck.'

His face fell. 'Engelbert Humperdinck? What about The Shadows? Doesn't she like The Shadows?'

'I don't think so.'

Eric dropped his head into his hand. 'I can't stand bloody Engelbert Humperdinck.' He looked up sulkily. 'And why have you stopped getting me pills?'

'Because I'm beginning to feel like a drug runner, that's why,' Tara replied. 'You don't need me; you can buy them off the internet.'

'Marion only lets us have ten minutes surfing the web. Any longer and she thinks we might get overexcited.'

Tara was disturbed. They *were* literally like prisoners living under Mad Marion's obnoxious rules. 'That's outrageous!'

Eric looked at her cunningly. 'So you'll get the pills?'

'I didn't say that!' She changed the subject before he could manipulate her any further, particularly when she was having so much fun doing it to him. 'By the way, you need to sort your act out and start shaving. Designer stubble only looks good if you're under thirty-five.'

'Eh?'

'Never mind.'

There was a burst of laughter from the group of women at the card table. Eric's eyes were automatically drawn to Lillian, a look of such longing on his face that Tara was surprised to discover she felt sorry for him. Getting to her feet, she dropped her handbag on Eric's lap and began pushing him towards the doors leading to the corridor, closely watched by Lillian Gillickson.

'Where are we going?' He curled his hands around the wheels, bringing them to an abrupt halt. *There's nothing wrong with your arms anyway*, Tara thought as she lurched over his shoulder. 'I'm taking you back to your apartment so you can shave and change your clothes. If you're serious about making headway with Lillian, you'd better make a start.'

'Oh. Righto.'

On the way to his apartment, Tara checked that Marion Popplewell wasn't lurking behind a potted palm tree and murmured, 'Eric, what exactly are you doing with all those pills?'

'They're not just for me; they're for the boys as well.'

She stopped so abruptly that Eric almost tipped out of his chair. 'Watch it!'

Tara scooted in front of him and, gripping the arms of the chair, thrust her face close to his. 'Tell me you're joking. You *are* joking, aren't you, Eric? You're not *really* handing them out to the other men?'

'How else do you think the boys get hold of them?'

The boys? *The boys?*

'Even I know those pills shouldn't be taken without checking with a doctor first. Why don't they get them from their GPs?' Tara demanded.

'Because their doctors won't give them a prescription.'

'Oh God . . .' Tara covered her face with her hands, unknowingly pushing her breasts together so that her cleavage swelled over the neckline of her pink dress. She opened her eyes to discover Eric staring brazenly. 'Stop that, you old pervert!' she cried, jerking her cardigan closed and straightening up. 'You've got to stop handing out those pills to anybody who asks for them.'

'Don't be such a girl, Tara. Can you think of a better way to go? We're all adults in here, not kids. If the boys are happy to take the risk, then who the hell is some wet-behind-the-ears doctor or you to tell them any different? It's done wonders for Fred and Felicity; he says Felicity is very—'

'No!' Tara waved her hands agitatedly. 'I *do not* want to hear about Fred Skinner and Felicity Ringwald's sex life.'

Eric smiled slyly. 'Just because you're not getting any doesn't mean the rest of us can't.'

'Shut *up*, Eric.'

'I don't know what's wrong with Gil!' he continued relentlessly. 'I know he likes to play his cards close to his chest about his women, but why travel all the way to Hamilton or Auckland when he's got someone like you on his doorstep?'

Tara was about to slap him when a movement behind his chair made her look up.

Gil stood in the middle of the strip of carpet, looking as if he wished he was anywhere else.

'Hello, Tara,' he said resignedly.

She made a sound of distress and looked away.

Eric twisted about in his chair. 'Bloody hell, two visitors in one day. Am I dying or something?'

Gil covered the distance between them and dumped a carrier bag from the bottle store on Eric's lap next to Tara's handbag. 'We should be so lucky.' He grabbed hold of the handles of the wheelchair and looked at Tara. ''Scuse *us*.'

She stepped hastily aside.

Gil began to wheel Eric along the corridor at breakneck speed, taking the corners on two wheels.

Tara watched them disappear around the corner and scuttled after them.

Eric roared and tried to grab the wheels of the chair to stop it, but Gil was far stronger than Tara. She ran behind, chuckling. When they finally reached Eric's apartment, she was laughing so hard she had to lean against the wall to catch her breath.

'I've got a good mind to report you two to Bevan Sargeson!' Eric howled. 'You're a pair of bloody lunatics! What do you think this is? The fucking wheelchair derby?'

He let out a squawk when Tara grabbed the key on the chain around his neck, yanked him unceremoniously forward and unlocked the door. 'You never *had* a good mind, Eric.'

'Just watch your mouth in future, you old devil,' Gil advised and wheeled him inside.

Tara closed the door and followed them into the lounge. 'Did you ever wonder what Lillian Gillickson would think if she found out you were running a black market in *erection pills*, Eric?' she asked sweetly.

Eric's eyes widened. 'You wouldn't!'

'I will if you don't watch what you say about Gil and me.' She crossed her arms and leant forward until they were nose to nose. 'We're not going to put up with it, Eric. I visit you even though I don't like you, and I'm sure Gil's got better things to do than drive into town and buy you beer.'

Eric scowled and dropped his gaze. Then his face brightened.

Tara looked down and saw that her cardigan had parted and her boobs were swelling over the top of her pink bodice again. She jerked upright and punched him in the shoulder.

'Oww!' he howled. 'I'm in a wheelchair!'

'I don't care!'

'What d'you expect a man to do when he's got a pair of ti— knoc— . . . eh . . . boobs shoved in his face?' He looked to Gil for support.

Gil was all out of male solidarity. Tara was right; he did have better things to do than run around buying Eric his favourite beer because it was on special. He had paddocks to fertilize, a maize crop to put down, drains that needed clearing, and a herd of cows needing artificial insemination. If he hadn't needed to collect a few things in town, he wouldn't have dropped into the bottle store to pick up the beer and come to Peacehaven.

Eric appealed to Gil. 'Gil, you know what I mean.'

'Don't try and drag me into it.'

Gil wasn't going to admit that Tara reminded him of an ice cream sundae in her pink dress and little red cardigan. The sight of her breasts spilling over the top of her bodice made him think of vanilla ice cream spilling out of a pink cone. He imagined stroking his tongue across those creamy, firm mounds.

'Unlike you, Eric,' Tara said tartly, 'Gil doesn't have a one-track mind.'

Gil busied himself putting the beer in the fridge.

'Hah!' Eric snorted. 'Pull the other one, it's got bells on.'

In the car park, Gil and Tara stood awkwardly by her car.

'Did you know he's running a black market in erection pills?' she asked.

Gil laughed. 'No.'

'It's not funny, Gil. What if one of them has a heart attack or stroke or something?'

'They're adults, Tara, not toddlers. And besides.' His smile deepened. 'I can think of worse ways to go.'

She felt the delicious, familiar tingling begin low in her belly. Why oh why did it have to be Richard's cousin who made her think about sex? 'You're as bad as Eric.'

More than you know. Gil changed the subject. 'What was all that about Miss Gillickson?'

'You mean Lillian?'

Gil nodded. He never referred to her as 'Lillian'; to him she would always be 'Miss Gillickson'.

Eric's boorish behaviour overthrew any qualms Tara had about discussing his personal business. Anyway, she wasn't at all sure that Lillian shouldn't be warned and offered a lift to the airport to make a getaway. 'Eric's in love with her.'

He frowned. 'Don't be stupid! Of course he isn't.'

'I'm afraid he is,' Tara replied in her snootiest voice.

Gil shook his head. 'That's disgusting! Miss Gillickson isn't like that.'

'For your information, not only is Miss Gillickson *like that*, she's enjoying making Eric work damned hard to catch her. But I've no doubt she intends to be caught,' Tara insisted.

Gil was thunderstruck. 'You don't know what you're talking about.'

Tara shrugged and unlocked her car. 'Suit yourself.'

She slid into the driver's seat, taking care not to flash an eyeful of knickers but giving Gil a gorgeous display of the tops of those lovely breasts and her legs with the pretty, dainty pink sandals strapped around her ankles. The one-track mind Gil wasn't supposed to have imagined what it would feel like to stroke his hand from the inside of one delicate ankle to the top of Tara's thigh. Everything about her turned him on, even the polish on her toenails that was exactly the same shade as her little cardigan. As for that cardigan, it was playing hell with Gil's imagination by parting and closing as she spoke. Gil decided he had a big problem if a cardie made him feel horny. He needed Tara Whitehead to go away and stay away before he did something even more serious than dump her in a wheelbarrow. He slammed the door and stepped away from the Lexus.

Tara fastened her seat belt and lowered the window. 'When could you start giving me those riding lessons?'

Gil's face fell.

Tara looked hurt and humiliated. Fumbling with the keys, she started the car and began to reverse out of the parking space.

Gil wrapped his hand around the window. 'Tara! Stop!'

She wouldn't look at him. 'It was *your* suggestion, not mine! I didn't even want to have riding lessons. Now let go of the car before I run you over!'

Gil felt awful. She was so upset that she wasn't even using her newsreader's voice. It wasn't her fault he couldn't get his brain out of his pants, and it *had* been his suggestion that she have riding lessons. The only problem was those weren't the kind of riding lessons he wanted to give her.

He walked beside the car, clutching the window. 'I'm sorry, Tara. What Eric said . . . I felt awkward — embarrassed!'

Tara took her foot off the gas pedal and looked up at him uncertainly through the window.

Gil braced his hands on the roof and leaned down to look at her. 'Tomorrow morning,' he said. 'Come over tomorrow morning.'

She hesitated. 'I've got something else planned.'

'Well, unplan it,' he insisted stubbornly. 'Nine o'clock tomorrow morning on the dot. Bring a riding helmet and no high heels.'

She glared at him. 'I'm not a complete idiot, Sorensen.'

So they were back to 'Sorensen', were they? Probably just as well, Gil thought. 'We'll find out tomorrow, won't we?'

Lillian Gillickson and Felicity Ringwald stood in the communal lounge watching Tara Whitehead and Gil Sorensen through the window.

'So that's the way the wind blows,' Felicity remarked.

Lillian smiled. 'I hope so. Gil has been on his own for far too long. I like what I've seen of her — she's got plenty of spunk and seems to be intelligent. He could do a lot worse.'

Felicity nodded. 'It would certainly put Glenys Tweedie's nose out of joint.'

They looked at one another and laughed.

Lillian slowly turned away from the window, leaning heavily on her walking frame. She wasn't sure what she hated more, the stupid frame or the chronic, grinding pain that never left her swollen, useless knee. Felicity waited patiently until Lillian had made the turn, and together they walked over to some armchairs bathed in afternoon sunlight on the opposite side of the room. Felicity was a diabetic with high blood pressure, but like Lillian she refused to let her health problems slow her down; unlike many of the other residents, who frequently spent entire evenings discussing their illnesses and what medications they were taking for them. Lillian, Felicity and Fred Skinner refused to join in.

Once they were both sitting, Felicity asked tentatively, 'Do you think it's time to let Eric off the hook?'

'No, I don't,' Lillian replied firmly. 'Not yet.'

'Don't you think he's suffered enough already? He looks *so* miserable in that wheelchair, Lillian.'

Lillian shrugged; her eyes steely. 'It serves him right for being so deceitful.'

Felicity shook her head and sighed. 'I still can't believe he would do something like that.'

A fortnight after the fiasco at the Long Drop Pub, she and Lillian had made a visit to a mutual friend who lived in a house on the ridge behind Peacehaven. Normally the view to the apartments below was blocked by several large trees, but on this particular day they were being cut back. As Lillian and Felicity sat by the large picture window in the lounge of their friend's house while she made coffee, they spied a man perched on the retaining wall of one of the small gardens attached to the Peacehaven apartments. He was balanced on the wall with his arms on his knees, casually smoking a cigarette.

Lillian peered at the man and frowned. 'Felicity? Who's that?'

'Who, love?'

She pointed. 'Is that who I think it is?'

Felicity gasped. 'Why, that old devil! It's Eric Whitehead! I thought he couldn't walk!'

'He doesn't seem to have any problem climbing!' Lillian cried furiously.

Eric's mobility had taken a turn for the worse soon after the day at the pub, and he'd been forced to give up his walking frame for a wheelchair. After his behaviour and obvious enjoyment at causing so much trouble, Lillian had been distant, but her manner had softened somewhat when Eric took to the wheelchair. It was awful to see such a big, strong man reduced to sitting helplessly in a chair, reliant on other people for help. Lillian was very even-tempered and slow to anger. Forty years of teaching fractious, tearful new entrants had given her enormous patience and understanding, but, like others who seldom lost their temper, when she did she wasn't to be trifled with.

Felicity suddenly began to laugh.

'What on earth do you find funny? He's been pulling the wool over our eyes and treating us like idiots. I'm sure he doesn't even need a walking frame, let alone a wheelchair!' Lillian's eyes were shooting flames.

'I think it's romantic.' Felicity searched her handbag for a handkerchief to wipe her eyes. 'This is all about *you,* Lillian. Eric Whitehead is sweet on you.'

'Don't be so ridiculous! Anyway, I can't bear the man!'

Felicity wiped her eyes and smiled knowingly. 'Mmm.'

'What on earth is that supposed to mean?'

'Nothing, nothing . . .'

Eric climbed off the wall, dropped his cigarette and ground it beneath his shoe. He stretched his long arms and arched his strong back before strolling back into his apartment.

'You've got to admit, Lillian, he's a fine figure of a man.'

Lillian didn't have to admit any such thing.

'Felicity, are you doing any crocheting at the moment?'

'Only a tea cosy for Fred. Why?'

Lillian smiled coolly. 'Because I'm sure Eric Whitehead could do with a nice rug to keep his knees warm during all those long hours he's going to be spending in that wheelchair.'

Felicity's brown eyes widened and her lips twitched. 'Lillian! That's cruel.'

'Is it?' she replied serenely. 'Good.'

Felicity watched Lillian as they sat in the warm sunshine, and wondered how much longer she was going to make Eric Whitehead pay. Judging by the look on Lillian's face, she wasn't even close to giving in. Felicity laid her head against the back of her chair, smiling as she thought about Eric and Lillian's relationship. It was nothing like the warm, steady feeling she shared with Fred. When Eric and Lillian were in the same room, it was all thunder and lightning bolts. It was thrilling to watch. Felicity couldn't wait to see how things played out and hoped that there would be a happy ending. She closed her eyes.

'You look like a Cheshire cat,' Lillian said. 'What's put that smile on your face?'

'Love.'

'Oh.'

Felicity knew that Lillian assumed she was thinking of Fred.

Chapter 23

'This is Magnum.'

Tara looked uneasily at the large red-brown horse. Magnum slouched, one hind foot propped and a bored expression on his long face.

'He's big,' she said doubtfully.

'Not too big,' Gil replied brusquely. 'Don't worry; you'll be fine. He's twenty-three and very patient. He'll take care of you.'

Tara glanced at Gil uncertainly. He'd been like that, brusque and unsmiling, ever since she'd arrived ten minutes earlier, right on the dot of nine, yet he was the one who'd insisted she come today when she'd made it clear she wanted to call the whole thing off. The only thing stopping her leaving was her need to talk to Gil about Jen's crush. It was the only explanation Tara could think of for the lip gloss and the time Jen spent in front of the mirror every time she had a riding lesson or any reason to visit the Sorensen farm. Jen also rushed to her bedroom to run a brush through her hair when Gil arrived to fix the tractor or lay fertilizer on the paddocks. When Tara mentioned she was going to have riding lessons with Gil, Jennifer hadn't been at all pleased.

How could I have been so dense and why did I think this was a good idea? Tara wondered as she studied Gil's closed expression. *And why did I spend the better part of an hour worrying about whether my bum looks big in these damned jodhpurs?* And why had the mere thought of seeing him given her butterflies in her stomach as she walked through the underpass? She was as bad as her daughter.

Gil's frame of mind was no better. He had decided he was making a big deal out of nothing. After all, he'd taught lots of people to ride over the years, and Tara Whitehead would be no different; but the moment she wandered up the driveway dressed in white jodhpurs that clung to her hips and thighs as though they'd been sprayed on, and a thin white shirt that showed her lacy white bra beneath, Gil knew he was in trouble. Without her high heels she looked small and fragile. Everybody else kept their white jodhpurs for turnout at shows and wore their old dark riding clothes for lessons, but Tara wasn't everybody. Only she would think that it was appropriate to wear a silk shirt and a tortoiseshell clip to hold back her blonde hair as if she was doing a photo shoot for a fashion magazine. Gil's hackles rose and he turned uncharacteristically surly.

He spent a good half-hour showing her how to groom and tack up Magnum, putting off for as long as possible the moment when she would actually climb aboard, because it meant that he'd have to touch her, but fortunately she managed to hop aboard without any help. When Gil finally led her out to the big oval sand arena behind the barn and began to explain what they were going to do, Tara seemed distracted and he had to keep repeating things.

'Are you paying attention?' he demanded.

'I'm trying!' she cried.

Gil took a calming breath. 'At the beginning there are going to be lots of times when I'll have to touch you to move your arms or legs into the correct position.'

Tara nodded warily.

He took hold of her left knee and ankle, and she immediately became as stiff as a board. Gil shook her leg. 'Relax! Your leg should be in this position.' He rearranged her leg and held it in place. 'If the horse disappeared from under you, you should land on your feet.'

'I don't *want* the horse disappearing from under me!'

'He *won't.* I'm just trying to paint a picture in your head of how you should sit on him.'

'The picture in my head is of me flat on my back in the sand with the wind knocked out of me.'

Gil blew out his lips and closed his eyes. Now he had a picture in his head of her flat on her back, but she wasn't in the sand and she wasn't alone. He rubbed a hand across his face. 'Let's try that again.'

Tara did her best to ignore the feel of Gil's hand wrapped around her knee and the inside of her thigh, but it was difficult. While he was describing how to sit properly, Tara was miles away noticing how the sunshine brought out deep shades of mahogany in his thick dark hair and that his eyes were flecked with gold and green and were in fact more hazel than brown.

'Your eyes are hazel.'

Gil stopped mid-sentence. 'What?'

'I just — um — noticed you haven't got brown eyes.' Tara reddened. 'They're hazel.'

'Are you listening to a word I'm saying?'

'Yes,' she lied.

'What did I just say?' Gil demanded.

Tara's temper rose to match his. 'I heard you! You said, "What did I just say?"'

Gil took a long breath and slowly exhaled. His patience was generally inexhaustible, but he'd never had a pupil like Tara before. Magnum's long ears flickered and he moved restlessly in response to the tension he sensed in his rider. Gil reached out and gently took hold of the bridle. 'Just relax, Tara.'

'I'm trying,' she said in a small voice.

Tara really did try for the rest of the lesson. Gil stood in the middle of the arena and Magnum plodded around and around him, stopping every once in a while so Gil could rearrange Tara's arms and legs, and, on one memorable occasion, sandwich her abdomen and lower back between his palms to tilt her pelvis into the correct position.

'You're sitting on your fork, which is why you keep tipping forward.'

'My fork? What's my fork?' Tara clutched the reins and wished he would let go of her. She felt as if she was going to ignite from the internal heat his hands generated. She kept trying to tell herself that there was nothing sexual about the way Gil was touching her, but her body wasn't getting the message.

'The front of your pelvis,' Gil explained patiently. If he said her fanny she'd probably punch him in the nose.

'Oh . . . you mean my . . .'

'*Yes!*' He walked back to the middle of the arena. 'Now change the rein and go large around the arena.' When he looked back, Magnum hadn't moved.

'I've forgotten what that means.'

'Change direction and go right around the outside.'

She did as he asked, but it was hopeless. Magnum arched his neck and began to jog on the spot.

'Nice piaffe.' Gil tried not to stare as Tara's breasts bounced enticingly beneath her shirt. Didn't she own a decent bra to keep things under control?

'I'm sorry!' she cried miserably. 'I know it's me — I'm as stiff as a board!'

You and me both. Gil was thankful for the old baggy grey T-shirt he was wearing over his jeans.

'What's a piaffe?'

'It's a dressage movement.' He watched Magnum and Tara continue to bounce around on the spot. 'I think we'll call it a day.'

She slumped with relief and Magnum immediately stopped jogging. Gil led the way back to the round barn and showed her how to remove the saddle and bridle and wipe off any accumulated sweat, although it was debatable who was most in of a lather — Tara, Gil or Magnum.

'I've got a carrot for him.' She held it out to Gil.

'OK, I'll put it in his feed.'

'Jen told me to bring it.'

He nodded and went to rinse the metal bit under a nearby tap.

It's now or never: don't be such a coward.

Tara gritted her teeth. 'Jen . . . really *likes* having lessons from you.'

Gil shut off the tap. 'Uh huh.'

She took a deep breath. 'Gil, I think Jen's got a crush on you.'

He stared at the bit in his hands. 'I know.'

'You do?' Tara exclaimed. 'So I'm not imagining it?'

'I don't think so.'

He looked so uncomfortable she felt sorry for him. 'It's not your fault, Gil. She's looking for a replacement for Richard, and I guess it was inevitable that she'd latch on to you.'

Gil eyed her curiously. She so seldom mentioned Richard. 'Hey, I'm flattered. She's a lovely girl.'

Tara smiled, but even in the semi-shadow of the barn he could see how worried she was. He used to think her pale eyes were freaky; now he was fascinated by how they reflected the light, making them appear luminous at times.

'I don't know what to do,' Tara said. 'I should have been paying more attention to Jen instead of being so wrapped up in my own concerns.'

Gil watched her silently. There was so much more to this than a marriage break-up, of that he was certain. 'If it makes you feel any better, I was on another planet for at least a year after my wife died. If I hadn't had help from my parents, Jake could have disappeared for hours before I'd have even noticed he'd gone.'

That was stretching the truth a bit, but he *had* operated in a fog for a long time after Louise died.

Tara's face softened. 'What was her name?'

'Louise.'

She hesitated. 'How long has she been dead?'

'Almost fourteen years.'

'That's a long time.'

Gil nodded and hung up the bridle. 'Sometimes it feels just like yesterday.'

Tara felt ashamed. What had happened with Richard was painful and difficult, but it didn't compare to what Gil must have gone through, losing his wife so young and being left to raise a small child.

'For what it's worth, I agree that Jen's not so much infatuated as looking for a father figure,' he offered.

Tara nodded and tried to ignore the way her nose prickled and her eyes stung. 'I don't really know what to do about it. I hope she isn't bothering you?'

'Not at all; she's great. Anybody would be proud to have a kid like Jen.' Gil watched in dismay as Tara's bottom lip suddenly wobbled and she blinked furiously. 'Tara?' He started across the barn towards her.

She shook her head violently, concentrating hard on the dust coating her shiny new riding boots. Strands of pale blonde hair had escaped from the tortoiseshell clip and fallen forward to brush her cheeks. 'I've made such a mess of things,' she whispered.

Gil watched helplessly as she struggled to contain her tears. 'No, you haven't. It isn't easy.' He watched her sink her teeth into her lower lip. 'Tara—'

'Don't,' she pleaded, a sob in her voice. *'Please* don't try and make me feel better!'

Gil watched a tear slide down her cheek and was undone. He reached out and pulled her into his arms.

Tara struggled briefly before burying her face in his chest and giving in to the misery inside her, her slim body heaving against his.

Gil stared grimly at the cobwebs coating the wall of the barn opposite, wondering what the hell Richard could have done to cause her such agony. The only thing he could think of was another woman, but the notion that any man would turn his back on Tara was beyond his comprehension. Her tears soaked his T-shirt. Gil cradled her, his hands gently stroking her hair and back, trying to keep the front of his jeans from coming into contact with the front of her jodhpurs.

Tara's sobs dwindled to hiccups. She leaned wearily against Gil, her hands tangled in the sides of his T-shirt, feeling lulled by the steady thud of his heart beneath her ear and the soothing sweep of his hands up and down her back. He smelled of the laundry powder he'd used on his T-shirt and a faint whiff of deodorant. He felt warm and solid and dependable and — Tara pressed closer and her drooping lids snapped open — *sexually aroused.*

Gil caught her hips and tried to put some distance between their lower bodies. The last thing she wanted or needed at a time like this was a guy hitting on her.

Tara hesitated and stepped closer, pressing herself against him.

While Gil was trying to make sense of the messages her body was sending his — not an easy task when most of his blood was diverted away from his brain — Tara was waging a war with her conscience. It was telling her that no decent woman would recover sufficiently to be thinking about making use of what Gil had to offer, and in principle she agreed, but her principles had no control over the way her body responded to this man. Tara's crying spate hadn't only relieved her misery; it seemed to have also released her inhibitions.

Gil didn't move. He barely breathed, waiting to see what she would do next.

Reaching up, Tara took his face between her hands and kissed him.

At first Gil was too stunned to respond, but the touch of Tara's tongue against his woke his brain, which began firing off orders to the rest of his body. He caught the back of her thighs and lifted her from the ground. Tara clutched at his shoulders and hooked her legs around his waist. The sensations were so exquisite she tightened her legs and, wrenching her mouth from Gil's, began to kiss her way down his throat, dragging at the neck of his T-shirt to dip her tongue into the hollow of his shoulder bone.

When Tara made a sound of frustration because the worn old T-shirt was getting in her way, Gil said hoarsely, 'Rip it.'

She looked up at him, a shocked expression on her face.

'Dare you,' he urged.

She grabbed it in her fist and yanked. Stitches popped and the old fabric tore. 'Oh . . .' she murmured as her eyes travelled across muscle, sinew and a dusting of dark hair. Tara leaned forward and bit him on the collarbone.

Gil grunted in surprise and cupped her buttocks. Tara crossed her ankles and pressed herself against him. He could feel the tremors building in her and was backing towards the hay bales when a voice called, *'Gi-iill!! Gi-illl! Are you here, Gil?'*

He froze mid-stride.

Tara stopped sucking his neck and looked up at him, her eyes soft and unfocused.

Gil closed his eyes and groaned. 'Ah, hell! It's my mother.'

She listened without comprehension, teetering on the precipice of an orgasm. His words slowly made sense.

'W-whaat? Did you say *your mother?*'

Gil covered her mouth with his hand and nodded.

'Gil? Are you there?' called the voice from just outside the barn.

Tara leapt off Gil as if he was on fire. 'She mustn't see me!'

'Hang on, Mum! I'll be out in a moment. Wait right there,' Gil called back. He lowered his voice. 'Why don't you just bite the bullet and come meet her?'

'Are you *mad?*' She flapped her hands at him. 'Your shirt is ripped! She'll think I'm a nymphomaniac! Go away! Take her inside so I can make a run for it!'

Gil decided she was probably right. She was rumpled and tousled, her lips wet and red, and her nipples stood out against the thin white shirt like bullets. Gil wanted to howl with frustration, but suddenly he could see the funny side and his shoulders began to shake with silent laughter.

Tara was outraged. 'This *isn't* funny!' she hissed, darting glances towards the wide, shadowy doorway of the barn. She backed away into the shadows.

'Gil?' his mother called uncertainly.

Gil grabbed the back of his T-shirt and pulled it over his head. He was rewarded by a soft moan from Tara. With a final, regretful look towards her, he stepped out into the sunlight holding the bunched-up remains of his shirt at the level of his zipper.

'Hi. When did you get back? Is Dad with you?'

Tara hid until Gil had led his mother into the house before making her getaway, all but slithering along the driveway on her belly and zig-zagging down to the underpass bent at the waist like a commando. When she reached Eric's, she collapsed against the gate to Magic's paddock gasping for air, a hand flattened against her breastbone, 'What on earth was I thinking?'

Magic poked his nose over the gate to see if any titbits were on offer, retreating grumpily when there was nothing forthcoming.

Just thinking about what had happened in the barn sent Tara's heart skittering around in her chest. If his mother hadn't arrived, she knew she would be lying naked with Gil among the hay bales having torrid sex while Magnum chomped on the contents of his feed bucket.

Gil was Richard's *cousin.* He was the man living across the road who looked at Tara as if she shouldn't be allowed out without adult supervision and who always managed to be around when she made a total fool of herself, thereby confirming his opinion. Tara *was not* attracted to men who wore brown clothes three seasons out of fashion. She liked urbane, charming, witty men who could tell the difference between Armani and Hugo Boss, men like Richard — or at least, the man Richard used to be.

But Gil possessed the legendary Whitehead charm. *In spades.* His easygoing manner was even more lethal than Richard's gilded, smiling beauty, because it snuck up and blindsided the unwary. Beneath the awful clothes was a gorgeous, *fully functioning* male body, honed from years spent outdoors doing hard physical labour. Those too-brief moments spent in the barn had blown Tara's socks off. Gil Sorensen kissed like a dream. He felt wonderful, and just the thought of him made the most intimate parts of her body quiver and weep.

Unbidden, a low, sultry voice slunk into Tara's head.

I want that man . . .

Chapter 24

'Have you heard from Richard Whitehead?' Gil casually asked his mother as they shared a cup of coffee in the kitchen. Despite her abysmal timing, he was pleased to see her and had lifted her off her feet in a bear hug when he emerged from the barn.

Connie had buried her nose in his arm and sniffed ostentatiously as he walked her towards the house.

'What are you doing?'

'Nothing.' She lifted her face and beamed at him. 'Just checking you're mine.'

For a moment, Gil thought that Tara had left some trace of herself on him. His relief was short-lived when Connie frowned at his neck. 'Why are you running around half-naked? And you've got a red mark on your neck,' she said, touching it with her fingertip.

Gil brushed her hand away. 'It's a bee-sting. I ripped my shirt taking it off. Fancy a coffee?'

In the kitchen, Connie watched as he threw his shirt into the bin and grabbed a clean one from a pile of clothes on a chair. She filled Gil in on what she and his father had been doing in the months they'd been away, sitting at the wooden table in the kitchen with her elbows propped on the surface and her chin resting on the backs of her hands, watching Gil trying not to fiddle with the mark on his neck.

Connie Sorensen was fifty-nine years old, below medium height, with full breasts and a round bottom. Her dark hair was cropped short and touched with grey at the temples, and her eyes sparkled with mischief and humour. She wore three-quarter-length orange pants and a gauzy shirt patterned with lime, orange and bronze parrots over an orange sleeveless tank top. Gold hoops hung from her ears, and rings decorated most of her fingers, while an assortment of bangles clanged and rattled on her right arm. It was a family joke that Connie could never sneak up on anybody because her clanking jewellery would give her away, but Gil reflected that she could have been beating a big bass drum and he still wouldn't have noticed when he was in the barn with Tara. The touch and feel of Tara had obliterated everything else.

'Love one, dear. I'll just use the bathroom first.'

When she returned, Gil casually asked after Richard.

'No, I haven't. Why do you ask?'

He lounged against the kitchen sink, holding a coffee mug in one hand, the other buried in the front pocket of his jeans. 'He's split up with his wife.'

Connie's mouth fell open. 'No! That lovely girl, Tara? When?'

Gil told her what had happened in her absence.

She was so shocked that she didn't say anything for several moments. It took a lot to render Connie Sorensen speechless. 'Good Lord!'

Gil took a swallow of his cooling coffee.

'Eric? In *Peacehaven?*'

'Yep.'

'And Richard's wife, Tara, and his little girl *across the road?* In *Eric's house?*'

'Yep, although Jennifer isn't so little any more. She's fifteen.'

'Well, I'll be jiggered.' Connie leapt to her feet. 'I'll go over and see her right now.'

'No!' Gil said hastily. He didn't think Tara would be in the mood for a visitor so soon after what had or, more annoyingly, *hadn't* taken place in the barn. 'I'm pretty sure she said she'd be out today.'

'Oh.' Connie tilted her head to one side. 'When did you last see her?'

Gil turned to rinse his cup in the kitchen sink. 'A day or so ago. Eric asked me to keep an eye on the place and help out with the horses. Why don't you go and see Eric? He wasn't too happy last time I visited.'

'That's a good idea, sweetheart. I think I will.' Connie slid an arm through the gold handles of a large orange handbag and headed towards the back door, pausing to pat Gil on the cheek as she went by. 'Be back at three when Jake gets home. I'll do dinner. I do love you.'

Gil smiled fondly. 'Love you, too.' He glanced down at her feet and saw she was wearing orange beaded slippers in some sort of shiny fabric. Gil shook his head. Tara and his mother should get on like a house on fire if for no other reason than their shared obsession with shoes.

Connie headed towards her lime-green Honda Accord, a satisfied smile on her lips.

So the blonde she'd seen scurrying through the underpass like Rambo, and who was making her dairy farmer son smell of Trésor perfume, was Richard's ex-wife. *Bee-sting, my arse*; she knew a lovebite when she saw one. Connie had seen Tara's clumsy escape and, using the excuse of needing the bathroom, she'd hot-footed it along the hallway and, standing on the toilet lid, had shoved her head out the bathroom window just in time to see a slender blonde wearing white jodhpurs and shirt disappear through the underpass.

Climbing down from her perch, Connie had waited for a few minutes before flushing the toilet, running the tap and returning to the kitchen. On one hand, she was absolutely delighted that a woman had finally caught Gil's interest — his women in Hamilton and Auckland didn't count, although Connie wasn't supposed to know about them. But on the other hand, she was worried that Gil's attention had been caught by Richard's estranged wife. Gil didn't get *involved* with local women.

Connie started the car, waved at Gil where he stood watching her through the big dining-room window, and headed down the driveway. She'd have to warn Malcolm to make a lot of noise and take his time getting out of the car when he visited Gil's house in future, in case their son was in the barn with Tara. Connie's suspicions had been instantly aroused when he'd taken so long to come out of the barn, and she'd idly thought how nice it would be if there was a woman in his life.

She was astonished, however, when she realized that Gil really *was* in the barn with a woman. She could tell the moment he walked out of the shadowy interior into the sunshine. His short, dark hair was tousled, his shirt clutched in his hand at groin level. Although she knew her son *was* pleased to see her, Connie knew she wasn't the one to put the sparkle in his eyes. She headed towards Divine and Peacehaven Retreat, singing along to the Dixie Chicks CD Jake had given her for Mother's Day the year before. As she hummed along to 'Long Time Gone', Connie reflected that she was more than willing to forget that Tara was Richard's wife if Tara made Gil happy, but first she needed information. She needed the dirt on exactly what had ended Tara and Richard's marriage, and she needed to know if it was permanent or just a trial separation.

If anybody in Divine knew the intimate details, it would be Eric.

Malcolm Sorensen and Dick Cathcart sat with their feet propped up on opposite sides of Dick's large, untidy desk with glasses of the fine single-malt whisky Dick kept in the bottom drawer cradled in their hands. Dick kept a bottle of inferior whisky in the filing cabinet to offer people he didn't like but had to entertain. The contents of Dick Cathcart's desk and filing cabinet were part of the fabric of Divine life, and people had come to expect to be offered a tot of whisky.

Dick was fifty-eight, of average height and a solid build that was going soft around the middle. He had sparkling brown eyes and long, grizzled sideburns, a leftover from the 'seventies when they'd been jet black and sexy. Dick favoured tweed jackets and bow ties, and had the phenomenal memory and sharp wit of a seasoned journalist. Only the very brave or very stupid tried to best Dick Cathcart in a verbal exchange, which was why Barney Bigelow hated him — Dick always made him look a fool.

Malcolm Sorensen was sixty-three and an older version of Gil. He had the same calm, unassuming manner and understated charm. His greying dark hair was still thick and he had bright green eyes. Connie often said that the greying hair and green eyes made Malcolm look like a distinguished cat.

'You mean an old tom?' Mal asked in amusement.

'More like Snagglepuss,' Connie replied, sliding her arms about him to snuggle against his chest. '*My* Snagglepuss.'

Dick and Malcolm were the scourge of Simon Unwin and the Divine Town Council because of their propensity for playing elaborate practical jokes on anybody in a position of power and influence they considered fair game; and in their opinion, their vain, pompous mayor was definitely fair game. The moment word got out that Dick and Malcolm were reunited, Simon would start sweating in the mayoral office and try to find a way to slope off for a few weeks. Nobody would miss him. Elaine Selwyn ran Simon's office; Simon merely signed the papers that she put in front of him, which Barney had already vetted. Simon turned up for photo opportunities where he got to wear his mayoral chain and robes, and spent a lot of time on the nineteenth at the Divine Golf Club.

'If our illustrious mayor's brains were made of elastic they wouldn't make a set of garters for a one-legged budgie,' Malcolm had once observed.

'Yes, but isn't he fun to have around?' Dick had replied gleefully.

Simon still hadn't forgiven either of them for their April Fool's Day prank the previous year. Malcolm and Dick had placed an advert in the *Flyer* advising that the AGM of the Divine Nude Tree Climbers Association was due and that members were advised to look up their dates. The ad included a post office box number for anybody wanting to make submissions to council about the proposed ten-year plan for future tree-planting, with specific reference to the following proposal: 'That no trees with thorns be planted, that gardens be planted beneath any trees to break any falls, and, most important, that priority be given to planting evergreens as they are easier to climb.' It was signed by April F. Day, who had a Degree in Public Parking from the University of Canterbury, and copies were sent on Divine Town Council letterhead to Mayor Unwin and local councillors, among others.

Malcolm and Dick then sat back to enjoy the fallout.

An emergency meeting was called by the president of the Chamber of Commerce, and, not to be outdone, Simon called an emergency meeting of the council. It wasn't until one of the councillors wearily pointed out the date and name on the letter that Simon and the president of the Chamber of Commerce realized their error. The president had sworn a bit, but Simon still hadn't been on speaking terms with either Dick or Malcolm by the time Malcolm and Connie had embarked on their trip away.

For the past hour, Dick had been bringing Malcolm up to date on the recent goings-on in Divine, including Eric's removal to Peacehaven Retreat and the feud with Mad Marion and Barney, and Tara Whitehead's arrival in town, beginning with the story about the blowjob at the All Saints PTA meeting. Malcolm was convulsed with laughter, wiping his eyes.

'I didn't think Annabelle Archer knew what a blowjob was.'

'The only blowjob Annabelle ever gave would involve plenty of soap and bubbles,' Dick agreed. 'Rumour has it,' he continued mischievously, 'that Barney asked Gil to take care of Tara and use his influence to point her in the direction of the Waikato Expressway and Auckland. When I say "take care", Barney meant it in the biblical sense, if you get my drift.'

Malcolm was clearly amazed. 'He asked Gil to sleep with Richard's wife? My Gil?'

Dick nodded and laughed. 'Apparently Gil told Barney to take a hike. Although—' he leaned forwards to slide his glass between the piles of paper littering his desk and tug open the bottom drawer, '—providing Tara Whitehead with tea and sympathy wouldn't be a hardship by any stretch of the imagination.' Unscrewing the cap on the bottle of Glenfiddich, he splashed some into Malcolm's glass before topping up his own and settling back into his chair. 'She's a lovely-looking woman. So's her daughter, Jennifer; she and your grandson are as thick as thieves.'

Malcolm's brows rose with interest. 'I only saw Tara once, years ago. She was very pretty; full of life.'

'Hmm. I wouldn't say she looks full of life these days, but then I've only seen her from a distance. I'm not that popular with her.' Dick put down his glass and rifled among the piles on his desk. 'Have a look at that.' He handed Malcolm a clipping taken from the front page of the *Flyer*.

Malcolm looked at the photograph of Eric perched on a mobility scooter grinning at the camera while a slender blonde with high cheekbones and angry eyes shouted at him. Marion Popplewell, Bevan Sargeson and several of the residents from Peacehaven made up the rest of the group. Once he'd got over the shock of seeing Eric on a mobility scooter, Malcolm looked again at Tara. The pretty girl had grown into a beautiful woman.

'Chook Larby offered to stand in for Gil. I think he was only half-joking,' Dick said.

'Ngaire would kill him.'

There was a knock at the door and Connie came in, bangles rattling.

Dick launched himself off his chair and hurried around the desk to scoop her into a hug. 'Darling Connie! You're a sight for sore eyes!'

'Hello, Dick, love. How are you?' She smiled up at him.

'All the better for seeing you, Connie.' Dick frowned. 'You look upset. Would you like a splash of whisky?'

'No, thank you, it's a bit early for me.'

Dick gave the large enamel-faced clock on the wall beside his desk a baffled look. It was decorated in the orange and brown colours of the Divine Rugby Club and bore the words *Divine Diggers* in black italic script. He could never understand what the time of day had to do with having a drink. It wasn't as if the cap wouldn't come off the bottle until after five o'clock.

Malcolm studied Connie's pensive expression. 'What's the matter? Is there something wrong with Gil and Jake?'

'No, they're both fine. I told Gil we'd be back to see them after Jake gets home from school.' She paused. 'I've been to see Eric.'

'Did he make you listen to his Shadows records?'

'No,' Connie replied. 'He doesn't live at home any more. He's moved into Peacehaven Retreat.'

'So I've heard. Dick's been filling me in.'

Connie sighed. 'Believe me — Dick only knows half the story. Come with me and I'll tell you the rest.'

Dick stood to attention, his journalistic nose twitching. 'What did Eric tell you? I promise I won't tell a word, Connie.'

'As if!' she snorted, borrowing one of Jake's favourite phrases. 'Come on.' She urged Malcolm towards the door, calling over her shoulder, 'Tell Corrine — dinner at our house tomorrow night.'

Malcolm exchanged glances with Dick over her head, a look of resigned amusement on his face as the door closed behind them.

'Bugger!' Dick said.

Jennifer Whitehead came over while Connie and Malcolm were visiting Jake and Gil later that afternoon, and immediately offered to leave them alone so they could catch up in peace. They were all seated around the table in the garden, drinking coffee and stuffing themselves with apple turnovers.

Connie looked at Jennifer and thought to herself that she'd have to keep her eye on Jake as well. Eric's revelations about the reasons for Richard's separation from his wife had utterly shocked her and Malcolm. Connie didn't know how any woman could recover from such a devastating emotional blow, and her heart went out to Tara.

She was even more concerned about Gil's relationship with Tara, and suspected he hadn't received a letter from Richard. Connie had picked up the mail from the post office and found one for her and Malcolm among the pile. The contents made her cry. It was one of the saddest, bravest and most thoughtless letters she had ever received. Sad and brave of Richard to write it, but entirely thoughtless, because of what publicizing his decision would do to his wife and daughter. Richard had decided to come out and had given his family no choice but to follow him.

Gil saw the doubtful look on Connie's face as Jake and Jen disappeared inside the house with an apple turnover each, and tried to reassure her. 'Jen and Jake are just good friends.'

'I know,' she said. 'She's got a crush on you instead.'

Gil was put out. Why were women like that? Why did they see all the things that men didn't even notice unless they were attached to an anvil and dropped on their heads?

'Her mother knows. We've discussed it. Jen's just looking for a father figure.'

Connie pursed her lips. *Another* good reason for Gil not to get involved with Tara. She decided to change the subject. 'Has he made any progress with Melanie Larby?'

Gil considered. 'Where was he before you went away?'

'He still hadn't got up the courage to ask her out.'

Gil nodded. 'Sounds about right.'

'What's the matter with that son of yours?' Connie complained. 'Girls are tripping over themselves to go out with him and he's too shy to ask out the one he likes!'

'He's just taking his time, and I notice he's *my son* when he's done something wrong and *your grandson* when he's done something right.'

Connie ignored him. 'I blame you and your stupid *don't date Divine women* rule. You've put Jake off.'

Gil looked to his father for support, but Malcolm shrugged. He wasn't getting involved. Instead, he asked, 'Have you seen Alison?'

'Not recently,' Gil replied.

Connie brightened. 'She called me almost as soon as we got off the plane. Wasn't that nice? I'm going to see her tomorrow.'

Gil nodded.

He looked across at his mother's pensive expression, thinking she was still worrying about Jake, Jen and Melanie Larby — never dreaming that Connie was far more concerned about his own romantic life.

Chapter 25

When Gil checked his neck in the mirror and saw the lovebite Tara had given him, he was shocked. It was the first time he'd ever been given a hickey. Who would have believed prim and proper Mrs Whitehead would be the one to do it?

He suspected Tara would try to avoid him, and if she couldn't, she'd pretend the incident in the barn hadn't happened. He had no intention of letting her do either. She reminded him of a nervous horse ready to bolt, but he was very good at soothing frightened or nervous animals, good at slowly building up their confidence until they were doing exactly what he wanted. It perplexed Gil that a sensual, intelligent woman like Tara had such low self-esteem, but he wasn't surprised when almost a week went by without her arranging another riding lesson.

'How's your mother?' he asked Jen casually.

'She was really sore after that lesson you gave her. I think she decided she's never going to be any good at riding.'

Five days after the riding lesson, Gil saddled Magnum and rode over to Eric's house. It was October. The days were bright with sunshine, and summer seemed just around the corner, but for the last few days a sudden cool wind had blown up from the South Island, reminding them all that Mother Nature could be fickle.

Gil's only concession to the drop in temperature was to change his shorts for jeans. As he rode through the underpass, he saw Tara come out of the round barn further up the race, wearing a thick, fleecy blue sweatshirt and blue jeans. He was glad she'd got the message that white jeans and farms don't mix.

She watched as he rode towards her and stopped Magnum beside the grey corrugated-iron barn.

Gil dipped his chin in greeting. 'Morning.'

'Hello,' Tara replied warily and patted Magnum on the neck.

The silence stretched between them.

'I decided it'd be a good idea for you to keep Magnum over here,' he said.

Tara looked baffled. 'Why? What am I going to do with him?'

'Ride him.'

She shook her head. 'No, I don't think that's a good idea.'

'Why not? I said I'd help you.'

Gil dismounted and led Magnum towards the barn.

Tara scuttled after him. 'But I don't want to learn to ride! I don't like it.'

'That's funny,' he mused. 'I thought you did. In fact, I thought you were a natural.'

Tara watched in mounting frustration as Gil replaced Magnum's bridle with a blue halter she hadn't noticed he was carrying. 'Why are you doing this? I *don't want* to learn to ride!'

He stripped the saddle and blanket from the horse's back. 'If you're going to make a success of this business, you need to learn as much as you can about horses. Now stop whining and help me put this gear away in the barn.'

Tara glowered. Perhaps what he was saying *did* make sense and maybe she *was* behaving like a brat, but the sight of him after so many days of wanting to see him, of lying in bed at night reliving those moments in his barn and wanting to run across the road and finish what they'd started, had unnerved Tara. It had been a lot easier when he was brown and boring. Why couldn't he stay brown and boring?

As he released Magnum into a nearby paddock, Tara wondered

irritably how he could make an old blue T-shirt and threadbare jeans look so good.

Gil handed her the bridle and walked ahead of her into the barn, carrying the saddle. She dragged her heels. Why couldn't he have love handles? She wanted flaws. She *needed* flaws. Stepping into the shadowy interior of the barn, Tara ploughed straight into Gil's back.

He turned and caught her. 'You OK?'

She grabbed his shoulder and the neck of his shirt dipped to reveal the red mark on his throat. 'Did *I* do that?'

'Pretty sure it was you. I haven't had anybody else biting my neck lately.'

Tara watched as Gil hooked the saddle on to one of the racks. It infuriated her that he remained so unruffled.

'Where are your brown overalls?' she demanded angrily.

He regarded her quizzically. 'I thought you didn't like my overalls.' There was no making sense of the woman. 'I decided to dazzle you with my sartorial elegance.'

Tara stared silently at him, taking in his broad shoulders and lean waist, thinking to herself that if he really wanted to dazzle her he'd forget the clothes.

'You don't seem very grateful,' Gil said. 'I've gone to all the trouble of bringing Magnum over to you—'

'I don't want him!'

'—unsaddling him and putting him in the paddock—'

'I don't want him in my paddock!'

'—offering to teach you how to ride—'

Tara was about to say he could stick his riding lessons, but something in Gil's voice told her that the conversation had taken an interesting turn and the riding lessons he was talking about didn't involve a horse. She searched his face for clues. What she saw made her toes curl inside her flowery gumboots.

'You're — you're trying to *seduce me?*' Her voice rose in disbelief.

He smiled his one-cornered smile. 'That's the general idea.'

Tara felt as if she was standing in front of a woodburner with the door open. Gil Sorensen was a problem, a big, beautiful problem. She desperately wanted to finish what they'd started in his barn. The problem was that letting him inside her body would allow him inside her mind, and then Gil would find out there was something fundamentally wrong with her as a woman.

'I'm no good at any of that,' Tara said miserably.

He was incredulous. 'Who the hell told you that?'

'The other day was just a — a —'

'An act?'

'No!' As if!

'An aberration? That's a fluke, if you didn't—'

'I know what an aberration is, you smart-arse!'

Gil's smile was tinged with relief. He could handle her anger and smart mouth better than the whipped, sad look she'd had in her eyes.

'Tara, stop making this so damned hard.' He gathered her against him and kissed her.

For a second Tara was too surprised to react, but then it was as if they'd taken up right where they'd left off in the barn. She greedily kissed him back. Gil rested his forehead against Tara's, his chest heaving. 'For a woman who doesn't think she's any good at this, you catch on pretty quick.'

'I shouldn't be doing this!' She had her hand up inside his T-shirt, stroking his chest.

'Stop trying to rationalize everything,' Gil lowered his head and kissed the pulse beating frantically at the base of her throat.

Tara closed her eyes and moaned. She tipped back her head, purring like a cat until she realized that Gil was giving her a hickey. She grabbed his hair. 'Stop that!'

'Ow! Why?' Gil said against her neck. 'You didn't hear me complaining, even when my mother spotted it.'

'Your *mother* spotted it?'

Gil began to laugh. He ducked when Tara took a swipe at him and caught her wrists, trapping her hands between his. 'I forgive you. I told her it was a bee-sting.'

'A *bee-sting?* Was that the best you could do?'

He looked offended. 'I wasn't exactly thinking clearly. And neither were you, judging by your Rambo impersonation as you ran down the hill. What were you dodging? Snipers?'

'Ha! Ha!' She gave Gil a shove and was disappointed when he let her push him away.

He went and sat on some hay bales. 'Why don't you tell me what you *do* want me to do? You can call the shots.'

Tara stared. 'You don't mean that.'

'Yes, I do.'

'You'll do whatever I want you to?' She looked sceptical.

Gil spread his knees and folded his arms, prepared to wait her out, although he wasn't feeling nearly as confident as he looked.

Tara replayed her recent fantasies. She didn't think he'd go along if she told him she wanted to see him naked and touch him. The thought of making herself physically available to a man other than Richard, and of him finding out what a failure she was as a woman, made Tara want to run and hide. She couldn't do it — she couldn't allow a man to get close enough to see her as she really was, especially not a man as observant as Gil. But while she wanted *him* very, very much, she was equally sure he would soon lose interest once he realized how little she offered in return. She pulled herself back from her reverie. It was time to get this charade over with.

'OK,' she said briskly. 'Take your clothes off.'

Gil rose slowly to his feet. 'Does this arrangement work both ways?'

'No.'

Tara waited impatiently for him to walk out.

Gil reached over his head and pulled off his T-shirt. He sat back down on the hay and began to remove his boots and socks.

Tara stared.

He stood to unzip his jeans and slid them downwards to reveal heavily muscled legs. Tara decided Sian's remark about him being able to rise to the trot for hours was probably true. When Gil hooked his thumbs into the elastic waistband of his black underwear and began to slide them off, Tara panicked.

'No! Stop!'

He looked up. 'Stop?'

'Yes! I mean *no!* I mean . . .'

Gil took a deep breath. 'What's it going to be? Yes or no?'

She looked at the hard ridge of flesh under his briefs and wet her lips. 'OK.'

He lowered the briefs.

'Stop!'

'For crissakes, Tara! Make up your mind!'

'I'm sorry! I'm sorry! I *really* am!'

Why couldn't she be more like her sister? Kim would've had Gil naked and stretched out on the hay by now while she played Ride 'em Farmer. Faced with a man as — Tara glanced at the front of Gil's briefs — ready for action as Gil Sorensen, Kim wouldn't have wasted any time debating the ethics of the situation.

'Tara?' Gil's voice was strained. 'What exactly is the problem? It isn't as if you haven't seen one before.'

'I know that! It's — it's just that once I see *yours* I won't be able to change my mind,' she replied nervously.

The green flecks in his eyes deepened. 'I'm not going to force you!'

'Oh Gil, I know *that!*' Tara cried. 'I know you wouldn't hurt me.'

At least, not physically.

'What I meant was I don't think *I'll* be able to stop.'

She went to him and laid a hand tentatively on his chest. 'I've been with the same man for almost twenty years.'

Gil tried to concentrate on what she was saying, but it was difficult when she was touching him. The confusion in her voice made him wanted to hug her and tell her everything would be all right. He understood how she was feeling, recalled the pain and self-loathing he'd felt the first time he'd slept with a woman after Louise died. They both needed to lighten up a little.

Gil caught her hand and raised it to his mouth. 'Tara?' He gently bit the tip of one finger.

'Yes?' she replied faintly, watching his mouth and her finger.

'Promise you'll be gentle with me.'

Tara began to laugh.

He touched his underwear. 'Is it OK to take these off now?'

'Yes.'

He dropped them on top of the rest of his clothes.

Tara stared. He was beautiful. And, for the moment, he was all hers. She crossed her arms over her tingling breasts and pressed her thighs together, her usual good sense overridden by pure lust at the sight of him. For so many years she'd been a good wife, mother, daughter, sister and friend. Tara was sick and tired of being good.

A tiny patch of sunlight found its way between the roof and the wall of the barn and fell on Gil. He waited for her silently, his hands hanging loosely by his thighs, watching intently as the expressions chased each other across her face — incredulity, passion and, finally, *hunger.*

'I can't believe you actually did it,' she murmured.

'I'm a man of my word,' Gil replied gravely and she grinned.

He was charmed by her naïvety. What man would turn down the chance to get naked for a woman like Tara?

'Does *Take your clothes off, I want to see you naked* mean something different in Auckland?' He gestured to his jeans. 'Because I can put them back on if you want.'

Tara grabbed the jeans and threw them across the barn. 'I don't think so!'

Gil laughed.

She wanted to touch him all over, to sink her teeth into his muscles and see if they were as hard as they looked. If he ever gave up dairy farming he'd be a shoo-in as a male stripper.

Tara noticed his expectant look and her heart sank. 'I suppose you want me to take my clothes off, too?'

'Do you want to?'

She shook her head and her ponytail swung from side to side.

Gil swallowed his disappointment. The ponytail and those wide, worried grey eyes made her look about eighteen. He wanted her to enjoy what happened between them, which meant he needed to keep a tight rein on his libido and let Tara continue to set the pace. *I deserve a medal*, he thought.

'Keep them on, then.' He held his hands out at his sides and wiggled his brows. 'I'm all yours.' A gust of wind suddenly found its way through the gap in the roof and he shivered.

Tara felt guilty. 'You're cold.'

'Warm me up.'

She looked down and arched a brow. "You look pretty warmed up to me.'

'My motor's only idling, but you're welcome to take a test drive.'

Tara was startled into laughter. She walked behind him and ran her palms across his shoulders and down his arms to his hands. Gil shuddered in response. Tara slid her fingers between his and clasped his hands. As his fingers closed around hers, Tara stepped closer and pressed her lips against his shoulder blade.

Gil arched his back and his head dropped backwards, inhaling deeply as Tara gently bit him.

'You're beautiful.' She let go of one of his hands to run her fingers down the shallow indentation of his spine.

He didn't answer. He couldn't speak, could barely even breathe.

'Mr Sorenson,' she murmured, 'you've got great buns.'

Gil clenched his teeth. She was *killing* him. 'Promise you won't stick me in the arse again with those nails.'

Tara lightly drew pictures on him with the tip of her finger. 'Are you planning on throwing me into a wheelbarrow?'

'Not today.'

'You'll behave yourself?'

'Uh huh,' he nodded jerkily. 'Will you?'

'No.'

He groaned as Tara rose on tiptoe to stroke her tongue upwards along his shoulder blade. Gil didn't know how much more he could take before he embarrassed himself like a randy schoolboy. He was surprised when Tara suddenly pushed him backwards on the hay bales and straddled his thighs.

She risked a peep at Gil. He gazed back steadily, smiling faintly. Tara blushed and looked away, feeling his leg quivering against her as he laughed silently. When she turned away to glare at the barn wall, he began to laugh out loud. Tara took a half-hearted swing at him. 'Oh shut up!'

Gil caught her hand and flipped her over on her back. He rolled on top of her and, catching her other hand, gently stretched them both above her head.

'Get off me!'

He released her hands, to trace circles on the insides of her wrists with his thumbs. 'Tell me why you're feeling so guilty?'

'I'm not.'

Gently he stroked her cheek. 'Liar—'

Tara shifted so that their hips were aligned and caressed his butt. He really did have a gorgeous bum.

Gil tried to ignore the stirrings in his groin. 'What's the matter? Were you thinking about Richard?'

Tara stopped stroking. 'No.'

Gil was silent, knowing he'd trespassed into a no-go area. While he didn't want to talk about Richard, he hated the way Richard seemed to hover between them like a spectre.

'How long was it after Louise died before you . . .'

Gil propped his cheek on his hand. 'About two years.'

'Two years! I haven't even lasted one!'

He watched her through half-closed eyes, amused by the look on her face. He sucked in a breath as her hands closed around him and reared up off the hay. 'Shit!'

Tara pushed him onto his back again and sat up to release her hair. It rained down around her shoulders like pale silk. She began to kiss her way down Gil's chest, and when she reached his groin she blew softly. She was overwhelmed by his patience and kindness — most men would have been trying to get her naked and on her back by now. But she also wanted this for herself. She just hoped she didn't botch it.

Gil sank his hands into the hay and groaned. Tara wasn't nearly as experienced as he'd expected, but what she lacked in finesse she more than made up for with enthusiasm. When she eventually sat up, Gil felt as if he'd been wrung out like a dishcloth, his body humming with pleasure and his mind wandering drunkenly in a sexual haze.

Tara climbed off him to sit on her heels in the hay. Gil watched as she delicately dabbed the corners of her mouth with a fingertip, first one side then the other. He could tell by the way she avoided his eyes that she was feeling embarrassed and uncertain, and he was swamped by an unexpected wave of tenderness.

Tara was wondering if she was more like Kim than she'd realized. She hardly knew Gil, but that hadn't stopped her behaving like a brazen hussy.

Gil decided to take a chance. 'This isn't Monopoly, Tara. You don't pass go and collect two hundred dollars for being celibate the longest.'

Her face cleared.

He didn't know what to make of her. Any other woman would have kneed him in the groin. 'Do you think I should put Glenys Tweedie and Annabelle Archer straight?' Gil asked.

'Straight?' She frowned. 'About what?'

'About where you *did* give me a blowjob.'

When she went to bed that night, Tara couldn't stop thinking about what had happened in the barn. She didn't regret it — well only if she let the sanctimonious, perfect Tara out to shake her finger, *tsk tsk*, and generally be a pain in the bum. Having a fit, virile, gorgeous man spread-eagled naked in a hay barn would probably rate pretty highly in a lot of women's fantasies, right up there with the visit from the hunky plumber with the well-equipped tool-belt.

Tara had loved being in charge, had adored calling the shots and watching Gil come apart. She'd been about to take her clothes off when Gil suddenly checked his watch and sat up.

'Got a meeting with the stock agent in five minutes,' he announced, pulling on his clothes.

'Is that it?' Tara looked pointedly at the erection he was trying to zip back inside his jeans. She had an itch that only Gil could scratch. The look on his face told her that he knew it, but wasn't about to help her out — at least not right now.

'That's entirely up to you, surfer girl.' Gil kissed the tip of her nose, smiled and strolled out of the barn.

Tara threw a boot at the door. 'Bastard!'

It was a while before she calmed down enough to figure out that Gil was telling her that he was leaving it up to her to decide where, when and even *if* things would go any further. While she was touched by Gil's consideration, Tara baulked at demanding he have sex with her. She was a fairly traditional girl when it came to sex — she liked a shared arrangement, and quite enjoyed being chased.

Apparently Gil expected her to do the chasing.

Chapter 26

Two mornings after the barn incident, Tara got up as usual, made breakfast for Jen, packed her lunch and waved her off to catch the school bus.

She felt too nervous to eat anything, and instead filled the bath with scented bubbles and shaved her legs before exfoliating every inch of her body and rubbing scented lotion into her skin. Tara washed and blowdried her hair until it gleamed, before twisting it into a loose knot on the top of her head and securing it with golden combs, leaving tendrils to brush her cheeks and the back of her neck. She dug out a pale gold, almost transparent silk bra embroidered with tiny lavender flowers, and a matching thong, and added a pair of sheer stockings with lacy tops that hugged her thighs and didn't need a suspender belt to keep them up.

Tara slid on the saffron high heels with their saucy ankle chains and stood before the long cheval mirror in her bedroom. Her eyes looked huge and scared. She worried that all the weight she had lost since the break-up made her look like a scarecrow in high heels, but there wasn't a lot she could do about that. And besides, once she was flat on her back would it really matter? Turning away from the mirror she reached for a deep yellow coat with a wide collar, full skirt, and a belt that cinched tightly around her waist. It matched the saffron sandals perfectly.

Tara checked her watch. Nine o'clock. Jake and Jen would be at school and, from what Jen had told her of Gil and Jake's daily routine, Gil would have finished milking and be eating his breakfast while reading the morning paper. She sprayed her favourite Trésor perfume behind her ears, on her pulse points, between her breasts and on the inside of each thigh. A dab of clear lip gloss and touch of mascara, and she was ready. She looked out the window and saw that a light rain had begun to fall. She frowned.

It was too bad. She couldn't chicken out now.

Five minutes later she reached Gil's house, her hips swaying sinuously from side to side as she glided along on the spiky heels of the saffron sandals, the gold chains bouncing against the backs of her ankles with each step.

Gil was sitting at the dining-room table drinking a cup of tea with the newspaper spread out before him, the remnants of his and Jake's breakfast strewn about. He was chewing some toast and trying to concentrate on the paper, but his mind kept filling with images of Tara sprawled in the hay. Gil wasn't sure how long he could wait for her to make a move without bursting a blood vessel. He didn't know how the hell he'd managed to walk away when she'd obviously wanted to have sex, but somehow he had. While his brain told him he'd done the right thing, other parts of his anatomy strongly disagreed.

As if on cue, he suddenly saw Tara through the big picture window beside the dining table, striding along the driveway like a bloody model on a catwalk. She was wearing a short yellow coat belted around her waist that ended at mid-thigh, revealing her legs as she tripped along on a pair of high heels. Gil's mouth went dry, the toast suddenly feeling like a wad of flannel. Nobody wore a pair of high heels like Tara Whitehead.

She spotted him through the window and waved and gestured for him to stay where he was, indicating she would let herself in. Gil was surprised — she'd never been inside before — but he obediently sat back down, listening as the front door opened and closed and the tap-tap of her heels on the granite tiles came closer.

'Gil?' She sounded nervous.

He took a gulp from Jake's water glass and forced down the toast. 'Through here, in the dining room. Just keep coming,' he called back hoarsely.

Tara appeared in the doorway.

Gil put the glass on the table and slowly sat back in his chair, feeling like he'd been cow-kicked in the gut.

She was covered in a fine sheen of moisture from the rain, making her porcelain skin appear pearly. She'd done something with her hair so that it looked as if it was about to fall down from the loose knot on the top of her head. Her eyes looked huge and her pink mouth vulnerable. The yellow coat didn't even deserve the name. It was even shorter than Gil had first thought, flirty, and never intended to keep the wearer dry judging by the dark patches of moisture staining the shoulders. His gaze dipped to her legs covered in pale, silky-looking stockings. *Please, God, if you are a man*, Gil prayed, *don't let them be pantyhose*. Her yellow shoes, which matched the silly little coat, were held in place by a strip of yellow leather across her toes and slim gold chains around her ankles.

Gil's heart pounded against his chest. 'Hi.'

Tara clutched the lapels of her coat. 'Hi.' A tendril of blonde hair slid from the top of her head to join some strands in front of her right ear. She looked as nervous as hell.

Gil frowned. 'Are you OK?'

She nodded again and looked about the room. His framed university degree caught her attention. 'Is that yours?'

He barely spared it a glance. 'Uh huh. Was there something you wanted?'

'Oh. Yes.' She took a deep breath and unfastened the belt and big yellow buttons on the front of the coat.

Gil watched as inch by inch more and more pale creamy skin was revealed. He wondered if he was dreaming or if he had died and gone to heaven, but the frantic beat of his heart told him that this was real.

Tara took another deep breath, closed her eyes and pushed the coat from her shoulders. It fell onto the carpet behind her.

Gil felt as if his lungs had seized. '*Jesus Christ*,' he whispered hoarsely.

Tara opened her eyes and swallowed. 'No, just me. I thought it only polite after what you did for me the other day.'

He got slowly to his feet and walked over to her. 'One striptease deserves another?'

She laughed shakily. 'Something like that.'

'Hell. Wish I'd known sooner,' he said unsteadily.

She was the answer to any red-blooded male's fantasies, and far more gorgeous than he'd dreamed. The pale yellow bra and thong were so sheer they revealed more than they concealed. Her breasts spilled over the edge of the low-cut bra, and tiny satin straps rode high on her hips. And she was wearing stockings.

Gil walked slowly around her, smiling a little as he saw the blush staining her fair, smooth skin. She fidgeted, looking everywhere but at him. Gil took his sweet time, figuring she owed him for the time he'd spent buck-naked in her barn while she checked him out from every angle. He smoothed a hand across one of her buttocks and she jumped.

'Do you want to check my teeth?' Tara demanded testily, twin red banners painting her cheekbones. This was a lot harder than she'd expected. She thought she might die of embarrassment.

'Maybe later,' Gil replied. He reached out to cup her breast, lifting its weight in his palm, and stroked his thumb across the silky fabric covering her nipple.

Tara gasped and squirmed. 'It's raining. I got wet.'

He looked into her eyes and murmured, 'How wet?'

Her face lit up even more. 'I — I —'

Gil continued to stroke her. 'Don't lose your nerve now, surfer girl. I'm counting on you.'

His taunt strengthened Tara's wavering resolve. He was toying with her, not just physically but mentally. She launched herself at him, taking satisfaction from the look of surprise on his face as she knocked him backwards onto the dining-room table, sending a river of tea across the newspaper.

Tara looked down at him through narrowed eyes. 'Take your clothes off.'

Gil captured her hands. 'I believe this time it's my turn.'

He sat Tara on the edge of the table and stripped off her bra and thong while she squirmed, finally letting go when her thong got caught up on the little gold chains at her ankles. Pulling Tara to her feet, he knelt to untangle the scrap of yellow silk, lifting first one foot and then the other free, and then stroked his hands up the outside of her thighs. He just about expired on the spot when he looked up at the picture she made standing naked above him.

When Tara tried to take off her shoes Gil stopped her. 'Uh uh, not those.' He touched the lace at the top of her stocking. 'Or these.'

'OK.' Her embarrassment had turned to excitement. 'Could you — uh — hurry up please, Gil?'

He stripped off his clothes.

Tara flung herself at him again, wrapping her arms about his neck and her legs about his waist. 'Finally . . .' she sighed, kissing him.

Gil was lost. Her skin was incredible, like the softest silk, but the need to cup her buttocks to keep her in place limited what he could get to. A tiny particle of his brain reminded him that at any moment somebody might walk or drive up to the house and see them through the dining-room window. It was clear that foreplay wasn't going to be a part of the equation; they both wanted one another too much. Still kissing her, he carried her from the dining room into the wide, light-filled hallway that led to the bedrooms and bathrooms at the other end of the house.

Tara was only vaguely aware that they were moving. With each step Gil took, the tip of his penis bounced against the inside of her thigh. She wriggled and lunged, trying to impale herself, but Gil tightened his grip and held her in place. When Tara persisted, he slapped her smartly on the bottom.

'Ow!' She reared back and glared at him. 'Why'd you do that?'

'Condom.'

She jabbed him in the hip with the heel of her shoe. 'Get a move on!'

As soon as they reached the bedroom, Gil dropped Tara unceremoniously on top of the duvet and wrenched the bedside drawer open so roughly that it fell on to the carpet, spilling its contents. Swearing, Gil got down on his hands and knees to sift through the mess. His fingers closed over a foil packet and he climbed back on to the bed to open it. Getting to her knees, Tara tried to help. Gil brushed her hands aside. 'Less haste, more speed, sweetheart.'

He fell between her thighs, tumbling her backwards into the pillows and catching his weight on his palms at the last moment. Trust Tara to be demanding. What surprised Gil was how much he liked it.

Tara lifted her hips, lunged at him and missed yet again. Gil was torn between lust and laughter. She mewled with frustration and tried again, this time finding her target and yelping a little at the roughness of his entry.

Gil's laughter died. He squeezed his eyes shut and clenched his jaw. She felt like heaven. He opened his eyes and looked down at her.

Tara gazed back, feeling the weight of him pressing her into the mattress and seeing the tension in his jaw and the intensity of his dark eyes. She was suddenly swamped with grief as Richard inexplicably intruded into her thoughts. Instead of savouring the heavenly sensation of Gil deep inside her, filling and stretching her, memories of sharing this intimacy with her husband brought tears to her eyes.

Gil watched the conflicting emotions chasing one another across Tara's face and knew she was thinking of Richard. Disappointment pierced him. He was certain he didn't have it wrong this time. 'Do you want me to stop?' he asked in a low voice.

She swallowed a sob. 'Yes — no — *I don't know!'*

He began to withdraw from her body.

Tara wrapped her legs around his waist and held him in place. 'Don't!' she whispered imploringly. 'Please . . .'

Please make me feel whole again.

'You're sure?' Gil asked.

Tara nodded and a tear spilled on to her cheek.

He stroked it away with his thumb. 'Old memories?'

She nodded again, her lower lip wobbling like a child's.

Gil rested his forehead against hers and looked into her teary eyes. 'If it's any help, I know how you feel.'

Tara sniffed. 'Does it get better?'

'Yes,' he smiled. 'Remember, Tara: it's only sex. It's not the same.'

She smiled back and the guilt receded. Tara squirmed a little under Gil's weight and caught her breath at the friction it created between their bodies. *'Oh!'* she moaned softly, her eyes drifting shut. She did it again. *'Ooohhh!'*

Gil took over. If he let her carry on bumping and grinding, it would be all over in no time and he wanted to savour every single moment of her. The room reverberated with the sound of their moans, gasps and breathless laughter. Gil thought fleetingly that it was just as well they lived in the country — he never would have guessed that cool, haughty Tara would be so vocal, or how much he would enjoy listening to her.

She held nothing back. If something pleased her, Tara let Gil know, and she was quick to notice what he liked. Sian had been right: Gil could rise to the trot for hours — at least it seemed that way. He kept up a steady, relentless rhythm until Tara was writhing beneath him, so desperate for release that she pounded him on the shoulder and gasped, *'N-now!!'*

He picked up the pace and Tara hurtled over the edge, lightning bolts of sensation exploding between her legs and outwards in slow, languorous waves.

Gil hovered above her, eyes closed, head tipped back and mouth grim as he moved one last time. His face contorted and his body shook.

Tara caught her breath as a couple more lightning bolts zapped her, and thought how beautiful he was. Gil collapsed against her, breathing raggedly, and Tara's breath whooshed from her lungs. He quickly levered himself upwards again. 'Sorry!'

'It's all right.' She tugged him back down and nestled against him.

'I'm not too heavy?'

Tara tucked her face into his shoulder. 'You're just right.'

He smiled; inexplicably pleased by her answer and the bashful way she'd said it. Tara moved and Gil was reminded of how small she was compared with him. He rolled to his side, pulling her against his chest. She made a sound of protest.

'It'll look suspicious if they find you suffocated in my bed,' he said.

Tara chuckled and snuggled against him.

Gil looked down at her face. Her eyes were closed. Strands of her long, fine, silvery hair were caught amongst his chest hair. He was fascinated by the contrast between them, not just the obvious differences between female and male — as if *those* weren't spectacular enough — but also by how pale her skin was compared with his olive complexion. Blue veins were visible just beneath Tara's skin whereas Gil's jutted above his, making a long ridged highway down the inside of his arm from his biceps to his wrist.

Tara was falling asleep. Gil rubbed his cheek gently across the top of her head, feeling her breasts rising and falling and her warm, slow breaths against his chest. He should be out on the farm. There was a blocked drain he needed to clear, but it could wait. Gil couldn't recall the last time he had climbed back into his bed in the middle of the morning . . .

Suddenly he could.

The last time had been when Louise was alive. Gil would return to the house when he'd finished the milking, and Lou would have the table set and breakfast ready and they'd sit together eating and chatting, and sometimes if they got lucky and Jake obliged by having a morning nap they'd climb back into the very bed he was lying in now and make love. The bed had been a wedding present from Louise's parents. Gil hadn't been able to bring himself to part with it for a bigger, more comfortable one, but he'd just made love to another woman in it — and not just any woman but his cousin's wife.

A framed photo of Louise holding Jake, taken a few weeks before she died, stood on a chest of drawers opposite the foot of the bed.

Don't look! Gil's mind urged. But he couldn't seem to stop himself. He turned his head and saw Louise's sweet face and laughing brown eyes. He flinched.

I can't remember how her skin felt! Gil thought desperately, his hands falling away from Tara's nakedness. *I've forgotten how she smelt!* He inhaled the unique scent of Tara mixed with sex. Gil struggled to recall Louise's voice, sweat breaking out in a fine film on his body as he tried and failed. He stared hard at her photo, frozen in time and forever young, and was filled with self-loathing. He had never brought a woman to this bed; never brought a woman home to the house he had built for Louise but never shared with her.

Tara stirred in his arms and frowned up at him, blinking. 'Gil?' His body was strung as tight as number-eight fencing wire, his attention directed to something at the end of the bed.

He suddenly released her, almost flinging her away as if he couldn't bear to touch her, and climbed from the bed.

Tara sat up, pushing hair from her eyes. 'Gil? What is it?'

He scooped his clothes from the floor. 'Nothing.' He thrust his leg into his jeans without bothering with his underwear.

Tara watched him, feeling confused. 'Where's the fire?' she joked awkwardly.

'Nowhere.' He dragged the jeans up his hips and reached for the zipper. 'I haven't got time to lie around in bed all day. I've got a farm to run.'

She gazed at him in bewilderment. What had she done? What was wrong? A few moments ago he had been cradling her against him, and now — well, now she felt like a tart being shown the door. She bit her lip to keep from crying as humiliation and betrayal flooded her. When would she learn? She *would not* let a man take away any more of her self-esteem and pride. She slid from the bed, taking the sheet with her, feeling stupid in her stockings and — dear Lord! — she still had her shoes on!

Gil watched her try to hide her nakedness from him and felt like the lowest form of human life. He wanted to explain, but he didn't know where to begin.

'Tara . . .'

Tara sank her teeth into her bottom lip, biting hard on it to keep from bursting into tears or screaming at him. 'Thanks for the shag,' she said and fled.

Gil let her go, so filled with self-loathing that he felt physically sick. His guilt and hang-ups weren't Tara's fault.

The sound of the front door slamming snapped him from his inertia.

He ran to the dining room and nearly fell flat on his face when his feet tangled in the sheet Tara had taken from his bed. Bracing his hands on the windowsill above his head, he watched as a flash of saffron yellow disappeared down the driveway towards the underpass, and digging his fingers into the wood he bellowed at the ceiling.

His bare foot brushed against something. On the carpet lay one of the golden combs he recalled sliding from Tara's hair. Gil picked it up and wrapped his fingers around it. He needed to talk to her and explain, but he wasn't up to the job right now. How could he explain when he didn't entirely understand his feelings himself?

'Shit ...' He pounded the heel of his hand against the wood. 'Shit . . . shit . . . *shit!*'

Chapter 27

It would have been easy to sit down and howl like a baby, but Tara deliberately cultivated her anger, nurturing it into a seething maelstrom that scared her battered self-esteem and lacerated feelings into a tiny corner of her mind where she slammed the door shut on them. She *would not* let any man break her — especially not another Whitehead. She'd been a fool. She'd fallen for Gil's nice-guy act, for his unexpected kindness and understanding, never realizing that when he said it was only sex he meant exactly that.

Tara filled the bathtub and ruthlessly scrubbed all trace of Gil Sorensen from her skin. She had just finished dressing when the phone rang. Tara sped into the kitchen with murder in her eyes. If Gil was the caller she would run back to his house and skewer his balls to the wall with Eric's pitchfork. Snatching up the phone she shouted, 'What?!'

'Tara? It's — uh — Rona from Superior Services. I'm just calling to remind you your shift begins in fifteen minutes.'

'Great,' Tara said through gritted teeth. *'Excellent!!'*

Rona hesitated. 'Are you OK?'

You bet I am, Tara thought. She was just in the mood to abuse a man — any man. 'Fire away!' she urged Rona. 'Bring 'em on! Go for it! The more the merrier.'

Tara balefully eyed the kitchen counters, imagining all the things she could do to Gil Sorensen's studly body. Toast his balls. Microwave his dick. Stick his clever tongue in a blender and feed it back to him as a health drink.

The phone rang.

Tara grabbed it. 'What?!'

'Mistress,' a voice whispered, 'I've been a very, *very* bad boy.'

'What the hell is the matter with you?' she snarled, pacing like a caged lioness, picturing Gil's body parts whirring and frying in and on various kitchen appliances. 'Haven't you got anything better to do than call up strange women and pant over the phone at them? GO AWAY!'

She slammed down the phone, kicked one of the kitchen units and . . . clapped a hand to her mouth as she realized what she'd just done. She'd just hung up on her client.

Tara was certain that wasn't in the training manual.

Five minutes later, the phone rang again.

She looked at it and chewed a nail. It rang and rang and rang. Eric didn't have an answering machine and Tara was too mean to buy one. The phone eventually stopped ringing. Tara's mobile began to ring instead. She sidled towards it. The service did not have her mobile number. Pressing the phone to her ear, she said tentatively, 'Hello?'

'Tara, *darling*,' Sian purred.

Tara closed her eyes and held her breath. She was going to get the sack.

'Tara, do you remember the golden rule I talked about on your training day?' asked Sian sweetly.

'Ah . . . keep the client on the phone as long as possible.'

'That's right! Well done!' Sian sounded as delighted as if Tara was nine and had just got all her spelling homework right. 'Because you get paid for every *minute* you keep the caller on the line, don't you? And so it follows that the more *minutes* they spend talking to you, the more *money* you'll make, doesn't it?'

'Yes, Sian.'

'So a thirteen-second conversation isn't going to do an awful lot for your bank balance, is it, Tara?'

'No, Sian.'

'It won't buy you so much as a blade of grass in Remuera, will it, darling? Let alone that nice big house with the swimming pool and tennis court you have your heart set on?'

'I'm sorry, Sian,' Tara mumbled. 'I'll resign at once.'

'Oh no, you won't!' Sian said tartly. 'Whatever you did in that oh-so-brief space of time absolutely thrilled the client. He thought you were wonderful and plans to recommend Mistress Fury to all his friends. He wants to call back.'

'He — he does?'

'*Yes.* So find somewhere comfortable and settle in for a nice *long* bitch at him. And if you set your mind to it, you should be able to keep him on the line for at least an hour. Now pull your finger out and remember we want quality *and quantity*, Tara. OK?'

'OK, Sian.'

There was a pause.

'What's wrong? Has something happened to Jennifer?'

'No. She's fine. She's at school.'

'So it's you.' Sian paused again. 'What's wrong, Tara?'

Tara sighed. 'Nothing I can't handle, Sian.'

'It's a man, isn't it?'

'Why does everything have to be about men?' Tara's defensive tone gave the game away.

'So I'm right.' Sian's manner softened. 'Do you want to give today a miss?'

'No.' Tara pinched the bridge of her nose when it stung with suppressed tears. 'I need the money. One of my regulars calls today.'

'Oh yes, Nial the knitter.'

Nial was a closet knitter, taught by his mother as a child, much to his now-deceased father's disgust. He went into detailed descriptions of what he planned to knit, including the colour, pattern and type of wool. At first Tara didn't have a clue what to say to him, until Nial mentioned the colours he had in mind for a Fair Isle jumper — fuchsia, black and sunshine yellow.

Tara was appalled. 'Tell me you're joking.'

'No, Mistress! That would be rude!'

'So will that jumper if you put those three colours together! What's wrong with you? Are you colour-blind?'

Nial was in heaven. He'd never had anybody take so much interest in his knitting before, and Mistress Fury was so wonderfully bossy. He often called wearing only a hat, gloves, scarf and socks.

'All right,' Sian said briskly. 'I'll allow you to speak to Nial, but the other caller will have to wait for another day.'

'You can't do that, Sian! He might not call back!'

'Of course he will, Tara; making him wait will only add to the excitement.'

'Are you sure?'

'I'm sure,' Sian replied firmly. 'And Tara?'

'Yes?'

'You know where I am if you need somebody to talk to.'

Tara felt tears prick her eyes again. 'Thanks, Sian.'

Nial had finished his Fair Isle jumper and was embarking on a hat-and-gloves set to match. 'It looks *so* much better in the ivory, pink and heather you chose, Mistress!' he cried ecstatically. 'I'm giving it to my mother for Christmas. Are you all right, Mistress? You sound like you might be getting a cold.'

'That's none of your business, Nial,' Tara snapped.

'Are you keeping warm, Mistress? Would you like me to knit you something?'

Tara looked out the window. The rain had stopped. A heat haze hung over the paddocks and the cicadas were in full voice. She'd managed to talk Nial down to his socks and gloves after finding out he was also wearing a balaclava, ski hat, scarf and skinny-rib jumper. 'Where on earth do you live, Nial? Antarctica?'

'No, Mistress. Bulls.'

Tara got through the rest of the call. Gil's treatment had been a body blow mentally and physically, but she wasn't going to let it destroy her. Over the past few months she had wrested back control of her life.

And clearly there was no place for a man in it.

Gil skipped breakfast the following morning and headed over to Tara's on the motorbike. He'd had no appetite for food ever since she'd run from his house the day before.

After a sleepless night spent with just his tortured, guilty thoughts and the lingering scent of Tara on his bed sheets for company, Gil was impatient for Jake and Jen to get off to school so that he could apologize to Tara and explain his behaviour. He didn't expect she'd make it easy for him, but he wanted to try.

His suspicions were confirmed when he drove through the underpass and up on to the race to see Tara in the distance riding Magnum in the direction of the river. Gil was surprised she'd managed to saddle the horse and that she felt confident enough to go for a ride alone after only one lesson.

He braked abruptly, the back wheel of the bike spinning sideways in the dirt. The noise made Tara glance over her shoulder. Spotting Gil, she kicked Magnum into a trot.

Gil headed after her. 'Tara!'

She ignored him, bouncing inelegantly in the saddle because Magnum was trotting too fast for her to keep the rhythm Gil had taught her, her long blonde ponytail bouncing up and down beneath her white riding helmet.

Gil followed at a distance. Magnum didn't like motorbikes, particularly Harley Davidsons — Gil hadn't realized they sounded any different from other bikes until he got to know the old horse. Magnum was a Harley Davidson expert from way back, and obviously he'd had a bad experience with one of them, although he tolerated other motorbikes so long as they respected his personal space.

'Tara?' Gil called over the throb of the motorbike engine. 'Can we please talk?'

She pushed Magnum into a canter.

Gil increased his speed, eyeing her hunched, insecure position with concern. 'For God's sake, stop before you fall off!'

Magnum had had his fair share of humans shouting and bouncing about on his back in his time, but a human riding a motorbike *and* shouting stretched the limits of his patience. He broke into a gallop, disappearing off down the brown ribbon of the race with Tara clinging to him.

'Oh shit!' Gil had two options: follow on the bike and risk panicking the horse even more, or ditch it and follow on foot without a hope of keeping up. He thought it highly unlikely the old horse would continue running for long — he was too sensible and too unfit. Cursing, Gil ditched the bike and sprinted after them.

Tara managed to stop Magnum before they reached the river, but by then she was completely out of breath and had lost both stirrups, most of her dignity and nearly her breakfast. The horse stopped as quickly as he'd started and dropped his head to graze, giving Tara the opportunity to dismount. She was leaning against his side when Gil ran up to her.

'What are you trying to do?' she yelled. 'Kill me?'

Gil was red-faced and sweating. Magnum had galloped a lot further than he'd expected. 'Are you OK?' he gasped.

'Yes!' Tara shouted. 'No thanks to you.'

She was furious with him; not because his stupid motorbike had turned Magnum into Phar Lap, but because the sight of Gil perspiring and his chest heaving from his sprint along the race reminded her of how he'd looked naked in his bed just after he'd come. Tara wanted to rip his ugly clothes off — awful khaki-green knee-length shorts with numerous holes, and a mangy-looking T-shirt that had probably once been black but had been through the washer so many times it had gone grey and lost its shape — to get at what she knew was hidden underneath. Despite his treatment of her the previous day, she was mortified to find that she was hungry for more.

Gil was just as put-out when he saw that Tara was wearing another one of her silk shirts, this one a pale shade of aqua, and her white jodhpurs tucked into glossy black riding boots. He felt a jolt of pure lust shoot him in the groin. Just like Tara, he now knew what lay beneath.

He offered his first olive branch. 'Sorry about spooking Magnum. You did well to stay on.'

'Did I? How nice of you to notice,' Tara replied sweetly. 'Now why don't you bugger off?'

Gil fought a smile.

'Don't laugh at me, you cheeky sod!' Tara shouted. 'You think having a horse bolt is funny?'

'No, I know it isn't.'

She decided it was better not to confide that once she realized she wasn't going to come off she'd quite enjoyed the gallop. Knowing Gil was in hot pursuit only added to the fun.

'I wanted to apologize.'

'Right, now bugger off.' Tara wished she could look away from his gorgeous eyes. Yesterday she'd discovered they were threaded with not only green and gold, but also amber.

'I meant about yesterday. I'm really sorry for what happened after we made love, Tara. I never meant to hurt you.'

Tara's cheeks burned. She looked away, surprised and confused by his apology. He looked and sounded sincere, but she didn't intend to let him off the hook that easily. 'You were an arsehole.'

'I know.'

Gil took Magnum's reins from her. 'Yesterday was the first time I've ever taken a woman home.'

She frowned and tilted her head. 'For sex?'

'For anything.'

Her eyes widened. 'Oh.'

Gil looked embarrassed. 'It was the bed.'

She squinted at him. 'The bed?'

'It's the bed Louise and I got from her parents as a wedding present. I've never got around to changing it. I probably should, but . . .' He shrugged.

Tara hadn't expected an apology, let alone such a surprising explanation. It was so off-the-wall that she actually believed him. If he was telling the truth, yesterday hadn't been about her at all. Tara decided Louise Sorensen had been a very lucky woman.

Gil was annoyed when Tara simply watched him thoughtfully, saying nothing. He didn't make a practice of spilling his guts and was beginning to wonder why he'd bothered. He held out Magnum's reins and said curtly, 'I'll let you get on with your ride.'

Tara reached for them. 'Thank you for telling me. I couldn't figure out what I'd done wrong. Up until then you didn't seem to have a problem with my behaviour.'

Gil's hand closed around hers. 'There was *nothing* wrong with your behaviour.'

She stared at their joined hands. 'Good. Because I didn't have any problems with yours either.'

'Thank you,' Gil replied gravely.

Tara cleared her throat. 'Do you want to continue with the — ah — arrangement?'

God, he loved it when she went all snooty and serious. 'Yes. Do you?'

'Yes.' She paused. 'But there'll have to be some conditions.'

'Absolutely.'

She scowled. 'You're taking the piss.'

'Damn. I thought I was hiding it better.' He looked at their hands. 'Do you want to shake on it?'

Tara snatched hers away.

Gil tucked his hands in his armpits. 'We're supposed to be embarking on a mad, torrid affair, not booking a dental appointment.'

She propped her fist on her hip and glared. 'Unlike *you*, I'm not accustomed to embarking on mad, torrid affairs.'

'What makes you think *I* am?' he exclaimed.

'I've heard all about your women,' she muttered.

His brows dipped. 'You don't want to believe all you hear.'

Tara snorted. 'To be honest, I don't care if you're keeping a harem in your barn, so long as you've been practising safe sex.' She peered up at him. 'You have, haven't you?'

Hell, this really was starting to feel like a visit to the dentist. 'Of course I have!'

'Good.' Tara rested a hand against Magnum's shoulder.

'Great,' Gil replied testily. 'Anything else?' He rocked back on his heels and blew a breath at the sky when she took him seriously.

'We'd have to be discreet. I wouldn't want Jen or — God forbid — *Divine* to find out about it.'

'*I* wouldn't want Jake or Divine to find out about it, either.'

And most definitely not Barney Bigelow, who would jump to the conclusion that Gil was fulfilling Barney's request that he sleep with Tara and persuade her to sell Eric's land. Gil most definitely did not want Tara hearing about that. After what happened yesterday, who knew what she'd do if she thought he had an ulterior motive. He still couldn't figure out how such a beautiful, intelligent woman could have such low self-esteem, and he wondered if Tara would ever trust him enough to tell him. She was getting under his skin.

If Jake found out about him and Tara, it would blow Gil's *don't get involved with a local woman* rule out of the water. For some reason all of Gil's rules and a good deal of his common sense went flying right out the window where Tara Whitehead was concerned, something else he preferred not to examine too closely.

'I understand how you feel about Louise's bed,' Tara said. 'But I'm afraid I've got a similar problem with Eric's house.'

'What sort of problem?'

She held some grass out to Magnum, shuddering delicately. 'All that flocked wallpaper reminds me of a bordello.'

Gil almost laughed himself sick.

'It's *not* funny! I know most men could shag in the middle of the bus lane on the Auckland Harbour Bridge at rush hour, but women are different. They like some ambience.' She was such a liar; all she needed was a naked Gil and a flat surface.

Gil crossed his arms over his horrible T-shirt. 'Where do you propose we go?'

Tara hesitated. 'The hay barn?'

'The hay barn?' His brows formed twin question marks. 'The hay barn has ambience?'

'Now you're being obtuse.'

No, he was being a saint. All this talk of the where and how made him want to get to the when. Gil almost expected Tara to whip out a contract and get him to sign here, here and here. Just for the hell of it, he said, 'I've got a few conditions of my own.'

That threw her. 'You have? What are they?'

'High heels.'

Tara swallowed. 'You — you want to wear them?'

'Of course I bloody don't! I want *you* to!' Gil exclaimed indignantly.

'Ohhh!' she laughed shakily. 'I thought you said my high heels were silly.'

He smiled intimately and Tara's insides turned little somersaults. 'Not when you're flat on your back, stark naked, with them wrapped around my waist.'

'I'm not looking for anything more from you than sex, Gil,' Tara insisted.

'Good. Because I'm not looking for a replacement for Louise.'

'So long as we understand one another.'

'I think we proved yesterday just how well we understand each other. Do you watch *Boston Legal?*' Gil asked.

The sudden change of subject confused her. 'Yes, it's one of my favourite programmes.'

'So you'll have heard the saying "friends with benefits"?'

'Is that what we're going to be? Friends with benefits?'

Gil smiled his crooked smile, and the slow burn began low in Tara's belly.

'Something even better; we're going to be *neighbours* with benefits.' He checked his watch. 'I don't have a lot of time to spare during the day. Yesterday was unusual.'

'I'm busy, too,' Tara said. 'I was only going to have a quick ride on Magnum. I've got paddocks to muck out.' *And men calling me for a spot of S&M.*

‘Do we have a deal?’

She held out her hand. ‘Deal.’

Gil’s large brown hand closed over hers. His voice lowered. ‘I can think of a better way to seal the deal.’

Tara didn’t want to seem to easy, even if the touch of his hand and the sound of his voice did make her want to drop Magnum’s reins and climb onto Gil instead.

‘I thought you were too busy?’

He tugged her towards him. ‘I’ll work late.’

Tara dragged her feet. ‘I hurt my fork when Magnum bolted.’

Gil slid his arms around her waist and smiled down at her. ‘Let me kiss it better.’

Chapter 28

The need for secrecy added to the fun. Anybody watching Tara and Gil passing the time of day in Divine's main street would never have believed what they got up to once Jen and Jake left on the school bus each morning.

The only person who suspected was Connie. Gil didn't realize until she remarked, 'I saw Tara Whitehead today. She had a bee-sting just like yours, Gil. Or maybe it was from a wasp?'

Gil looked her straight in the eye. 'Maybe it was a black widow.'

Connie took the hint and changed the subject, but later she told Malcolm.

'Why, after so many years of staying away from local women, does he have to get involved with Richard's wife?' she fretted.

'Because none of the others look like Tara, that's why.' Malcolm was due to tee off at the golf club with Dick in half an hour and was more worried about the possibility of rain than Gil's sex life.

'I might have known you'd be like that.' Connie followed him around to the driver's side of the car. 'I don't want him getting hurt. He doesn't know why Tara and Richard broke up, so he's got no idea how fragile Tara is at the moment.'

'If you ask me, any woman who's still standing after her husband says he's becoming a woman is definitely not fragile, Connie.' Malcolm climbed into the car. 'Gil's a big boy. Leave it alone.' He started the car and looked through the window at her. 'And don't go getting any ideas about telling Gil why Richard left Tara. The only person he should hear that from is her.'

Connie stuck her tongue out as Mal drove away. He saw her in the rear mirror and laughed.

She wasn't the only member of the family to suspect Gil was sharing more than neighbourly advice with Mrs Whitehead. Jake came across his father on the phone to Tara one evening with a towel wrapped around his hips and an erection tenting the front of it.

Gil had climbed out of the shower when his shouts for Jake to answer the phone brought no response. He'd spent a torrid half-hour with Tara in his hay barn earlier that day, and the sound of her voice had the same effect on his libido as the starting gun on runners in the blocks. Gil rose to the occasion.

Jake did a double-take at the front of his father's towel as he wandered down the hall towards his bedroom carrying a plate loaded with food.

Gil adjusted the towel self-consciously and, seeing a bag of chicken chips among Jake's stash, said automatically, 'Hang on a moment, Tara, will you?' He wanted to kick himself when he realized he'd just given away the name of his caller. He grabbed the bag of chips. 'You've just finished dinner!'

'I'm hungry.' Jake's gaze dipped below his father's waist.

Gil covered himself with the bag of chips. 'Have some fruit instead!'

Jake, too embarrassed to argue, fled to his room.

Gil decided it was wiser not to mention to Tara what Connie had said or what Jake had seen.

The only one who remained oblivious was Jennifer. She even told Gil she thought her mother was overdoing her riding lessons on Magnum because she was really sore.

At the appointed time, Tara would arrive at either Gil's or Eric's hay barn dressed in one of her prettiest, flimsiest summer dresses and high heels. Each time Gil saw her gliding towards him, he just about swallowed his tongue watching the sway of her hips and the gentle bounce of her breasts beneath the thin fabric of her dress. Knowing that beneath it she was naked apart from perhaps a pair of silky lace-top stockings made his palms sweat.

On one occasion when Tara appeared in the doorway of Gil's barn and wrapped her arms about his neck and kissed him, Gil couldn't wait. He dropped the reel of electric tape he held, lifted her legs around his waist, backed her against the wall of the barn and pushed himself inside her.

Tara made no complaint. She was every bit as desperate as Gil, and laughed when he apologized afterwards. 'I'm not complaining.'

As he set her on the ground, Gil noticed a tear in the shoulder of her dress. 'I'm sorry, it must have snagged on the wall. I'll buy you another.'

She shook her head. 'It's just a dress.'

Gil argued, but she wouldn't give in. She also wouldn't give in about Magic, who was waiting outside Gil's barn when they emerged.

'What's he doing here? He's not supposed to be able to escape any more.'

Tara looked vague and avoided Gil's eyes.

'You let him out, didn't you?' he accused. 'He's not a bloody dog, you know. He'll get fat if you don't restrict his diet, which is another reason he should be back in his paddock.'

'So? He's getting exercise.'

Tara didn't mention that Magic spent large parts of the day curled up in the back garden waiting for her to come out and sit down, or that if she took too long he wasn't above coming into the kitchen to find her. She decided it would also be wise not to mention that Magic was her drinking buddy and had the occasional can of Waikato Draught when she was having a glass of wine in her garden.

'Stop picking on him. He's no bother.'

Gil's eyebrows nearly disappeared into his hairline. 'You've changed your tune.'

He usually tried to grab a shower before he belted over to the hay barn to meet her, and apologized profusely if he hadn't had time to wash up.

Tara would laugh, press her lips against his salty skin and murmur, 'Mmmm … my bit of rough.'

She was funny, passionate, contrary, and wildly spontaneous; she literally took Gil's breath away. Gil was the most perceptive, centred person Tara had ever met. She loved his dry sense of humour and understated charm. She loved Gil's stillness, the way he let people finish what they had to say before asking questions. The laughter and conversations they shared soon became as important as the sex, which seemed to just get better and better. They became friends as well as lovers. Tara ran through the underpass or to Eric's hay barn each day, eager to see Gil. When she spotted him coming along the race towards her on the motorbike or Lazarus, her stomach fluttered as if she was fifteen again.

Gil taught Tara how to run Eric's place. She was curious, asking lots of questions about his dairy farm, and was surprised at how hard he worked. Gil answered patiently, revealing how much he hated milking after doing it morning and night for so many years, but how he wouldn't swap it for a life of sitting in traffic every morning and night and being chained to a desk and computer all day.

Tara's naïvety about farming was utterly priceless. When Gil mentioned that most dairy cows were impregnated via artificial insemination, Tara imagined dairy farmers up and down the country lurking in cow sheds armed with turkey basters. 'You mean the poor things get the goods without any of the fun?' she cried indignantly.

'Not all of them. I put in a pair of bulls to catch any of the ones that haven't taken,' Gil explained.

Tara's frown deepened. 'Why do you need two bulls? Don't they fight?'

'No. They've got other things on their mind. They work in pairs so they don't get too tired.'

'What?' she laughed. 'Like a tag team?'

Gil seemed to take Tara's criticism of his bulls' sexual prowess personally.

'It's bloody hard work servicing forty-odd cows. I have two pairs and change them every twelve hours so they get a rest.'

Tara rolled around the hay in her stockings and high heels roaring with laughter, until Gil growled and rolled her underneath him instead. She called later that night to complain about the noise one set of bulls were making in her paddock. They'd been sent over between stud duty to graze down some of her grass.

'Your bloody bull is bellowing his head off.'

Gil was already asleep when the phone rang. Morning milking meant he was in bed early most nights. 'They're only there for the night,' he said groggily.

'It's trying to dig a hole under my fence!'

'What's the other one doing?'

'He's curled up on the ground, snoring like a freight train. Obviously he got all the action today while his friend missed out. The one doing the digging tried to mount the one lying down, but he wasn't interested; that's probably why the digger is making so much noise — he's feeling rejected. I'm sure it's nothing that a beer and a man-to-man talk wouldn't sort out,' Tara sighed. 'I haven't got a hope of getting any sleep tonight with Romeo bawling his head off outside.' She paused. 'Did I wake you up?'

'*Yes.*'

'Oh. Sorry. I forgot you go to bed early.'

'That's all right.' Gil relaxed back against the pillows, wide awake now. 'Are you in bed?'

'No. In my jarmies, though.'

He was certain Tara's pyjamas wouldn't be like other women's. 'Where's Jen?'

'Staying the night at Melanie Larby's. They're doing a science project together.'

'What are your jarmies like?'

'Gil!' They'd never taken their games outside the hay barn before. 'Where's Jake?'

'In the lounge watching SKY and ignoring the bloody phone. Tell me about your jarmies,' Gil coaxed.

'I'll tell you about my jarmies if you'll come and get your bull.'

'Tomorrow,' he promised.

'OK.' She lowered her voice. 'Do you want me to describe what I'm wearing, Gil?'

'Uh huh.'

'Tomorrow.'

She hung up.

Gil overslept in the morning. He was greeted by a herd of loudly mooing cows, put out because their routine had been upset. Yawning, Gil followed behind the cows on the motorbike, thinking Tara Whitehead and her bloody pyjamas had a lot to answer for. He got his own back the next day by presenting Tara with a white container of gel and telling her she was responsible for washing Magnum's sheath.

'What's his sheath?'

'His penis.' Gil watched with satisfaction as Tara puffed up indignantly. 'And *no,* I'm not joking. Horses aren't like dogs; they can't lick their balls.'

'But how — how —' Her face was so red she looked ready to explode.

He pointed to the label, which read *Sheath Cleaning Gel*. 'Get him to drop and apply a coating of this. All it takes is a good hand action, and we both know you've got that.'

'You mean I have to *masturbate* a horse?' she choked.

'I wouldn't put it quite like that.' Gil left, calling over his shoulder, 'Make sure you warm the gel up if it's cold.'

Magnum was very coy about 'dropping', and Tara was forced to go into search-and-rescue mode, all the time casting frantic looks over her shoulder in case a car came up the driveway and she got caught at her humiliating task. Once she found her quarry and, grimacing, applied the gel and a good dose of elbow grease, Magnum seemed to be in heaven, raising his head, crossing his eyes and nibbling the air rapturously.

'Bloody men,' Tara muttered. 'You're all the same.'

She was amazed at how much she had in common with Gil and how easy it was to talk to him. When Tara revealed how disappointed she was that she'd never completed her degree, Gil asked why she didn't go back to university.

'Because it isn't the right time.'

'If you keep waiting for the right time, all you'll ever do is waste it.'

'That's all right for you to say,' Tara said. 'You had your mother and father and no doubt half the township to support you when you did your degree. I'll bet hardly a week went by when Glenys Tweedie wasn't on your doorstep with a casserole.'

Gil thought it better not to tell her that she was right. Instead, he said, 'You'd have plenty of help.'

'Who?' she demanded, annoyed at him for making it sound so easy and at herself for being jealous of Glenys Tweedie.

'I do a better roast dinner than casserole *and* . . .' he wriggled his brows, '. . . I'd provide lots of tea and sympathy.'

Tara stared at him in surprise. He meant it. The thought warmed the parts of her soul that had lain cold and barren for months. Then she remembered that her time in Divine was just an interlude, a speed bump on the highway of her life, which led straight back to Auckland. 'But — but I'm going back to Auckland!'

'Of course.' Gil's smiled faded. 'I forgot.'

It wasn't all one-way traffic. When Tara came upon Gil jump-schooling Lazarus in the arena one morning, she realized just how talented a rider he was. Lazarus was green and tended to rush the jumps, but Gil patiently worked with him, getting him to slow down and take his time, until the young horse was jumping cleanly and rhythmically, clearing the jumps with room to spare. They looked huge to Tara.

Gil shrugged: 'They're only a metre.' He patted Lazarus's sweaty neck. 'He hates touching the poles and has the ability to go a lot higher. He's quite talented. I really should sell him to somebody who'll do him justice.'

'Why can't you do him justice?' Tara asked.

'I don't compete any more. He needs to be out doing something.'

'Why can't you take him out and do something?'

Gil knew Tara was challenging him just as he'd challenged her about completing her degree. The idea of her going back to Auckland bothered him. He was sure that Tara would laugh if she knew, and would say he only cared because he'd miss the sex, but it wasn't that. Tara had never pretended she liked living in Divine. If anybody belonged in Auckland it was her, and Gil had never asked for anything more than the pleasure of her body, but the more he got to know her and delve beneath her prickly exterior the more he liked her.

'It takes a lot of time schooling a young horse up.' He paused. 'I'd need help.'

'I'd help.'

Gil swung down off Lazarus's back. 'You'll be in Auckland. Remember?'

'Oh. Yes. I don't know why I said it.'

Gil drew Tara like a magnet. She rushed through her work at Eric's so that she could spend time with him. It was inevitable that she started helping him around the farm; it meant Gil finished sooner and they had more time to spend together in the hay barn or, as the weather grew warmer, in the grass of one of the back paddocks or beneath the trees in a stand of native bush.

Gil loved watching Tara's ham-fisted attempts to master something new, usually with her eyes closed and mouth pinched tight in disgust. Louise had been raised on a farm and had always been gentle and accommodating. Tara was quick-tempered and mercurial. When she was around, the very air seemed to vibrate with her presence. She made the mundane, repetitive tasks Gil did day-in day-out fun; she was impatient with her ineptitude, but too stubborn to give in until she got the hang of something. The first time Jen and Jake were both away for the weekend, Gil took her with him to do the afternoon milking; he didn't think he would ever forget the look on Tara's face when he insisted she don a pair of his overalls to protect her clothes.

'Is this really necessary?' She stood on the concrete pad in front of the milking bays in her floral gumboots, dangling the overalls between finger and thumb. 'Or are you just having a laugh at my expense?'

Gil slipped a set of cups on to the udders of the nearest cow. 'Why do you think I'm wearing them?'

'Because you have a fetish for ugly brown clothing.'

'True,' he agreed. 'But that's not the only reason.'

Gil pointed at the green slime coating a cow's hindquarters and smiled. 'That's one of the reasons.'

'You're enjoying this!' she accused.

His smile widened. 'No, I'm not.'

Tara glowered.

'One other thing,' he advised. 'Keep your mouth closed when you're facing their back end.'

Tara looked up at the back end in front of her. 'Why?'

'You don't want to get splashed with your mouth open.'

'With wha—?'

The cow chose that moment to evacuate her bowel. The slimy jet hit the edge of the milking bay and splashed high in the air right in front of Tara.

Too late.

Chapter 29

Her remark about his brown clothing prompted Gil to ask Tara to come shopping for clothes with him in Hamilton.

'I thought you weren't going shopping 'til next year.'

'Things have worn out faster this time. I've a good mind to take them with me and ask for my money back,' Gil lied.

She hesitated. 'What if somebody from Divine sees us?'

Gil shrugged. He didn't care if they were recognized. 'You're doing me a favour, helping me pick out some clothes.'

They spent a wonderful few hours in Hamilton. Tara steered him into shops he would never have chosen, and Gil made Tara buy herself some overalls.

'What colours do they come in?' she asked the man behind the counter as if she expected him to whip out a catalogue with the latest spring/summer range.

'Brown,' he replied, eyeing with disbelief the glamorous creature in her high heels and pretty dress.

Tara's brow puckered. *'Brown? Nothing else?'*

The man looked helplessly at Gil. 'And blue.'

She sighed. 'It'll have to be blue, then.'

'I'm proud of you,' Gil teased as they left the store. 'We'll make a farmer of you yet.'

'They'll clash with my gumboots,' Tara complained.

Gil looked devastating in good clothes. Every time he stepped out of the fitting room wearing something new, Tara almost melted into a puddle on the shop floor. Seeing that wonderful body filling out various shirts and trousers, with Gil's dark, rugged face above, made her want to follow him back into the changing room and close the curtain.

'Your husband asked me to bring you his old clothes,' the shop assistant said when Gil was getting dressed. He handed Tara a large, green plastic bag.

Tara thought about correcting him, but instead she thanked him and took the bag. When Gil appeared in his new jeans and a dark-green striped shirt that picked out the green in his eyes, she found herself imagining what it would be like to be married to him. She thrust the thought aside.

Gil came forwards, one shoulder raised as he tucked his wallet into the back pocket of his jeans. 'Are you sure these aren't too tight?'

Tara hooked her arm through his. 'They're just new, that's all.'

He insisted on buying her a dress to replace the one she'd torn in his barn.

'I don't need a new dress. I've got loads of dresses!'

'Not one from me,' Gil replied stubbornly.

Tara tried to steer him into places that stocked cheaper clothing, but he knew her well enough by now to realize what she was doing. 'You don't wear this kind of stuff.'

'Yes, I do,' she insisted. 'For casual.'

Gil marched her further along the mall to a more upmarket boutique. 'In here.' He stood in the doorway and folded his arms. 'I'll wait.'

It was too much for Tara. Faced with racks of lovely clothes she spent the next hour dressing up and parading for him, and was surprised that Gil seemed to enjoy it, too. He sat on a velvet chaise longue by the changing rooms, chatting to the two shop assistants, who were clearly charmed by him, and waiting for Tara to appear.

Gil's opinions about her clothes were just as strong as Tara's about his.

His comments ranged from *Not that, What is that?* and *Bloody hell!* to a shrug, and finally silence, a smile and *That one!*

'I guess it's this.' Tara grinned at the shop assistant and smoothed a hand down the front of a silky dress with tiny straps in misty shades of pink, grey and lavender. It was her favourite, too.

'Your husband has wonderful taste,' said one of the women.

Gil and Tara's eyes met. They burst out laughing.

He dragged her outside and straight into the shoe shop next door.

'No!' Tara baulked. 'No more. The dress is enough.'

He dipped his head and crooned in her ear. '*Shoes, Tara . . . just look at them. Take a deep breath, Tara, and smell them. Look! There's a pink pair the same colour as your dress.*'

Tara followed his gaze and pulled a face. 'Don't be ridiculous — they're strawberry pink! Now *that's* the right shade of pink.' She pointed at another pair of sandals and was gone.

Gil had never had so much fun shopping for clothes. He got a kick out of watching Tara. She made him laugh. And she turned him on. It had taken a huge amount of self-control on his part to take her shoe shopping when all he wanted to do was take her home to bed. And that was another thing. He wanted to make love to Tara in a bed. Not have sex on the floor of a hay barn or against the wall, but *make love* in a *real bed.*

They got home well before the school bus was due. Gil cupped Tara's face between his hands and kissed her slowly, sliding his tongue gently into her mouth.

Tara pressed against him. She tipped her head back and smiled. 'Your barn is closest.'

He shook his head. 'Not the barn. Let's go to bed.'

She clutched his wrists. 'No. Not in Louise's bed. It wouldn't feel right.'

Gil led her to the guest bedroom instead. It was where Connie and Malcolm slept when they stayed, which made him feel a bit uncomfortable, but it was still better than his bed.

This time was different and they both knew it. Tara would have left her high heels on, but Gil took them off. They didn't dive on one another with an eye to the clock; they took their time. Afterwards, Gil lay on his side with Tara tucked in front of him and studied the contrast of his dark-skinned, hairy legs entwined with her smooth, pale ones.

'You make me look so white and sickly,' Tara observed sleepily. 'You're so dark and beautiful.'

Gil kissed her shoulder. 'You're not white and sickly. Your skin looks ivory and pink.'

'Why do you call me surfer girl?'

'Mum saw you at one of Eric's parties years ago and said you looked like you'd just stepped off a beach. When you laugh, I know what she means.'

Tara clutched his hand against her chest.

She didn't want to love him.

She didn't want to love any man ever again.

But Gil Sorensen wasn't just any man.

Tara was relieved when Jen started mentioning Gavin Archer, the head boy at All Saints, and he began calling. It took Tara a while to realize that Gavin was Annabelle Archer's son.

'You're welcome to invite Gavin around to hang out and have dinner if you want, provided he doesn't bring his mother,' she told Jen over dinner. 'Whatever you do, don't accept any offers from Mrs Archer to knit you a cardigan or you'll probably spend next winter dressed as a toucan.'

Jen began to laugh. She'd noticed Mrs Archer in a big striped zebra sweater that hung to her knees when she'd picked Gavin up from school.

Maybe, just maybe, Tara thought, *I'll be able to tell her about Gil and me.*

And you'll have some sort of a future together, a corner of her mind whispered seductively.

One of the things Tara didn't talk about with Gil was her employment with Superior Services. She continued to take calls at least three times a week, but was beginning to resent the time she spent on the phone when she could be with Gil. She got around her lack of enthusiasm by making her clients spend long periods waiting for her while she wandered off to hang out the washing, take a coffee break or paint her nails. It always amazed her that they were still waiting for her when she returned.

It didn't take Sian long to realize that her star pupil was playing hooky. 'You've changed. There's something different about you.'

'I have not!' Tara was alarmed by Sian's frightening talent for sniffing out the truth.

'You're sleeping with somebody,' Sian said slowly. '*I know!* You're sleeping with the DDF, aren't you?'

Tara tried denying it, but it was a lost cause.

'Well done, darling! I'm *so* proud of you,' Sian crowed. 'Tell me, *does* he rise to the trot for hours?'

'Sian!'

'Don't worry, darling,' Sian purred. 'Your secret is safe with me.'

Tara thought that the worst thing that could happen, apart from Gil and the town of Divine discovering Richard's new identity, would be Jennifer or Gil finding out about Mistress Fury. But the following Tuesday, somebody far worse discovered her secret. At the end of her afternoon session, after calls from Percy Feather and Walter the retired chicken farmer, she received a call from a new client. It started much the same as any other call.

'*Mistress Fury?*' The sibilant whisper reminded Tara of a snake, tongue flickering and darting.

'Yes?' she replied frostily, tucking the phone between her ear and shoulder as she spooned batter from a mixing bowl into muffin tins.

They were chocolate and caramel — Jake, Jen and Gil's favourites.

'I need your help, Mistress. I need some *serious* disciplining. Nothing you can say or do could be bad enough. I am slime, Mistress, the lowest of the low.'

Tara wrinkled her nose. This one certainly didn't waste any time getting to the point. The oily voice gave her the creeps: she would definitely tell Sian she didn't want to deal with this one again. She looked about for her watch to see how much longer she had before her shift was over, but couldn't find it, and the cuckoo was still doing time inside its wooden house.

'Who do you think you are, telling me you need disciplining?' Tara's voice dripped venom. '*I'll* be the one to decide if you'll be punished or not.'

The sound of the caller's excited breathing rattled down the phone.

'Sorry, Mistress! Of course, Mistress!'

Tara felt increasingly uneasy. There was something about the voice that tugged at her memory. If it were an old acquaintance from Auckland, Sian's reassurance that men in the throes of sexual excitement were unlikely to recognize the voice at the end of the phone meant that Tara was safe enough. Still . . . something about this caller worried her. She considered telling him to sit and wait, but decided it would be better to get rid of him instead.

'Tell me what you've done.'

He did. And what he wanted to do, none of which made for pleasant listening. Tara felt her stomach heave. This wasn't one of her usual callers; this guy was a real sicko. She suddenly saw a man's flushed, sweaty face pressed against a table top, the bulging eyes glittering with excitement because she'd just stabbed him in the leg with her high heel.

'Mistress, please tell me what I can do to make amends?'

Tara dropped the mixing bowl. She jabbed the off button twice on the phone before she managed to disconnect.

The caller was Barney Bigelow.

Tara hadn't heard from Sian in over a week, which was unusual. They'd become close friends and spoke regularly. Panicked about Barney, Tara called Rona and asked to speak to Sian. Rona was strangely elusive about Sian's whereabouts, and when Tara said she'd call Sian at home instead Rona was quick to put her off.

'She's not been well.'

'What's wrong with her?'

'Flu — a — a really bad dose of the flu.'

Tara smelt a rat almost as big as Barney Bigelow. 'Rona, I *need* to speak to Sian!'

'Don't we all?' Rona muttered.

'What does that mean?' Tara asked sharply. 'Has something happened to her?'

Rona sighed. 'I haven't seen her in a week, Tara. She isn't taking any calls, and when I went round to her house there was mail piled up in the letterbox and the neighbours hadn't seen her in days but her car was in the garage.'

'Break in! She might be sick and collapsed inside!'

'She isn't sick, Tara.'

'You don't know that!'

'I do.' Rona hesitated. 'I'm only telling you this because you're Sian's friend.'

'*Telling me what?*'

'Marcus Bancroft's wife, Susie, is pregnant again.'

Sian's dilemma drove all thoughts of Barney from Tara's mind. She gave Jennifer an abbreviated version of what Rona had said.

Jen was puzzled. 'But I thought they were divorced.'

'That doesn't mean she doesn't still love him.'

Tara told Gil what had happened and asked him if Jen could stay for a few days while she went to Auckland. 'Pat has promised to keep an eye on the place while I'm away, so you won't have to worry about the animals or the house.'

'That wouldn't have been a problem, and of course Jen can stay,' he said. 'But are you sure Sian will see you?'

'I'll make her see me,' Tara replied grimly. 'Even if I have to break down her front door.'

Gil nodded. 'Try not to get yourself arrested.'

Tara's black mood lifted briefly. In the same situation, Richard would have been advising caution. *Don't let your heart rule your head, Tara. You know what you're like. Far too impulsive!*

She smiled at Gil. 'Why? Would you come and bail me out?'

He smiled back. 'I might.'

Tara lingered, not wanting to leave. Her knock had interrupted his shower. His dark hair dripped on the collar of his hastily buttoned shirt, and beneath the hems of his faded jeans his feet were bare. Tara wished she could take him with her; wished she could have his quiet, steady presence beside her when she saw Sian.

Gil reached out and picked up a strand of her hair. He rubbed it between his fingers. 'Do you want me to come with you?'

Tara felt herself sway towards him. She backed away and shook her head. 'No, I'll be fine. You've got milking to do and maize to plant.'

'If I asked, Mum and Dad would come and stay, and Jake could cover the milking.'

'No, really,' Tara insisted. 'You don't have to come with me.'

'Maybe I want to,' Gil said.

And so do I, Tara thought. Alarmed, she backed further away. 'No, I'll be much better on my own.'

His lips twisted. 'Of course, I'd forgotten.'

As Tara drove towards Auckland, Gil's words and her response replayed in her head. She thumped the steering wheel. Why now? Why, when her life was at its shittiest in months, had Gil suddenly decided to change the rules? Tara wasn't lying when she said she didn't need Gil. The past few months had shown her she was quite capable of standing on her own two feet. She *wanted* Gil. That was the difference. Their 'neighbours with benefits' arrangement was a sham. Gil seemed to think so, too, but Tara wasn't as brave as him. She was too scared to admit to her feelings and trust him with her dirty little secrets.

You'll be hurt. You know *you will,* she thought. *It's just a matter of time . . .*

Chapter 30

Sian's house was trashed. Shards of glass, ceramics and china littered the floor of her beautiful living room. There were huge gashes in the seat and arms of the pink sofas where she and Tara had sat so many months before, foam and stuffing spilled on the floor like huge flakes of dandruff. It looked as if Sian had taken either a hammer or scissors to every photo she owned of Marcus Bancroft. When Sian wouldn't open the front door, Tara had climbed in through a window that she found open at the back of the house.

Sian was crouched in a corner of her bedroom, nursing a half-empty bottle of flat champagne. She was drunk, and the soles of her feet were covered in dried blood. The curtains were pulled and the windows closed. The room stank of stale booze and desperation. Tara stumbled on several empty bottles as she made her way across the bedroom to the figure crouched against the wall.

'Who's there?' Sian fumbled around on the floor beside her. 'How did you get in here?' She launched one of the empty bottles.

Tara just avoided getting struck in the shins. 'Sian! It's me — Tara!'

Sian's hand hovered above a second bottle. 'T-Tara? Is that you?'

'Yes. I've just broken the land-speed record from Divine, and I'd appreciate it if you didn't kneecap me.' Tara knelt on the carpet beside her.

Sian clutched her champagne bottle and whispered, 'He's got her pregnant again. His perfect, fertile little Susie is up the duff. He told me that they weren't sleeping together, that once the little boy was born that part of their marriage was over.'

She began to cry, great, heaving, dry sobs that shook her.

Tara gently took the bottle from her. 'I know, sweetie, I know. I'm *so* sorry.'

'I've been such a fool. Why did I believe him? Why? I'm so stupid.'

Tara wished she had an answer. She put Sian in the shower, washed and dressed her feet, and helped her into clean clothes. Sian didn't make a sound, even when Tara put antiseptic on the wounds on her feet and forced the tangles from her long, dark hair. Tara packed a bag and phoned Rona to say Sian was going on holiday and any essential calls were to be forwarded to Tara.

'I've turned her mobile off. If Marcus Bancroft phones, don't tell him where Sian is,' Tara said. 'Tell him — tell him —'

'I'll tell him to fuck off,' Rona snarled, shocking both herself and Tara. 'Perhaps not; I might get fired.'

'Sian won't fire you, Rona. She'll probably give you a raise.'

'Tell Sian not to worry about *anything*. I'll make sure everything carries on here as usual. I'll put you off for the week as well, shall I?'

Tara was relieved; at least Barney Bigelow wouldn't be able to call her. 'That'd be great. Thanks, Rona.'

After long months of pining for Auckland, Tara couldn't wait to get the hell out of the city. She found the noise and sheer volume of traffic daunting. Everybody was in such a rush, and the smell of car fumes and sticky tarmac made her feel sick. It wasn't until she hit the Waikato Expressway that she began to feel a little calmer, and at the turn-off at Taupiri she started to breathe more easily. Tara felt confused and upset. Auckland was her home. It was a beautiful city. She didn't want to become one of those people who moved away and then bagged it, but it had felt like a foreign country.

However, it wasn't just the city that had upset her; it was witnessing

Sian's utter devastation at Marcus Bancroft's duplicity. Like Tara, Sian had seen only what she wanted to see. Everybody had known the truth except her. Tara thought about the destruction of Sian's house, and knew that if she hadn't needed to put on a brave face for Jennifer she would likely have done the same thing to the house she'd shared with Richard, a house that, strangely, no longer seemed so perfect.

When did I stop missing it? Tara wondered.

About the time you started meeting Gil Sorensen in hay barns, when you began to look forward to sharing something funny in your day with him or grumbling about how frustrating it is to raise teenagers.

Sian was asleep in the passenger seat, her head propped against the window. Tara pulled over, folded her jacket and placed it between Sian's head and the glass. She stared into the darkness of the country road. It wouldn't take much for her to be right back where Sian was now. Bereft, adrift, overwhelmed with pain and the desolation of loss.

Gil Sorensen was no longer just the extremely attractive dairy farmer across the road, her 'neighbour with benefits'. He'd crept into her mind and soul. He was the first person Tara thought to turn to if she had a problem to discuss or needed help.

She looked at Sian, who looked just like she had in the first weeks after Richard had left. Tara couldn't face that kind of pain and disillusionment again.

She started the car and headed back on to the road, feeling as if she'd aged twenty years. A dull ache throbbed at Tara's temples, keeping perfect time with the one inside her chest.

Sian slept most of the way back to Divine. Without make-up and one of her glamorous suits, she looked old and hunched, as if a vampire had sucked the life out of her. Tara didn't feel much better.

They got back around two in the morning. Tara put Sian to bed in a spare bedroom decorated with purple swirls on the wallpaper and a canary yellow chenille bedspread on the old oak bedstead. For all the notice Sian took, Tara could have been loading her into a coal bunker. She climbed into bed like a docile toddler and took the two tablets Tara handed her for the pain in her feet, complaining that she'd rather have a whisky.

'Well, you can't.' Tara tucked the bedspread under her chin. 'Judging by the number of empty bottles lying around your house, you've drunk enough alcohol to supply a small country for an entire year. Shut up and go to sleep.'

'Yes, *mein Führer*,' Sian muttered with a glimmer of her usual fire, pulling a pillow over her face.

Tara went to bed, but couldn't sleep. She kept imagining what would happen if Barney Bigelow revealed she was a telephone sex worker, and was surprised to discover that she didn't really care for herself. Jen was a different matter. Tara agonized over the teasing and ugliness Jen would get at school if the word got out. And when she imagined the look on Gil's face when he heard the news, her bravado leaked away like air from a burst balloon.

Whichever way Tara looked at it, one thing was blindingly obvious. She had to end things with Gil. Before he realized how she felt about him. The pain made her feel as if she'd gashed her soul the way Sian had ripped open her feet.

Hugging her pillow, Tara bit down on her lip. She finally drifted off just before dawn, only to be awakened by the sound of sobbing from the spare bedroom. She went in, climbed on the bed beside Sian and hugged her.

Sian huddled against her. 'He told me h-he wasn't sleeping with her any more! He t-told me he only d-did it to get a son!'

Tara stroked her hair, 'Sian, Marcus is a shit. He always was.'

'I know.' Sian wiped her eyes on the yellow bedspread and then apologized.

'It's OK.' Gathering up a corner of the yellow bedspread, Tara made her blow her nose as well. 'I hate this bedspread anyway.'

Sian hiccupped and laughed.

'I never thought I'd be a victim again, yet I set myself up to be hurt.'

'Yes,' Tara replied softly. 'So what's the answer, Sian?'

Sian sighed. 'Stay out of the game.'

When Jennifer arrived back from Gil's she was extremely sweet to Sian. And utterly bloody to her mother.

'What on earth is the matter with you, Jennifer?' Tara demanded in exasperation. Jen wasn't prone to moodiness, but like any teenager she had her moments — and right now wasn't an ideal time for her to be having one.

When they were finally alone, Jen turned on her mother like a virago, blue eyes flashing and lips trembling with suppressed fury.

'How could you?' she shouted.

Tara was shaken. She'd never seen Jen like this before.

'How could I *what?*' she cried. 'Tell me what I've done!'

It all came boiling out of Jennifer in a dreadful, furious torrent. Jake had made references to his father liking Jen's mother in the past, but Jennifer had never taken it seriously, firm in her belief that Tara and Gil didn't like one another. When Jake mentioned something about their parents while she was staying at Gil's, Jen lost her temper.

'For God's sake, Jen, are you fifteen or five?' Jake snapped in return. '*My* father and *your* mother have been getting it on for weeks.'

'That's *disgusting!*'

'Whatever.' Jake shrugged. 'You can be such a child sometimes, Jen.'

Gil knew they'd had a fight, but couldn't find out what it had been about. Jen was nothing like her usual chirpy self and looked so wounded that even Jake began to feel guilty.

'What did you say?' Gil demanded.

Jake avoided his gaze. 'It was nothing — I mean, I didn't *mean* anything,' he muttered. 'How was I to know she'd go ballistic about it?'

'About *what*, Jake?'

'About you and Tara — you know . . .'

Gil closed his eyes and grimaced.

'Sorry, Dad! I thought she knew! I mean, why's it got to be some big secret?'

Gil shook his head. None of the reasons he could give made any sense.

'I'd better let Tara know.'

He tried but she didn't answer the phone, and Gil didn't want to go over to the house, because he knew Sian was there and wanted to give her some privacy.

In the meantime, Jennifer screamed at her mother, 'I hate you! You're a *slut!*'

Tara was devastated and knew that her decision to break things off with Gil was the right one. She doubted it would affect him all that much anyway; he'd probably miss the sex, but that was about all. Still, she kept putting off going across the road to tell him, ignored the phone when it rang, and concentrated on taking care of Sian.

Sian spent most of her time huddled in a deck chair in the garden, staring into space and picking at the food that Tara brought her. She fed some to Magic, who broke out of his paddock and curled up at her feet as if he sensed Sian's desolation.

Jennifer was refusing to speak with her mother, but not, apparently, with her father. She disappeared into her bedroom most nights with the telephone; another reason Gil could never get through. Tara discovered that Jen was talking to Richard when she tried to use the phone and overheard Jen say, 'Mum's behaved like a tart, Dad. She's got the cheek to preach to me about safe sex and all I've done is *talk* to Gavin Archer on the phone and gone out with him a couple of times! *She's* been *screwing* Gil Sorensen!'

'Jennifer!!' Richard's new feminine voice spoke sharply. 'I *will not* allow you to speak about your mother like that!'

'Why are you defending her?' Jen exclaimed. 'She's been *cheating* on you! And with your cousin! I hate Gil Sorensen! I hate him!'

Tara hung up the phone, shaking. Now Richard knew, too.

Sian found her gazing blankly at the red flocked wallpaper above the telephone table. She patted Tara's arm as she wandered by, saying listlessly, 'Don't worry, some new wallpaper would do wonders.'

When Tara didn't answer, Sian stopped and peered at her face. 'Tara? What's wrong?'

Tara started. 'Jen knows about Gil and me.'

'Is that a problem?'

'Of *course* it's a problem!' she burst out. 'Imagine how she feels! It's — it's the last thing she needs. First Richard leaves and then— '

'You start having sex with Gil?'

Tara rubbed her forehead wearily. 'No! Yes! I mean . . .' She dropped her hand and looked at Sian miserably. 'Jen has a crush on Gil.'

'Ahh . . . I see.' Sian nodded slowly. 'And she's had you all to herself for months now, hasn't she?'

'What does that mean?'

'All Jen talks about is that boy Gavin at her school. If she has a crush on anybody, Tara, I think it's him. I think it's more likely that Jen doesn't like the idea of having to share you with Gil.'

Tara looked doubtful.

'You're going to do something stupid, aren't you?' Sian asked.

'What does that mean?'

'I know how your mind works. You're a woman *and* a wife *and* a mother. You feel responsible for everything that goes wrong in your little universe. You're not in the right frame of mind to make any decisions at the moment.' Sian laughed hollowly. 'Believe me, I know. Don't rush into something you might regret. Jen's a big girl. She'll get over it.'

'It's not that simple,' Tara said.

Sian shuffled away to her room. 'It's as difficult as you make it.'

Gil had just finished ploughing a paddock when Tara suddenly appeared at the gate. He stopped the tractor and stared, thinking for a moment that he'd imagined her. He hadn't seen her since she'd left for Auckland. Gil wasn't sure if she was avoiding him because she was angry about Jennifer, or if it was something else.

Their parting had played on Gil's mind, worrying him. He knew Tara's body as well as his own; knew how she liked to be touched and what made her laugh. Getting to know the woman within was a different matter. Tara would talk about everything except Richard; if his name came up, she changed the subject. Gil felt as if Richard stood between them and had toyed with the idea of contacting him to find out what had happened to send Tara and Jen running to the Waikato. Gil wanted more than just sex from Tara. His feelings for her had deepened. Yes, the sex was outstanding; but the companionship and laughter and Tara's sheer contrariness energized and delighted Gil, making the world brighter.

He'd even offered Jake the old double bed.

Jake was surprised. 'You're getting a new bed?'

'Thinking about it.'

'Sweet as!' Jake hesitated. 'So . . . everything's OK with you and Tara?'

'Working on it.'

'Sorry Dad . . .'

'It's OK. Jen had to find out sooner or later.'

'I really like Tara.'

Gil looked at his son in surprise, wondering when Jake had taken that final step into manhood and how he'd missed it. He could see Louise in Jake's smile and his deep brown eyes. She'd left a part of herself behind when she died. Jake and their memories meant Louise lived on.

As Tara picked her way along the freshly turned earth towards him, Gil noticed how tired and careworn she looked, as if she carried the weight of the world, and wished she'd let him help shoulder some of her burden.

Gil expected her to be on the warpath about Jen, but the first thing Tara said was, 'I haven't come about Jen.'

He climbed from the tractor. 'I've tried to call you but the phone is either engaged or nobody answers. Jake is really sorry. He tried to apologize, but Jen won't speak to him.'

'She isn't talking to me either.'

Gil stripped his gloves off. 'That bad, huh?'

'That bad.' She looked away across the paddock. 'I've done a lot of thinking these past few days.'

He felt the first prickling of unease. 'Have you now?'

Tara took a deep breath. 'I can't continue with our . . . arrangement, Gil. I have to think of Jen. It's been . . .' She ground to a halt. What? Fun? A blast? The best sex she'd ever had? 'Nice.' She looked at him and winced.

His face was set like granite. 'What? You mean you've enjoyed yourself?'

Tara hunched her shoulders defensively. Why was he being so difficult? Because of Jake, she'd thought he would understand.

'You look upset, Tara,' Gil dropped his gloves on the seat of the tractor. 'Am I making this difficult for you?' he asked flatly.

Tara didn't know what to say. She'd never seen this side of Gil and hadn't expected him to be so angry. 'I've got to think of Jen. She's very confused and hurt at the moment. She misses her father and—'

'Are you going back to Richard?' Gil asked grimly.

Tara's mouth dropped open. 'Believe me, Gil! I will *never* get back with Richard!' she cried bitterly.

Gil was taken aback by her vehemence. 'Then what's the real reason? There's something more to this than Jen spitting the dummy because she's had to face the fact that her mother is a grown woman.'

'That's a horrible thing to say. Jen isn't like that!'

'She's had you all to herself, clucking like an anxious mother hen for months. It's hardly surprising she doesn't want to share,' Gil replied curtly. 'Tell me the truth — is it something to do with Richard?'

Tara's expression became shuttered. 'No.'

'I don't believe you.'

'I don't care!' she shouted, pale-faced and shaking, her hands clenched in fists by her sides.

Gil's defences crumbled. He stepped towards her. 'Tara—'

'Leave me alone!' She backed away. 'Stay away from me! I mean it! It's *over!*'

She turned and fled towards the gate, her floral gumboots scattering the ploughed earth in all directions.

Gil watched her go, despair and fury holding him immobile until, with a roar, he swung his fist and punched the side of the tractor.

Connie found him sitting in the kitchen holding a tea towel to a cut on one of his knuckles, his eyes burning with anger.

'What on earth is wrong?'

A muscle jumped in Gil's jaw. 'Tara just dumped me.'

'Oh, Gil. I'm so sorry.' She looked at the bloody tea towel. 'What did you do to your hand?'

'I punched the tractor.'

Connie bit her lip. The very thing she'd dreaded had happened: Gil was in love with Richard's wife.

He watched her closely. 'Do you know why Richard and Tara split up?'

She eyed him warily. 'Why?'

'Because I want to know why whenever anybody mentions Tara and Richard's break-up people get strange looks on their faces and change the subject — including Tara.'

Connie knew Gil wasn't going to give in until he got answers. He was easygoing to a fault, always had been, but if you put a barrier in his way Gil would always find a way around it. She sighed. 'You never got Richard's letter, did you?'

'What letter?'

Connie picked up the jug and carried it to the sink. 'I'll make us a cup of coffee and tell you all about it.'

Chapter 31

Sian was sitting in the deck chair in the garden feeding Magic her lunch when Tara returned to the house. Sian looked at her and said, 'You've done something stupid.'

Tara burst into tears and spilled the beans. 'I thought he'd understand! But he didn't seem to care how upset Jennifer is!'

She was flabbergasted when Sian said flatly, 'Sod Jennifer. In a few years she'll be up and gone to university or somewhere. Where does that leave you? *Alone* — that's where. Wake up and smell the roses. You can't spend the rest of your life blaming Richard for everything that's wrong in your life. *He* didn't have a choice. *You* do.'

Sian got to her feet and headed towards the back steps with Magic in close attendance. It was time for her to stop thinking about Marcus and her own predicament. With Tara's help, Sian was getting through the horrible black tunnel of misery and despair that she'd been in since hearing about Susie Bancroft's pregnancy. Now Tara needed her help. She'd been moping around playing the martyr for far too long. If Tara was too stupid to recognize what a rare and special man Gil Sorensen was, Sian would have to do something about it. Tara clearly needed a kick up the arse and Sian was only too happy to oblige.

When Jen got home, her mother was shut away in her bedroom refusing to speak to anybody — *including* Jen — and Sian was sitting in the kitchen nonchalantly smoking a cigarette. Jen was surprised;

Sian had only started smoking since the blow-up with Marcus, and her mother only put up with it because Sian was weaning herself off and smoked outside. A heavy, leaden atmosphere seemed to hang over the house, as if somebody had died.

'What's wrong with Mum?' Jen asked Sian.

Sian tilted her head and blew a perfect smoke-ring into the air. Her long, wavy sable brown hair brushed the back of her waist.

'Stay over there, darling, so you don't get polluted.' She smiled at Jen. 'What on earth makes you think something's wrong?'

'Well . . . Mum's locked herself in her room.'

Sian shrugged. 'So? You've been locked in *your* room ever since I got here, and your mother and I respected your need for privacy.' Her green eyes sharpened. 'It's what girls do when they're upset.'

Jen flushed uncomfortably.

Sian stubbed out the cigarette and inspected the chicken breasts defrosting on the kitchen counter. Going to the pantry, she checked Tara's supply of dried herbs.

'Why's Mum upset?' Jen asked.

'Hmm? Your mother? She just needs a little time to herself, sweetheart. She had to end things with Gil Sorensen — your neighbour?' Sian looked enquiringly at Jen, whose face turned a deeper shade of red. 'She told him they were over and, well, I'm sure she's made the right decision, but,' Sian lowered her voice, girl to girl, 'things didn't go well so she's recharging her batteries. I'm sure she'll be as right as rain by dinner time. Now tell me, darling,' she held up two containers of dried herbs, 'which do you prefer: thyme or sage?'

Over at Peacehaven Retreat Eric was in the midst of a crisis, and somehow he'd been cast as the villain.

'Marion and Barney are talking about turfing out poor old Stan,' Fred Skinner said. 'And it's all your bloody fault.'

'My fault? What'd I do?' Eric demanded indignantly.

'You put two fingers up at Barney by paying him five dollars a week, so he's picking on Stan. His son went bankrupt last year and owes money on Stan's rent. Marion's let it go up to now, because Stan saves her money on cleaning — he does a better job than that lot she gets in. But because Barney's too scared to do anything to you, he's taking it out on Stan.'

This situation hadn't done anything for Eric's standing with Lillian. She'd stopped speaking to him and spent her time writing letters to Dick Cathcart and phoning government agencies to see if there was any extra funding available for Stan. For the first time in his life, Eric's feelings were hurt — not only because of Lillian's reproachful silence, but also because of the way Fred Skinner was treating him. Fred was the first real friend Eric had ever had, apart from his brother Henry, whom he'd never liked anyway, because he was a fussy tosser.

At first Eric sulked, outraged that the Peacehaven residents dared criticize him — he was a *Whitehead* for God's sake! This bloody town wouldn't exist if it hadn't been for his family. But it didn't take him long to realize that Lillian, Fred, Felicity and the others didn't give a tinker's cuss about the Whiteheads.

'You'll go out in a wooden box the same as the rest of us,' Fred said.

'I'm having cardboard,' Felicity said. 'It's better for the environment.'

Eric sat in his apartment, feeling utterly bewildered until it dawned on him that *he* was going to have to change if he wanted to be readmitted to the fold. When he found Marion haranguing poor Stan for missing a cobweb in reception, Eric was galvanized into action.

'If you're so bothered about the bloody cobweb, why don't you get one of the cleaners to do it?' he snapped. 'Or, better still, get off your fat arse and clean it yourself.'

Marion rounded on him furiously, her hands clenched in fists and her little brown eyes almost disappearing in the folds of her fat face. 'You evil old bastard! How dare you speak to me like that?'

There was a heavy silence as Celia, the receptionist, and three residents overhead Marion's outburst. Marion's eyes swivelled left and right like balls in a pinball machine. 'I — I'm going to speak to

Barney about this!' She rushed away, the soles of her white nurse's shoes practically leaving scorch marks on the carpet.

Later that afternoon, Eric cornered Fred. 'I need you tonight.'

'What d'you mean?' Fred asked suspiciously.

'We need to get into the office after Celia's gone and have a nose around.'

Fred's rheumy blue eyes brightened. 'What're we looking for?'

'Something Marion and Barney have been cooking.'

'Eh?'

'*Books*.'

Eric was furious when Fred turned up at the appointed time and place with a large yellow torch — and Stan. 'What the hell did you bring him for?' he hissed, anxiously checking the corridor leading from the reception area to the apartments.

'He was polishing the elevator panel and saw me,' Fred explained.

'It's half past one in the morning! What's he doing polishing the bloody elevator panel?' Eric demanded angrily.

Stan read his lips. 'I CAN'T SLEEP AT NIGHT!' he yelled.

Both Eric and Fred clapped their hands over his mouth, nearly suffocating him.

It was then that Fred noticed that Eric was standing on his own two feet. 'Hang on a minute — you're walking!'

'Yeah,' Eric agreed. 'It's a miracle.'

'You crafty old bugger. It was all for Lillian's benefit, wasn't it?'

'Oh shuddup.' Eric headed towards the glass door behind the reception desk that led into the office, saying over his shoulder, 'You're responsible for keeping a lid on Megamouth.'

As Eric had expected, the door was locked. He looked at Fred. 'You worked at a garage, didn't you?' He could just make out Fred's nod in the darkness. 'You any good at picking locks?'

'No. I was a mechanic, not a bloody safe-cracker.'

Eric scowled.

Stan suddenly shoved Eric aside. Reaching into his little plastic box of cleaners and rags, he extracted a small set of tools and set to work on the lock. A few moments later the door clicked open.

Eric and Fred thumped him on the back. Stan beamed.

'What're we looking for?' Fred whispered once they were inside the office.

Eric began poking inside cupboards and drawers. 'Records, books, stuff like that.'

'Nobody uses books any more.' Fred pointed at the computer. 'It'll all be on there.'

'Did you come down in the last shower?' Eric snorted. 'The computer will show what Barney *wants* people to see. Trust me, there's another set of books around somewhere — or at least I hope there is.'

'What do you mean by that?' Fred asked uneasily.

'If they're not in here, they'll be hidden somewhere else, like under Marion's bed.'

Fred looked sick at the thought of searching under Marion's bed. Judging by the noises that came from her apartment when she entertained Barney, there was no knowing what you'd find under the old bag's frilly four-poster. Unlike Stan, not everybody at Peacehaven was deaf.

Stan shuddered. He'd been shining the torch back and forth so he could lip-read Fred and Eric's conversation and was every bit as appalled as Fred at the prospect of entering Marion's bedroom.

'Put that bloody torch down, Stan!' Eric snapped. 'What do you think this is? Stalag 13?'

Offended, Stan lowered the torch.

They located the hidden files at the back of a locked cabinet, which Stan had obligingly opened. Fred and Eric huddled over the ledgers with the torch while Stan peered short-sightedly over their shoulders. Fred whistled, pointing out names of former residents for whom Barney and Marion were still claiming subsidies.

'Vera Galloway — moved away two years ago. Milly Anderson — moved to Gisborne to live with her daughter. Johnny Miller — moved to Picton. They've only picked ones who've gone to live with relatives instead of new retirement villages or kicked the bucket.'

'WHAT? WHAT?' Stan yelled, making them both jump. Without the torch he couldn't lip-read.

'Shut up!' Eric and Fred snarled.

Eric refused to give up the torch, so Fred scribbled a quick note of explanation and held it in the pool of light for Stan to read.

'I HAVEN'T—'

They froze him with a look.

Stan did his best to whisper. 'I haven't got me glasses.'

'Ah, for crissakes!' Eric handed over his bifocals.

Stan read the note. 'The old cow!'

Marion's constant yapping was one of the reasons he kept his hearing aid turned off. The only time he turned it on was for his phone calls to Mistress Fury, who sadly had been unavailable for the past week. Stan missed her dreadfully, and wouldn't speak to anybody else the nice lady at Superior Services suggested.

'She should be back next week, Mr Feather,' she said kindly.

Stan hoped so. Christmas was only a matter of weeks away, and he had big plans for the manger and decorations displayed in reception, although he had a feeling Mistress Fury wouldn't let him string lights around the exposed roof beams.

Stan was jolted from his reverie when Eric poked him in the ribs.

'Givvus me glasses.' Eric put them on and tapped a page in one of the books. 'There you are: Stanley Percival Brown. How much did Barney say you owed?'

Fred scribbled a note. 'Give him yer glasses.'

Eric wrenched off his glasses. 'This is a fucking pantomime!'

Stan read the note. 'Three thousand, six hundred.'

'He's lying,' Eric said while Fred scribbled frantically. 'Your son paid two thousand dollars in September and he's been keeping up the payments. There's only fifteen hundred outstanding.' He looked at Fred and smiled his evil-genie smile. 'Better fire up the photocopier, Fred. We've got work to do.'

Gil wondered why it had never occurred to him before. After all, the signs had been there all along. Eric and the rest of the family had made poor Richard's life hell, and Gil had sometimes wondered if that was why Henry and Grace had moved away to Auckland. No wonder they had regarded Tara's arrival on the scene as a godsend.

'Why didn't you tell me about Richard's letter?' he asked his mother.

'Because you were in a relationship with Tara,' she replied.

'Wasn't that a good reason why you should have told me? You must have realized I had no idea.'

'Gil, I've lain awake at night worrying about whether I should tell you, but in the end I decided it was best not to interfere.'

'Why? It's never stopped you before.'

Gil was so angry that he stayed away from Tara for a couple of days to give himself a chance to calm down and plan what he wanted to say. He was damned if he would let her give up on them. Gil knew he was good for Tara, just as he knew Tara was good for him. All he had to do was figure out a way of convincing her.

He was surprised when Jen arrived on his doorstep, looking anxious.

'Hi, Gil.'

'Hi, Jen.' he forced a smile. 'Jake's moving the herd, but he should be back soon.'

She fiddled with a charm bracelet on her wrist. 'Actually, it was you I came to see. I wanted to say I was sorry for being such a pain about . . . you know.'

Any anger Gil had felt towards her dissolved. She was only a kid, and a damned good one, too. 'That's OK.'

'Are you angry with me?' Jen asked.

'Not any more. It takes guts to admit you've made a mistake.'

'Please can you make it up with Mum, Gil? She's so unhappy.'

Yes! Gil was immediately ashamed of how pleased he felt. 'It's not that easy, Jen.'

'Yes, it is!' Jen cried fiercely. 'She only dumped you because of me!'

Gil smiled wryly. So much for tact. 'Have you been out with Gavin Archer yet?' he asked.

'How d'you know about that?'

'I make it my business to know what you're up to,' Gil replied. 'You just make sure Gavin knows it, too.'

Tara's friend, Sian, was his next visitor. She arrived the following morning, swaying up the driveway in high heels and a slinky summer dress. Gil watched her through the dining-room window, wishing she was Tara. He opened the front door before she knocked.

'Morning, Sian. How are you?'

'I've been better.' She looked over Gil's shoulder into the house. 'Are you going to invite me in?'

He stood back, wondering if he was doing the right thing. What single man in his right mind turned down a visit from a beautiful, sexy woman like Sian? The problem was that somewhere along the line he'd stopped feeling single. Gil wasn't sure that entertaining Sian alone would send Tara the right message.

Apparently, Sian had the same idea. 'I made sure I gave you time to finish the morning milking.' She glanced at her watch. 'I think about an hour should do it.'

'Do what?' Gil asked warily.

'Why, make her jealous of course, darling.' Sian looked around. 'What a simply stunning house. I'd love to see the rest.' When Gil hesitated, she laid a hand on his arm and said soothingly, 'Trust me, Gil. I'm only going to rattle Tara's cage.'

Up close, Gil noticed the shadows beneath her eyes and the hipbones poking through the front of her dress, and remembered that Sian was in the middle of her own emotional crisis. 'After I've shown you the house, I'll make us both a coffee. There's some Louise cake in the pantry that my mother made.'

'Louise cake!' Sian's eyes lit up. 'My favourite.'

Chapter 32

Sian told Gil the most likely place to find Tara the following morning. 'She's taken to hiding out in the hay barn along the race. She says she's tidying up, but I have my doubts.'

When Gil reached the hay barn it sounded more as if things were being thrown around than sorted. He pushed open the door and went inside, ducking as a riding boot narrowly missed his head.

Tara stood in a corner beside a pile of junk, holding the other boot. She wore the most disreputable pair of shorts Gil had ever seen, jandals and a filthy pink singlet with a knot tied in one of the straps to hold it together. Her face was streaked with dirt and her loose hair was festooned with cobwebs. The jandals were the biggest shock — they weren't even floral.

Tara glared at Gil. She wanted to kill him. How dare he spend an hour alone with Sian? The end of their agreement obviously didn't bother him. Why should it when Tara's *good friend* Sian was obviously willing to step into her place? Gil's 'neighbours with benefits' arrangement would be right up Sian's street. She'd probably never leave Divine.

Common sense told Tara that Gil hadn't been shagging Sian, but it was hard to listen when Sian returned from her walk full of voluptuous sighs and secret smiles and just happened to mention she'd been to visit Gil.

'Your DDF really is rather gorgeous, Tara.'

'His name's Gil and he's *not* my DDF.'

'No,' Sian smiled. 'He isn't, is he?'

She sighed again and stretched luxuriantly, and Tara noticed the buttons on her dress were done up the wrong way. It was *too* obvious and just the sort of stunt Sian would pull to make Tara feel jealous and drive her back into Gil's arms. For all she knew, they were in cahoots together, but that didn't stop her spending most of the night imagining Sian wrapped around Gil's beautiful, naked body.

'Gil's got the most beautiful new sleigh bed,' Sian said.

Tara thought she'd misheard. 'Gil's got a new bed?'

'Yes.'

'What sort of a bed?'

'The sort you sleep in, Tara.'

'No . . . I mean — what's he done with the old one?'

'I think he said he gave it to his son,' Sian's brow puckered. 'Jack?'

'Jake.' Tara felt more confused. It was only later that she realized she hadn't asked how Sian knew Gil had a new bed.

Don't get your hopes up, she told herself. *It's over — finished. You did the right thing. You have to think of Jennifer.* The new bed probably meant nothing. *At least Gil won't have to worry about where to shag Sian*, Tara thought nastily. Still, he kept throwing her off-balance by doing the unexpected.

Tara looked at Gil standing on the other side of the barn and snapped, 'What do you want?'

He propped his hands on his hips. 'To talk to you.'

'Piss off!' She threw the other boot at him.

Gil ducked. 'I'm warning you, the next thing you throw is coming right back.' His eyes were shooting green sparks. Tara wondered why *he* was so angry. *She* was the one who'd been wronged. She snatched up an old plastic bucket.

'You dare . . .' Gil growled.

Tara measured the distance between her and the barn door.

'You'll never make it,' he said grimly.

Tara threw the bucket, jumped over some bales of hay and ran for the door.

Gil caught her as she cleared the hay bales, swung her on to his hip and carried her back to the hay.

Tara fought and kicked. 'Let go of me! Put me down!'

He threw her on to the hay bales. She struggled upright, spitting hay and hair. One of her jandals was gone, and the knot in the strap of her top had broken. If Gil hadn't been so furious with her, he would have laughed.

Tara grabbed the strap. 'Now look what you've done!'

'Shut up!' he roared. 'You are the most painful, exasperating, difficult damned woman I've ever met! Sian's right, you *do* need a kick up the arse!'

'Don't you talk to me about Sian, you bastard. My back wasn't turned five minutes before you were going at it with my so-called best friend!'

His brows rose in disbelief. 'I never thought it would work — Sian said you'd be jealous.'

'I *knew* Sian was up to something!' Tara yelled. 'What does she mean I need a kick up the arse?'

'What do you mean I was "going at it" with your best friend?' Gil cried furiously, but then became distracted as Tara's bodice began to slide down her breast.

'I don't have to listen to this!' She began to climb off the hay.

Gil caught her behind the knees and flipped her back onto her back. 'Oh yes you do. You're not running off to hide and sulk this time.'

'What do you mean *this time?*' She struggled to sit up.

'Like you have ever since you arrived from Auckland.' He leant over her, a hand on either side of her hips. 'Like you have ever since Richard told you he wanted to live as a woman.'

Tara stopped wriggling and stared up at him. The colour anger had painted in her cheeks leached away. She was so pale that even her lips were bloodless. Suddenly she was short of breath and little sparkles of light danced before her eyes. From a distance, Tara thought she heard Gil say, 'Oh shit.' When she tried to get up he pushed her down again.

'Close your eyes and take some slow, deep breaths.'

Tara did as he said. The dizziness slowly receded and she stopped feeling as if an elephant was sitting on her chest. She took a shuddering breath and opened her eyes. Gil loomed above her, looking anxious. 'Are you OK?'

She nodded.

He knelt on the hay beside her. 'Only you could faint while you're lying down.'

'It's a talent,' Tara replied hollowly. She slowly sat up.

Gil hovered, ready to catch her if she toppled off the hay. 'That's how bad it's been?'

'That's how bad it's been,' she admitted wearily. 'Who told you? Sian?'

'No, my mother.'

Her mouth twisted. 'I thought Connie knew.'

'She wanted to come and see you, but . . .'

'Didn't feel she could,' Tara finished. 'You never got a letter?'

'Everybody except me.' He studied her. 'Are you sure you're OK?'

Tara nodded and reached for him.

Gil stood, wincing as the blood flowed back into his legs, and didn't see her gesture.

Tara hastily drew back her hand. 'Gil, I'm sorry.'

He nodded. 'Me, too.'

She swallowed. 'Where — where does that leave us?'

'You dumped me, remember?'

Tara flushed. 'Only because I was worried about Jen and what you'd do if . . .'

'If I found out about Richard?' Gil held his hands out at his sides, palms up. 'I've found out, Tara. Has the earth stopped spinning? Has the sun stopped shining?'

'It's just been hard—' she began.

'Of course it's bloody hard!' he snapped. 'When somebody you love is suddenly gone, it hurts like hell!'

Tara thought of Louise and felt ashamed. 'I feel so responsible—'

He interrupted her again, which told her how furious he was. 'Was I responsible for Louise's brain haemorrhage? Was it my fault because she was my wife?'

'Of course not.'

'So why are *you* responsible for Richard's decision to become a woman? Why does it mean you've failed as a woman? Surely the fact that he managed to live as your husband for all those years says a lot about how Richard felt about you. You couldn't stop Richard from doing what he did, Tara. He was born that way!' Gil shook his head and muttered, 'I don't know why I never saw it. The signs were always there.'

Tara felt as if she was seeing him for the first time.

He was still Gil Sorensen. Most of the time he wore awful clothes — tattered jean-shorts and an amber Diggers singlet with a hole in the side today. Not that Tara could talk; ever since she'd broken things off with Gil, she'd let herself go completely. But Gil's atrocious dress sense was as much a part of him as the glowing hazel eyes watching her so intently and the one-cornered smile so peculiarly his own.

'I'm sorry I hurt you.'

'I'm sorry you've been hurt,' he replied.

'What do you want to do?' she asked.

'I'm not going to do anything. It's up to you what happens. I can't fix things for you. The way I see it, you've got two choices: you can stay in your rut and be a martyr to the past, or you can get off your arse and grab hold of your future.'

His words stung.

'What future?'

Gil held out his hands as if to say she was looking at it. 'That's up to you. When you're acting like a spoilt brat, only your mother would want you,' he said flatly. 'On the other hand, when you're kicking Barney Bigelow or forcing yourself to learn how to do things you hate . . .' His face softened. 'When you're fighting your corner and Jen's, and marching through the mud in flowery gumboots kicking horseshit — well then, I guess just about anybody would want you.'

His words warmed her, but hearing Barney's name reminded Tara of her vulnerability. 'When people find out, they'll crucify Jen.'

Gil didn't know she wasn't just talking about Richard. 'You're both strong enough to weather the storm and your friends — your *real* friends — won't desert you. It won't make any difference to them. You'll just have to put your trust in people,' he said, and left Tara sitting on the hay.

Eric summoned Barney to a meeting at Peacehaven Retreat to tell him what they'd found in the other set of ledgers that Marion kept hidden in the office.

Barney was beside himself with fury. Why had the stupid cow left the books in the office when he'd given her explicit instructions to keep them under her bed?

'But I can't get down on my hands and knees any more!' Marion quaked at the rage burning in Barney's bulging eyes. 'You *know* I can't, Barney! Because of my back!'

She was referring to the curtailing of one of Barney's favourite sexual games, in which they both spent a lot of time on their hands and knees. Barney had been furious when Marion's bad back had spoiled his fun.

'You pathetic, fat old cow! You're as bad as them.' He jerked his head in the direction of the residents' apartments. 'But at least they pop off, whereas you just hang about getting fatter and stupider.'

'Barney!' Marion sobbed. *'You don't mean that!'*

'Don't I?' He slammed the door as he left.

Barney was petrified that Eric would show Bevan the photocopies and that Barney would get a visit from the Serious Fraud Office. He felt sick. Everything he'd worked for would come tumbling down like a pack of cards because of the paltry few thousand dollars he pocketed each year from Peacehaven. Even worse, it might jeopardize his real plans for the Country Corners development. Barney had no intention of building houses on his land; it had always been earmarked for a shopping mall, which was why Eric Whitehead's land was so important.

And now it looked as if that old bastard might scupper it.

Eric acted as if he'd worked alone, but Barney was certain he must have had help, not that Eric would ever admit to it.

'Stan Brown's son owes you some money for Stan's rent,' Eric said. 'I'd take it as a personal favour if you forgot about it, especially now that Stan's boy is paying each month, regular as clockwork.'

Eric was seated in the big armchair in his apartment — the apartment on which he *still* owed rent and was paying off at five dollars a week — while Barney squirmed on a hard blue plastic chair in front of him, feeling like a prisoner in the dock. He could tell that Eric was enjoying himself. Barney wished he had a gun. It would have been worth going to prison just for the pleasure of putting a bullet in the old bastard.

Eric then proceeded to lay out a list, written by Lillian, outlining the changes the residents wanted made to the running of Peacehaven Retreat. Their demands included a book at reception for signing in and out, which would allow residents to come and go as they liked, and permission for residents wishing to live together as couples to be allocated apartments on the same basis as married couples.

'This is blackmail!' Barney hissed.

Eric smiled. 'Yes, and you're an expert at that, aren't you, Barn?'

Just before Barney stormed out, Eric reminded him, 'If anything happens to me that looks even the slightest bit dodgy, I've left instructions with my lawyer to take a look at the special file I've given him and act accordingly. He's a smart lad is my lawyer — and by the way —' Eric paused. 'He's not the one I use here in town, so don't think you can pull a swifty by giving somebody a backhander or breaking into my local lawyer's office.'

'You bastard,' Barney snarled.

Eric's smile deepened. 'Just so we understand one another.'

After Barney had gone, Eric walked to Lillian's apartment, where Lillian, Fred, Felicity, Stan and several of the other residents waited. He'd owned up to Lillian about his fake paralysis, knowing she would find out from Fred; besides, it had been a relief to be able to get up and walk about. Eric had been surprised at how forgiving everybody had been, and he began running a few errands for the more infirm and doing odd jobs like fixing stuck windows or broken door hinges.

Lillian's response had confused Eric when he apologized.

'I always told my students that admitting you've made a mistake and learning from it could do them a lot more good than never making the mistake in the first place.'

'I did it so I could move in here and see more of you. I thought I'd be able to make you like me, but I've made a mess of everything and I'm very sorry about that,' Eric said abjectly, looking every one of his seventy-two years. 'I'm going to hang around for a little longer, just to make sure Barney doesn't pull a fast one, and then I'll move back to my house.'

'I see.' Lillian pursed her lips. 'What about Tara and Jennifer? Will you ask them to go?'

'Of course not! They're family.'

Lillian smiled.

When Eric told them all about the upshot of his meeting with Barney, there were celebrations all round.

'Put the jug on, Lillian!' Felicity cried. 'Let's all have a cup of tea.'

'Bugger the jug,' Fred winked at Eric. 'Let's have a whisky.'

They toasted their success and made Eric repeat several times exactly what Barney had agreed to.

'You're a hero, Eric!' Stan had turned his hearing aid on specially and felt happier than he had in days, although sadly Mistress Fury was still on leave.

Eric smiled, but his eyes looked sad. He couldn't bear to look at Lillian. She looked so pretty in her pale blue-and-pink patterned dress, with her hair in a silver halo about her lovely face. Soon he would see her only if he bumped into her when he visited Fred or Stan.

The rest of the group charged their glasses and Fred made a toast.

'To Eric!'

Lillian sipped her whisky and watched Eric thoughtfully over the rim of her glass.

Chapter 33

Elaine Selwyn felt sick. Barney had finally gone too far and even she couldn't look the other way. She wished somebody else had been the one to discover exactly what Barney had planned for Divine, somebody brave and fearless like Gil Sorensen or his father Malcolm, or Dick Cathcart.

Elaine hated it when Barney lost his temper, which had been happening more and more often lately; and for the first time in all the years they'd been together, he'd backhanded her across the face when she wouldn't back down but kept demanding answers to her questions.

It had all started when Fred Skinner had called, asking to speak to Simon Unwin.

'You sort it out, Elaine.' Simon swiftly put on his jacket and fled, saying he had a meeting.

He was still sulking because Elaine had refused to buy his hairnets. They were on special: three for the price of two. Elaine knew very well that Simon didn't have a meeting, because she kept his diary, near enough washed and dressed him, *and* wrote all his speeches and dealt with any difficult business. Like DAMSAG business. Elaine listened patiently to Fred Skinner's complaints and promised to find a spot in Simon's diary for him to meet with the group to discuss how Divine could be made more user-friendly for disabled people. She knew Simon would kill her, but, frankly, Elaine didn't care. She was sick and tired of covering for him, and Fred Skinner and his friends weren't asking for anything more than they deserved.

'Bless you, Elaine,' Fred said before he rang off. 'You're an angel. You know, you should be the mayor, not bloody Oily Unwin.'

Elaine thanked him, but there was no way the townspeople would vote for Barney Bigelow's mistress as mayor and risk upsetting the Whiteheads, particularly Alison Whitehead, who acted as if Elaine was invisible when their paths happened to cross. Eric was all right, and Tara Whitehead had proven to be nice enough in a distant sort of way, but she didn't have the clout Alison did.

As Elaine hung up the phone, she knocked an unmarked yellow folder off the edge of Simon's desk. Blueprints, geological reports and resource consent applications spilled out across the mulberry-and-pink patterned carpet. Sighing, Elaine got down on her knees to gather them up. When she realized what the documents were about, her hands slowed and she sat back on her heels to read the contents more closely.

Part of it appeared to be about the Country Corners lifestyle blocks, but the site plan was different. Instead of lots marked up in three- to ten-acre blocks, this plan included pockets of high-density housing, rows and rows of sections, some of them only six hundred square metres, with streets laid out, including a school, a playground and . . . a shopping mall. A shopping mall would sound the death knell for the businesses in Divine. They could never compete with a mall five minutes up the road.

Elaine's gaze wandered across the correspondence, reports and applications she had spread out on the floor around her. Barney and Simon appeared to be the only people in Divine who were involved in this part of the venture and, judging by the dates on the letters, it had been planned for a long time. She didn't recognize the names of the other people, but they were from a company that specialized in building shopping malls. Elaine was certain that Gil, Norris, Dave and Chook knew nothing about any of it. Her lips compressed when she saw the name of the street leading to the mall entrance that would run directly through Eric Whitehead's land: *Bigelow Boulevard.*

That was when she finally understood that Barney would never be satisfied; he would always be looking for ways to rub his success in everybody's faces. Nothing would ever assuage his bitterness over a father who was the town drunk and a mother who had abandoned them, who had left them all to suffer the humiliation of charity and handouts. His bitterness and deep-seated anger were so ingrained that he would never stop trying to settle his score with the Whiteheads and the people of Divine.

When Barney popped into the council offices later that afternoon, Elaine began asking him about what she'd discovered, insisting that the mall would be a disaster for local business.

Barney had just come from his meeting with Eric. He was already livid, and Elaine unwittingly provided the spark that exploded the powder keg of his fury. Barney wouldn't dare lay a hand on Eric Whitehead, but Elaine was another matter. He owned her. Without him, she was nothing. How *dare* she poke her nose into things that she didn't understand and that were none of her business?

'I don't give a flying fuck about Divine!' he roared, making himself heard all the way to the reception area. 'That mall will make ten times the amount a few piddling country shops do *and* increase the value of the Country Corners sections!'

That was when Elaine lost her temper. 'You'll *ruin* people! They'll lose their livelihoods and their homes all because of your determination to settle old scores.'

Barney was so dumbfounded by her uncharacteristic show of defiance that for a moment he didn't react. When he did, his blow sent Elaine flying across Simon's office to crash into his desk, sending papers spilling onto the floor.

Elaine slowly sat up, her head throbbing, and her elbow and ribs vibrating with pain from where she'd hit Simon's desk. All the noise and shouting had brought Lois rushing in from the front desk. The receptionist hovered in the doorway, her horrified gaze darting between Elaine, crumpled on the floor, and Barney, who was on his knees beside her, frenziedly scooping up the contents of the yellow folder.

'What do you want?' he snarled at Lois.

'Is — is Elaine all right?' Lois faltered.

'Of course she's all right.' Barney looked at Elaine, his eyes narrowing. 'She tripped.'

Before Barney left, he used Simon's phone to call Glenys Tweedie. He didn't seem to care that Elaine could overhear the conversation. By then, Elaine had dragged herself into a chair and was holding to her aching jaw the cold towel that Lois had brought her. Lois had wanted to call an ambulance, but Elaine refused, knowing Barney would come along in case she told the doctor the truth about how she'd been injured.

'I'm fine, Lois,' she lied while Barney stood over her, daring her to say anything different.

She was surprised when Lois argued: 'You don't look fine.'

Barney was surprised too. What the hell had got into the women in this town? First Marion and Elaine, and now bloody Lois Thompson daring to stand up to him.

'Haven't you got work to do, Lois?' he snarled.

Lois refused to back down. 'Don't you speak to me like that!'

'Lois! *Please!* Just go back to reception.' Elaine was terrified Barney would lose his temper and hurt Lois, too. 'I'll be fine — honestly.'

Reluctantly, Lois departed.

It was then that Barney made his call to Glenys, and Elaine heard him tell an outrageous story about Tara Whitehead's husband, Richard.

When he hung up, Barney smiled at her. He wasn't going to take a hiding from Eric Whitehead without fighting back, particularly when he had so much dirt on Tara Whitehead, alias Mistress Fury. Whenever Barney phoned Superior Services they said she was on leave, but he was sure she had recognized his voice before she hung up. He'd mentioned to Glenys that he'd heard from a friend that Tara was moonlighting as a dominatrix called Mistress Fury. Glenys had a gob the size of Lake Taupo, and almost as big a chip on her shoulder as Barney. He knew he could rely on her to fire the verbal bullets he provided, leaving him looking squeaky clean, and causing public humiliation for Tara and enraging Eric. It would also put the final nail in Glenys's coffin. She was beginning to get too big for her boots and wanted a higher commission for the Country Corners development. When Eric found out that Glenys was the one who'd let the cat out of the bag about Richard, he'd bury her professionally.

It was so perfect, Barney sighed with pleasure.

He eyed Elaine dispassionately, thinking how pathetic she was. 'If you tell anybody one word of what you've heard me say or what you've seen in this folder, I'll make you wish you'd never been born. You're a stupid bitch if you think you can mess with me and win. I'll make mincemeat of you. You and I both know I'm the only reason anybody in Divine puts up with you, and don't you forget it. You're nothing but the town slut.'

His words caused Elaine more pain than the blow to her face or the throb in her elbow and ribs. She suspected Barney was right; yet at the same time, the way Lois had stood up for her had surprised her more than she could say. Elaine felt a spark of defiance, and was glad that she'd had the foresight to photocopy the entire contents of the yellow folder before she spoke to Barney.

It would have been easy to leave early for the day to crawl home and hide, but Elaine knew Barney had to be stopped. She called Gil's house, but Jake said Gil was away in Auckland and he didn't know when he'd be back.

'Sometimes he drops in to see Uncle Eric on the way through town.'

Eric. Like Gil, Eric Whitehead had no fear of Barney.

Elaine put the envelope containing the photocopies in her handbag and, still holding the wet towel to her face, left the council offices to drive to Peacehaven, refusing Lois's offer to take her to the doctor or at least give her a lift.

'Maureen will cover reception while I'm gone.'

'No. Thanks all the same, Lois, but this is something I need to do alone,' Elaine mumbled, trying not to reopen the split in her lip, which had only just stopped bleeding.

'At least let me call you a cab,' Lois insisted. 'I really don't think you should be driving.'

Reluctantly, Elaine gave in. 'All right. I'm going to Peacehaven.'

'Right.' Lois reached for the phone. 'I'll call Celia in reception there and tell her you're not well, and she's to call you a taxi when it's time to leave. Don't worry about your car. Maureen and I will see it gets back to your house when we come to check on you.'

Elaine nodded in surprise. 'OK.'

The moment she walked into the reception area at Peacehaven, Celia came rushing around the front of her desk. 'Elaine! Are you all right?'

'Yes, thank you,' Elaine attempted a smile. She didn't dare ask what Lois had told Celia about her injuries. 'Which apartment is Eric Whitehead's?'

'Number thirty-two, but they're having a bit of a get-together at Miss Gillickson's and she's in number forty-four. Just turn left at the end of the corridor instead of right.' Celia lowered her voice. 'And while you're down there, tell them to keep it quiet, will you? I think they're having a bit of a drink and a party, and if Marion finds out there'll be hell to pay.'

Eric, Felicity and Fred were the only ones still at Lillian's when Elaine knocked on the door. They were appalled at the sight of her swollen face and fussed over her, making her sit in Lillian's most comfortable chair.

Protesting that she was all right, Elaine lowered herself carefully into the chair, an arm braced against her side to support her aching ribs.

'You don't bloody look all right,' said Fred.

Eric, who had fallen off many a horse in his day and knew first-hand what broken ribs looked and felt like, came to stand beside her. 'You need those ribs x-rayed.' He gently touched her swollen elbow beneath the short sleeve of her shirt. Elaine winced.

'Lillian, have you got a couple of safety pins and something we could use as a sling?' Eric asked. 'Don't get up,' he said when she began to struggle to her feet. 'Just tell me where to look.'

'In the top right-hand drawer of my dressing table there's a cream-and-pink shawl that should do the trick, and some safety pins in the little glass tray on the top.'

Felicity was in the kitchen making an ice pack and a cup of tea for Elaine. Her brows rose. Lillian must be softening towards Eric if she was letting him see inside her knicker drawer.

'You should be at the doctor's, not here visiting us,' Felicity scolded, once Eric had applied the makeshift sling and the ice pack with a surprisingly gentle hand.

Elaine took the two painkillers Lillian pressed on her, and the cup of tea from Fred. They were being so kind she was struggling not to burst into tears. 'I'll do that later, I promise, but right now I need to talk to Eric. Hold on—' She looked at him in astonishment. 'You're walking!'

'Yes. It's a miracle,' chimed Lillian, Felicity and Fred in unison.

Eric reddened and changed the subject. 'What did you want to see me about, Elaine? Must be important if it couldn't wait while you went to the doctor.'

Elaine glanced at Lillian, Felicity and Fred, and hesitated.

'Whatever you say won't go beyond these walls, love. I can promise you that,' Eric said.

They listened in silence while Elaine explained what she'd found on Simon's desk and showed them the photocopies. Lillian and Felicity gasped and tutted. Eric and Fred were more vocal, both snarling '*Bastard!*' several times and then apologizing to the women.

'Oh for goodness' sake!' Lillian cried impatiently. 'Will you stop apologizing? Barney Bigelow *is* a bastard!'

Felicity gasped and Fred's eyebrows would have disappeared into his hairline if he'd still had one.

'*Lillian!*' Eric cried.

'Do you think you're the only one who ever uses bad language, Eric Whitehead?' She turned to Elaine. 'Is there anything else we need to know, dear?'

'No, I think that's it — oh! Except for a phone call Barney made to Glenys Tweedie before he left Simon's office.' Elaine looked at Eric. 'I *really* think you might like to hear this in private, Eric. It was something about your nephew Richard.'

'What? That he's turned into a woman?'

Fred, Felicity and Lillian gaped.

Eric waved a hand airily. 'I know all about that.'

'You do?' Elaine asked. 'And that Tara is supposed to have been working for a telephone sex service?'

Eric's jaw slackened. 'I don't believe it.'

There was a stunned silence as everybody digested this latest piece of news.

'Telling Glenys Tweedie is as good as putting a banner up in the main street. You need to let Tara and Gil know, Eric!' Lillian exclaimed.

'Yes.' He tugged distractedly on his ear and looked about the room. 'Where's the phone book, Lillian? I'll call Glenys first and let her know I won't be too pleased if she starts spreading rumours about Richard *or* Tara.'

While the phone book was being located, Fred said to Elaine, 'Barney did that to you, didn't he, Elaine? He hit you.'

Elaine's stricken expression was all the answer they needed. She had never felt so ashamed, not even after the first time she'd slept with Barney, knowing he was married.

Eric gripped the arms of his chair tightly. '*Scumbag. Lowlife fucking scumbag.*'

Elaine flinched, but for once didn't defend the scumbag in question.

'I'm going to phone Gil as well, and fill him in on all this,' Eric snarled. 'Between us, we'll finally kick Barney Bigelow's fat arse into touch.'

'Gil's away in Auckland, Eric. I tried calling him earlier,' said Elaine.

'We'll deal with Glenys first, then.'

Celia phoned to say that Dr Rewi, one of the local GPs, was in the building visiting a resident and had agreed to take a look at Elaine.

'Who's sick?' Fred asked.

'Cyril Rowlandson,' Lillian replied. 'Apparently he took some pills he shouldn't have. He won't say where he got them from.'

Fred and Felicity looked everywhere but at one another. Eric didn't hear; he was still on the phone trying to contact Glenys.

Dr Rewi ordered some x-rays for Elaine after he'd seen her, suspecting that she had indeed broken her ribs. He hadn't come down in the last shower and didn't buy her story that she'd slipped in the bathroom. 'What do I put down as the cause on the ACC form, Elaine? The *real* cause,' he asked, after they'd left Lillian's bedroom where he'd conducted his examination.

There was a pregnant silence.

Elaine swallowed. 'I was assaulted.'

'Good girl,' Lillian said approvingly.

'If that's the case, you need to speak to Bevan Sargeson,' Dr Rewi said firmly. He had a fair idea who the culprit was.

Elaine panicked. 'I can't do that!'

'Yes, you can,' Eric said. 'How else will you stop him from doing it again?'

'Look how brave you've been today, dear,' Felicity said. 'You're not going to let that bully win, are you? Do you want Lillian and me to come to the police station with you, after you've had your x-rays?'

Tears filled Elaine's eyes at their kindness.

Barney was wrong. She *wasn't* the town slut.

Eric couldn't get hold of Glenys, and tried Gil for good measure.

'I've just remembered they're having the Guy Fawke's celebrations at the community hall tonight,' Lillian said.

'Bit late, isn't it?' Eric asked. 'It's December.'

'They were redoing the tennis courts at the beginning of November and had to put it off,' Lillian explained. 'Glenys always goes. Do you think Tara and Jennifer will?'

'Aw hell! Probably,' Eric agreed. He looked at his watch. 'Bugger! The doc's gone and I haven't got a car. I'll have to call a cab.'

'You can't. Ron Walker's wife had a hysterectomy today. He'll be at Waikato Hospital.'

When it came to women's problems, Eric wasn't interested in the details. Much as he liked the equipment, he didn't really want to know how it was fixed when it broke down.

'One-horse bloody town!'

'You're wasting time.' Lillian got painfully to her feet. 'You need to get to the hall.'

Eric hesitated. 'What about you?'

'Just go. Don't wait for me.' She shuffled towards her walking frame.

'Are you sure?' he asked anxiously.

'Positive, love.' She smiled and reached up to pat his cheek. 'Please *just go.*'

Eric felt like the sun and the moon and the stars had all come out at once. She had called him 'love'; his darling Lillian cared about him, after all! Bending down, he gently kissed her on the cheek and looked deep into her eyes. 'As soon as I get this lot sorted out, I'm paying for you to get that knee fixed, Lillian. No arguments.'

Fred was in reception talking to Celia, who was closing up for the night.

He braced his palms on either side of his knobbly spine and stared at the swirls on the carpet thoughtfully. 'The only car is Mad Marion's.'

'Where is it?' Eric asked.

'She keeps it in the car port beside her flat.'

'You can't steal the matron's car!' Celia cried.

'Oh do be quiet, Celia.' Lillian had just reached the reception area.

News had spread among the residents that Eric had to get to an important meeting and planned to steal Marion's car. Help arrived; people who hardly left their apartments were showing up to watch Marion's flat and sound the alarm if she came out. At this hour she'd be eating her dinner with her feet propped up, watching her favourite games show.

Eric looked at the elderly Ford Escort in disgust. 'Piece of junk.'

'It goes. What more d'you want?' Fred demanded.

He climbed creakily beneath the steering column to hotwire it, and after a few attempts the engine spluttered to life. Fred pumped the accelerator with his hand and it roared, sending black smoke belching from the exhaust. He climbed out one body part at a time and scowled at the smoke. 'I don't know how many times I've told her to get the rings and bearings done,' he said, rubbing his back.

'Have you put it out again, Freddie?' Felicity asked in concern, massaging his back through his zip-up cardigan. 'I'll give it a rub for you after dinner.'

The ranch slider at the front of Marion's flat suddenly opened and she appeared on the porch, minus her starched cap and white shoes, holding a fork. 'What are you all doing out here? You're supposed to be in your rooms.' Suddenly noticing her car was running, she pointed her fork at it. 'What are you doing with my car?!'

Eric looked up at her and smiled his evil-genie smile. 'Nicking it.'

'What Eric *means*, Matron,' Lillian interjected smoothly, 'is that he needs to borrow your vehicle for an emergency.'

'You can't take my car!' Marion shrieked. 'I won't let you.'

Before Eric roared off, he grumbled to Lillian, 'It'll probably fall apart and Marion will make me foot the bill. It should have gone to the wrecker's yard years ago.'

'Be quiet,' Lillian retorted. 'And fasten your seat belt!'

The remaining residents clustered about the porch just in case a furious, swearing Marion decided to give chase. Later, she tearfully told a disbelieving Bevan Sargeson that she had feared for her life.

'They were so menacing! Nesta Godfrey swooped in and parked her mobility scooter right across the bottom of my porch steps, cutting off my only avenue of escape, while the rest of them stood along the perimeter. They knew I couldn't get my leg over the top of the railing.'

Bevan really didn't want to think about Marion getting her leg over. It was a blessing she couldn't get over the metal handrail, because it would have buckled under the strain. Then she would have fallen and squashed the life out of the residents, triumphing where two world wars, heart disease, and old age had so far failed.

Chapter 34

Tara and Sian reluctantly accompanied Jennifer to the Guy Fawke's celebration at the local hall. Pat had invited them, along with instructions to bring a plate, so Tara had made sushi and Sian a lemon flan, because she said it showed how she felt — a sour old tart.

Sian and Jennifer knew that Tara and Gil had argued in Eric's hay barn, and Tara had been very quiet ever since. Jennifer was upset because she thought Gil had broken things off with Tara, despite her apology for her behaviour.

'It's got nothing to do with you, love,' Tara assured her.

She told Sian that Gil knew about Richard.

'How do you feel about that?'

'Relieved, I guess. I'm tired of waiting for somebody to let the cat out of the bag.'

'How did he take it?'

'He said he wasn't really all that surprised.' Tara paused. 'I've decided to tell him about Superior Services, Sian. I'd rather he heard it from me rather than from Barney Bigelow.'

Sian nodded. 'I agree.'

Tara touched her arm. 'I'm not ashamed of working for you, but I think I'll be retiring.'

Sian smiled. 'No longer hankering for that big house in Auckland?'

Tara shook her head. 'No.'

She knew Gil was still angry when he'd left her in the barn, but she hadn't expected to hear he'd taken himself off to Auckland. When Tara had decided to tell Gil how she earned extra cash working for Sian, it was Connie who opened the door.

'He left about lunchtime yesterday,' Connie explained.

Tara thought of the rumours she'd heard about Gil's women in Auckland, and wondered if she had misread him the day before. 'Do you know when he's coming back?'

'In a couple of days.' Connie looked sympathetic. 'He said he needed to see somebody.'

Tara couldn't speak.

'Why don't you come in? I've got a lovely bottle of wine in the fridge.'

She summoned a smile. 'Thanks anyway, Connie, but I'll leave it.'

'I promise I'll let you know as soon as Gil gets back.'

Tara nodded and headed home. Gil hadn't made any promises. He hadn't told her he loved her. What she didn't know was that Sian had told him that under no circumstances was he to tell Tara how he felt about her.

'It's too soon after Richard. If you tell her you love her, she'll bolt.'

'What makes you think I love her?' Gil hedged.

'Nobody goes to that much trouble for sex.'

'Are you some kind of an expert on what people will and won't do for sex?' he demanded.

'Abso-bloody-lutely,' replied Sian.

Tara headed into the community hall, carrying the clingfilm-wrapped platter. She was vaguely aware that community meetings were held there, but it was the first time she had been in the hall.

Jennifer pointed at the wooden sign above the front doors, which had *Whitehead Community Hall* written on it in black letters, and said, 'You know, Sarah Whitehead — my great-great-great-grandmother — was responsible for the original hall being built.'

'You've been spending too much time with Eric,' said Tara.

Connie, Malcolm, Corrine and Dick were already inside. Tara introduced Sian, and Dick and Malcolm poured glasses of wine, and some cola for Jen, who disappeared outside to join Jake and Melanie Larby. Small children ran about the room and in and out of the doors leading to the grassy area beside the fenced tennis courts.

Connie handed Tara her glass of wine. 'Gil called. He's on his way home.'

Tara's pulse rate went from a slow waltz to a cha-cha.

'I don't know if he plans to come over when he gets back. I told him you and Jen were coming. He sounded tired,' Connie said.

Tara's lips tightened. He was probably exhausted from shagging his girlfriend in Auckland. She'd worn the dress and shoes that Gil had bought her in case he showed up, and now she felt like a fool.

Pat Warner was fluffing around two trestle tables in the middle of the room and hurried over to tell them where to put their plates of food. Tara watched her eye up Sian's purple voile halter-neck top and hipster jeans. Pat was wearing a pair of hipster jeans herself, but unlike Sian, who had a tiny waist and looked slinky and feminine, Pat didn't have a waist and looked like a bloke. The green-and-white shirt with horizontal stripes tucked into them didn't help, nor did the chunky black belt sporting a massive brass buckle that wouldn't have looked out of a place at a rodeo. At least Pat was going to the hairdresser now instead of cutting her hair herself.

'Who *is* that woman?' Pat whispered.

'Sian Bancroft, a friend of mine from Auckland.'

Pat nodded and went off to greet Chook and Ngaire Larby, and Dave and Trish Richards.

'Is that a woman?' Sian asked, staring after her.

Tara waved to the others. 'Pat Warner. She's been a very good friend to Jen and me since we moved here.'

Sian raised a brow. 'Then your taste in friends has obviously improved.' She surveyed the tables. 'I feel robbed. There isn't a pink lamington or sausage roll in sight.'

Tara kept glancing at the door, but Gil didn't show.

Malcolm came over with a man Tara hadn't seen before. 'This is Kevin McNaughton. He moved into the place next to Annabelle's about a month ago.'

Kevin McNaughton was a large, auburn-haired man somewhere between fifty and sixty, with deep brown eyes and expensive clothes. Until recently he'd owned several businesses in Wellington. He sold them all following a heart attack when his cardiologist explained that, if he didn't wake up and make some lifestyle changes, the next time he had chest pain he quite possibly wouldn't wake up at all.

Divorced, with children and grandchildren, he'd been raised in Taranaki but no longer had any family in his hometown. When he stuck a pin in a map of the North Island and it landed on Divine, he promptly bought a house and twenty acres. He still had an apartment in Wellington, but hadn't been back since he moved into his country home. Kevin had spent the past weeks walking a lot, listening to music and starting a vegetable garden, which gave him more satisfaction than he'd felt in years. He'd lost weight and relished the solitude — or almost-solitude. His new neighbour Annabelle Archer, and Glenys Tweedie, the estate agent who'd sold him his house, kept on popping in to see him despite his determined efforts to discourage them.

Boredom had driven Kevin along tonight, and if he hadn't met Malcolm Sorensen and Dick Cathcart by the barbecue he would have left an hour earlier. As he looked at the silvery-eyed blonde and the sultry, moody-looking brunette Mal was introducing him to, Kevin was even more pleased he'd stayed — until he saw Annabelle Archer and Glenys Tweedie heading their way.

Glenys was annoyed to see Tara Whitehead and an unknown brunette hogging Kevin McNaughton's attention. Tara wore a lovely gauzy dress in pink and lavender, and with her long, blonde hair trailing down her back and her big, silvery eyes, she looked like she'd stepped out of Lothlorien. Glenys wore a white suede skirt with fringing on the hem, and a pair of matching white, fringed ankle boots. At home, in her mirror, the outfit had looked good; but beside Tara Whitehead and the brunette, Glenys felt like a cheap version of Dolly Parton.

'Nobody told me it was fancy dress,' Chook complained loudly. 'If I'd known, I'd have worn my Roy Rogers suit.'

'It makes you realize where the saying "dressed to kill" came from, doesn't it?' Corrine said sweetly.

Glenys searched the crowd for Gil. If he was here, tonight would be the perfect opportunity to put Tara Whitehead in her place and squash any attraction he felt for her.

Sian wished she'd stayed at home with her book and a glass of wine. She could see the interest in Kevin McNaughton's eyes, and set out to put him off by behaving as badly as possible.

Annabelle and Glenys were headed their way.

'Tara,' Sian said in a pained voice. 'Please don't tell me they're your friends as well, because I'm afraid that toucan is the absolute limit.'

Annabelle Archer was wearing a knitted jerkin that reached to her knees and was decorated with a big yellow-and-black toucan. Its huge beak ended on her left breast, looking for all the world as if the bird was trying to bite her nipple.

Tara remembered her comment to Jen about the toucan.

'Hello, Kevin.' Glenys smiled at him when she reached them, and looked suspiciously at Tara, who was coughing, and Sian, who was patting her back. Kevin buried his face in his beer. Malcolm had been called away to light sparklers for the smaller children.

'I don't think we've met,' Glenys said, looking directly at Sian.

'No.' Sian stared at Glenys's ankle boots. 'I would have remembered.'

Glenys carried a plate of pink lamingtons and Annabelle a plate of sausage rolls.

'What *lovely* food,' Sian drawled.

Tara dragged her away. 'Come and get a drink.'

'I've got one.'

'Have another one,' Tara insisted.

'I promised to help with the fireworks,' Kevin said, and escaped outside.

Glenys was even more determined to spill the beans about Tara

Whitehead, and decided to give Gil a little longer.

As darkness descended, the fireworks were lit on the tennis courts surrounded by a high mesh-wire fence beside the hall, while the children watched from a safe distance on the grass beside the courts. Malcolm and Dick were in charge, although somehow Tara, Sian and Kevin had been roped into doing the actual work while Connie and Corrine manned the water and sand buckets.

Sian held the torch so Kevin could light the fuse on a rocket. 'I'm warning you: if my silk top gets ruined, I'll stick a rocket up somebody's arse and light it.'

The rocket whizzed off into the black sky towards the Southern Cross.

'Beautiful,' said Kevin.

Sian and Tara lifted their faces to watch.

'As long as you stay on this side of the fence, you should be safe, Kevin,' Malcolm warned.

'Safe?' Kevin echoed.

Malcolm nodded at Glenys Tweedie watching them from the other side of the fence.

Tara searched the crowd for Gil.

'Annabelle Archer puts the fear of God into me.' Kevin lit a Catherine wheel stuck to a nail on a post and stepped back. The crowd oohed and aahed as it spun and flashed. 'Give me a hostile company takeover any day. What line of business are you in?' he asked Sian.

'I sell my body for cash,' she replied. 'I also accept all major credit cards.'

Tara rolled her eyes and went to light some more sparklers for the kids.

Sian riffled through a box of fireworks. 'Oh look! Double-happies! Shall we light a few and drop them down Glenys's ankle boots?'

'Later,' Kevin laughed. 'Right now I need you to hold the torch so I can light this rocket.'

Sian sauntered towards him. 'Never let it be said that I stopped a man lighting his rocket.'

The kids had just walked away from Tara with their sparklers alight when Glenys appeared on the opposite side of the fence.

'You really are amazing,' she said tightly.

Tara was tired and depressed and not in the mood. 'Thank you, Glenys, but I'm sure you could light sparklers if you put your mind to it.'

'Don't you get smart with me. I know you're a prostitute and your husband is a sexual deviant.'

Tara felt as if she was being sucked backwards into a tunnel. The noise of the fireworks, the excited chatter and shrieks of the children, and the laughter receded. She seemed to hear and see Glenys across a great distance. 'I'm not a prostitute.'

Connie had just told Sian about Glenys Tweedie's ambitions to become Mrs Sorensen when Sian saw Tara talking to Glenys and instantly smelt trouble. She thrust the torch at Kevin. 'You'll have to get somebody else to light your rockets.' She set off across the court.

Connie and Corrine were right behind her.

'Oi!' Malcolm shouted. 'Where're you . . .' He trailed off as he noticed Glenys and Tara. Even from a distance he could see the tension in Tara's shoulders and the way she was clutching the mesh fence. Fortunately, the crowd further up the slope was oblivious.

'What's wrong?' Kevin demanded.

Malcolm searched the crowd. 'Where's Gil?' He looked at Kevin. 'You said you knew where my son Gil's farm was?'

Kevin nodded.

'Do me a favour and see if he's back from Auckland, will you? If he is, tell him to get over here right away. Tell him Glenys is on the warpath and Tara's in the firing line. I haven't got time to explain.'

As Kevin left, Malcolm called out, 'And tell Chook we need him to give us a hand with the fireworks.'

Glenys was furious when Sian, Connie and Corrine joined them at the fence and Gil's mother began to champion Tara. 'Did you hear me, Connie?' Glenys shrieked. 'She's a *prostitute!*'

Tara had gathered her scattered wits. Her biggest fear was that Jen would overhear, but Jen was watching the fireworks with her friends on the slope. Tara would also have preferred Gil's mother to stay away, but was touched by Connie's spirited defence.

'I'm not a prostitute, Glenys. My speciality is telephone sex. There *is* a difference, although subtlety clearly isn't your strong point.'

Connie and Corrine exchanged incredulous looks, and Corrine began to giggle.

'I can vouch for that,' Sian drawled. 'She's one of my best employees.'

Glenys's mouth fell open.

'You're a *madam?*' Connie squeaked.

'I prefer to think of myself as an expert in customer services.'

'That's fascinating!' Corrine cried.

'It's disgusting!' Glenys screeched. This wasn't going the way she'd planned. 'Connie, Richard's a sexual deviant — he's getting a sex change and everything!'

Connie eyed her with disgust. 'I know.'

On the other side of the courts, Malcolm, Dick and Chook continued to light fireworks as fast as they could so nobody would notice the drama playing out further down the slope.

'I don't believe this!' Just like the fireworks, Glenys's plans were going up in smoke. She was furious and frustrated at being cast as the villain of the piece, while Tara Whitehead with her snooty voice and blonde prettiness became the damsel in distress. Gil's mother didn't even seem to *care* that Tara worked in the sex industry.

Glenys turned on Tara, desperate to score a hit. 'Gil only slept with you so you'd sell Eric's land to a lifestyle development he's involved with. Barney told him to.'

Tara gazed at her blankly as the *crack-crack-crack* of fireworks forced them to stop speaking.

'What absolute rubbish!' Connie snapped as the noise died away. 'Gil wouldn't spit on Barney if he was on fire!'

'If Barney could order Gil to sleep with women, you'd have got your leg over Gil years ago,' Corrine said.

Glenys sucked in a breath. *'You bitch!'*

Sian smiled at Corrine and looked down her nose at Glenys. 'Glenys, you're becoming tedious.' She gestured languidly at Tara. 'Do you seriously think any man would need to be bribed to sleep with *her?*'

Tara was still grappling with the news that Barney had asked Gil to sleep with her.

The sky turned pink and red as rockets burst overhead.

Glenys thrust her face against the fence and hissed, 'Your husband is a pervert! You lived with him for years and all the time he wanted to be a woman. How sick is that? How did you explain that to your daughter?'

The mention of Jen got Tara's attention.

'And Graham had to leave *you*, Glenys, or risk being emasculated!' Connie shouted.

Dick heard her shout and thrust a handful of rockets at Chook. 'Line 'em up and light 'em! Quick!'

Chook shoved the rockets in the bucket of sand. 'What the hell is going on?'

'Believe me, you don't want to know.'

Glenys slapped the fence beside Connie's head. 'You've got no right to speak to me like that!'

Connie leapt backwards.

'Leave her alone!' Tara rushed through the gap in the fence towards Glenys. 'Pick on somebody your own size!'

Sian, Connie and Corrine hurried after her.

'Are you threatening me?' Glenys shrieked.

'No, just reminding you that you're half her age, twice her size and ugly as hell!' Tara snarled.

'Uh oh!' said Sian.

Glenys lunged at Tara, who ducked, took a wild swing and managed to bitch-slap Glenys into the fence. The fringe on Glenys's skirt and one of her boots caught in the wire mesh and she tripped and fell.

'Bloody hell,' Chook said. 'This is better than *Survivor*.'

Gil and Kevin came running down the slope from the hall, followed by a substantial crowd, including Jen and Jake.

Gil stopped beside Tara and caught her arm. 'Are you OK?'

She nodded mutely.

'She assaulted me!' Glenys wailed.

Gil glanced down at her and back at Tara. 'What the hell has she been saying?'

Glenys looked up at the circle of faces. 'Tara Whitehead assaulted me! You're all witnesses! Somebody help me get up! Somebody call Bevan Sargeson!'

Eric suddenly arrived, panting. 'What happened? Am I too late?'

Connie looked at his clothes. 'Why are you covered in grease?'

'Marion's bloody car broke down. Are you all right, Tara? Where's Jen?' He looked down at Glenys. 'What's she doing down there? Whatever she's said, don't believe a word of it. I tried to ring you, Tara, but there was no answer.'

Bevan Sargeson walked down the slope from the hall. He was wearing his uniform. 'What's been going on here?'

Glenys struggled to her feet and pointed at Tara. 'She assaulted me! She pushed me into the fence! I think I've cracked some ribs.' She clutched her side.

'Shame it wasn't her vocal cords,' somebody said.

'What're you doing here?' Eric asked Bevan.

'Looking for you,' he replied. 'Marion reported you'd stolen her car.'

Eric's face sagged in disbelief.

'You'd better come down to the station,' Bevan said. He looked at Tara. 'You'd better come too, Mrs Whitehead.'

Eric and Tara were detained at the Divine Police Station while Bevan took everyone's statements. As far as he knew, it was the first time that one, let alone two, of the Whitehead family had been a guest of the Divine Police.

Eric was outraged that he *could* be arrested.

Tara was so ashamed she barely said a word, unaware that Gil was waiting for her in reception.

Marion was adamant that Eric had stolen her car.

And Glenys was equally adamant that Tara had assaulted her.

However, nobody at Peacehaven Retreat or the community hall had seen anything to support their stories. The residents at Peacehaven swore that Marion had given Eric permission to borrow her car because of a sudden emergency. And practically everybody at the fireworks hadn't noticed anything unusual, and those who were nearby claimed Glenys had attacked Tara, who'd acted in self-defence.

'Bloody Whiteheads!' Glenys cried bitterly when Bevan explained the situation. 'They've even got you in their pocket!'

'Be very careful what you say, Glenys. I don't work for Eric Whitehead *or* Barney Bigelow,' he said pointedly. 'If I can find enough evidence to charge somebody I'll do it — simple as that.'

Lillian and Fred came to collect Eric when he and Tara were released the following morning. Fred had borrowed his nephew's car.

Eric was mortified when he saw Lillian. 'What must you think of me? I've never been arrested in my life. Never even had a parking ticket.'

Lillian braced a hand on her walking frame and reached up to pat his face. 'I think you're a very obstinate, kind, foolish, loyal man.' She smiled into his eyes. 'Nothing that can't be fixed by a firm hand on the tiller.'

Eric stared at her. 'You mean you're not angry?'

'Angry?' she laughed. 'No. I'm just sorry I had to miss out on all the fun. But I suspect there'll never be a dull moment with you around, Eric Whitehead.'

The first thing Tara noticed about Gil was that he was wearing some of the clothes they'd bought together in Hamilton. Like Eric, she was deeply embarrassed, and wished he'd go away. By now he must know everything Glenys had said.

As soon as he saw her, Gil asked, 'Are you all right?'

Tara nodded, and then frowned as something occurred to her. 'You didn't have to pay bail to get me out, did you?'

Gil managed to keep a straight face. 'You weren't accused of drug running, Tara.'

She pursed her lips.

'You look tired,' he said.

'So do you,' Tara replied.

'I haven't had much sleep the last couple of nights.'

She gritted her teeth. 'Really?'

Gil held the door open and followed her out of the police station and into the car park. 'Bevan said there were no charges against you.'

'Yes,' Tara said tartly. 'I think my offer to sleep with him helped.'

Gil caught her arm and pulled her around to face him. 'What's that supposed to mean?'

She snatched her arm away. 'Haven't you heard? I'm a sex worker. I'm sure it's all over town by now.'

He pushed his hands into the pockets of his jeans and counted slowly to five. She was as combustible as any fire-cracker. 'The way I heard it, you worked for Sian, providing telephone sex.'

'Yes.' Tara stared at him defiantly. 'I did. And I'm not ashamed of it.'

'There's no reason you should be.'

She blinked. 'Pardon?'

'I said there's no reason you should be,' Gil repeated.

'You don't mind?'

He shrugged. 'I can't say I wasn't surprised when Sian told me, but I can imagine how much her customers liked hearing your snooty voice, especially when you're in a strop.'

Tara rubbed her forehead in confusion. 'Glenys said Barney Bigelow told you to sleep with me so I'd sell you Eric's land.'

'And what did you think of that?' he asked.

She looked at him through her fingers. 'I didn't believe it. Nobody could make you do anything you didn't want to.'

'I *did* want to do *you*, Tara.'

She turned pink and fidgeted. 'Yes, well . . .'

'Jennifer doesn't know anything about you working for Sian.'

'She doesn't?'

'The only people close enough to hear were Mum, Corrine and Sian, and if Glenys opens her mouth they'll deny it. I don't think Glenys will be living in Divine for much longer.'

She closed her eyes. 'Thank God.'

Gil reached out and cupped her cheek. 'Why are you angry at me?'

'I'm n—'

'Don't lie, Tara. I know you too well.'

Her high heels dangled from her fingers by her side. As usual, without her shoes, she looked small and fragile. Gil felt a wave of tenderness.

Tara stared up at him. It was the truth. Gil *did* know her very well. He had waited patiently for hours and didn't have a single word of rebuke for her behaviour, whereas Richard would have had plenty to say and none of it would have been good. The last of her defences crumbled. '*Where* have you been, Gil? Were you with a woman in Auckland?'

Gil looked stunned and then angry. 'Don't you know me better than that?'

'Yes . . . No . . . I don't know!' Tara hooked her hair behind her ears and licked her lips. 'I don't trust my feelings or my instincts any more. I used to think I knew people, that I was a good judge of character, but . . .' She shrugged helplessly.

'You mean because of Richard?' Gil asked. 'That's where I've been for the past couple of days, Tara. In Auckland, with Richard — I mean, Rachel.'

She stared at him, too shocked to speak. The crushing weight of disappointment and loss she'd been carrying since she'd found out Gil had left for Auckland slowly dissipated. 'Why?' she whispered.

'You wouldn't talk to me, so I went to see Richard.' He paused. 'Do you still love him, Tara?'

'I'll always love Richard.' Tara gathered her courage. 'But I'll never feel about him the way I feel about you.'

His expression turned fierce. 'Really?'

'Yes. *Really.* I didn't want to feel anything for you — the sex was great, and I kidded myself that that was all there was between us. I don't need somebody to lean on. I can take care of Jen and myself without anybody else's help.'

Gil nodded. 'I know.'

Tara straightened her spine and lifted her chin. 'I think we need to upgrade our "neighbours with benefits" agreement.'

'Do you?' His lips twitched. 'What did you have in mind?'

She swung her shoes gently to and fro at her side. 'I hear you have a new bed.'

'Damn. You can't keep anything secret in this town.'

Tara smiled. 'And I think I'm going to be homeless soon.'

Gil frowned. 'Not Eric and Miss Gillickson?'

'Yes.'

Gil shook his head. 'Unbelievable.'

'Eric's all right — a bit rough around the edges, but Lillian will sort that out.' Tara changed the subject. 'If I move in with you, I'm available for afternoon milking but I don't do mornings.'

Gil caught her wrist and drew her gently against him. 'Tara, you can't live in the country and not "do" mornings.'

'Just watch me.' She leant into him. 'I'm going to get a part-time job and I want to go back to university.'

He linked his hands in the small of her back. 'No more Mistress Fury?'

'I'm hanging up my phone. What about you? Are you willing to forego the excitement of being the town gigolo?'

'Yes, and I'm willing to buy you a cuckoo clock just like Eric's and redecorate the living room in red flock wallpaper to make you feel at home.' He leant forward and kissed her. 'I'm going to say it, Tara.'

'No! Don't! It's too soon.' She tried to shut him up with a kiss, but Gil still managed to say *I love you* against her lips.

He lifted his head and smiled. 'Come on, now. I know you can do it.'

'I didn't want to fall in love with you,' she complained.

'We all have our cross to bear,' Gil replied. 'Look at me — I've got you.'

Tara watched him anxiously. 'I'm scared. I've fallen so fast for you.'

'Don't be afraid, surfer girl, I'll catch you.'

Epilogue

Nearly three years later, members of the Sorensen, Whitehead and Kemp families sat in the audience at the Founders Theatre in Hamilton to watch Tara receive her degree from the University of Waikato.

So much had happened in the past few years that if anybody had asked them to list everything it would be impossible not to miss something out. But every one of them would also have agreed that their lives had become richer and brighter, and that, both individually and as a family, they had been blessed.

Lillian Gillickson's wedding to Eric Whitehead was still a talking point in Divine. Who would have dreamt that sweet, saintly Miss Gillickson would take up with that reprobate Eric Whitehead? If that hadn't been a big enough shock, the wedding ceremony had been unusual to say the least. The bride, given away by Fred Skinner, had walked up the aisle to Engelbert Humperdinck's 'The Last Waltz' accompanied by her attendants Felicity Ringwald and Tara and Jennifer Whitehead, and down the aisle with her new husband to The Shadows' 'Apache'.

Gil Sorensen stood up as Eric's best man, which was just as well when the groom had a sudden attack of nerves about the wedding night. 'I've never had a virgin before! What if I mess it up?' Eric fretted. 'Louise must've been a virgin. Tell me what to do.'

'Just do the opposite of whatever you usually do.'

'The opposite?'

'Yes.'

When it became clear that Eric didn't have a clue what he meant, Gil added, 'You know: not rip — shit — and,' he winced, '— *bust*.'

'Right.' Eric nodded. 'Gotcha.'

The following day, when he tentatively mentioned to his lovely new wife that he thought 'The Last Waltz' had been a bit morbid for a couple their age, Lillian replied tranquilly, 'It's a lot more romantic than the song you chose for the walk down the aisle. I've had to learn to compromise over the years, and so will you.'

When Eric and Lillian moved into his house, the cuckoo was liberated from its clock. 'I don't think Tara's all there,' Eric grumbled. 'Whoever heard of a wooden cuckoo needing a break?'

Lillian smiled sweetly. Little did Eric know that the cuckoo's days were numbered.

As soon as Lillian had recovered from her knee operation, Eric whipped her off for an extended honeymoon, which included a stop at Las Vegas to see Engelbert perform. 'Wishy-washy prat,' Eric confided to Gil when they got home. 'But Lillian loved it.'

Barney Bigelow was charged with assault and fraud and went to prison, Bevan Sargeson allowing himself a rare smile as he arrested him.

It turned out that the deeds to Peacehaven Retreat were still in the name of Alison's father, Bill Whitehead. Alison sold it to Eric, who turfed Mad Marion out and put Celia the receptionist in charge. She instigated a far more flexible regime, making it a much happier place for the residents, who could come and go as they pleased. Fred and Felicity finally moved into their apartment, although Eric didn't entirely approve when they declared they had no intention of ever getting married and planned to live — and die — in sin.

Bigelow Towers was gutted in a mysterious accident involving a welding torch. As soon as the insurance money was paid out, Alison knocked it down and built a much nicer, smaller house beside her studio and developed the rest of the extensive grounds into a sculpture park and arboretum. Among the first pieces she erected at the top of her drive was one of her penis sculptures.

Tiffany was, if not reformed, then certainly easier to get along with. She loved the fact that her new bedroom had corners, and, although her mother wasn't as open-handed as her father had been, Tiffany was a lot happier, knowing that Alison cared enough to want to know where she was, who she was with and what she was doing. There were still screaming matches from time to time, but Alison, with her artistic temperament, could throw even bigger tantrums than Tiffany. The biggest surprise of all was the discovery that Tiffany had inherited some of her mother's talent, which soon flourished under Alison's guidance.

With Tara's encouragement, Pat Warner finally got out of her jodhpurs and boots and into a dress. She was in a long-term relationship with a dairy farmer from Matamata that looked promising. Pat assured her that when Bernie popped the question she would let Tara help choose the wedding dress.

In the next local elections, Simon Unwin was ousted. Elaine Selwyn obliterated him at the polls after a clever, colourful campaign largely orchestrated by Alison Whitehead, who went to see Elaine when she heard that Barney had assaulted her and that Elaine had blown the whistle on the shopping mall. Barney was enraged when his soon-to-be ex-wife showed up at court to support his ex-mistress as he was prosecuted for her assault.

'Poetic justice,' Alison said with relish when he was sentenced.

The last anybody heard of Simon, he was running a real estate agency with Glenys Tweedie, who had seen the writing on the wall and left town. People weren't prepared to forgive her when they heard she'd been in cahoots with Barney to build a shopping mall on their doorstep. Her son, Neville, went to live with his father, Graham.

Elaine Selwyn revitalized the local council. She raised the profile of Divine as a great place to live and raise a family, and revised the Country Corners lifestyle development, which went ahead on a much smaller scale, sticking to the original plan of three- to ten-acre blocks. Chook and Ngaire made enough money to get out of debt and move into a nice house in town, and Dave Richards sold off fifty acres and splashed out by buying Trish a genuine cubic zircon ring. Norris Jenkins decided to pull out, because he valued his privacy too much; and Eric refused to move, which meant a road had to be built on the other side of the development.

Nial, Stan and Walter never forgot Mistress Fury, and Sian used her as an example of excellent customer service in the company training manual. She replaced her with a retired headmistress from England, known professionally as Miss Spankwell. Nial and Stan adored her because she gave double detentions for dropped stitches or missed cobwebs. Sian still received an occasional enquiry about Mistress Fury, but told clients she had only one client now, which made Gil laugh.

Sian and Kevin McNaughton were living together, dividing their time between Wellington, where Sian had set up a new branch of Superior Services, and their home in Divine while Rona ran the operation in Auckland. Sian called Kevin 'Mr McNaughty', and he was helping her develop a business plan to take Superior Services global. They were very happy together. With Sian's encouragement, Kevin had established contact with his sons and grandchildren, who, after some initial reservations, got on well with her. After all, it wasn't every day that your father introduced his new girlfriend as a madam.

'Who would have guessed it?' Sian asked Tara. 'I'm a stepmother *and* a step-grandmother.'

Gil trained and competed with Lazarus to intermediate level before selling him for loads of money to a wonderful young rider who was looking for a horse to take her to the next Olympics. He still competed on a much smaller scale, bringing through young horses before sending them on to new owners and new heights. Tara ended up being a lot better around the farm than he would have guessed, and was soon a dab hand at milking, drenching and driving the tractor — although she still drew the line at morning milking.

As Gil watched the graduates step on to the stage to accept their degrees, Tara gave him a little wave from where she stood at the bottom of the steps in her gown, waiting for her name to be called. He was so proud of her and what she'd achieved. It had taken her a little longer to complete her degree than she'd originally intended, thanks to an unplanned little hiccup named Zack Sorensen, who had just turned one and was currently perched on his big sister's knee, sucking his fingers.

Gil could still remember his shock and the stunned expression on Tara's face when she told him she'd was pregnant.

'But . . . we used . . .'

'I *know* that,' she said.

'So how on earth . . . ?'

'I *don't* know that.'

Once the initial shock had worn off and Tara's morning sickness had stopped, she and Gil had thoroughly enjoyed her pregnancy and had fallen in love with Zack when he was born after a five-hour labour. He weighed in at nine pounds, and was an easy, happy baby who was in danger of being spoilt rotten by his big brother and sister, both sets of grandparents and Great-uncle Eric and Great-auntie Lillian.

Before Zack was born, Gil had put his foot down and insisted that Tara marry him; something she had been leery of, even after her divorce from Richard had come through.

'You are not jinxed,' Gil insisted. 'There is nothing you could have done to stop Rachel being the way she is. She was born that way.'

'I know that.'

'So why won't you marry me?'

Tara was almost seven months pregnant before she gave in and they were married in Gil's garden. She wore a beautiful off-white gown from her favourite local designer, Ooby Ryn, with a strapless, pleated bodice that stepped upwards to the centre of her collar bones and down again, drawing attention away from her belly beneath the high empire waistline of the softly draped skirt.

'You look wonderful,' Gil said quietly when she finally stood beside him in front of the celebrant.

'So do you.' Tara looked at his smart charcoal-grey suit, blue shirt and blue-grey striped silk tie. 'I was convinced you'd wear a brown suit.'

He smiled his one-cornered smile and dipped his head to look into her eyes. 'I couldn't get my old brown one drycleaned in time. I hope you're not too disappointed.'

She laughed and pressed her forehead against his. 'I'll get over it.'

Rachel, who was sitting in the audience wearing a large, grey picture-hat on her sleek blonde bob, wept buckets during the ceremony. 'She always looks wonderful when she's pregnant!'

Eric hadn't realized who Rachel was, seeing only a tall, blonde woman with a nice set of knockers and long legs. He was mortified when she suddenly winked as they were being introduced and said, 'Hi, Uncle Eric', and he'd realized it was Richard, who'd undergone sex reassignment surgery in Colorado the previous year. Watching her, it was hard to know Rachel had been born a boy. Eric spent more time staring at her than at the happy couple, until Lillian patted his hand reassuringly and said, 'I think your *niece* is very lovely.'

Rachel later told Tara that Eric was a lot nicer to her now she was his niece than he had been when she was his nephew.

Tara's sister Kim was delighted to hear that her little sister was knocked up and getting married. 'I knew I was going to like you, Gil, the moment I met you,' she told him approvingly. 'Good on you.'

Gil was amused. 'Thanks. I think.'

'Why don't you introduce me to one of the local dairy farmers, Tara?' Kim asked, knocking back wine as if a grape blight had been announced.

'What a great idea,' Tara agreed. 'I'll introduce you to Norris Jenkins.'

There was a sudden rattle as Zack knocked an open bag of lollies out of Jennifer's handbag and onto the floor. She'd just started her first year at Waikato, had split with Gavin Archer after two years going steady, and was playing the field. Gil was like a bear with a sore head whenever she brought a new boyfriend home.

'Why are you so horrible to them?' Tara demanded. 'They're scared stiff of you.'

'Good,' Gil retorted. 'That's the way I want it. At least that way they'll think twice before they try anything out of order.'

'No, you little monkey!' Jen cried, grabbing a pilfered peppermint from Zack. She looked down at the mess on the floor. 'Bum!'

Zack bounced up and down on her lap and clapped his hands.

Gil leant forward to smile down the row at his baby son. 'Come here, trouble.'

Spotting his father, Zack held out his arms and crawled or was lifted across the row of laps, stopping along the way for kisses and hugs from Nana Sandra and Grandad Trev, before spending an extra few minutes with his big brother, Jake, who was up from Otago university. Sian, Kevin, Eric, Lillian, Connie and Malcolm were back at the house preparing a celebration dinner. Jake's girlfriend of three years, Melanie Larby, was with them. Jake passed his little brother to Gil, who looked up and saw that Tara was next to go on stage.

'Tara Elizabeth Sorensen . . .'

He stood and perched Zack on his shoulder so Zack could see his mother climb the stairs in her long gown and sway across the stage in the brand-new pair of Jimmy Choos that Gil had bought her as a graduation present.

As Tara shook hands with the chancellor and accepted her degree, everybody in the row of seats stood and cheered. She turned to wave at them, her face wreathed in smiles as she donned her mortar board and spotted her precious little boy on her husband's shoulder. Zack was the image of Gil, with his dark hair and merry hazel eyes, but there was a touch of her in the tilt of his nose and his smile. She waved again.

'Look!' Gil pointed. 'There's Mummy!'

Zack raised his little arms and crowed, 'Bum!'